Washington Irving's Tales of the Supernatural

Washington Irving's Tales of the Supernatural

Selected and with an
Introduction by
EDWARD WAGENKNECHT
Illustrated by
R.W. Alley

Stemmer
House

Publishers, Inc.
Owings Mills, Maryland

Illustrations copyright © 1982 by R.W. Alley
Introduction copyright © 1982 by Edward Wagenknecht

Stemmer House™

Inquiries should be directed to
Stemmer House Publishers, Inc.
2627 Caves Road
Owings Mills, Maryland 21117

Published simultaneously in Canada by Houghton Mifflin Canada Ltd., Markham, Ontario

A Barbara Holdridge book
Printed and bound in the United States of America
First Edition

Library of Congress Cataloging in Publication Data

Irving, Washington, 1783–1859.
    Washington Irving's Tales of the supernatural.

    CONTENTS: The Devil and Tom Walker.--The bold dragoon.--The spectre bridegroom.--[etc.]
    1. Supernatural--Fiction. I. Wagenknecht, Edward Charles, 1900– . II. Title. III. Title: Tales of the supernatural.
PS2053.W3 1982   813'.2   80–29313
ISBN 0–916144–64–X   AACR2
ISBN 0–916144–65–8 (pbk.)

Contents

Introduction

American literature may be said to have begun to be a part of world literature with the publication of *The Sketch Book* of Washington Irving in 1819–20, and the first collection of William Cullen Bryant's *Poems* and James Fenimore Cooper's first novel of consequence, *The Spy*, both in 1821. Except for *Diedrich Knickerbocker's History of New York from the Beginning of the World to the End of the Dutch Dynasty*, most of Irving's creative writing, in the narrower sense of the term, appeared in five miscellanies: *The Sketch Book, Bracebridge Hall* (1822), *Tales of a Traveller* (1824), *The Alhambra* (1832), and *Wolfert's Roost* (1855). All these works contain some fiction, though *Tales of a Traveller* is the only one entirely devoted to it, and all save *Bracebridge Hall* have been drawn upon for the collection of tales of the supernatural with which the reader is presented in this volume.

Washington Irving very narrowly escaped being a colonial; he was born in New York on April 3, 1783, the youngest of the numerous children of a strict Presbyterian business man. He never went to college, but he read law in several law offices and even passed his bar examination. Much more important than this, however, so far as his writing was concerned, was his browsing in the library of his friend Henry

Brevoort, where he developed some of his characteristic interests and discovered some of his themes.

Though he contributed to the *Morning Chronicle*, as Jonathan Oldstyle, Gent., as early as 1802, his real beginnings as an author date from 1807–1808, when he joined with James K. Paulding and his own brother William to publish at irregular intervals twenty numbers of a *Spectator*-like miscellany called the *Salmagundi Papers*. In 1809 he scored the first of his two greatest triumphs as a writer (*The Sketch Book* would be the second) with the Knickerbocker *History*. Not only was this a tremendously successful book, but it created a figure who was to personify New York City thenceforth and forevermore. It was prepared for by one of the cleverest hoaxes in the history of publishing, and there had been no advance indication that it was to be a humorous work. First, the *New York Evening Post* announced the "distressing" disappearance of "a small, elderly gentleman, dressed in an old black coat and cocked hat, by the name of Knickerbocker." Eleven days later, "A Traveller" reported having seen him on the Albany stagecoach. Next, his landlord announced that "a very curious kind of a written book" had been found in his room, and that if he did not return at once to settle his account, this would be sold to the booksellers to cover the cost of his board and lodging. Publication followed in due course.

Irving did not yet, however, regard himself as a professional writer. He shared with his brothers the administration of the family hardware business, and in 1815 he went to England to assist his brother Peter in managing the Liverpool branch. It was not until the business had failed that he began to look to his pen for support. Sir Walter Scott helped him to get *The Sketch Book* published; it appeared on both sides of the Atlantic, and his succeeding miscellanies followed as has been indicated above.

In later years, however, Irving turned increasingly to historical writing—the multivolumed biographies of Columbus and Washington (1828 and 1855–59), *The Conquest of Granada* (1829), the *Voyages and Discoveries of the Companions of Columbus* (1831), and the much less ambitious biographies of Oliver Goldsmith (1840) and Mohammed (1841), as well as the memoir of a young American poet, Margaret Miller Davidson (1841). In 1832 he returned to America, after many years' residence in Europe (in France, Germany and especially Spain), and settled at "Sunnyside," which is located at Tarrytown on the Hudson, the place most closely associated with his memory. He was now regarded as not only a great man of letters but an important figure in public affairs. He might have been a congressman or mayor of New York; he might also have had the secretaryship of the Navy in Van Buren's cabinet. Out of his travels on the frontier and his friendship with John Jacob Astor came a number of books on Western themes: *A Tour on the Prairies* (1835), *Astoria* (1836), and *Adventures of Captain Bonneville* (1837). Between 1842 and 1846 he served as United States Minister to Spain, and in 1845 he went to England in connection with the Oregon Boundary dispute. In 1848 he began work on the final revision of his writings. He died on November 28, 1859.

Our volume opens with three tales from *The Sketch Book,* all derived from German sources. One, "The Spectre Bridegroom," Irving left on its native heath; the others he so ingeniously transplanted to the Hudson River country that with them he virtually began the history of the American short story, and with one of them, "Rip Van Winkle," he created the piece of American folklore which, beyond any other, has become a vital portion of our cultural inheritance.

It must be admitted that both "The Spectre Bridegroom" and "The Legend of Sleepy Hollow" adhere to the mock-supernaturalism of the eighteenth century, as exemplified primarily in Mrs. Radcliffe, when the ladies and gentlemen of the "Enlightenment" insisted upon tickling their imagination with "horrid" thrills, taking care at the same time to keep their skirts clean of any taint of "superstition." Though this is a type of story which contemporary aficionados of ghostly tales are inclined to reject, Irving succeeds pretty well in steering a course he can sail with reasonable hope of coming safely into harbor. Nor is this by any means wholly nor even mainly because the mock-supernaturalism itself is not original with him but carries over from his German sources. It is the schoolmaster himself whom we remember longest from "The Legend of Sleepy Hollow," and the whimsical tone with which Irving invests him and his associates seems just right for the author's temperament and the effect he seeks to create. Obviously he knew the region he was writing about as well as the forces contending in American life at the time of his writing, yet he so steeps the narrative in the "local tales and superstitions" which "thrive best" in such "sheltered, long-settled retreats" as Sleepy Hollow ("this is perhaps the reason," he remarks slyly, "why we so seldom hear of ghosts except in our long-established Dutch communities") that Ichabod's misapprehension about the Headless Horseman (whom the United States Government honored with a postage stamp in 1974) is wholly convincing. All seems quite in harmony with Lowell's point about "credulity as a mental and moral phenomenon" manifesting itself "in widely different ways, according as it chances to be the daughter of fancy or terror." It is helpful too that Ichabod should, like Walter de la Mare's Miss M., simply disappear at the end. Reasonable hypotheses are suggested to account for this, but Irving commits himself to none of them, and characters who disappear in literature, since they never die, always hold a reasonable purchase upon immortality. Perhaps, after all, we ought not to be surprised at one scholar's thesis that the story is "a rollicking parody of ancient Greek myths and rites of Greek fertility cults, a *comic* story of death and rebirth, fertility and immortality."[1] I should hate to stake my life upon it that Irving held all Ms. Bruner's parallels in his mind, but she has observed so many of them and presents her findings so reasonably that it is difficult to believe they can all be coincidental.

"The Spectre Bridegroom" lacks the charactery of "The Legend of Sleepy Hollow." But though it becomes quite clear in retrospect that the cause of the later events was the baron's rehearsal of "the history of the goblin horseman that carried away the fair Leonora" (Irving himself observes at the end that the reader must have known the truth all the while), we are not formally let in on the secret until the end, and the spectre's behavior is surely gloomy and mysterious enough to retain at least a reasonable modicum of the authentic Gothic thrill. It is clear that Irving is still playing with the mock-documentation he had used so effectively in *Knicker-bocker's History* when he gravely informs us that "events of the kind are extremely common in Germany, as many well-authenticated histories bear witness." If "The Spectre Bride-groom" is by no means so good a story as either "Rip" or "Sleepy Hollow," it is still a not unworthy third member of the group, and I can never forget how it enthralled me as a child. Even now, I am by no means sure that, as one scholar has argued, Irving intended it as a burlesque.

But of course it must go without saying that "Rip Van Winkle," which is said to have been written at high speed in a single night, is the *pièce de résistance*. Irving's vagueness in indicating his sources occasioned controversy and accusations of plagiarism even in his own time. But he knew, as Chaucer and Shakespeare had known before him, that literary materials which circulate in the blood of the race belong to him

[1] Marjorie W. Bruner, "*The Legend of Sleepy Hollow*: A Mythological Parody," *College English*, 25 (1963–64), 274–83.

who can use them best, and that all other considerations are irrelevant. Essentially, "Rip Van Winkle" was based on the story of Peter Klaus in the *Volkssagen* of Otmar (pseud. J. C. C. Nachtigal), but apparently Irving's direct source was J. G. Büsching's *Volks-Sagen, Märchen, und Legenden*, a copy of which he brought to America and which is still among his books at Sunnyside.

Peter was a goatherd who was lured into a deep dell where twelve knights were playing at skittles, and where he drank and fell asleep for twenty years. But Irving's story is four times as long as "Peter Klaus," and he did a remarkable job of Americanizing his materials. He changed the European knights to the ghosts of Henry Hudson and his crew, he transferred the scene to the Catskills, he added humor, and he built up Rip's domestic background. The twenty years' sleep he passed over in a single sentence, and devoted half his space to what happened after the old man returned home.

The sleep-motif in "Rip Van Winkle," however, has roots which run far back of Otmar. There was Epimenides, who, in the seventh or sixth century, B.C., retired to a cave to escape the heat of the day, when he should have been watching his flock, and slept there not for twenty years but for fifty-seven. But the Seven Sleepers of Ephesus remained in hibernation for some 360 years, and presumably Arthur, Charlemagne, Frederick Barbarossa, and other worthies who are supposed to return to succor their people in time of need are sleeping still. Once a pair of lovers visited Frederick in the Kyffhäuser to borrow crockery for their wedding feast; but when they returned home, they found that they had been away for two centuries. Sir Walter Scott told Irving about Thomas the Rhymer, who was carried off by the Fairy Queen, and at Inverness, when he was in Scotland, he heard of the two fiddlers of Strathspey, who were lured into that hill and detained there for a hundred years. They recognized nothing and were recognized by no one when they finally emerged, and they crumbled to dust when the Scriptures were read in church. Different sleep-motifs occur in such stories as those of Brünnhilde and the Sleeping Beauty in the Wood, as Kenneth Walter Cameron[2] and others have pointed out, and Cameron relates how the explorer Nansen told J. M. Barrie a story about a monk who wandered out into the fields one spring day, which may well have contained the germ of what the dramatist developed in *Mary Rose*:

He heard a lark singing. He had never heard a lark sing before, and he stood there in the field until the bird and its song had become part of the heavens. Then he walked back to the monastery and found there a door-keeper whom he did not know and who did not recognize him. Other monks came along, and they were strangers to him. He told them that he was Father Anselm, but that was no help. Finally, they looked through the records of the monastery, and these revealed there had been a Father Anselm there some hundred years before. Time had been blotted out while the monk listened to the lark sing!

The terror of falling out of time, of losing identity, of surviving into a world we never made informs all these tales, and all this must be taken into account if we are to understand why the story of a friendly, henpecked old ne'er-do-well, as Irving tells it, should move us as it does.

To be sure, in these days when so many critics find it more important to be "original" than to get things right, and greatly prefer interpreting the story the author didn't write to considering what he did, it is not surprising that attempts can be made to desupernaturalize even "Rip Van Winkle." Thus, according to one learned article, the story is "a brilliant satire on the gothic mind." Rip never slept in the mountains; he merely deserted his termagant wife, wandered for twenty

---

[2] Kenneth Walter Cameron, "The Long Sleep-and-Changed-World Motif in 'Rip Van Winkle,'" *Emerson Society Quarterly*, No. 19 (1960), pp. 35–36.

years, and then returned "with a bit of gothic nonsense designed to amuse the town and avoid its scorn." And that, of
course, is the reason why he did not always tell his story the
same way and why different auditors took up different atti-
tudes toward it. The argument founders on the fact that the
story is not told from Rip Van Winkle's point of view but
from that of the omniscient author. The reader, unlike the
villagers, was there with Rip in the mountains; he *knows* what
happened! As for the doubts of the villagers and such, this
is conventional in tales involving the supernatural; even Sir
Walter's "Wandering Willie's Tale," probably the greatest
narrative of its kind extant, leaves a little crack in the door
open at the end for a naturalistic explanation of the phenom-
ena that have been related. It is not only in religion that, as
Browning says, you must mix some doubt with faith if you
would have faith be. And since there is nothing new that is
not also very old, it is interesting to note that the history of
Epimenides himself was "rationalized" as far back as the eighteenth century by "some Authors" who

discountenanced this story of his long Dream; and make him to
have wandered all that Time, in order to be improving his Natural
Philosophy by the Experience of *Simples*. But perhaps the Sleep
might be only a Politick Fiction of his, to gain Authority to his Art.
For we are told, he used commonly to put a much greater Fallacy
on the People; pretending, as often as the Fit took him, to die, and
revive again at his Pleasure.

This is not to say, however, that the tale contains no authentic subtleties. Every reader remembers how confused
Rip was when, upon returning to his old town on Election
Day, he finds that General Washington's portrait has replaced
that of King George III on the sign which used to hang before
"the quiet little Dutch inn" he knew so well and which now
graced the Union Hotel. But it remained for Robert H.

Woodward[3] to alert us all to the fact that the day under consideration is that on which Washington was chosen President. Hudson explored the river which bears his name in 1609, and according to the legend he and his men return every twenty years. As a simple arithmetical operation will demonstrate, the last year during which Rip could have encountered them during the Colonial Period was 1769, and since he slept for twenty years, this would bring him back in 1789. All this was appropriate enough on the part of an author who had not only been named for the President but, as a small child, had been blessed by him when young Irving's nurse audaciously presented him in a New York shop, and who, not content with that, became one of Washington's important biographers.

In his second miscellany, *Bracebridge Hall*, Irving developed the English aspect of *The Sketch Book* by taking himself off for a book-length visit to the family he had already introduced to his readers in the Christmas papers included in the earlier book. The character sketches included, and the description of the family life, interests and recreations bring us to the verge of fiction; but Irving warns us we must not look to him for continuity. It is an attractive picture of English rural life, viewed from the upper class standpoint which he presents, but he does not neglect rural superstitions and May Day customs, and this side of the book is developed further through bringing in a band of gipsies. He departs from these matters only long enough to regale us with four tales, whose presence is justified on the ground that the stories were told at Bracebridge Hall. Though they are good stories of their kind, none is quite suited to a collection of his tales of the supernatural.

Tales of a Traveller is very much "another story"; indeed

---

[3] Robert H. Woodward, "Dating the Action of 'Rip Van Winkle,'" *New York Folklore Quarterly*, 15 (1959), 70.

it is many stories. It is divided into four sections: "Strange Stories of a Nervous Gentleman," "Buckthorne and his Friends," "The Italian Banditti" and "The Money-Diggers." "Buckthorne" is Irving's longest and most varied narrative; it derives from both reading and his own observations in England and Germany; Buckthorne's theatrical passion is like Wilhelm Meister's, and his affair with Columbine takes off from Wilhelm's with Mariana. This narrative contains ample material for a wide-ranging historical romance that might well run to a thousand pages, and while I am not suggesting that Irving develops it, it is rather remarkable that no writer has ever come along to take up his clues and create it. "The Italian Banditti" is conventional romanticism of the kind one might expect under that title, and "The Money-Diggers" is American material, centered around the idea of digging for pirate gold or gaining wealth by diabolical means. Our book takes four linked tales from "Strange Stories of a Nervous Gentleman" and one—"The Devil and Tom Walker," Irving's finest tale after "Rip Van Winkle"—from "The Money-Diggers."

"The Adventure of My Aunt" is a very slight mock-supernatural tale, but the more elaborate "Adventure of My Uncle" calls for more careful consideration. Here, the ghost who appears in my uncle's chamber at the Marquis' old chateau seems real enough, for the lady "has been dead more than a hundred years," and "my uncle" learns her history when he comes across her portrait while being shown through the building the next day. Perhaps Irving slightly misleads the reader by having her warm herself at the fireplace, "for your ghosts, if ghost it really was, are apt to be cold," and by having the old valet, when my uncle questions him in the morning, reply that "it was not for him to know anything of *les bonnes fortunes* of Monsieur." But all this is quite in line with a method of story-telling which, in this instance, almost moves beyond sophistication to perversity. Surely the atmosphere is quite as thick as anything we could ask for in a ghost story; my uncle goes to sleep in "the kind of comfortable apartment that a ghost . . . would single out for its favorite lounge," and it contains "just such an old clock as ghosts are fond of," which my uncle was confident struck thirteen; moreover he afterwards learned that the night marked the anniversary of that when the ill-starred duchess had occupied the chamber. All in all, "The Adventure of My Uncle" is about the simplest ghost story with the most elaborate build-up of any such tale I know (the situation is very different from that in "The Stout Gentleman" of *Bracebridge Hall*, where the fact that the build-up leads to nothing is the very point of the story), and Irving is evasive at the end, not so much about the supernatural manifestation itself but rather about another aspect of the history of the duchess to which he has at this point rather impishly deflected the reader's attention.

"The Bold Dragoon" is a light-hearted fantasy whose author boldly disdains any attempt to achieve what Coleridge called "that willing suspension of disbelief for a moment which constitutes poetic faith." Though Irving here invokes Sterne, he is more likely to remind the modern reader of Dickens' anthropomorphizing gifts and even of Disney's *Fantasia*. And if there are suggestions of innuendo in "My Uncle" and "My Aunt," there are more of them here.

At the close of "The Bold Dragoon," "the old gentleman with the haunted head observed that the stories hitherto related had rather a burlesque tendency" and himself proposed to relate a tale "of a very grave and singular nature." This "The Adventure of the German Student" certainly is, though the narrator's promise to vouch for its truth is seriously weakened by the conclusion, for, despite the atmosphere of necrophilia which hovers over it, this rather powerful French Revolutionary tale is as much a study of temperament as either a horror story or a ghost story. It has a dream which anticipates experience, quite in the manner cultivated by many more recent writers, and the ending in a madhouse suggests the great German film, *The Cabinet of Dr. Caligari.* "Could Wolfgang have found a corpse near the guillotine and imposed his fantasy upon it?" asks Kelly Griffith, Jr.[4] "Could he have carried it home and accepted it there as his bride, believing all the while that it was the sentient embodiment of his ideal?" Griffith rightly admits that his interpretation is "unavoidably based on inference," but surely this time Irving's evasiveness is not that of Radcliffian rationalism but has much more in common with Hawthorne's skilful, subtle, and deliberate ambiguity. There are suggestions of Poe about the story also, and though the two narratives differ in many ways, I do not believe that any reader of Marjorie Bowen's "The Fair Hair of Ambrosine" could read Irving's story without being reminded by it of the much later tale.

Though "The Devil and Tom Walker" is one of the classic tales built around the bargain with Satan, Charles G. Zug, III,[5] has rightly dissented from the usual description of it as a kind of minor New England *Faust* on the ground that Tom, unlike Faust, is not seeking to extend the bounds of human knowledge. He shows too that Irving began with the legends of Captain Kidd and his buried treasure and that he grafted upon this material a much wider variety of motifs drawn from German folklore than had previously been realized. There is no single main source here, as in "Rip Van Winkle"; the devil himself, for example, is a compound of German, American Indian and Puritan elements. Here, as in "Rip," Irving created American folklore, and here too he drew suggestions from his reading of Cotton Mather. The devil runs true to form; he keeps the letter of his bargain, and this time he is

---

[4] "Ambiguity and Gloom in Irving's 'Adventure of the German Student,' " *CEA Critic*, 38, November 1975, pp. 10–13.

[5] "The Construction of 'The Devil and Tom Walker': A Study of Irving's Later Use of Folklore," *New York Folklore Quarterly*, 24 (1968), 243–60.

not cheated of his prize. Simple as the tale seems, its skilfully developed images of desolation and sterility deserve more analysis as well as praise than they have always received. Again Irving builds up the hero's domestic background; he also includes many references to and much satire of colonial society in the Boston of 1727, showing clearly that though he did not write as a reformer, he was not blind to either social or economic abuses, or unaware that piety and respectability are often only a facade. Thus we are told of Deacon Peabody that he "had waxed wealthy by driving shrewd bargains with the Indians," and Tom Walker himself resolutely rejects the devil's first condition, that he should employ his newly acquired wealth by fitting out a slave ship: "he was bad enough in all conscience; but the devil himself could not tempt him to turn slave-trader." The misogyny suggested by the presence of Dame Van Winkle in an earlier tale reappears in the considerably more revolting wife of Tom Walker, and there was to be another much like her later, in "Guests from Gibbet Island." Not all the females in "The Spectre Bridegroom" are reverentially treated either, nor are those in the Alhambra tales. If we are tempted to read autobiography into this, however, we shall find ourselves far astray, for though Irving never married, he did carry about with him a heart "handsomely cracked," as Sir Walter expressed it in another connection, from his early bereavement in the death of Matilda Hoffman, and he confessed that he was always more or less in love with every charming woman he met.

Irving began his writing under eighteenth-century influences, but Romantic impulses appeared early, and were already strongly in evidence, at least as a leavening influence, in *The Sketch Book*. *The Alhambra* is generally thought of as his complete capitulation to romance, and it is quite true that the legends contained in it are an *Arabian Nights* kind of material, glowing with the richest colors and highly stimulating to the imagination. Most of the first volume, however, is devoted to describing the Alhambra itself as it was when Irving visited there, and this is all honest reporting. As he himself puts it, "Every thing in the work relating to myself and to the actual inhabitants of the Alhambra is unexaggerated fact; it was only in the legends themselves that I indulged in *romancing*."

Of the eight pieces Irving labels legends, all save one are reprinted here, "Legend of the Three Beautiful Princesses" being excluded as not sufficiently a supernatural tale. He supplemented his observations by research in Spanish libraries, but the sources of these tales have not been very satisfactorily or exhaustively traced. Some of his materials he may well have received orally, and he may even have used remnants of his old German accumulations.

Here are magic spells, underground caverns containing priceless treasures and enchanted beings, and even a flying carpet. Here also we encounter a wondrous book of knowledge buried in a sepulchral chamber in a mighty pyramid, a bronze figure of a horseman which turns on a pivot to give warning of the approach of invaders who, while still distant, may be defeated and slain by striking their effigies, a mystic hand which, by reaching forth to seize upon a fated key, can dissolve the charm holding an enchanted mountain in thrall, and an enchanted garden, cursed of old because of the presumption of its creator, which may still appear at intervals to a wanderer. A prince who has been guarded against all knowledge and experience of love learns of it through becoming familiar with the language of birds; he is then guided and advised by a raven skilled in the black arts and a parrot who has all the learning of the East at the tip of his tongue. A Moorish talisman leads into a world of supernatural wonder, including a sight of the Alhambra "as it was in the days of its glory," when the great Boabdil was alive, and there is an incantation which opens belts, bars and caverns, and a magic taper which will keep them open so long as it shall burn. And

there is much, much more out of the same bolt of cloth, as
the reader of the following pages will enjoy learning for himself.

Yet even the Alhambra legends are not all supernaturalism;
Irving was too good an artist for that. He knew that undiluted
wonders cloy, and that marvels lose their power over the
imagination when there is no homely reality to set over
against them. One of the best stories, "Legend of the Moor's
Legacy," begins quite realistically, on the plane of charactery.
The first hint of coming wonders enters only with the san-
dalwood box bequeathed to the henpecked little water carrier
by the dying Moor whom he has befriended, and even then
we do not know what will come of it. Only the epilogue of
the "Legend of Don Munio Sancho de Hinojosa" is supernatural, and love in a highly romantic setting is the only
wonder of the "Legend of the Rose of the Alhambra" until
the spirit of the love-deprived Zorahayda rises at last from
the fountain. In "The Legend of the Enchanted Soldier," on
the other hand, the note of wonder is sounded in the very
first paragraph, then promptly fades out into a reasonable
account of the wandering life of the student of Salamanca
who finds the seal marked with the Star of David. From here
we pass on to his infatuation with the padre's "pet lamb," and
supernaturalism does not really take over until he encounters
the soldier who belongs to the royal guard of Ferdinand and
Isabella, three centuries back, and whom he can deliver from
enchantment only with the aid of a stainless priest and
maiden.

The emphasis throughout is on yarning and atmosphere
rather than character development, though the lower-class
characters are, not surprisingly, more likely to be presented
in some detail than the more conventionalized protagonists
of romantic adventures. The water carrier of "The Moor's
Legacy" perhaps comes closest to being a real character, and
there are some interesting glimpses of those associated with

him. But if developed character determines incident less in these tales than modern critics tend to prefer, it should still be understood that wonder and reality do not merely lie one on the other like the layers of a cake; the combination is much more subtle than that. By means of magic, the Arabian Astrologer has learned how to prolong his life indefinitely, but since "he did not discover the secret until well stricken in years, he could only perpetuate his gray hairs and wrinkles," in spite of which he still fails to control an old man's fruitless passion for young beauty. And the quarrels between the raven and the parrot who are both so important to Prince Ahmed, because one cares only for poetry and the other for metaphysics, might well have been relished by Chaucer.

Nor, for that matter, is the kind of social criticism we have seen elsewhere wholly excluded from the Alhambra legends. Having conquered everything in sight, the King of Granada "desired nothing more than to live at peace with all the world, to husband his laurels, and to enjoy in quiet the possessions he had wrested from his neighbors." With princes, religion "is always a point of pride and etiquette," and nobody can doubt that the Alcalde by whom Peregil is confronted "set a high value upon justice, for he sold it at its weight in gold." Nor is the church herself spared in either the person of the greedy Fray Simon of the "Discreet Statues" or the priest in "The Legend of the Enchanted Soldier," who was "certainly a mirror of good if not of holy living." And if any reader has ever doubted that this worthy's "pet lamb" is actually his mistress, it must certainly be dispelled when she bears her first child, a sturdier and more robust specimen than any which follow, only seven months after her marriage.

Irving's final miscellany, *Wolfert's Roost*, was a collection of flotsam and jetsam—"garrett-trumpery," he called it—which his publisher Putnam "enticed" from his desk and old periodicals. His contemporaries loved it, and although the very title is unfamiliar to many who still love *The Sketch Book*, it contains much good reading, reflecting a wide variety of Irving's interests. Only one of its stories is included in this collection. "Guests From Gibbet Island" is a yarn influenced by his researches into the literary remains of the old Dutch settlers, though, according to Henry A. Pochmann, it is based on the Grimms' much shorter story, "The Gallows Guests." Pluto (as his name suggests) has seemed more than a merely human character from the beginning, but his claims in that direction seem undercut at the end, and the story does not really turn supernatural until the hanged buccaneers accept Vanderscamp's drunken invitation, as defiant and as ill-advised as Don Giovanni's to the statue, and come to dinner at his mansion.

Washington Irving was far from being a naive or unsophisticated story teller; like Chaucer's, his apparent naiveté is a part of his art. As early as 1823 he wrote his brother:

There are such quantities of the legendary and romantic tales now littering from the presses, both in England and in Germany, that one must take care not to fall into the commonplaces of the day. Scott's manner must likewise be avoided. In short, I must strike out some way of my own, suited to my own way of thinking and writing.

Later he gave some indication of the direction in which he planned to move:

I fancy that much of what I value myself upon in writing, escapes the observation of the great mass of my readers: who are intent more upon the story than the way in which it is told. For my part I consider a story merely as a frame on which to stretch my materials. It is the play of thought, and sentiment and language; the weaving in of characters, lightly yet expressively delineated; the familiar and faithful exhibition of scenes of common life; and the half concealed vein of humor that is often playing through the whole—these are among what I aim at, and upon which I felicitate myself in proportion as I think I succeed. . . . I believe the works

I have written will be oftener reread than any novel of the size that I could have written.

His art nevertheless is an art that conceals art, and this adds to his value in a day when so many writers have apparently so completely lost the ability to distinguish between a story and a crossword puzzle. Not only must we read through the first half of an avant-garde novel, but we must even sit through such popular art as films and television shows, trying to figure out who so-and-so is and how some new element can possibly be fitted into what we thought we had known before. If Irving valued "the play of thought, and sentiment and language" above the plot as plot, he was still too intelligent not to know that in art, absorption in method for method's sake spells decadence. Essentially the method that was good enough for Scheherazade and the folk tales was good enough for him: he lays out his properties beforehand and guides the reader every step of the way. You do not piece the situation together out of scattered hints; neither need you be afraid that if you allow your attention to wander for a moment, you will miss the whole point of the narrative. Instead you can curl up in his lap like a tired child and listen to his clear, pleasant, cultivated voice going on and on but never too long. This does not mean that there are no subtleties and refinements that will repay repeated readings, but it does mean that you are dealing with an author who never forgets that art is communication, and who gives no reasonable excuse for weird misinterpretations of his meaning, though, as we have seen, even this has not always saved him from them.

EDWARD WAGENKNECHT

West Newton, Massachusetts
February 1982

Washington Irving's Tales of the Supernatural

Rip Van Winkle

A Posthumous Writing of Diedrich Knickerbocker

By Woden, God of Saxons,
From whence comes Wensday, that is Wodensday,
Truth is a thing that ever I will keep
Unto thylke day in which I creep into
My sepulchre—

Cartwright

[The following Tale was found among the papers of the late Diedrich Knickerbocker, an old gentleman of New York, who was very curious in the Dutch history of the province, and the manners of the descendants from its primitive settlers. His historical researches, however, did not lie so much among books as among men; for the former are lamentably scanty on his favorite topics; whereas he found the old burghers, and still more their wives, rich in that legendary lore so invaluable to true history. Whenever, therefore, he happened upon a genuine Dutch family, snugly shut up in its low-roofed farmhouse, under a spreading sycamore, he looked upon it as a little clasped volume of black-letter, and studied it with the zeal of a book-worm.

The result of all these researches was a history of the province during the reign of the Dutch governors, which he published some years since. There have been various opinions as to the literary character of his work, and, to tell the truth, it is not a whit better than it should be. Its chief merit is its scrupulous accuracy, which indeed was a little questioned on its first appearance, but has since been completely established; and it is now admitted into all historical collections as a book of unquestionable authority.

The old gentleman died shortly after the publication of his work; and now that he is dead and gone, it cannot do much harm to his memory to say that his time might have been much better employed in weightier labors. He, however, was apt to ride his hobby his own way; and though it did now and then kick up the dust a little in the eyes of his neighbors, and grieve the spirit of some friends, for whom he felt the truest deference and affection, yet his errors and follies are remembered "more in sorrow than in anger," and it begins to be suspected that he never intended to offend. But however his memory may be appreciated by critics, it is still held dear by many folk whose good opinion is well worth having; particularly by certain biscuit-makers, who have gone so far as to imprint his likeness on their New-Year cakes; and have thus given him a chance for immortality, almost equal to being stamped on a Waterloo Medal, or a Queen Anne's Farthing.]

WHOEVER has made a voyage up the Hudson must remember the Kaatskill mountains. They are a dismembered branch of the great Appalachian family, and are seen away to the west of the river, swelling up to a noble height, and lording it over the surrounding country. Every change of season, every change of weather, indeed, every hour of the day, produces some change in the magical hues and shapes of these mountains, and they are regarded by all the good wives, far and near, as perfect barometers. When the weather is fair and settled, they are clothed in blue and purple, and print their bold outlines on the clear evening sky; but sometimes, when the rest of the landscape is cloudless, they will gather a hood of gray vapors about their summits, which, in the last rays of the setting sun, will glow and light up like a crown of glory.

At the foot of these fairy mountains, the voyager may have descried the light smoke curling up from a village, whose shingle-roofs gleam among the trees, just where the blue tints of the upland melt away into the fresh green of the nearer landscape. It is a little village, of great antiquity, having been founded by some of the Dutch colonists in the early times of the province, just about the beginning of the government of the good Peter Stuyvesant, (may he rest in peace!) and there were some of the houses of the original settlers standing within a few years, built of small yellow bricks brought from Holland, having latticed windows and gable fronts, surmounted with weathercocks.

In that same village, and in one of these very houses (which, to tell the precise truth, was sadly time-worn and weather-beaten), there lived, many years since, while the country was yet a province of Great Britain, a simple, good-natured fellow, of the name of Rip Van Winkle. He was a descendant of the Van Winkles who figured so gallantly in the chivalrous days of Peter Stuyvesant, and accompanied him to the siege of Fort Christina. He inherited, however, but little of the martial character of his ancestors. I have observed that he was a simple, good-natured man; he was, moreover, a kind neighbor, and an obedient, hen-pecked husband. Indeed, to the latter circumstance might be owing that meekness of spirit which gained him such universal popularity; for those men are most apt to be obsequious and conciliating abroad, who are under the discipline of shrews at home. Their tempers, doubtless, are rendered pliant and malleable in the fiery furnace of domestic tribulation; and a curtain-lecture is worth all the sermons in the world for teaching the virtues of patience and long-suffering. A termagant wife may, therefore, in some respects, be considered a tolerable blessing; and if so, Rip Van Winkle was thrice blessed.

Certain it is, that he was a great favorite among all the good wives of the village, who, as usual with the amiable sex, took his part in all family squabbles; and never failed, whenever they talked those matters over in their evening gossipings, to lay all the blame on Dame Van Winkle. The children of the village, too, would shout with joy whenever he approached. He assisted at their sports, made their playthings, taught them to fly kites and shoot marbles, and told them long stories of ghosts, witches, and Indians. Whenever he went dodging about the village, he was surrounded by a troop of them, hanging on his skirts, clambering on his back, and playing a thousand tricks on him with impunity; and not a dog would bark at him throughout the neighborhood.

The great error in Rip's composition was an insuperable aversion to all kinds of profitable labor. It could not be from the want of assiduity or perseverance; for he would sit on a wet rock, with a rod as long and heavy as a Tartar's lance, and fish all day without a murmur, even though he should not be encouraged by a single nibble. He would carry a fowling-piece on his shoulder for hours together, trudging through woods and swamps, and up hill and down dale, to shoot a few squirrels or wild pigeons. He would never refuse to assist a neighbor even in the roughest toil, and was a foremost man at all country frolics for husking Indian corn, or building stone fences; the women of the village, too, used to employ him to run their errands, and to do such little odd jobs as their less obliging husbands would not do for them. In a word, Rip was ready to attend to anybody's business but his own; but as to doing family duty, and keeping his farm in order, he found it impossible.

In fact, he declared it was of no use to work on his farm; it was the most pestilent little piece of ground in the whole country; everything about it went wrong, and would go wrong, in spite of him. His fences were continually falling to pieces; his cow would either go astray, or get among the cabbages; weeds were sure to grow quicker in his fields than anywhere else; the rain always made a point of setting in just as he had some out-door work to do; so that though his patrimonial estate had dwindled away under his management, acre by acre, until there was little more left than a mere patch of Indian corn and potatoes, yet it was the worst conditioned farm in the neighborhood.

His children, too, were as ragged and wild as if they belonged to nobody. His son Rip, an urchin begotten in his own likeness, promised to inherit the habits, with the old clothes, of his father. He was generally seen trooping like a colt at his mother's heels, equipped in a pair of his father's cast-off galligaskins, which he had much ado to hold up with one hand, as a fine lady does her train in bad weather.

Rip Van Winkle, however, was one of those happy mortals, of foolish, well-oiled dispositions, who take the world easy, eat white bread or brown, whichever can be got with least thought or trouble, and would rather starve on a penny than work for a pound. If left to himself, he would have whistled life away in perfect contentment; but his wife kept continually dinning in his ears about his idleness, his carelessness, and the ruin he was bringing on his family. Morning, noon and night, her tongue was incessantly going, and everything he said or did was sure to produce a torrent of household eloquence. Rip had but one way of replying to all lectures of the kind, and that, by frequent use, had grown into a habit. He shrugged his shoulders, shook his head, cast up his eyes, but said nothing. This, however, always provoked a fresh volley from his wife; so that he was fain to draw off his forces, and take to the outside of the house—the only side which, in truth, belongs to a hen-pecked husband.

Rip's sole domestic adherent was his dog Wolf, who was as much hen-pecked as his master; for Dame Van Winkle regarded them as companions in idleness, and even looked upon Wolf with an evil eye, as the cause of his master's going so often astray. True it is, in all points of spirit befitting an honorable dog, he was as courageous an animal as ever scoured the woods; but what courage can withstand the ever-enduring and all-besetting terrors of a woman's tongue? The moment Wolf entered the house his crest fell, his tail drooped to the ground, or curled between his legs, he sneaked about with a gallows air, casting many a sidelong glance at Dame Van Winkle, and at the least flourish of a broomstick or ladle he would fly to the door with yelping precipitation.

Times grew worse and worse with Rip Van Winkle as years of matrimony rolled on; a tart temper never mellows with age, and a sharp tongue is the only edged tool that grows keener with constant use. For a long while he used to console himself, when driven from home, by frequenting a kind of perpetual club of the sages, philosophers, and other idle personages of the village, which held its sessions on a bench before a small inn, designated by a rubicund portrait of His Majesty George the Third. Here they used to sit in the shade through a long, lazy summer's day, talking listlessly over village gossip, or telling endless sleepy stories about nothing.

But it would have been worth any statesman's money to have heard the profound discussions that sometimes took place, when by chance an old newspaper fell into their hands from some passing traveller. How solemnly they would listen to the contents, as drawled out by Derrick Van Bummel, the schoolmaster, a dapper learned little man, who was not to be daunted by the most gigantic word in the dictionary; and how sagely they would deliberate upon public events some months after they had taken place.

The opinions of this junto were completely controlled by Nicholas Vedder, patriarch of the village, and landlord of the inn, at the door of which he took his seat from morning till night, just moving sufficiently to avoid the sun and keep in the shade of a large tree; so that the neighbors could tell the hour by his movements as accurately as by a sun-dial. It is true he was rarely heard to speak, but smoked his pipe incessantly. His adherents, however (for every great man has his adherents), perfectly understood him, and knew how to gather his opinions. When anything that was read or related displeased him, he was observed to smoke his pipe vehemently, and to send forth short, frequent, and angry puffs; but when pleased, he would inhale the smoke slowly and tranquilly, and emit it in light and placid clouds; and sometimes, taking the pipe from his mouth, and letting the fragrant vapor curl about his nose, would gravely nod his head in token of perfect approbation.

From even this stronghold the unlucky Rip was at length routed by his termagant wife, who would suddenly break in upon the tranquillity of the assemblage and call the members all to naught; nor was that august personage, Nicholas Vedder himself, sacred from the daring tongue of this terrible virago, who charged him outright with encouraging her husband in habits of idleness.

Poor Rip was at last reduced almost to despair; and his only alternative, to escape from the labor of the farm and clamor of his wife, was to take gun in hand and stroll away into the woods. Here he would sometimes seat himself at the foot of a tree, and share the contents of his wallet with Wolf, with whom he sympathized as a fellow-sufferer in persecution. "Poor Wolf," he would say, "thy mistress leads thee a dog's life of it, but never mind, my lad, whilst I live thou shalt never want a friend to stand by thee!" Wolf would wag his tail, look wistfully in his master's face, and if dogs can feel pity, I verily believe he reciprocated the sentiment with all his heart.

In a long ramble of the kind on a fine autumnal day, Rip had unconsciously scrambled to one of the highest parts of the Kaatskill mountains. He was after his favorite sport of squirrel-shooting, and the still solitudes had echoed and re-echoed with the reports of his gun. Panting and fatigued, he threw himself, late in the afternoon, on a green knoll, covered with mountain herbage, that crowned the brow of a precipice. From an opening between the trees he could overlook all the lower country for many a mile of rich woodland. He saw at a distance the lordly Hudson, far, far below him, moving on its silent but majestic course, with the reflection of a purple cloud, or the sail of a lagging bark, here and there sleeping on its glassy bosom, and at last losing itself in the blue highlands.

On the other side he looked down into a deep mountain glen, wild, lonely, and shagged, the bottom filled with fragments from the impending cliffs, and scarcely lighted by the reflected rays of the setting sun. For some time Rip lay musing on this scene; evening was gradually advancing; the mountains began to throw their long blue shadows over the valleys; he saw that it would be dark long before he could reach the village, and he heaved a heavy sigh when he thought of encountering the terrors of Dame Van Winkle.

As he was about to descend, he heard a voice from a distance, hallooing, "Rip Van Winkle, Rip Van Winkle!" He looked around, but could see nothing but a crow winging its solitary flight across the mountain. He thought his fancy must have deceived him, and turned again to descend, when he heard the same cry ring through the still evening air: "Rip Van Winkle! Rip Van Winkle!"—at the same time Wolf bristled up his back, and giving a low growl, skulked to his master's side, looking fearfully down into the glen. Rip now felt a vague apprehension stealing over him; he looked anxiously in the same direction, and perceived a strange figure slowly toiling up the rocks, and bending under the weight of something he carried on his back. He was surprised to see any human being in this lonely and unfrequented place; but supposing it to be some one of the neighborhood in need of his assistance, he hastened down to yield it.

On nearer approach he was still more surprised at the singularity of the stranger's appearance. He was a short, square-built old fellow, with thick bushy hair, and a grizzled beard. His dress was of the antique Dutch fashion,—a cloth jerkin strapped around the waist—several pair of breeches, the outer one of ample volume, decorated with rows of buttons down the sides, and bunches at the knees. He bore on his shoulders a stout keg, that seemed full of liquor, and made signs for Rip to approach and assist him with the load. Though rather shy and distrustful of this new acquaintance,

Rip complied with his usual alacrity; and mutually relieving one another, they clambered up a narrow gully, apparently the dry bed of a mountain torrent. As they ascended, Rip every now and then heard long, rolling peals, like distant thunder, that seemed to issue out of a deep ravine, or rather cleft, between lofty rocks, toward which their rugged path conducted. He paused for an instant, but supposing it to be the muttering of one of those transient thunder-showers which often take place in mountain heights, he proceeded. Passing through the ravine, they came to a hollow, like a small amphitheatre, surrounded by perpendicular precipices, over the brinks of which impending trees shot their branches, so that you only caught glimpses of the azure sky and the bright evening cloud. During the whole time Rip and his companion had labored on in silence; for though the former marvelled greatly what could be the object of carrying a keg of liquor up this wild mountain, yet there was something strange and incomprehensible about the unknown, that inspired awe and checked familiarity.

On entering the amphitheatre, new objects of wonder presented themselves. On a level spot in the centre was a company of odd-looking personages playing at ninepins. They were dressed in a quaint, outlandish fashion; some wore short doublets, others jerkins, with long knives in their belts, and most of them had enormous breeches, of similar style with that of the guide's. Their visages, too, were peculiar: one had a large beard, broad face, and small piggish eyes; the face of another seemed to consist entirely of nose, and was surmounted by a white sugar-loaf hat, set off with a little red cock's tail. They all had beards, of various shapes and colors. There was one who seemed to be the commander. He was a stout old gentleman, with a weather-beaten countenance; he wore a laced doublet, broad belt and hanger, high crowned hat and feather, red stockings, and high-heeled shoes, with roses in them. The whole group reminded Rip of the figures in an old Flemish painting, in the parlor of Dominie Van Shaick, the village parson, and which had been brought over from Holland at the time of the settlement.

What seemed particularly odd to Rip was, that, though these folks were evidently amusing themselves, yet they maintained the gravest faces, the most mysterious silence, and were, withal, the most melancholy party of pleasure he had ever witnessed. Nothing interrupted the stillness of the scene but the noise of the balls, which, whenever they rolled, echoed along the mountains like rumbling peals of thunder.

As Rip and his companion approached them, they suddenly desisted from their play, and stared at him with such fixed, statue-like gaze, and such strange, uncouth, lack-lustre countenances, that his heart turned within him, and his knees smote together. His companion now emptied the contents of the keg into large flagons, and made signs to him to wait upon the company. He obeyed with fear and trembling; they quaffed the liquor in profound silence, and then returned to their game.

By degrees Rip's awe and apprehension subsided. He even ventured, when no eye was fixed upon him, to taste the beverage, which he found had much of the flavor of excellent Hollands. He was naturally a thirsty soul, and was soon tempted to repeat the draught. One taste provoked another; and he reiterated his visits to the flagon so often that at length his senses were overpowered, his eyes swam in his head, his head gradually declined, and he fell into a deep sleep.

On waking, he found himself on the green knoll whence he had first seen the old man of the glen. He rubbed his eyes—it was a bright sunny morning. The birds were hopping and twittering among the bushes, and the eagle was wheeling aloft, and breasting the pure mountain breeze. "Surely," thought Rip, "I have not slept here all night." He recalled the occurrences before he fell asleep. The strange man with a keg of liquor—the mountain ravine—the wild retreat among the rocks—the woe-begone party at ninepins—the flagon— "Oh! that flagon! that wicked flagon!" thought Rip, "what excuse shall I make to Dame Van Winkle?"

He looked round for his gun, but in place of the clean, well-oiled fowling-piece, he found an old firelock lying by him, the barrel encrusted with rust, the lock falling off, and the stock worm-eaten. He now suspected that the grave roisters of the mountains had put a trick upon him, and, having dosed him with liquor, had robbed him of his gun. Wolf, too, had disappeared, but he might have strayed away after a squirrel or partridge. He whistled after him, and shouted his name, but all in vain; the echoes repeated his whistle and shout, but no dog was to be seen.

He determined to revisit the scene of the last evening's gambol, and if he met with any of the party, to demand his dog and gun. As he rose to walk, he found himself stiff in the joints, and wanting in his usual activity. "These mountain beds do not agree with me," thought Rip, "and if this frolic should lay me up with a fit of the rheumatism, I shall have a blessed time with Dame Van Winkle." With some difficulty he got down into the glen: he found the gully up which he and his companion had ascended the preceding evening; but to his astonishment a mountain stream was now foaming down it, leaping from rock to rock, and filling the glen with babbling murmurs. He, however, made shift to scramble up its sides, working his toilsome way through thickets of birch, sassafras, and witch-hazel, and sometimes tripped up or entangled by the wild grape-vines that twisted their coils or tendrils from tree to tree, and spread a kind of network in his path.

At length he reached to where the ravine had opened through the cliffs to the amphitheatre; but no traces of such opening remained. The rocks presented a high, impenetrable wall, over which the torrent came tumbling in a sheet of feathery foam, and fell into a broad deep basin, black from the shadows of the surrounding forest. Here, then, poor Rip was brought to a stand. He again called and whistled after his dog; he was only answered by the cawing of a flock of idle crows, sporting high in air about a dry tree that overhung a sunny precipice; and who, secure in their elevation, seemed to look down and scoff at the poor man's perplexities. What was to be done? the morning was passing away, and Rip felt famished for want of his breakfast. He grieved to give up his dog and gun; he dreaded to meet his wife; but it would not do to starve among the mountains. He shook his head, shouldered the rusty firelock, and, with a heart full of trouble and anxiety, turned his footsteps homeward.

As he approached the village he met a number of people, but none whom he knew, which somewhat surprised him, for he had thought himself acquainted with every one in the country round. Their dress, too, was of a different fashion from that to which he was accustomed. They all stared at him with equal marks of surprise, and whenever they cast their eyes upon him, invariably stroked their chins. The constant recurrence of this gesture induced Rip, involuntarily, to do the same, when, to his astonishment, he found his beard had grown a foot long!

He had now entered the skirts of the village. A troop of strange children ran at his heels, hooting after him, and pointing at his gray beard. The dogs, too, not one of which he recognized for an old acquaintance, barked at him as he passed. The very village was altered; it was larger and more populous. There were rows of houses which he had never seen before, and those which had been his familiar haunts had disappeared. Strange names were over the doors—strange faces at the windows—everything was strange. His mind now misgave him; he began to doubt whether both he and the world around him were not bewitched. Surely this was his native village, which he had left but the day before. There stood the Kaatskill mountains—there ran the silver Hudson at a distance—there was every hill and dale precisely as it had always been. Rip was sorely perplexed. "That flagon last night," thought he, "has addled my poor head sadly!"

It was with some difficulty that he found the way to his own house, which he approached with silent awe, expecting every moment to hear the shrill voice of Dame Van Winkle. He found the house gone to decay—the roof fallen in, the windows shattered, and the doors off the hinges. A half-starved dog that looked like Wolf was skulking about it. Rip called him by name, but the cur snarled, showed his teeth, and passed on. This was an unkind cut indeed. "My very dog," sighed poor Rip, "has forgotten me!"

He entered the house, which to tell the truth, Dame Van Winkle had always kept in neat order. It was empty, forlorn, and apparently abandoned. This desolateness overcame all his connubial fears—he called loudly for his wife and children—the lonely chambers rang for a moment with his voice, and then all again was silence.

He now hurried forth, and hastened to his old resort, the village inn, but it too was gone. A large rickety wooden building stood in its place, with great gaping windows, some of them broken and mended with old hats and petticoats, and over the door was painted, "The Union Hotel, by Jonathan Doolittle." Instead of the great tree that used to shelter the quiet little Dutch inn of yore, there now was reared a tall naked pole, with something on top that looked like a red night-cap, and from it was fluttering a flag, on which was a singular assemblage of stars and stripes—all this was strange and incomprehensible. He recognized on the sign, however, the ruby face of King George, under which he had smoked so many a peaceful pipe; but even this was singularly metamorphosed. The red coat was changed for one of blue and buff, a sword was held in the hand instead of a sceptre, the head was decorated with a cocked hat, and underneath was painted in large characters, GENERAL WASHINGTON.

There was, as usual, a crowd of folk about the door, but none that Rip recollected. The very character of the people seemed changed. There was a busy, bustling, disputatious tone about it, instead of the accustomed phlegm and drowsy tranquillity. He looked in vain for the sage Nicholas Vedder, with his broad face, double chin, and fair long pipe, uttering clouds of tobacco-smoke instead of idle speeches; or Van Bummel, the schoolmaster, doling forth the contents of an ancient newspaper. In place of these, a lean, bilious-looking fellow, with his pockets full of handbills, was haranguing vehemently about rights of citizens—elections—members of congress—liberty—Bunker's Hill—heroes of seventy-six—and other words, which were a perfect Babylonish jargon to the bewildered Van Winkle.

The appearance of Rip, with his long, grizzled beard, his rusty fowling-piece, his uncouth dress, and an army of women and children at his heels, soon attracted the attention of the tavern-politicians. They crowded round him, eying him from head to foot with great curiosity. The orator bustled up to him, and, drawing him partly aside, inquired "On which side he voted?" Rip stared in vacant stupidity. Another short but busy little fellow pulled him by the arm, and, rising on tiptoe, inquired in his ear, "Whether he was Federal or Democrat?" Rip was equally at a loss to comprehend the question; when a knowing, self-important old gentleman, in a sharp cocked hat, made his way through the crowd, putting them to the right and left with his elbows as he passed, and planting himself before Van Winkle, with one arm akimbo, the other resting on his cane, his keen eyes and sharp hat penetrating, as it were, into his very soul, demanded in an austere tone, "What brought him to the election with a gun on his shoulder, and a mob at his heels; and whether he meant to breed a riot in the village?"—"Alas! gentlemen," cried Rip, somewhat dismayed, "I am a poor quiet man, a native of the place, and a loyal subject of the King, God bless him!"

Here a general shout burst from the by-standers—"A tory! a tory! a spy! a refugee! hustle him! away with him!" It was with great difficulty that the self-important man in the cocked hat restored order; and, having assumed a tenfold austerity of brow, demanded again of the unknown culprit, what he came there for, and whom he was seeking? The poor man humbly assured him that he meant no harm, but merely came there in search of some of his neighbors, who used to keep about the tavern.

"Well—who are they?—name them."

Rip bethought himself a moment, and inquired, "Where's Nicholas Vedder?"

There was a silence for a little while, when an old man replied, in a thin piping voice, "Nicholas Vedder! why, he is dead and gone these eighteen years! There was a wooden tombstone in that churchyard that used to tell all about him, but that's rotten and gone too."

"Where's Brom Dutcher?"

"Oh, he went off to the army in the beginning of the war; some say he was killed at the storming of Stony Point—others say he was drowned in a squall at the foot of Antony's Nose. I don't know—he never came back again."

Where's Van Bummel, the schoolmaster?"

"He went off to the wars too, was a great militia general, and is now in congress."

Rip's heart died away at hearing of these sad changes in his home and friends, and finding himself thus alone in the world. Every answer puzzled him too, by treating of such enormous lapses of time, and of matters which he could not understand: war—congress—Stony Point—he had no courage to ask after any more friends, but cried out in despair, "Does nobody here know Rip Van Winkle?"

"Oh, Rip Van Winkle!" exclaimed two or three. "Oh, to be sure! that's Rip Van Winkle yonder, leaning against the tree."

Rip looked, and he beheld a precise counterpart of himself, as he went up the mountain; apparently as lazy, and certainly as ragged. The poor fellow was now completely confounded. He doubted his own identity, and whether he was himself or another man. In the midst of his bewilderment, the man in the cocked hat demanded who he was, and what was his name.

"God knows," exclaimed he, at his wit's end; "I'm not myself—I'm somebody else—that's me yonder—no—that's somebody else got into my shoes—I was myself last night, but I fell asleep on the mountain, and they've changed my gun, and everything's changed, and I'm changed, and I can't tell what's my name, or who I am!"

The by standers began now to look at each other, nod, wink significantly, and tap their fingers against their foreheads. There was a whisper, also, about securing the gun, and keeping the old fellow from doing mischief, at the very suggestion of which the self-important man in the cocked hat retired with some precipitation. At this critical moment a fresh, comely woman pressed through the throng to get a peep at the gray-bearded man. She had a chubby child in her arms, which, frightened at his looks, began to cry. "Hush, Rip," cried she, "hush, you little fool; the old man won't hurt you." The name of the child, the air of the mother, the tone of her voice, all awakened a train of recollections in his mind. "What is your name, my good woman?" asked he.

"Judith Gardenier."

"And your father's name?"

"Ah, poor man, Rip Van Winkle was his name, but it's twenty years since he went away from home with his gun, and never has been heard of since—his dog came home without him; but whether he shot himself, or was carried away by the Indians, nobody can tell. I was then but a little girl."

Rip had but one question more to ask; but he put it with a faltering voice:

"Where's your mother?"

"Oh, she too died but a short time since; she broke a bloodvessel in a fit of passion at a New England peddler."

There was a drop of comfort, at least, in this intelligence. The honest man could contain himself no longer. He caught his daughter and her child in his arms. "I am your father!" cried he—"Young Rip Van Winkle once—old Rip Van Winkle now!—Does nobody know poor Rip Van Winkle?"

All stood amazed, until an old woman, tottering out from among the crowd, put her hand to her brow, and peering under it in his face for a moment, exclaimed, "Sure enough! it is Rip Van Winkle—it is himself! Welcome home again, old neighbor. Why, where have you been these twenty long years?"

Rip's story was soon told, for the whole twenty years had been to him but as one night. The neighbors stared when they heard it; some were seen to wink at each other, and put their tongues in their cheeks: and the self-important man in the cocked hat, who, when the alarm was over, had returned to the field, screwed down the corners of his mouth, and shook his head—upon which there was a general shaking of the head throughout the assemblage.

It was determined, however, to take the opinion of old Peter Vanderdonk, who was seen slowly advancing up the road. He was a descendant of the historian of that name, who wrote one of the earliest accounts of the province. Peter was the most ancient inhabitant of the village, and well versed in all the wonderful events and traditions of the neighborhood. He recollected Rip at once, and corroborated his story in the most satisfactory manner. He assured the company that it was a fact, handed down from his ancestor the historian, that the Kaatskill mountains had always been haunted by strange beings. That it was affirmed that the great Hendrick Hudson, the first discoverer of the river and country, kept a kind of vigil there every twenty years, with his crew of the *Half-moon;* being permitted in this way to revisit the scenes of his enterprise, and keep a guardian eye upon the river and the great city called by his name. That his father had once seen them in their old Dutch dresses playing at ninepins in a hollow of the mountain; and that he himself had heard, one summer afternoon, the sound of their balls, like distant peals of thunder.

To make a long story short, the company broke up and returned to the more important concerns of the election. Rip's daughter took him home to live with her; she had a snug, well-furnished house, and a stout, cheery farmer for a husband, whom Rip recollected for one of the urchins that used to climb upon his back. As to Rip's son and heir, who was the ditto of himself, seen leaning against the tree, he was employed to work on the farm; but evinced an hereditary disposition to attend to anything else but his business.

Rip now resumed his old walks and habits; he soon found many of his former cronies, though all rather the worse for the wear and tear of time; and preferred making friends among the rising generation, with whom he soon grew into great favor.

Having nothing to do at home, and being arrived at that happy age when a man can be idle with impunity, he took his place once more on the bench at the inn-door, and was reverenced as one of the patriarchs of the village, and a chronicle of the old times "before the war." It was some time before he could get into the regular track of gossip, or could be made to comprehend the strange events that had taken place during his torpor. How that there had been a revolutionary war—that the country had thrown off the yoke of old England—and that, instead of being a subject of his Majesty George the Third, he was now a free citizen of the United States. Rip, in fact, was no politician; the changes of states and empires made but little impression to him; but there was one species of despotism under which he long groaned, and that was—petticoat government. Happily that was at an end; he had got his neck out of the yoke of matrimony, and could go in and out whenever he pleased, without dreading the tyranny of Dame Van Winkle. Whenever her name was mentioned, however, he shook his head, shrugged his shoulders, and cast up his eyes; which might pass either for an expression of resignation to his fate, or joy at his deliverance.

He used to tell his story to every stranger that arrived at Mr. Doolittle's hotel. He was observed, at first, to vary on some points every time he told it, which was, doubtless, owing to his having so recently awaked. It at last settled down precisely to the tale I have related, and not a man, woman,

or child in the neighborhood but knew it by heart. Some always pretended to doubt the reality of it, and insisted that Rip had been out of his head, and that this was one point on which he always remained flighty. The old Dutch inhabitants, however, almost universally gave it full credit. Even to this day they never hear a thunderstorm of a summer afternoon about the Kaatskill, but they say Hendrick Hudson and his crew are at their game of ninepins; and it is a common wish of all hen-pecked husbands in the neighborhood, when life hangs heavy on their hands, that they might have a quieting draught out of Rip Van Winkle's flagon.

NOTE.

The foregoing Tale, one would suspect, had been suggested to Mr. Knickerbocker by a little German superstition about the Emperor Frederick *der Rothbart,* and the Kypphäuser mountain: the subjoined note, however, which he had appended to the tale, shows that it is an absolute fact, narrated with his usual fidelity.

"The story of Rip Van Winkle may seem incredible to many, but nevertheless I give it my full belief, for I know the vicinity of our old Dutch settlements to have been very subject to marvellous events and appearances. Indeed, I have heard many stranger stories than this, in the villages along the Hudson; all of which were too well authenticated to admit of a doubt. I have even talked with Rip Van Winkle myself, who, when last I saw him, was a very venerable old man, and so perfectly rational and consistent on every other point, that I think no conscientious person could refuse to take this into the bargain; nay, I have seen a certificate on the subject taken before a country justice and signed with a cross, in the justice's own handwriting. The story, therefore, is beyond the possibility of doubt.

"D.K."

POSTSCRIPT.

The following are travelling notes from a memorandum-book of Mr. Knickerbocker.

The Kaatsberg, or Catskill Mountains, have always been a region full of fable. The Indians considered them the abode of spirits, who influenced the weather, spreading sunshine or clouds over the landscape, and sending good or bad hunting-seasons. They were ruled by an old squaw spirit, said to be their mother. She dwelt on the highest peak of the Catskills, and had charge of the doors of day and night to open and shut them at the proper hour. She hung up the new moons in the skies, and cut up the old ones into stars. In times of drought, if properly propitiated, she would spin light summer clouds out of cobwebs and morning dew, and send them off from the crest of the mountain, flake after flake, like flakes of carded cotton, to float in the air; until, dissolved by the heat of the sun, they would fall in gentle showers, causing the grass to spring, the fruits to ripen, and the corn to grow an inch an hour. If displeased, however, she would brew up clouds black as ink, sitting in the midst of them like a bottle-bellied spider in the midst of its web; and when these clouds broke, woe betide the valleys!

In old times, say the Indian traditions, there was a kind of Manitou or Spirit, who kept about the wildest recesses of the Catskill Mountains, and took a mischievous pleasure in wreaking all kinds of evils and vexations upon the red men. Sometimes he would assume the form of a bear, a panther, or a deer, lead the bewildered hunter a weary chase through tangled forests and among ragged rocks; and then spring off with a loud ho! ho! leaving him aghast on the brink of a beetling precipice or raging torrent.

The favorite abode of this Manitou is still shown. It is a great rock or cliff on the loneliest part of the mountains, and, from the flowering vines which clamber about it, and the wild flowers which abound in its neighborhood, is known by the name of the Garden Rock. Near the foot of it is a small lake, the haunt of the solitary bittern, with water-snakes basking in the sun on the leaves of the pond-lilies which lie on the surface. This place was held in great awe by the Indians, insomuch that the boldest hunter would not pursue his game within its precincts. Once upon a time, however, a hunter who had lost his way, penetrated to the Garden Rock, where he beheld a number of gourds placed in the crotches of trees. One of these he seized and made off with it, but in the hurry of his retreat he let it fall among the rocks, when a great stream gushed forth, which washed him away and swept him down precipices, where he was dashed to pieces, and the stream made its way to the Hudson, and continues to flow to the present day; being the identical stream known by the name of the Kaaterskill.

The Legend of Sleepy Hollow

Found Among the Papers of the Late Diedrich Knickerbocker

A pleasing land of drowsy head it was,
  Of dreams that wave before the half-shut eye,
And of gay castles in the clouds that pass,
  For ever flushing round a summer sky.

Castle of Indolence

IN the bosom of one of those spacious coves which indent the eastern shore of the Hudson, at that broad expansion of the river denominated by the ancient Dutch navigators the Tappan Zee, and where they always prudently shortened sail, and implored the protection of St. Nicholas when they crossed, there lies a small market-town or rural port, which by some is called Greensburgh, but which is more generally and properly known by the name of Tarry Town. This name was given, we are told, in former days, by the good house-wives of the adjacent country, from the inveterate propensity of their husbands to linger about the village tavern on market-days. Be that as it may, I do not vouch for the fact, but merely advert to it for the sake of being precise and authentic. Not far from this village, perhaps about two miles, there is a little valley, or rather lap of land, among high hills, which is one of the quietest places in the whole world. A small brook glides through it, with just murmur enough to lull one to repose; and the occasional whistle of a quail, or tapping of a woodpecker, is almost the only sound that ever breaks in upon the uniform tranquillity.

I recollect that, when a stripling, my first exploit in squirrel-shooting was in a grove of tall walnut-trees that shades one side of the valley. I had wandered into it at noon-time, when all nature is particularly quiet, and was startled by the roar of my own gun, as it broke the Sabbath stillness around, and was prolonged and reverberated by the angry echoes. If ever I should wish for a retreat, whither I might steal from the world and its distractions, and dream quietly away the remnant of a troubled life, I know of none more promising than this little valley.

From the listless repose of the place, and the peculiar character of its inhabitants, who are descendants from the original Dutch settlers, this sequestered glen has long been known by the name of SLEEPY HOLLOW, and its rustic lads are called the Sleepy Hollow Boys throughout all the neighboring country. A drowsy, dreamy influence seems to hang over the land, and to pervade the very atmosphere. Some say that the place was bewitched by a high German doctor, during the early days of the settlement; others, that an old Indian chief, the prophet or wizard of his tribe, held his pow-wows there before the country was discovered by Master Hendrick Hudson. Certain it is, the place still continues under the sway of some bewitching power, that holds a spell over the minds of the good people, causing them to walk in a continual reverie. They are given to all kinds of marvellous beliefs; are subject to trances and visions; and frequently see strange sights, and hear music and voices in the air. The whole neighborhood abounds with local tales, haunted spots, and twilight superstitions; stars shoot and meteors glare oftener across the valley than in any other part of the country, and the nightmare, with her whole ninefold, seems to make it the favorite scene of her gambols.

The dominant spirit, however, that haunts this enchanted region, and seems to be commander-in-chief of all the powers of the air, is the apparition of a figure on horseback without a head. It is said by some to be the ghost of a Hessian trooper, whose head had been carried away by a cannon-ball, in some nameless battle during the Revolutionary War, and who is ever and anon seen by the country folk, hurrying along in the gloom of night, as if on the wings of the wind. His haunts are not confined to the valley, but extend at times to the adjacent roads, and especially to the vicinity of a church at no great distance. Indeed, certain of the most authentic historians of those parts, who have been careful in collecting and collating the floating facts concerning this spectre, allege that the body of the trooper, having been buried in the churchyard, the ghost rides forth to the scene of battle in nightly quest of his head; and that the rushing speed with which he sometimes passes along the Hollow, like a midnight blast, is owing to his being belated, and in a hurry to get back to the churchyard before daybreak.

Such is the general purport of this legendary superstition, which has furnished materials for many a wild story in that region of shadows; and the spectre is known, at all the country firesides, by the name of the Headless Horseman of Sleepy Hollow.

It is remarkable that the visionary propensity I have mentioned is not confined to the native inhabitants of the valley, but is unconsciously imbibed by every one who resides there for a time. However wide awake they may have been before they entered that sleepy region, they are sure, in a little time, to inhale the witching influence of the air, and begin to grow imaginative, to dream dreams, and see apparitions.

I mention this peaceful spot with all possible laud; for it is in such little retired Dutch valleys, found here and there embosomed in the great State of New York, that population, manners, and customs remain fixed; while the great torrent of migration and improvement, which is making such incessant changes in other parts of this restless country, sweeps by them unobserved. They are like those little nooks of still water which border a rapid stream; where we may see the straw and bubble riding quietly at anchor, or slowly revolving in their mimic harbor, undisturbed by the rush of the passing current. Though many years have elapsed since I trod the drowsy shades of Sleepy Hollow, yet I question whether I should not still find the same trees and the same families vegetating in its sheltered bosom.

In this by-place of nature, there abode, in a remote period of American history, that is to say, some thirty years since, a worthy wight of the name of Ichabod Crane; who sojourned, or, as he expressed it, "tarried," in Sleepy Hollow, for the purpose of instructing the children of the vicinity. He was a native of Connecticut, a State which supplies the Union with pioneers for the mind as well as for the forest, and sends forth yearly its legions of frontier woodsmen and country schoolmasters. The cognomen of Crane was not inapplicable to his person. He was tall, but exceedingly lank, with narrow shoulders, long arms and legs, hands that dangled a mile out of his sleeves, feet that might have served for shovels, and his whole frame most loosely hung together. His head was small, and flat at top, with huge ears, large green glassy eyes, and a long snipe nose, so that it looked like a weathercock perched upon his spindle neck, to tell which way the wind blew. To see him striding along the profile of a hill on a windy day, with his clothes bagging and fluttering about him, one might have mistaken him for the genius of famine descending upon the earth, or some scarecrow eloped from a corn-field.

His school-house was a low building of one large room, rudely constructed of logs; the windows partly glazed, and partly patched with leaves of old copy books. It was most ingeniously secured at vacant hours by a withe twisted in the handle of the door, and stakes set against the window-shutters; so that, though a thief might get in with perfect ease, he would find some embarrassment in getting out: an idea most probably borrowed by the architect, Yost Van Houten, from the mystery of an eel-pot. The school-house stood in a rather lonely but pleasant situation, just at the foot of a woody hill, with a brook running close by, and a formidable birch-tree growing at one end of it. From hence the low murmur of his pupils' voices, conning over their lessons, might be heard on a drowsy summer's day, like the hum of a bee-hive; interrupted now and then by the authoritative voice of the master, in the tone of menace or command; or, peradventure, by the appalling sound of the birch, as he urged some tardy loiterer along the flowery path of knowledge. Truth to say, he was a conscientious man, and ever bore in mind the golden maxim, "Spare the rod and spoil the child."—Ichabod Crane's scholars certainly were not spoiled.

I would not have it imagined, however, that he was one of those cruel potentates of the school, who joy in the smart of their subjects; on the contrary, he administered justice with discrimination rather than severity, taking the burden off the backs of the weak, and laying it on those of the strong. Your mere puny stripling, that winced at the least flourish of the rod, was passed by with indulgence; but the claims of justice were satisfied by inflicting a double portion on some little, tough, wrong-headed, broad-skirted Dutch urchin, who sulked and swelled and grew dogged and sullen beneath the birch. All this he called "doing his duty" by their parents; and he never inflicted a chastisement without following it by the assurance, so consolatory to the smarting urchin, that "he would remember it, and thank him for it the longest day he had to live."

When school-hours were over, he was even the companion and playmate of the larger boys; and on holiday afternoons would convoy some of the smaller ones home, who happened to have pretty sisters, or good housewives for mothers, noted for the comforts of the cupboard. Indeed it behooved him to keep on good terms with his pupils. The revenue arising from his school was small, and would have been scarcely sufficient to furnish him with daily bread, for he was a huge feeder, and, though lank, had the dilating powers of an anaconda; but to help out his maintenance, he was, according to country custom in those parts, boarded and lodged at the houses of the farmers, whose children he instructed. With these he lived successively a week at a time; thus going the rounds of the neighborhood, with all his worldly effects tied up in a cotton handkerchief.

That all this might not be too onerous on the purses of his rustic patrons, who are apt to consider the costs of schooling a grievious burden, and schoolmasters as mere drones, he had various ways of rendering himself both useful and agreeable. He assisted the farmers occasionally in the lighter labors of their farms; helped to make hay; mended the fences; took the horses to water; drove the cows from pasture; and cut wood for the winter fire. He laid aside, too, all the dominant dignity and absolute sway with which he lorded it in his little empire, the school, and became wonderfully gentle and ingratiating. He found favor in the eyes of the mothers, by petting the children, particularly the youngest; and like the lion bold, which whilom so magnanimously the lamb did hold, he would sit with a child on one knee, and rock a cradle with his foot for whole hours together.

In addition to his other vocations, he was the singing-master of the neighborhood, and picked up many bright shillings by instructing the young folks in psalmody. It was a matter of no little vanity to him, on Sundays, to take his station in front of the church-gallery, with a band of chosen singers; where, in his own mind, he completely carried away the palm from the parson. Certain it is, his voice resounded far above all the rest of the congregation; and there are peculiar quavers still to be heard in that church, and which may even be heard half a mile off, quite to the opposite side of the mill-pond, on a still Sunday morning, which are said to be legitimately descended from the nose of Ichabod Crane. Thus, by divers little makeshifts in that ingenious way which is commonly denominated "by hook and by crook," the worthy pedagogue got on tolerably enough, and was thought, by all who understood nothing of the labor of headwork, to have a wonderfully easy life of it.

The schoolmaster is generally a man of some importance in the female circle of a rural neighborhood; being considered a kind of idle, gentleman-like personage, of vastly superior taste and accomplishments to the rough country swains, and, indeed, inferior in learning only to the parson. His appearance, therefore, is apt to occasion some little stir at the tea-table of a farm-house, and the addition of a supernumerary dish of cakes or sweet-meats, or, peradventure, the parade of a silver tea-pot. Our man of letters, therefore, was peculiarly happy in the smiles of all the country damsels. How he would figure among them in the churchyard, between services on Sundays! gathering grapes for them from the wild vines that overrun the surrounding trees; reciting for their amusement all the epitaphs on the tombstones; or sauntering, with a whole bevy of them, along the banks of the adjacent mill-pond; while the more bashful country bumpkins hung sheepishly back, envying his superior elegance and address.

From his half itinerant life, also, he was a kind of travelling gazette, carrying the whole budget of local gossip from house to house: so that his appearance was always greeted with satisfaction. He was, moreover, esteemed by the women as a man of great erudition, for he had read several books quite through, and was a perfect master of Cotton Mather's *History of New England Witchcraft,* in which, by the way, he most firmly and potently believed.

He was, in fact, an odd mixture of small shrewdness and simple credulity. His appetite for the marvellous, and his powers of digesting it, were equally extraordinary; and both had been increased by his residence in this spellbound region. No tale was too gross or monstrous for his capacious swallow. It was often his delight, after his school was dismissed in the afternoon, to stretch himself on the rich bed of clover bordering the little brook that whimpered by his school-house, and there con over old Mather's direful tales, until the gathering dusk of the evening made the printed page a mere mist before his eyes. Then, as he wended his way, by swamp and stream, and awful woodland, to the farm-house where he happened to be quartered, every sound of nature, at that witching hour, fluttered his excited imagination; the moan of the whippoorwill* from the hill-side, the boding cry of the tree-toad, that harbinger of storm; the dreary hooting of the screech-owl, or the sudden rustling in the thicket of birds frightened from their roost. The fire-flies, too, which sparkled most vividly in the darkest places, now and then startled him, as one of uncommon brightness would stream across his path; and if, by chance, a huge blockhead of a beetle came winging his blundering flight against him, the poor varlet was ready to give up the ghost, with the idea that he was struck with a witch's token. His only resource on such occasions, either to drown thought or drive away evil spirits, was to sing

---

*The whippoorwill is a bird which is only heard at night. It receives its name from its note, which is thought to resemble those words.

psalm-tunes; and the good people of Sleepy Hollow, as they sat by their doors of an evening, were often filled with awe, at hearing his nasal melody, "in linkèd sweetness long drawn out," floating from the distant hill, or along the dusky road.

Another of his sources of fearful pleasure was, to pass long winter evenings with the old Dutch wives, as they sat spinning by the fire, with a row of apples roasting and spluttering along the hearth, and listen to their marvellous tales of ghosts and goblins, and haunted fields, and haunted brooks, and haunted bridges, and haunted houses, and particularly of the headless horseman, or Galloping Hessian of the Hollow, as they sometimes called him. He would delight them equally by his anecdotes of witchcraft, and the direful omens and portentous sights and sounds in the air, which prevailed in the earlier times of Connecticut; and would frighten them wofully with speculations upon comets and shooting-stars, and with the alarming fact that the world did absolutely turn round, and that they were half the time topsy-turvy!

But if there was a pleasure in all this, while snugly cuddling in the chimney-corner of a chamber that was all of a ruddy glow from the crackling wood-fire, and where, of course, no spectre dared to show his face, it was dearly purchased by the terrors of his subsequent walk homewards. What fearful shapes and shadows beset his path amidst the dim and ghastly glare of a snowy night!—With what wistful look did he eye every trembling ray of light streaming across the waste fields from some distant window!—How often was he appalled by some shrub covered with snow, which, like a sheeted spectre, beset his very path!—How often did he shrink with curdling awe at the sound of his own steps on a frosty crust beneath his feet; and dread to look over his shoulder, lest he should behold some uncouth being tramping close behind him!—and how often was he thrown into complete dismay by some rushing blast, howling among the trees, in the idea that it was the Galloping Hessian on one of his nightly scourings!

All these, however, were mere terrors of the night, phantoms of the mind that walk in darkness; and though he had seen many spectres in his time, and been more than once beset by Satan in divers shapes, in his lonely perambulations, yet daylight put an end to all these evils; and he would have

passed a pleasant life of it, in despite of the devil and all his works, if his path had not been crossed by a being that causes more perplexity to mortal man than ghosts, goblins, and the whole race of witches put together, and that was—a woman.

Among the musical disciples who assembled, one evening in each week, to receive his instructions in psalmody, was Katrina Van Tassel, the daughter and only child of a substantial Dutch farmer. She was a blooming lass of fresh eighteen; plump as a partridge; ripe and melting and rosy-cheeked as one of her father's peaches, and universally famed, not merely for her beauty, but her vast expectations. She was withal a little of a coquette, as might be perceived even in her dress, which was a mixture of ancient and modern fashions, as most suited to set off her charms. She wore the ornaments of pure yellow gold, which her great-great-grandmother had brought over from Saardam; the tempting stomacher of the olden time; and withal a provokingly short petticoat, to display the prettiest foot and ankle in the country around.

Ichabod Crane had a soft and foolish heart towards the sex; and it is not to be wondered at that so tempting a morsel soon found favor in his eyes; more especially after he had visited her in her paternal mansion. Old Baltus Van Tassel was a perfect picture of a thriving, contented, liberal-hearted farmer. He seldom, it is true, sent either his eyes or his thoughts beyond the boundaries of his own farm; but within those everything was snug, happy, and well-conditioned. He was satisfied with his wealth, but not proud of it; and piqued himself upon the hearty abundance rather than the style in which he lived. His stronghold was situated on the banks of the Hudson, in one of those green, sheltered, fertile nooks in which the Dutch farmers are so fond of nestling. A great elm-tree spread its broad branches over it; at the foot of which bubbled up a spring of the softest and sweetest water, in a little well, formed of a barrel; and then stole sparkling away through the grass, to a neighboring brook, that bubbled along among alders and dwarf willows. Hard by the farmhouse was a vast barn, that might have served for a church; every window and crevice of which seemed bursting forth with the treasures of the farm; the flail was busily resounding within it from morning till night; swallows and martins skimmed twittering about the eaves; and rows of pigeons, some with one eye turned up, as if watching the weather, some with their heads under their wings, or buried in their bosoms, and others swelling, and cooing, and bowing about their dames, were enjoying the sunshine on the roof. Sleek unwieldy porkers were grunting in the repose and abundance of their pens; whence sallied forth, now and then, troops of sucking pigs, as if to snuff the air. A stately squadron of snowy geese were riding in an adjoining pond, convoying whole fleets of ducks; regiments of turkeys were gobbling through the farm-yard, and guinea fowls fretting about it, like ill-tempered housewives, with their peevish discontented cry. Before the barn-door strutted the gallant cock, that pattern of a husband, a warrior, and a fine gentleman, clapping his burnished wings, and crowing in the pride and gladness of his heart—sometimes tearing up the earth with his feet, and then generously calling his ever-hungry family of wives and children to enjoy the rich morsel which he had discovered.

The pedagogue's mouth watered, as he looked upon this sumptuous promise of luxurious winter fare. In his devouring mind's eye he pictured to himself every roasting-pig running about with a pudding in his belly, and an apple in his mouth; the pigeons were snugly put to bed in a comfortable pie, and tucked in with a coverlet of crust; the geese were swimming in their own gravy; and the ducks pairing cozily in dishes, like snug married couples, with a decent competency of onion-sauce. In the porkers he saw carved out the future sleek side of bacon, and juicy relishing ham; not a turkey but he beheld daintily trussed up, with its gizzard under its wing, and, peradventure, a necklace of savory sausages; and even bright chanticleer himself lay sprawling on his back, in a side-dish, with uplifted claws, as if craving that quarter which his chivalrous spirit disdained to ask while living.

As the enraptured Ichabod fancied all this, and as he rolled his great green eyes over the fat meadow-lands, the rich fields of wheat, of rye, of buckwheat, and Indian corn, and the orchard burdened with ruddy fruit, which surrounded the warm tenement of Van Tassel, his heart yearned after the damsel who was to inherit these domains, and his imagination expanded with the idea how they might be readily turned into cash, and the money invested in immense tracts of wild land, and shingle palaces in the wilderness. Nay, his busy fancy already realized his hopes, and presented to him the blooming Katrina, with a whole family of children, mounted on the top of a wagon loaded with household trumpery, with pots and kettles dangling beneath; and he beheld himself bestriding a pacing mare, with a colt at her heels, setting out for Kentucky, Tennessee, or the Lord knows where.

When he entered the house, the conquest of his heart was complete. It was one of those spacious farm-houses, with high-ridged, but lowly-sloping roofs, built in the style handed down from the first Dutch settlers; the low projecting eaves forming a piazza along the front, capable of being closed up in bad weather. Under this were hung flails, harness, various utensils of husbandry, and nets for fishing in the neighboring river. Benches were built along the sides for summer use; and a great spinning-wheel at one end, and a churn at the other, showed the various uses to which this important porch might be devoted. From this piazza the wandering Ichabod entered the hall, which formed the centre of the mansion and the place of usual residence. Here, rows of resplendent pewter, ranged on a long dresser, dazzled his eyes. In one corner stood a huge bag of wool ready to be spun; in another a quantity of linsey-woolsey just from the loom; ears of Indian corn, and strings of dried apples and peaches, hung in gay festoons along the walls, mingled with the gaud of red peppers; and a door left ajar gave him a peep into the best parlor, where the claw-footed chairs and dark mahogany tables shone like mirrors; and irons, with their accompanying shovel and tongs, glistened from their covert of asparagus tops; mock-oranges and conch-shells decorated the mantel-piece; strings of various colored birds' eggs were suspended above it, a great ostrich egg was hung from the centre of the room, and a corner-cupboard, knowingly left open, displayed immense treasures of old silver and well-mended china.

From the moment Ichabod laid his eyes upon these regions of delight, the peace of his mind was at an end, and his only study was how to gain the affections of the peerless daughter of Van Tassel. In this enterprise, however, he had more real difficulties than generally fell to the lot of a knight-errant of yore, who seldom had anything but giants, enchanters, fiery dragons, and such like easily conquered adversaries, to contend with; and had to make his way merely through gates of iron and brass, and walls of adamant, to the castle-keep, where the lady of his heart was confined; all which he achieved as easily as a man would carve his way to the centre of a Christmas pie; and then the lady gave him her hand as a matter of course. Ichabod, on the contrary, had to win his way to the heart of a country coquette, beset with a labyrinth of whims and caprices, which were forever presenting new difficulties and impediments; and he had to encounter a host of fearful adversaries of real flesh and blood, the numerous rustic admirers, who beset every portal to her heart; keeping a watchful and angry eye upon each other, but ready to fly out in the common cause against any new competitor.

Among these the most formidable was a burly, roaring, roistering blade, of the name of Abraham, or, according to

the Dutch abbreviation, Brom Van Brunt, the hero of the country round, which rang with his feats of strength and hardihood. He was broad-shouldered and double-jointed, with short, curly black hair, and a bluff but not unpleasant countenance, having a mingled air of fun and arrogance. From his Herculean frame and great powers of limb, he had received the nickname of BROM BONES, by which he was universally known. He was famed for great knowledge and skill in horsemanship, being as dexterous on horseback as a Tartar. He was foremost at all races and cockfights; and, with the ascendency which bodily strength acquires in rustic life, was the umpire in all disputes, setting his hat on one side, and giving his decisions with an air and tone admitting of no gainsay or appeal. He was always ready for either a fight or a frolic; but had more mischief than ill-will in his composition; and, with all his over-bearing roughness, there was a strong dash of waggish good-humor at the bottom. He had three or four boon companions, who regarded him as their model, and at the head of whom he scoured the country, attending every scene of feud or merriment for miles round. In cold weather he was distinguished by a fur cap, surmounted with a flaunting fox's tail; and when the folks at a country gathering descried this well-known crest at a distance, whisking about among a squad of hard riders, they always stood by for a squall. Sometimes his crew would be heard dashing along past the farm-houses at midnight, with whoop and halloo, like a troop of Don Cossacks; and the old dames, startled out of their sleep, would listen for a moment till the hurry-scurry had clattered by, and then exclaim, "Ay, there goes Brom Bones and his gang!" The neighbors looked upon him with a mixture of awe, admiration, and good-will; and when any madcap prank, or rustic brawl, occurred in the vicinity, always shook their heads, and warranted Brom Bones was at the bottom of it.

This rantipole hero had for some time singled out the blooming Katrina for the object of his uncouth gallantries; and though his amorous toyings were something like the gentle caresses and endearments of a bear, yet it was whispered that she did not altogether discourage his hopes. Certain it is, his advances were signals for rival candidates to retire, who felt no inclination to cross a line in his amours; insomuch, that, when his horse was seen tied to Van Tassel's paling on a Sunday night, a sure sign that his master was courting, or, as it is termed, "sparking," within, all other suitors passed by in despair, and carried the war into other quarters.

Such was the formidable rival with whom Ichabod Crane had to contend, and, considering all things, a stouter man than he would have shrunk from the competition, and a wiser man would have despaired. He had, however, a happy mixture of pliability and perseverance in his nature; he was in form and spirit like a supple-jack—yielding, but tough; though he bent, he never broke; and though he bowed beneath the slightest pressure yet, the moment it was away—jerk! he was as erect, and carried his head as high as ever.

To have taken the field openly against his rival would have been madness; for he was not a man to be thwarted in his amours, any more than that stormy lover, Achilles. Ichabod, therefore, made his advances in a quiet and gently insinuating manner. Under cover of his character of singing-master, he had made frequent visits at the farm-house; not that he had anything to apprehend from the meddlesome interference of parents, which is so often a stumbling-block in the path of lovers. Balt Van Tassel was an easy, indulgent soul; he loved his daughter better even than his pipe, and, like a reasonable man and an excellent father, let her have her way in everything. His notable little wife, too, had enough to do to attend to her housekeeping and manage her poultry; for, as she sagely observed, ducks and geese are foolish things, and must be looked after, but girls can take care of themselves. Thus while the busy dame bustled about the house, or plied her spinning-wheel at one end of the piazza, honest Balt would sit smoking his evening pipe at the other, watching the achievements of a little wooden warrior, who, armed with a sword in each hand, was most valiantly fighting the wind on the pinnacle of the barn. In the meantime, Ichabod would carry on his suit with the daughter by the side of the spring under the great elm, or sauntering along in the twilight,—that hour so favorable to the lover's eloquence.

I profess not to know how women's hearts are wooed and

won. To me they have always been matters of riddle and admiration. Some seem to have but one vulnerable point or door of access, while others have a thousand avenues, and may be captured in a thousand different ways. It is a great triumph of skill to gain the former, but a still greater proof of generalship to maintain possession of the latter, for the man must battle for his fortress at every door and window. He who wins a thousand common hearts is therefore entitled to some renown; but he who keeps undisputed sway over the heart of a coquette, is indeed a hero. Certain it is, this was not the case with the redoubtable Brom Bones; and from the moment Ichabod Crane made his advances, the interests of the former evidently declined; his horse was no longer seen tied at the palings on Sunday nights, and a deadly feud gradually arose between him and the preceptor of Sleepy Hollow.

Brom, who had a degree of rough chivalry in his nature, would fain have carried matters to open warfare, and have settled their pretensions to the lady according to the mode of those most concise and simple reasoners, the knights-errant of yore—by single combat; but Ichabod was too conscious of the superior might of his adversary to enter the lists against him: he had overheard a boast of Bones, that he would "double the schoolmaster up, and lay him on a shelf of his own school-house"; and he was too wary to give him an opportunity. There was something extremely provoking in this obstinately pacific system; it left Brom no alternative but to draw upon the funds of rustic waggery in his disposition, and to play off boorish practical jokes upon his rival. Ichabod became the object of whimsical persecution to Bones and his gang of rough riders. They harried his hitherto peaceful domains; smoked out his singing-school, by stopping up the chimney; broke into the school-house at night, in spite of its formidable fastenings of withe and window-stakes, and turned everything topsy-turvy: so that the poor schoolmaster began to think all the witches in the country held their meetings here. But what was still more annoying, Brom took opportunities of turning him into ridicule in presence of his mistress, and had a scoundrel dog whom he taught to whine in the most ludicrous manner, and introduced as a rival of Ichabod's to instruct her in psalmody.

In this way matters went on for some time, without producing any material effect on the relative situation of the contending powers. On a fine autumnal afternoon, Ichabod, in pensive mood, sat enthroned on the lofty stool whence he usually watched all the concerns of his little literary realm. In his hand he swayed a ferule, that sceptre of despotic power; the birch of justice reposed on three nails, behind the throne, a constant terror to evil-doers; while on the desk before him might be seen sundry contraband articles and prohibited weapons, detected upon the persons of idle urchins; such as half-munched apples, pop-guns, whirligigs, fly-cages, and whole legions of rampant little paper game-cocks. Apparently there had been some appalling act of justice recently inflicted, for his scholars were all busily intent upon their books, or slyly whispering behind them with one eye kept upon the master; and a kind of buzzing stillness reigned throughout the school-room. It was suddenly interrupted by the appearance of a negro, in tow-cloth jacket and trousers, a round-crowned fragment of a hat, like the cap of Mercury, and mounted on the back of a ragged, wild, half-broken colt, which he managed with a rope by way of halter. He came clattering up to the school-door with an invitation to Ichabod to attend a merry-making or "quilting frolic," to be held that evening at Mynheer Van Tassel's; and having delivered his message with that air of importance, and effort at fine language, which a negro is apt to display on petty embassies of the kind, he dashed over the brook, and was seen scampering away up the Hollow, full of the importance and hurry of his mission.

All was now bustle and hubbub in the late quiet school-room. The scholars were hurried through their lessons, without stopping at trifles; those who were nimble skipped over half with impunity, and those who were tardy had a smart application now and then in the rear, to quicken their speed, or help them over a tall word. Books were flung aside without being put away on the shelves, inkstands were overturned, benches thrown down, and the whole school was turned loose an hour before the usual time, bursting forth like a legion of young imps, yelping and racketing about the green, in joy at their early emancipation.

The gallant Ichabod now spent at least an extra half-hour at his toilet, brushing and furbishing up his best and indeed only suit of rusty black, and arranging his locks by a bit of broken looking-glass, that hung up in the school-house. That he might make his appearance before his mistress in the true style of a cavalier, he borrowed a horse from the farmer with whom he was domiciliated, a choleric old Dutchman, of the name of Hans Van Ripper, and, thus gallantly mounted, issued forth, like a knight-errant in quest of adventures. But it is meet I should, in the true spirit of romantic story, give some account of the looks and equipments of my hero and his steed. The animal he bestrode was a broken-down plough-horse, that had outlived almost everything but his viciousness. He was gaunt and shagged, with a ewe neck and a head like a hammer; his rusty mane and tail were tangled and knotted with burrs; one eye had lost its pupil, and was glaring and spectral; but the other had the gleam of a genuine devil in it. Still he must have had fire and mettle in his day, if we may judge from the name he bore of Gunpowder. He had, in fact, been a favorite steed of his master's, the choleric Van Ripper, who was a furious rider, and had infused, very probably, some of his own spirit into the animal; for, old and broken-down as he looked, there was more of the lurking devil in him than in any young filly in the country.

Ichabod was a suitable figure for such a steed. He rode with short stirrups, which brought his knees nearly up to the pommel of the saddle; his sharp elbows stuck out like grass-hoppers'; he carried his whip perpendicularly in his hand, like a sceptre, and, as his horse jogged on, the motion of his arms was not unlike the flapping of a pair of wings. A small wool hat rested on the top of his nose, for so his scanty strip of forehead might be called; and the skirts of his black coat fluttered out almost to the horse's tail. Such was the appearance of Ichabod and his steed, as they shambled out of the gate of Hans Van Ripper, and it was altogether such an apparition as is seldom to be met with in broad daylight.

It was, as I have said, a fine autumnal day, the sky was clear and nature wore that rich and golden livery which we always associate with the idea of abundance. The forests had put on their sober brown and yellow, while some trees of the tenderer kind had been nipped by the frosts into brilliant dyes of orange, purple, and scarlet. Streaming files of wild ducks began to make their appearance high in the air; the bark of the squirrel might be heard from the groves of beech and hickory nuts, and the pensive whistle of the quail at intervals from the neighboring stubble-field.

The small birds were taking their farewell banquets. In the fulness of their revelry, they fluttered, chirping and frolicking, from bush to bush, and tree to tree, capricious from the very profusion and variety around them. There was the honest cockrobin, the favorite game of stripling sportsmen, with its loud querulous notes; and the twittering blackbirds flying in sable clouds; and the golden-winged woodpecker, with his crimson crest, his broad black gorget, and splendid plumage; and the cedar-bird, with its red-tipt wings and yellow-tipt tail, and its little monteiro cap of feathers; and the blue jay, that noisy coxcomb, in his gay light-blue coat and white underclothes, screaming and chattering, nodding and bobbing and bowing, and pretending to be on good terms with every songster of the grove.

As Ichabod jogged slowly on his way, his eye, ever open to every symptom of culinary abundance, ranged with delight over the treasures of jolly autumn. On all sides he beheld vast store of apples; some hanging in oppressive opulence on the trees; some gathered into baskets and barrels for the market; others heaped up in rich piles for the cider-press. Farther on he beheld great fields of Indian corn, with its golden ears peeping from their leafy coverts, and holding out the promise of cakes and hasty-pudding; and the yellow pumpkins lying beneath them, turning up their fair round bellies to the sun, and giving ample prospects of the most luxurious of pies; and anon he passed the fragrant buckwheat fields, breathing the odor of the bee-hive, and as he beheld them, soft anticipations stole over his mind of dainty slapjacks, well buttered, and garnished with honey or treacle, by the delicate little dimpled hand of Katrina Van Tassel.

Thus feeding his mind with many sweet thoughts and "sugared suppositions," he journeyed along the sides of a range of hills which look out upon some of the goodliest scenes of the mighty Hudson. The sun gradually wheeled his broad disk down into the west. The wide bosom of the Tappan Zee lay motionless and glossy, excepting that here and there a gentle undulation waved and prolonged the blue shadow of the distant mountain. A few amber clouds floated in the sky, without a breath of air to move them. The horizon was of a fine golden tint, changing gradually into a pure apple-green, and from that into the deep blue of the mid-heaven. A slanting ray lingered on the woody crests of the precipices that overhung some parts of the river, giving greater depth to the dark-gray and purple of their rocky sides. A sloop was loitering in the distance, dropping slowly down with the tide, her sail hanging uselessly against the mast; and as the reflection of the sky gleamed along the still water, it seemed as if the vessel was suspended in the air.

It was toward evening that Ichabod arrived at the castle of the Heer Van Tassel, which he found thronged with the pride and flower of the adjacent country. Old farmers, a spare leathern-faced race, in homespun coats and breeches, blue stockings, huge shoes, and magnificent pewter buckles. Their brisk withered little dames, in close crimped caps, long-waisted shortgowns, homespun petticoats, with scissors and pin-cushions, and gay calico pockets hanging on the outside. Buxom lasses, almost as antiquated as their mothers, excepting where a straw hat, a fine ribbon, or perhaps a white frock, gave symptoms of city innovation. The sons, in short square-skirted coats with rows of stupendous brass buttons, and their hair generally queued in the fashion of the times, especially if they could procure an eel-skin for the purpose, it being esteemed, throughout the country, as a potent nourisher and strengthener of the hair.

Brom Bones, however, was the hero of the scene, having come to the gathering on his favorite steed, Daredevil, a creature, like himself, full of mettle and mischief, and which no one but himself could manage. He was, in fact, noted for preferring vicious animals, given to all kinds of tricks, which kept the rider in constant risk of his neck, for he held a tractable well-broken horse as unworthy of a lad of spirit.

Fain would I pause to dwell upon the world of charms that burst upon the enraptured gaze of my hero, as he entered the state parlor of Van Tassel's mansion. Not those of the bevy of buxom lasses, with their luxurious display of red and white; but the ample charms of a genuine Dutch country tea-table, in the sumptuous time of autumn. Such heaped-up platters of cakes of various and almost indescribable kinds, known only to experienced Dutch housewives! There was the doughty doughnut, the tenderer oly koek, and the crisp and crumbling cruller; sweet cakes and short cakes, ginger-cakes and honey-cakes, and the whole family of cakes. And then there were apple-pies and peach-pies and pumpkin-pies; besides slices of ham and smoked beef; and moreover de-lectable dishes of preserved plums, and peaches, and pears, and quinces; not to mention broiled shad and roasted chick-ens; together with bowls of milk and cream, all mingled hig-gledy-piggledy, pretty much as I have enumerated them, with the motherly tea-pot sending up its clouds of vapor from the midst—Heaven bless the mark! I want breath and time to discuss this banquet as it deserves, and am too eager to get on with my story. Happily, Ichabod Crane was not in so great a hurry as his historian, but did ample justice to every dainty.

He was a kind and thankful creature, whose heart dilated in proportion as his skin was filled with good cheer; and whose spirits rose with eating as some men's do with drink. He could not help, too, rolling his large eyes round him as he ate, and chuckling with the possibility that he might one day be lord of all this scene of almost unimaginable luxury and splendor. Then, he thought, how soon he'd turn his back upon the old school-house; snap his fingers in the face of Hans Van Ripper, and every other niggardly patron, and kick any itinerant pedagogue out-of-doors that should dare to call him comrade!

Old Baltus Van Tassel moved about among his guests with a face dilated with content and good-humor, round and jolly as the harvest-moon. His hospitable attentions were brief, but expressive, being confined to a shake of the hand, a slap on the shoulder, a loud laugh, and a pressing invitation to "fall to, and help themselves."

And now the sound of the music from the common room, or hall, summoned to the dance. The musician was an old gray-headed negro, who had been the itinerant orchestra of the neighborhood for more than half a century. His instrument was as old and battered as himself. The greater part of the time he scraped on two or three strings, accompanying every movement of the bow with a motion of the head; bowing almost to the ground, and stamping with his foot whenever a fresh couple were to start.

Ichabod prided himself upon his dancing as much as upon his vocal powers. Not a limb, not a fibre about him was idle; and to have seen his loosely hung frame in full motion, and clattering about the room, you would have thought Saint Vitus himself, that blessed patron of the dance, was figuring before you in person. He was the admiration of all the negroes; who, having gathered, of all ages and sizes, from the farm and the neighborhood, stood forming a pyramid of shining black faces at every door and window, gazing with delight at the scene, rolling their white eyeballs, and showing grinning rows of ivory from ear to ear. How could the flogger of urchins be otherwise than animated and joyous? the lady of his heart was his partner in the dance, and smiling graciously in reply to all his amorous oglings; while Brom Bones, sorely smitten with love and jealousy, sat brooding by himself in one corner.

When the dance was at an end, Ichabod was attracted to a knot of the sager folks, who, with old Van Tassel, sat smoking at one end of the piazza, gossiping over former times, and drawing out long stories about the war.

This neighborhood, at the time of which I am speaking, was one of those highly favored places which abound with chronicle and great men. The British and American line had run near it during the war; it had, therefore, been the scene of marauding, and infested with refugees, cow-boys, and all kinds of border chivalry. Just sufficient time has elapsed to enable each story-teller to dress up his tale with a little becoming fiction, and, in the indistinctness of his recollection, to make himself the hero of every exploit.

There was the story of Doffue Martling, a large blue-bearded Dutchman, who had nearly taken a British frigate with an old iron nine-pounder from a mud breastwork, only that his gun burst at the sixth discharge. And there was an old gentleman who shall be nameless, being too rich a mynheer to be lightly mentioned, who, in the battle of White Plains, being an excellent master of defense, parried a musket-ball with a small sword, insomuch that he absolutely felt it whiz round the blade, and glance off at the hilt; in proof of which he was ready at any time to show the sword, with the hilt a little bent. There were several more that had been equally great in the field, not one of whom but was persuaded that he had a considerable hand in bringing the war to a happy termination.

But all these were nothing to the tales of ghosts and apparitions that succeeded. The neighborhood is rich in legendary treasures of the kind. Local tales and superstitions thrive best in these sheltered long-settled retreats; but are trampled underfoot by the shifting throng that forms the population of most of our country places. Besides, there is no encouragement for ghosts in most of our villages, for they have scarcely had time to finish their first nap, and turn themselves in their graves before their surviving friends have travelled away from the neighborhood; so that when they turn out at night to walk their rounds, they have no acquaintance left to call upon. This is perhaps the reason why we so seldom hear of ghosts, except in our long-established Dutch communities.

The immediate cause, however, of the prevalence of supernatural stories in these parts was doubtless owing to the vicinity of Sleepy Hollow. There was a contagion in the very air that blew from the haunted region; it breathed forth an atmosphere of dreams and fancies infecting all the land. Several of the Sleepy Hollow people were present at Van Tassel's and, as usual, were doling out their wild and wonderful legends. Many dismal tales were told about funeral trains, and mourning cries and wailings heard and seen about the great tree where the unfortunate Major André was taken, and which stood in the neighborhood. Some mention was made also of the woman in white, that haunted the dark glen at Raven Rock, and was often heard to shriek on winter nights before a storm, having perished there in the snow. The chief part of the stories, however, turned upon the favorite spectre of Sleepy Hollow, the headless horseman, who had been heard several times of late, patrolling the country; and, it was said, tethered his horse nightly among the graves in the churchyard.

The sequestered situation of this church seems always to

have made it a favorite haunt of troubled spirits. It stands on a knoll, surrounded by locust-trees and lofty elms, from among which its decent white-washed walls shine modestly forth, like Christian purity beaming through the shades of retirement. A gentle slope descends from it to a silver sheet of water, bordered by high trees, between which, peeps may be caught at the blue hills of the Hudson. To look upon its grass-grown yard, where the sunbeams seem to sleep so quietly, one would think that there at least the dead might rest in peace. On one side of the church extends a wide woody dell, along which raves a large brook among broken rocks and trunks of fallen trees. Over a deep black part of the stream, not far from the church, was formerly thrown a wooden bridge; the road that led to it, and the bridge itself, were thickly shaded by overhanging trees, which cast a gloom about it, even in the daytime, but occasioned a fearful darkness at night. This was one of the favorite haunts of the headless horseman; and the place where he was most frequently encountered. The tale was told of old Brouwer, a most heretical disbeliever in ghosts, how he met the horseman returning from his foray into Sleepy Hollow, and was obliged to get up behind him; how they galloped over bush and brake, over hill and swamp, until they reached the bridge; when the horseman suddenly turned into a skeleton, threw old Brouwer into the brook, and sprang away over the tree-tops with a clap of thunder.

This story was immediately matched by a thrice marvellous adventure of Brom Bones, who made light of the galloping Hessian as an arrant jockey. He affirmed that, on returning one night from the neighboring village of Sing Sing, he had been overtaken by this midnight trooper; that he had offered to race with him for a bowl of punch, and should have won it too, for Daredevil beat the goblin horse all hollow, but, just as they came to the church bridge, the Hessian bolted, and vanished in a flash of fire.

All these tales, told in that drowsy undertone with which men talk in the dark, the countenances of the listeners only now and then receiving a casual gleam from the glare of a pipe, sank deep in the mind of Ichabod. He repaid them in kind with large extracts from his invaluable author, Cotton Mather, and added many marvellous events that had taken place in his native State of Connecticut, and fearful sights which he had seen in his nightly walks about the Sleepy Hollow.

The revel now gradually broke up. The old farmers gathered together their families in their wagons, and were heard for some time rattling along the hollow roads, and over the distant hills. Some of the damsels mounted on pillions behind their favorite swains, and their light-hearted laughter, mingling with the clatter of hoofs, echoed along the silent woodlands, sounding fainter and fainter until they gradually died away—and the late scene of noise and frolic was all silent and deserted. Ichabod only lingered behind, according to the custom of country lovers, to have a *tête-à-tête* with the heiress, fully convinced that he was now on the high road to success.

What passed at this interview I will not pretend to say, for in fact I do not know. Something, however, I fear me, must have gone wrong, for he certainly sallied forth, after no very great interval, with an air quite desolate and chop-fallen.— Oh, these women! these women! Could that girl have been playing off any of her coquettish tricks?—Was her encouragement of the poor pedagogue all a mere sham to secure her conquest of his rival?—Heaven only knows, not I!—Let it suffice to say, Ichabod stole forth with the air of one who had been sacking a hen-roost, rather than a fair lady's heart. Without looking to the right or left to notice the scene of rural wealth on which he had so often gloated, he went straight to the stable, and with several hearty cuffs and kicks, roused his steed most uncourteously from the comfortable quarters in which he was soundly sleeping, dreaming of mountains of corn and oats, and whole valleys of timothy and clover.

It was the very witching time of night that Ichabod, heavy-hearted and crestfallen, pursued his travel homewards, along the sides of the lofty hills which rise above Tarry Town, and which he had traversed so cheerily in the afternoon. The hour was as dismal as himself. Far below him, the Tappan Zee spread its dusky and indistinct waste of waters, with here and there the tall mast of a sloop riding quietly at anchor under the land. In the dead hush of midnight he could even hear the barking of the watch-dog from the opposite shore of the Hudson; but it was so vague and faint as only to give an idea of his distance from this faithful companion of man. Now and then, too, the long-drawn crowing of a cock, accidentally awakened, would sound far, far off, from some farm-house away among the hills—but it was like a dreaming sound in his ear. No signs of life occurred near him, but occasionally the melancholy chirp of a cricket, or perhaps the gutteral twang of a bull-frog, from a neighboring marsh, as if sleeping uncomfortably, and turning suddenly in his bed.

All the stories of ghosts and goblins that he had heard in the afternoon, now came crowding upon his recollection. The night grew darker and darker; the stars seemed to sink deeper in the sky, and driving clouds occasionally hid them from his sight. He had never felt so lonely and dismal. He was, moreover, approaching the very place where many of the scenes of the ghost-stories had been laid. In the centre of the road stood an enormous tulip-tree, which towered like a giant above all the other trees of the neighborhood, and formed a kind of landmark. Its limbs were gnarled, and fantastic, large enough to form trunks for ordinary trees, twisting down almost to the earth, and rising again into the air. It was connected with the tragical story of the unfortunate André, who had been taken prisoner hard by; and was universally known by the name of Major André's tree. The common people regarded it with a mixture of respect and superstition, partly out of sympathy for the fate of its ill-starred namesake, and partly from the tales of strange sights and doleful lamentations told concerning it.

As Ichabod approached this fearful tree, he began to whistle: he thought his whistle was answered—it was but a blast sweeping sharply through the dry branches. As he approached a little nearer, he thought he saw something white, hanging in the midst of the tree—he paused and ceased whistling; but on looking more narrowly, perceived that it was a place where the tree had been scathed by lightning, and the white wood laid bare. Suddenly he heard a groan—his teeth chattered and his knees smote against the saddle: it was but the rubbing of one huge bough upon another, as they were swayed about by the breeze. He passed the tree in safety; but new perils lay before him.

About two hundred yards from the tree a small brook crossed the road, and ran into a marshy and thickly wooded glen, known by the name of Wiley's swamp. A few rough logs, laid side by side, served for a bridge over this stream. On that side of the road where the brook entered the wood, a group of oaks and chestnuts, matted thick with wild grapevines, threw a cavernous gloom over it. To pass this bridge was the severest trial. It was at this identical spot that the unfortunate André was captured, and under the covert of those chestnuts and vines were the sturdy yeomen concealed who surprised him. This has ever since been considered a haunted stream, and fearful are the feelings of the school boy who has to pass it alone after dark.

As he approached the stream, his heart began to thump;

he summoned up, however, all his resolution, gave his horse half a score of kicks in the ribs, and attempted to dash briskly across the bridge; but instead of starting forward, the perverse old animal made a lateral movement, and ran broadside against the fence. Ichabod, whose fears increased with the delay, jerked the reins on the other side, and kicked lustily with the contrary foot: it was all in vain; his steed started, it is true, but it was only to plunge to the opposite side of the road into a thicket of brambles and alder bushes. The schoolmaster now bestowed both whip and heel upon the starveling ribs of old Gunpowder, who dashed forward, snuffling and snorting, but came to a stand just by the bridge, with a suddenness that had nearly sent his rider sprawling over his head. Just at this moment a plashy tramp by the side of the bridge caught the sensitive ear of Ichabod. In the dark shadow of the grove, on the margin of the brook, he beheld something huge, misshapen, black, and towering. It stirred not, but seemed gathered up in the gloom, like some gigantic monster ready to spring upon the traveller.

The hair of the affrighted pedagogue rose upon his head with terror. What was to be done? To turn and fly was now too late; and besides, what chance was there of escaping ghost or goblin, if such it was, which could ride upon the wings of the wind? Summoning up, therefore, a show of courage, he demanded in stammering accents—"Who are you?" He received no reply. He repeated his demand in a still more agitated voice. Still there was no answer. Once more he cudgelled the sides of the inflexible Gunpowder, and, shutting his eyes, broke forth with involuntary fervor into a psalm-tune. Just then the shadowy object of alarm put itself in motion, and, with a scramble and a bound, stood at once in the middle of the road. Though the night was dark and dismal, yet the form of the unknown might now in some degree be ascertained. He appeared to be a horseman of large dimensions, and mounted on a black horse of powerful frame. He made no offer of molestation or sociability, but kept aloof on one side of the road, jogging along on the blind side of old Gunpowder, who had now got over his fright and waywardness.

Ichabod, who had no relish for this strange midnight companion, and bethought himself of the adventure of Brom Bones with the Galloping Hessian, now quickened his steed, in hopes of leaving him behind. The stranger, however, quickened his horse to an equal pace. Ichabod pulled up, and fell into a walk, thinking to lag behind—the other did the same. His heart began to sink within him; he endeavored to resume his psalm-tune, but his parched tongue clove to the roof of his mouth, and he could not utter a stave. There was something in the moody and dogged silence of this pertinacious companion, that was mysterious and appalling. It was soon fearfully accounted for. On mounting a rising ground, which brought the figure of his fellow-traveller in relief against the sky, gigantic in height, and muffled in a cloak, Ichabod was horror-struck, on perceiving that he was headless!—but his horror was still more increased, on observing that the head, which should have rested on his shoulders, was carried before him on the pommel of the saddle: his terror rose to desperation; he rained a shower of kicks and blows upon Gunpowder, hoping, by sudden movement to give his companion the slip—but the spectre started full jump with him. Away then they dashed, through thick and thin; stones flying, and sparks flashing at every bound. Ichabod's flimsy garments fluttered in the air, as he stretched his long lank body away over his horse's head, in the eagerness of his flight.

They had now reached the road which turns off to Sleepy Hollow; but Gunpowder, who seemed possessed with a demon, instead of keeping up it, made an opposite turn, and plunged headlong downhill to the left. This road leads through a sandy hollow, shaded by trees for about a quarter of a mile, where it crosses the bridge famous in goblin story, and just beyond swells the green knoll on which stands the white-washed church.

As yet the panic of the steed had given his unskilful rider an apparent advantage in the chase; but just as he had got half-way through the hollow, the girths of the saddle gave way, and he felt it slipping from under him. He seized it by the pommel, and endeavored to hold it firm, but in vain; and had just time to save himself by clasping old Gunpowder round the neck, when the saddle fell to the earth, and he heard it trampled underfoot by his pursuer. For a moment, the terror of Hans Van Ripper's wrath passed across his mind—for it was his Sunday saddle; but this was no time for petty fears; the goblin was hard on his haunches; and (unskilful rider that he was!) he had much ado to maintain his seat; sometimes slipping on one side, sometimes on another, and sometimes jolted on the high ridge of his horse's backbone, with a violence that he verily feared would cleave him asunder.

An opening in the trees now cheered him with the hopes that the church-bridge was at hand. The wavering reflection of a silver star in the bosom of the brook told him that he was not mistaken. He saw the walls of the church dimly glaring under the trees beyond. He recollected the place where Brom Bones' ghostly competitor disappeared. "If I can but reach that bridge," thought Ichabod, "I am safe." Just then he heard the black steed panting and blowing close behind him; he even fancied that he felt his hot breath. Another convulsive kick in the ribs, and old Gunpowder sprang upon the bridge; he thundered over the resounding planks; he gained the opposite side; and now Ichabod cast a look behind to see if his pursuer should vanish, according to rule, in a flash of fire and brimstone. Just then he saw the goblin rising in his stirrups, and in the very act of hurling his head at him. Ichabod endeavored to dodge the horrible missile, but too late. It encountered his cranium with a tremendous crash,—he was tumbled headlong into the dust, and Gunpowder, the black steed, and the goblin rider, passed by like a whirlwind.

The next morning the old horse was found without his saddle, and with the bridle under his feet, soberly cropping the grass at his master's gate. Ichabod did not make his appearance at breakfast;—dinner-hour came, but no Ichabod. The boys assembled at the school-house, and strolled idly about the banks of the brook; but no schoolmaster. Hans Van Ripper now began to feel some uneasiness about the fate of poor Ichabod, and his saddle. An inquiry was set on foot, and after diligent investigation they came upon his traces. In one part of the road leading to the church was found the saddle trampled in the dirt; the tracks of horses' hoofs deeply dented in the road, and evidently at furious speed, were traced to the bridge, beyond which, on the bank

of a broad part of the brook, where the water ran deep and black, was found the hat of the unfortunate Ichabod, and close beside it a shattered pumpkin.

The brook was searched, but the body of the schoolmaster was not to be discovered. Hans Van Ripper, as executor of his estate, examined the bundle which contained all his worldly effects. They consisted of two shirts and a half; two stocks for the neck; a pair or two of worsted stockings, an old pair of corduroy small-clothes; a rusty razor; a book of psalm-tunes, full of dogs' ears; and a broken pitch-pipe. As to the books and furniture of the school-house, they belonged to the community, excepting Cotton Mather's *History of Witchcraft*, a *New England Almanac,* and a book of dreams and fortune-telling; in which last was a sheet of foolscap much scribbled and blotted in several fruitless attempts to make a copy of verses in honor of the heiress of Van Tassel. These magic books and the poetic scrawl were forthwith consigned to the flames by Hans Van Ripper; who from that time forward determined to send his children no more to school; observing, that he never knew any good come of this same reading and writing. Whatever money the schoolmaster possessed, and he had received his quarter's pay but a day or two before, he must have had about his person at the time of his disappearance.

The mysterious event caused much speculation at the church on the following Sunday. Knots of gazers and gossips were collected in the churchyard, at the bridge, and at the spot where the hat and pumpkin had been found. The stories of Brouwer, of Bones, and a whole budget of others, were called to mind; and when they had diligently considered them all, and compared them with the symptoms of the present case, they shook their heads, and came to the conclusion that Ichabod had been carried off by the Galloping Hessian. As he was a bachelor, and in nobody's debt, nobody troubled his head any more about him. The school was removed to a different quarter of the Hollow, and another pedagogue reigned in his stead.

It is true, an old farmer, who had been down to New York on a visit several years after, and from whom this account of the ghastly adventure was received, brought home the intelligence that Ichabod Crane was still alive; that he had left the neighborhood, partly through fear of the goblin and Hans Van Ripper, and partly in mortification at having been suddenly dismissed by the heiress; that he had changed his quarters to a distant part of the country; had kept school and studied law at the same time, had been admitted to the bar, turned politician, electioneered, written for the newspapers, and finally had been made a justice of the Ten Pound Court. Brom Bones too, who shortly after his rival's disappearance conducted the blooming Katrina in triumph to the altar, was observed to look exceedingly knowing whenever the story of Ichabod was related, and always burst into a hearty laugh at the mention of the pumpkin; which led some to suspect that he knew more about the matter than he chose to tell.

The old country wives, however, who are the best judges of these matters, maintain to this day that Ichabod was spirited away by supernatural means; and it is a favorite story often told about the neighborhood round the winter evening fire. The bridge became more than ever an object of superstitious awe, and that may be the reason why the road has been altered of late years, so as to approach the church by the border of the millpond. The school-house, being deserted, soon fell to decay, and was reported to be haunted by the ghost of the unfortunate pedagogue; and the ploughboy, loitering homeward of a still summer evening, has often fancied his voice at a distance, chanting a melancholy psalm-tune, among the tranquil solitudes of Sleepy Hollow.

POSTSCRIPT,

Found in the Handwriting of Mr. Knickerbocker.

The preceding Tale is given, almost in the precise words in which I heard it related at a Corporation meeting of the ancient city of Manhattoes, at which were present many of its sagest and most illustrious burghers. The narrator was a pleasant, shabby, gentlemanly old fellow, in pepper-and-salt clothes, with a sadly humorous face; and one whom I strongly suspected of being poor—he made such efforts to be entertaining. When his story was concluded, there was much laughter and approbation, particularly from two or three deputy aldermen, who had been asleep the greater part of the time. There was, however, one tall, dry-looking old gentleman, with beetling eyebrows, who maintained a grave and rather severe face throughout; now and then folding his arms, inclining his head, and looking down upon the floor, as if turning a doubt over in his mind. He was one of your wary men, who never laugh, but on good grounds—when they have reason and the law on their side. When the mirth of the rest of the company had subsided and silence was restored, he leaned one arm on the elbow of his chair, and sticking the other akimbo, demanded, with a slight but exceedingly sage motion of the head, and contraction of the brow, what was the moral of the story, and what it went to prove.

The story-teller, who was just putting a glass of wine to his lips, as a refreshment after his toils, paused for a moment, looked at his inquirer with an air of infinite deference, and, lowering the glass slowly to the table, observed, that the story was intended most logically to prove:

"There is no situation in life but has its advantages and pleasures—provided we will but take a joke as we find it;

"That, therefore, he that runs races with goblin troopers is likely to have rough riding of it.

"*Ergo,* for a country schoolmaster to be refused the hand of a Dutch heiress, is a certain step to high preferment in the state."

The cautious old gentleman knit his brows tenfold closer after this explanation, being sorely puzzled by ratiocination of the syllogism; while, methought, the one in pepper-and-salt eyed him with something of a triumphant leer. At length he observed, that all this was very well, but still he thought the story a little on the extravagant—there were one or two points on which he had his doubts.

"Faith, sir," replied the story-teller, "as to that matter, I don't believe one-half of it myself."

D.K.

The Adventure of My Uncle

MANY years since, some time before the French Revolution, my uncle passed several months at Paris. The English and French were on better terms in those days than at present, and mingled cordially in society. The English went abroad to spend money then, and the French were always ready to help them: they go abroad to save money at present, and that they can do without French assistance. Perhaps the travelling English were fewer and choicer than at present, when the whole nation has broke loose and inundated the continent. At any rate, they circulated more readily and currently in foreign society, and my uncle, during his residence in Paris, made many very intimate acquaintances among the French noblesse.

Some time afterwards, he was making a journey in the winter-time in that part of Normandy called the Pays de Caux, when, as evening was closing in, he perceived the turrets of an ancient chateau rising out of the trees of its walled park; each turret with its high conical roof of gray slate, like a candle with an extinguisher on it.

"To whom does that chateau belong, friend?" cried my uncle to a meagre but fiery postilion, who, with tremendous jack-boots and cocked hat, was floundering on before him.

"To Monseigneur the Marquis de ——," said the postilion, touching his hat, partly out of respect to my uncle, and partly out of reverence to the noble name pronounced.

My uncle recollected the Marquis for a particular friend in Paris, who had often expressed a wish to see him at his paternal chateau. My uncle was an old traveller, one who knew well how to turn things to account. He revolved for a few moments in his mind, how agreeable it would be to his friend the Marquis to be surprised in this sociable way by a pop visit; and how much more agreeable to himself to get into snug quarters in a chateau, and have a relish of the Marquis's well-known kitchen, and a smack of his superior Champagne and Burgundy, rather than put up with the miserable lodgment and miserable fare of a provincial inn. In a few minutes, therefore, the meagre postilion was cracking his whip like a very devil, or like a true Frenchman, up the long, straight avenue that led to the chateau.

You have no doubt all seen French chateaus, as everybody travels in France nowadays. This was one of the oldest; standing naked and alone in the midst of a desert of gravel walks and cold stone terraces; with a cold-looking, formal garden, cut into angles and rhomboids; and a cold, leafless park, divided geometrically by straight alleys; and two or three cold-looking noseless statues; and fountains spouting cold water enough to make one's teeth chatter. At least such was the feeling they imparted on the wintry day of my uncle's visit; though, in hot summer weather, I'll warrant there was glare enough to scorch one's eyes out.

The smacking of the postilion's whip, which grew more and more intense the nearer they approached, frightened a flight of pigeons out of a dove-cot, and rooks out of the roofs, and finally a crew of servants out of the chateau, with the Marquis at their head. He was enchanted to see my uncle, for his chateau, like the house of our worthy host, had not many more guests at the time than it could accommodate. So he kissed my uncle on each cheek, after the French fashion, and ushered him into the castle.

The Marquis did the honors of the house with the urbanity of his country. In fact, he was proud of his old family chateau, for part of it was extremely old. There was a tower and chapel which had been built almost before the memory of man; but the rest was more modern, the castle having been nearly

demolished during the wars of the league. The Marquis dwelt upon this event with great satisfaction, and seemed really to entertain a grateful feeling towards Henry the Fourth, for having thought his paternal mansion worth battering down. He had many stories to tell of the prowess of his ancestors; and several skull-caps, helmets, and cross-bows, and divers huge boots and buff jerkins, to show, which had been worn by the leaguers. Above all, there was a two-handed sword, which he could hardly wield, but which he displayed, as a proof that there had been giants in his family.

In truth, he was but a small descendant from such great warriors. When you looked at their bluff visages and brawny limbs, as depicted in their portraits, and then at the little Marquis, with his spindle shanks, and his sallow lantern vis-age, flanked with a pair of powdered earlocks, or *aîles de*

pigeon, that seemed ready to fly away with it, you could hardly believe him to be of the same race. But when you looked at the eyes that sparkled out like a beetle's from each side of his hooked nose, you saw at once that he inherited all the fiery spirit of his forefathers. In fact, a Frenchman's spirit never exhales, however his body may dwindle. It rather rarefies, and grows more inflammable, as the earthly particles diminish; and I have seen valor enough in a little fiery-hearted French dwarf to have furnished out a tolerable giant.

When once the Marquis, as was his wont, put on one of the old helmets stuck up in his hall, though his head no more filled it than a dry pea its peascod, yet his eyes flashed from the bottom of the iron cavern with the brilliancy of carbuncles; and when he poised the ponderous two-handed sword of his ancestors, you would have thought you saw the doughty little David wielding the sword of Goliath, which was unto him like a weaver's beam.

However, gentlemen, I am dwelling too long on this description of the Marquis and his chateau, but you must excuse me; he was an old friend of my uncle; and whenever my uncle told the story, he was always fond of talking a great deal about his host.—Poor little Marquis! He was one of that handful of gallant courtiers who made such a devoted but hopeless stand in the cause of their sovereign, in the chateau of the Tuileries, against the irruption of the mob on the sad tenth of August. He displayed the valor of a *preux* French chevalier to the last; flourishing feebly his little court-sword with a *ça-ça!* in face of a whole legion of *sans-culottes*; but was pinned to the wall like a butterfly, by the pike of a *poissarde,* and his heroic soul was borne up to heaven on his *aîles de pigeon.*

But all this has nothing to do with my story. To the point, then. When the hour arrived for retiring for the night, my uncle was shown to his room in a venerable old tower. It was the oldest part of the chateau, and had in ancient times been the donjon or stronghold; of course the chamber was none of the best. The Marquis had put him there, however, because he knew him to be a traveller of taste, and fond of antiquities; and also because the better apartments were already occupied. Indeed, he perfectly reconciled my uncle to his quarters by mentioning the great personages who had once inhabited them, all of whom were, in some way or other, connected with the family. If you would take his word for it, John Baliol, or as he called him, Jean de Bailleul, had died of chagrin in this very chamber, on hearing of the success of his rival, Robert de Bruce, at the battle of Bannockburn. And when he added that the Duke de Guise had slept in it, my uncle was fain to felicitate himself on being honored with such distinguished quarters.

The night was shrewd and windy, and the chamber none of the warmest. An old long-faced, long-bodied servant, in quaint livery, who attended upon my uncle, threw down an armful of wood beside the fireplace, gave a queer look about the room, and then wished him *bon repos* with a grimace and a shrug that would have been suspicious from any other than an old French servant.

The chamber had indeed a wild, crazy look, enough to strike any one who had read romances with apprehension and foreboding. The windows were high and narrow, and had once been loop-holes, but had been rudely enlarged, as well as the extreme thickness of the walls would permit; and the ill-fitted casements rattled to every breeze. You would have thought, on a windy night, some of the old leaguers were tramping and clanking about the apartment in their huge boots and rattling spurs. A door which stood ajar, and, like a true French door, would stand ajar in spite of every reason and effort to the contrary, opened upon a long dark corridor, that led the Lord knows whither, and seemed just made for ghosts to air themselves in, when they turned out of their graves at midnight. The wind would spring up into a hoarse murmur through this passage, and creak the door to and fro, as if some dubious ghost were balancing in its mind whether to come in or not. In a word, it was precisely the kind of comfortless apartment that a ghost, if ghost there were in the chateau, would single out for its favorite lounge.

My uncle, however, though a man accustomed to meet with strange adventures, apprehended none at the time. He made several attempts to shut the door, but in vain. Not that he apprehended anything, for he was too old a traveller to be daunted by a wild-looking apartment; but the night, as I have said, was cold and gusty, and the wind howled about the old turret pretty much as it does round this old mansion at this moment, and the breeze from the long dark corridor came in as damp and as chilly as if from a dungeon. My uncle, therefore, since he could not close the door, threw a quantity of wood on the fire, which soon sent up a flame in the great wide-mouthed chimney that illumined the whole chamber; and made the shadow of the tongs on the opposite wall look like a long-legged giant. My uncle now clambered on the top of the half-score of mattresses which form a French bed, and which stood in a deep recess; then tucking himself snugly in, and burying himself up to the chin in the bedclothes, he lay looking at the fire, and listening to the wind, and thinking how knowingly he had come over his friend the Marquis for a night's lodging—and so he fell asleep.

He had not taken above half of his first nap when he was awakened by the clock of the chateau, in the turret over his chamber, which struck midnight. It was just such an old clock as ghosts are fond of. It had a deep, dismal tone, and struck so slowly and tediously that my uncle thought it would never have done. He counted and counted till he was confident he counted thirteen, and then it stopped.

The fire had burnt low, and the blaze of the last fagot was almost expiring, burning in small blue flames, which now and then lengthened up into little white gleams. My uncle lay with his eyes half closed, and his nightcap drawn almost down to his nose. His fancy was already wandering, and began to mingle up the present scene with the crater of Vesuvius, the French Opera, the Coliseum at Rome, Dolly's chop-house in London, and all the farrago of noted places with which the brain of a traveller is crammed—in a word, he was just falling asleep.

Suddenly he was roused by the sound of footsteps, slowly pacing along the corridor. My uncle, as I have often heard him say himself, was a man not easily frightened. So he lay quiet, supposing this some other guest, or some servant on his way to bed. The footsteps, however, approached the door; the door gently opened; whether of its own accord, or whether pushed open, my uncle could not distinguish: a figure all in white glided in. It was a female, tall and stately, and of a commanding air. Her dress was of an ancient fashion, ample in volume, and sweeping the floor. She walked up to the fireplace, without regarding my uncle, who raised his nightcap with one hand, and stared earnestly at her. She remained for some time standing by the fire, which, flashing up at intervals, cast blue and white gleams of light, that enabled my uncle to remark her appearance minutely.

Her face was ghastly pale, and perhaps rendered still more so by the bluish light of the fire. It possessed beauty, but its beauty was saddened by care and anxiety. There was the look of one accustomed to trouble, but of one whom trouble could not cast down nor subdue; for there was still the predominating air of proud, unconquerable resolution. Such at least was the opinion formed by my uncle, and he considered himself a great physiognomist.

The figure remained, as I said, for some time by the fire, putting out first one hand, then the other; then each foot

alternately, as if warming itself; for your ghosts, if ghost it really was, are apt to be cold. My uncle, furthermore, remarked that it wore high-heeled shoes, after an ancient fashion, with paste or diamond buckles, that sparkled as though they were alive. At length the figure turned gently round, casting a glassy look about the apartment, which, as it passed over my uncle, made his blood run cold, and chilled the very marrow in his bones. It then stretched its arms towards heaven, clasped its hands, and wringing them in a supplicating manner, glided slowly out of the room.

My uncle lay for some time meditating on this visitation, for (as he remarked when he told me the story) though a man of firmness, he was also a man of reflection, and did not reject a thing because it was out of the regular course of events. However, being, as I have before said, a great traveller, and accustomed to strange adventures, he drew his nightcap resolutely over his eyes, turned his back to the door, hoisted the bedclothes high over his shoulders, and gradually fell asleep.

How long he slept he could not say, when he was awakened by the voice of some one at his bedside. He turned round, and beheld the old French servant, with his ear-locks in tight buckles on each side of a long lantern face, on which habit had deeply wrinkled an everlasting smile. He made a thousand grimaces, and asked a thousand pardons for disturbing Monsieur, but the morning was considerably advanced. While my uncle was dressing, he called vaguely to mind the visitor of the preceding night. He asked the ancient domestic what lady was in the habit of rambling about this part of the chateau at night. The old valet shrugged his shoulders as high as his head, laid one hand on his bosom, threw open the other with every finger extended, made a most whimsical grimace which he meant to be complimentary, and replied, that it was not for him to know anything of *les bonnes fortunes* of Monsieur.

My uncle saw there was nothing satisfactory to be learned in this quarter. After breakfast, he was walking with the Marquis through the modern apartments of the chateau, sliding over the well-waxed floors of silken saloons, amidst furniture rich in gilding and brocade, until they came to a long picture-gallery, containing many portraits, some in oil and some in chalks.

Here was an ample field for the eloquence of his host, who had all the pride of a nobleman of the *ancien régime*. There was not a grand name in Normandy, and hardly one in France, which was not, in some way or other, connected with his house. My uncle stood listening with inward impatience, resting sometimes on one leg, sometimes on the other, as the little Marquis descanted, with his usual fire and vivacity, on the achievements of his ancestors, whose portraits hung along the wall; from the martial deeds of the stern warriors in steel, to the gallantries and intrigues of the blue-eyed gentlemen, with fair smiling faces, powdered ear-locks, laced ruffles, and pink and blue silk coats and breeches—not forgetting the conquests of the lovely shepherdesses, with hooped petticoats, and waists no thicker than an hour-glass, who appeared ruling over their sheep and their swains, with dainty crooks decorated with fluttering ribbons.

In the midst of his friend's discourse, my uncle was startled on beholding a full-length portrait, the very counterpart of his visitor of the preceding night.

"Methinks," said he, pointing to it, "I have seen the original of this portrait."

"*Pardonnez moi*," replied the Marquis politely, "that can hardly be, as the lady has been dead more than a hundred years. That was the beautiful Duchess de Longueville, who figured during the minority of Louis the Fourteenth."

"And was there anything remarkable in her history?"

Never was question more unlucky. The little Marquis immediately threw himself into the attitude of a man about to tell a long story. In fact, my uncle had pulled upon himself the whole history of the civil war of the Fronde, in which the beautiful Duchess had played so distinguished a part. Turenne, Coligni, Mazarin, were called up from their graves to grace his narration; nor were the affairs of the Barricadoes, nor the chivalry of the Port Cochères forgotten. My uncle began to wish himself a thousand leagues off from the Marquis and his merciless memory, when suddenly the little man's recollections took a more interesting turn. He was relating the imprisonment of the Duke de Longueville with the Princes Condé and Conti in the chateau of Vincennes, and the ineffectual efforts of the Duchess to rouse the sturdy Normans to their rescue. He had come to that part where she was invested by the royal forces in the Castle of Dieppe.

"The spirit of the Duchess," proceeded the Marquis, "rose from her trials. It was astonishing to see so delicate and beautiful a being buffet so resolutely with hardships. She determined on a desperate means of escape. You may have seen the château in which she was mewed up—an old ragged wart of an edifice, standing on the knuckle of a hill, just above the rusty little town of Dieppe. One dark unruly night she issued secretly out of a small postern gate of the castle, which the enemy had neglected to guard. The postern gate is there to this very day; opening upon a narrow bridge over a deep fosse between the castle and the brow of the hill. She was followed by her female attendants, a few domestics, and some gallant cavaliers, who still remained faithful to her fortunes. Her object was to gain a small port about two leagues distant, where she had privately provided a vessel for her escape in case of emergency.

"The little band of fugitives were obliged to perform the distance on foot. When they arrived at the port the wind was high and stormy, the tide contrary, the vessel anchored far off in the road, and no means of getting on board but by a fishing-shallop which lay tossing like a cockle-shell on the edge of the surf. The Duchess determined to risk the attempt. The seamen endeavored to dissuade her, but the imminence of her danger on shore, and the magnanimity of her spirit, urged her on. She had to be borne to the shallop in the arms of a mariner. Such was the violence of the wind and waves that he faltered, lost his foothold, and let his precious burden fall into the sea.

"The Duchess was nearly drowned, but partly through her own struggles, partly by the exertions of the seamen, she got to land. As soon as she had a little recovered strength, she insisted on renewing the attempt. The storm, however, had by this time become so violent as to set all efforts at defiance. To delay, was to be discovered and taken prisoner. As the only resource left, she procured horses, mounted with her female attendants, *en croupe*, behind the gallant gentlemen who accompanied her, and scoured the country to seek some temporary asylum.

"While the Duchess," continued the Marquis, laying his

forefinger on my uncle's breast to arouse his flagging attention, "while the Duchess, poor lady, was wandering amid the tempest in this disconsolate manner, she arrived at this chateau. Her approach caused some uneasiness; for the clattering of a troop of horse at dead of night up the avenue of a lonely chateau, in those unsettled times, and in a troubled part of the country, was enough to occasion alarm.

"A tall, broad-shouldered chasseur, armed to the teeth, galloped ahead, and announced the name of the visitor. All uneasiness was dispelled. The household turned out with flambeaux to receive her, and never did torches gleam on a more weather-beaten, travel-stained band than came tramping into the court. Such pale, careworn faces, such bedraggled dresses, as the poor Duchess and her females presented, each seated behind her cavalier: while the half-drenched, half-drowsy pages and attendants seemed ready to fall from their horses with sleep and fatigue.

"The Duchess was received with a hearty welcome by my ancestor. She was ushered into the hall of the chateau, and the fires soon crackled and blazed, to cheer herself and her train; and every spit and stew-pan was put in requisition to prepare ample refreshment for the wayfarers.

"She had a right to our hospitalities," continued the Marquis, drawing himself up with a slight degree of stateliness, "for she was related to our family. I'll tell you how it was. Her father, Henry de Bourbon, Prince of Condé—"

"But did the Duchess pass the night in the chateau?" said my uncle rather abruptly, terrified at the idea of getting involved in one of the Marquis's genealogical discussions.

"Oh, as to the Duchess, she was put into the very apartment you occupied last night, which at that time was a kind of state-apartment. Her followers were quartered in the chambers opening upon the neighboring corridor, and her favorite page slept in an adjoining closet. Up and down the corridor walked the great chasseur who had announced her arrival, and who acted as a kind of sentinel or guard. He was a dark, stern, powerful-looking fellow; and as the light of a lamp in the corridor fell upon his deeply marked face and sinewy form, he seemed capable of defending the castle with his single arm.

"It was a rough, rude night; about this time of the year—apropos!—now I think of it, last night was the anniversary of her visit. I may well remember the precise date, for it was a night not to be forgotten by our house. There is a singular tradition concerning it in our family." Here the Marquis hesitated, and a cloud seemed to gather about his bushy eyebrows. "There is a tradition—that a strange occurrence took place that night.—A strange, mysterious, inexplicable occurrence—" Here he checked himself, and paused.

"Did it relate to that lady?" inquired my uncle eagerly.

"It was past the hour of midnight," resumed the Marquis, "when the whole chateau—" Here he paused again. My uncle made a movement of anxious curiosity.

"Excuse me," said the Marquis, a slight blush streaking his sallow visage. "There are some circumstances connected with our family history which I do not like to relate. That was a rude period. A time of great crimes among great men: for you know high blood, when it runs wrong, will not run tamely, like blood of the *canaille*—poor lady!—But I have a little family pride, that—excuse me—we will change the subject, if you please—"

My uncle's curiosity was piqued. The pompous and magnificent introduction had led him to expect something wonderful in the story to which it served as a kind of avenue. He had no idea of being cheated out of it by a sudden fit of unreasonable squeamishness. Besides, being a traveller in quest of information, he considered it his duty to inquire into everything.

The Marquis, however, evaded every question.

"Well," said my uncle, a little petulantly, "whatever you may think of it, I saw that lady last night."

The Marquis stepped back and gazed at him with surprise.

"She paid me a visit in my bedchamber."

The Marquis pulled out his snuff-box with a shrug and a smile; taking this no doubt for an awkward piece of English pleasantry, which politeness required him to be charmed with.

My uncle went on gravely, however, and related the whole circumstance. The Marquis heard him through with profound attention, holding his snuff-box unopened in his hand. When the story was finished, he tapped on the lid of his box deliberately, took a long, sonorous pinch of snuff—

"Bah!" said the Marquis, and walked towards the other end of the gallery.

Here the narrator paused. The company waited for some time for him to resume his narration; but he continued silent.

"Well," said the inquisitive gentleman, "and what did your uncle say then?"

"Nothing," replied the other.

"And what did the Marquis say farther?"

"Nothing."

"And is that all?"

"That is all," said the narrator, filling a glass of wine.

"I surmise," said the shrewd old gentleman with the waggish nose—"I surmise the ghost must have been the old housekeeper, walking her rounds to see that all was right."

"Bah!" said the narrator. "My uncle was too much accustomed to strange sights not to know a ghost from a housekeeper."

There was a murmur round the table, half of merriment, half of disappointment. I was inclined to think the old gentleman had really an after-part of his story in reserve; but he sipped his wine and said nothing more; and there was an odd expression about his dilapidated countenance which left me in doubt whether he were in drollery or earnest.

"Egad," said the knowing gentleman, with the flexible nose, "this story of your uncle puts me in mind of one that used to be told of an aunt of mine, by the mother's side; though I don't know that it will bear a comparison, as the good lady was not so prone to meet with strange adventures. But any rate you shall have it."

The Adventure of My Aunt

MY aunt was a lady of large frame, strong mind, and great resolution: she was what might be termed a very manly woman. My uncle was a thin, puny little man, very meek and acquiescent, and no match for my aunt. It was observed that he dwindled and dwindled gradually away, from the day of his marriage. His wife's powerful mind was too much for him; it wore him out. My aunt, however, took all possible care of him: had half the doctors in town to prescribe for him; made him take all their prescriptions, and dosed him with physic enough to cure a whole hospital. All was in vain. My uncle grew worse and worse the more dosing and nursing he underwent, until in the end he added another to the long list of matrimonial victims who have been killed with kindness.

"And was it his ghost that appeared to her?" asked the inquisitive gentleman, who had questioned the former story-teller.

"You shall hear," replied the narrator.—My aunt took on mightily for the death of her poor dear husband. Perhaps she felt some compunction at having given him so much physic, and nursed him into the grave. At any rate, she did all that a widow could do to honor his memory. She spared no expense in either the quantity or quality of her mourning weeds; wore a miniature of him about her neck as large as a little sun-dial, and had a full-length portrait of him always hanging in her bed-chamber. All the world extolled her conduct to the skies; and it was determined that a woman who behaved so well to the memory of one husband deserved soon to get another.

It was not long after this that she went to take up her residence in an old country-seat in Derbyshire, which had long been in the care of merely a steward and housekeeper. She took most of her servants with her, intending to make it her principal abode. The house stood in a lonely wild part of the country, among the gray Derbyshire hills, with a murderer hanging in chains on a bleak height in full view.

The servants from town were half frightened out of their wits at the idea of living in such a dismal, pagan-looking place; especially when they got together in the servants' hall in the evening, and compared notes on all the hobgoblin stories picked up in the course of the day. They were afraid to venture alone about the gloomy, black-looking chambers. My lady's maid, who was troubled with nerves, declared she could

never sleep alone in such a "gashly rummaging old building";
and the footman, who was a kind-hearted young fellow, did
all in his power to cheer her up.

My aunt was struck with the lonely appearance of the
house. Before going to bed, therefore, she examined well
the fastnesses of the doors and windows; locked up the plate
with her own hands, and carried the keys, together with a
little box of money and jewels, to her own room; for she was
a notable woman, and always saw to all things herself. Having
put the keys under her pillow, and dismissed her maid, she
sat by her toilet arranging her hair; for being, in spite of her
grief for my uncle, rather a buxom widow, she was somewhat
particular about her person. She sat for a little while looking
at her face in the glass, first on one side, then on the other,
as ladies are apt to do when they would ascertain whether
they have been in good looks; for a roistering country squire
of the neighborhood, with whom she had flirted when a girl,
had called that day to welcome her to the country.

All of a sudden she thought she heard something move
behind her. She looked hastily round, but there was nothing
to be seen. Nothing but the grimly painted portrait of her
poor dear man, hanging against the wall.

She gave a heavy sigh to his memory, as she was accustomed
to do whenever she spoke of him in company, and then went
on adjusting her night-dress, and thinking of the squire. Her
sigh was re-echoed, or answered by a long-drawn breath. She
looked round again, but no one was to be seen. She ascribed
these sounds to the wind oozing through the ratholes of the
old mansion, and proceeded leisurely to put her hair in papers, when, all at once, she thought she perceived one of the
eyes of the portrait move.

"The back of her head being towards it!" said the story-
teller with the ruined head. "Good!"

"Yes, sir!" replied dryly the narrator, "her back being towards the portrait, but her eyes fixed on its reflection in the
glass."—Well, as I was saying, she perceived one of the eyes
of the portrait move. So strange a circumstance, as you may
well suppose, gave her a sudden shock. To assure herself of
the fact, she put one hand to her forehead as if rubbing it;
peeped through her fingers, and moved the candle with the

other hand. The light of the taper gleamed on the eye, and was reflected from it. She was sure it moved. Nay, more, it seemed to give her a wink, as she had sometimes known her husband to do when living! It struck a momentary chill to her heart; for she was a lone woman, and felt herself fearfully situated.

The chill was but transient. My aunt, who was almost as resolute a personage as your uncle, sir, (turning to the old story-teller,) became instantly calm and collected. She went on adjusting her dress. She even hummed an air, and did not make even a single false note. She casually overturned a dressing-box; took a candle and picked up the articles one by one from the floor; pursued a rolling pin-cushion that was making the best of its way under the bed; then opened the door; looked for an instant into the corridor, as if in doubt whether to go; and then walked quietly out.

She hastened down-stairs, ordered the servants to arm themselves with the weapons first at hand, placed herself at their head, and returned almost immediately.

Her hastily levied army presented a formidable force. The steward had a rusty blunder-buss, the coachman a loaded whip, the footman a pair of horse-pistols, the cook a huge chopping-knife, and the butler a bottle in each hand. My aunt led the van with a red-hot poker, and in my opinion she was the most formidable of the party. The waiting-maid, who dreaded to stay alone in the servants' hall, brought up the rear, smelling to a broken bottle of volatile salts, and expressing her terror of the ghostesses. "Ghosts!" said my aunt, resolutely. "I'll singe their whiskers for them!"

They entered the chamber. All was still and undisturbed as when she had left it. They approached the portrait of my uncle.

"Pull down that picture!" cried my aunt. A heavy groan, and a sound like the chattering of teeth, issued from the portrait. The servants shrunk back; the maid uttered a faint shriek, and clung to the footman for support.

"Instantly!" added my aunt, with a stamp of the foot.

The picture was pulled down, and from a recess behind it, in which had formerly stood a clock, they hauled forth a round-shouldered, black-bearded varlet, with a knife as long as my arm, but trembling all over like an aspen-leaf.

"Well, and who was he? No ghost, I suppose," said the inquisitive gentleman.

"A Knight of the Post," replied the narrator, "who had been smitten with the worth of the wealthy widow; or rather a marauding Tarquin who had stolen into her chamber to violate her purse, and rifle her strong box, when all the house should be asleep. In plain terms," continued he, "the vagabond was a loose idle fellow of the neighborhood, who had once been a servant in the house, and had been employed to assist in arranging it for the reception of its mistress. He confessed that he had contrived this hiding-place for his nefarious purpose, and had borrowed an eye from the portrait by way of a reconnoitring-hole."

"And what did they do with him?—did they hang him?" resumed the questioner.

"Hang him!—how could they?" exclaimed a beetle-browed barrister, with a hawk's nose. "The offense was not capital. No robbery, no assault had been committed. No forcible entry or breaking into the premises—"

"My aunt," said the narrator, "was a woman of spirit, and apt to take the law in her own hands. She had her own notions of cleanliness also. She ordered the fellow to be drawn through the horse-pond, to cleanse away all offences, and then to be well rubbed down with an oaken towel."

"And what became of him afterwards?" said the inquisitive gentleman.

"I do not exactly know. I believe he was sent on a voyage of improvement to Botany Bay."

"And your aunt," said the inquisitive gentleman. "I'll warrant she took care to make her maid sleep in the room with her after that."

"No, sir, she did better; she gave her hand shortly after to the roistering squire; for she used to observe, that it was a dismal thing for a woman to sleep alone in the country."

"She was right," observed the inquisitive gentleman, nodding sagaciously; "but I am sorry they did not hang that fellow."

It was agreed on all hands that the last narrator had brought his tale to the most satisfactory conclusion, though a country clergyman present regretted that the uncle and aunt, who figured in the different stories, had not been married together; they certainly would have been well matched.

"But I don't see, after all," said the inquisitive gentleman, "that there was any ghost in this last story."

"Oh! If it's ghosts you want, honey," cried the Irish Captain of Dragoons, "if it's ghosts you want, you shall have a whole regiment of them. And since these gentlemen have given the adventures of their uncles and aunts, faith, and I'll even give you a chapter out of my own family-history."

The Bold Dragoon

or *The Adventure of My Grandfather*

M Y grandfather was a bold dragoon, for it's a profession, d' ye see, that has run in the family. All my forefathers have been dragoons, and died on the field of honor, except myself, and I hope my posterity may be able to say the same; however, I don't mean to be vainglorious. Well, my grandfather, as I said, was a bold dragoon, and had served in the Low Countries. In fact, he was one of that very army, which according to my uncle Toby, swore so terribly in Flanders. He could swear a good stick himself; and moreover was the very man that introduced the doctrine Corporal Trim mentions of radical heat and radical moisture, or, in other words, the mode of keeping out the damps of ditchwater by burnt brandy. Be that as it may, it's nothing to the purport of my story. I only tell it to show you that my grandfather was a man not easily to be humbugged. He had seen service, or, according to his own phrase, he had seen the devil—and that's saying everything.

Well, gentlemen, my grandfather was on his way to England, for which he intended to embark from Ostend—bad luck to the place! for one where I was kept by storms and headwinds for three long days, and the devil of a jolly companion or pretty girl to comfort me. Well, as I was saying, my grandfather was on his way to England, or rather to Ostend—no matter which, it's all the same. So one evening, towards night fall, he rode jollily into Bruges.—Very like you all know Bruges, gentlemen; a queer old-fashioned Flemish town, once, they say, a great place for trade and money-making in old times, when the Mynheers were in their glory; but almost as large and as empty as an Irishman's pocket at the present day.—Well, gentlemen, it was at the time of the annual fair. All Bruges was crowded; and the canals swarmed with Dutch boats, and the streets swarmed with Dutch merchants; and there was hardly any getting along for goods, wares, and merchandises, and peasants in big breeches, and women in half a score of petticoats.

My grandfather rode jollily along, in his easy, slashing way, for he was a saucy, sunshiny fellow—staring about him at the motley crowd, the old houses with gable ends to the street, and storks' nests in the chimneys; winking at the yafrows who showed their faces at the windows and joking the women right and left in the street; all of whom laughed, and took it in amazing good part; for though he did not know a word of the language, yet he had always a knack of making himself understood among the women.

Well, gentlemen, it being the time of the annual fair, all the town was crowded, every inn and tavern full, and my grandfather applied in vain from one to the other for admittance. At length he rode up to an old rickety inn, that looked ready to fall to pieces, and which all the rats would have run away from, if they could have found room in any other house to put their heads. It was just such a queer building as you see in Dutch pictures, with a tall roof that reached up into the clouds, and as many garrets, one over the other, as the seven heavens of Mahomet. Nothing had saved it from tumbling down but a stork's nest on the chimney, which always brings good luck to a house in the Low Countries; and at the very time of my grandfather's arrival, there were two of these long-legged birds of grace standing like ghosts on the chimney-top. Faith, but they've kept the house on its legs to this very day, for you may see it any time you pass through Bruges, as it stands there yet, only it is turned into a brewery of strong Flemish beer—at least it was so when I came that way after the battle of Waterloo.

My grandfather eyed the house curiously as he approached. It might not have altogether struck his fancy, had he not seen in large letters over the door,

HEER VERKOOPT MAN GOEDEN DRANK

My grandfather had learnt enough of the language to know that the sign promised good liquor. "This is the house for me," said he, stopping short before the door.

The sudden appearance of a dashing dragoon was an event in an old inn frequented only by the peaceful sons of traffic. A rich burgher of Antwerp, a stately ample man in a broad Flemish hat, and who was the great man and great patron of the establishment, sat smoking a clean long pipe on one side of the door; a fat little distiller of Geneva, from Schiedam,

sat smoking on the other; and the bottle-nosed host stood
in the door, and the comely hostess, in crimped cap, beside
him; and the hostess's daughter, a plump Flanders lass, with
long gold pendants in her ears, was at a side-window.

"Humph!" said the rich burgher of Antwerp, with a sulky
glance at the stranger.

"De duyvel!" said the fat little distiller of Schiedam.

The landlord saw, with the quick glance of a publican, that
the new guest was not at all to the taste of the old ones; and,
to tell the truth, he did not like my grandfather's saucy eye.
He shook his head. "Not a garret in the house but was full."

"Not a garret!" echoed the landlady.

"Not a garret!" echoed the daughter.

The burgher of Antwerp, and the little distiller of Schiedam, continued to smoke their pipes sullenly, eying the enemy askance from under their broad hats, but said nothing.

My grandfather was not a man to be browbeaten. He threw
the reins on his horse's neck, cocked his head on one side,
stuck one arm akimbo—"Faith and troth!" said he, "but I'll
sleep in this house this very night."—As he said this he gave
a slap on his thigh, by way of emphasis—the slap went to the
landlady's heart.

He followed up the vow by jumping off his horse, and
making his way past the staring Mynheers into the public
room.—Maybe you've been in the bar-room of an old Flemish
inn—faith, but a handsome chamber it was as you'd wish to
see; with a brick floor, and a great fireplace, with the whole
Bible history in glazed tiles; and then the mantel-piece, pitching itself head foremost out of the wall, with a whole regiment
of cracked tea-pots and earthen jugs paraded on it; not to
mention half a dozen great Delft platters, hung about the
room by way of pictures; and the little bar in one corner, and
the bouncing bar-maid inside of it, with a red calico cap, and
yellow ear-drops.

My grandfather snapped his fingers over his head, as he
cast an eye round the room—"Faith, this is the very house
I've been looking after," said he.

There was some further show of resistance on the part of
the garrison; but my grandfather was an old soldier, and an
Irishman to boot, and not easily repulsed, especially after he

had got into the fortress. So he blarneyed the landlord, kissed the landlord's wife, tickled the landlord's daughter, chucked the bar-maid under the chin; and it was agreed on all hands that it would be a thousand pities, and a burning shame into the bargain, to turn such a bold dragoon into the streets. So they laid their heads together, that is to say, my grandfather and the landlady, and it was at length agreed to accommodate him with an old chamber that had been for some time shut up.

"Some say it's haunted," whispered the landlord's daughter; "but you are a bold dragoon, and I dare say don't fear ghosts."

"The devil a bit!" said my grandfather, pinching her plump cheek. "But if I should be troubled by ghosts, I've been to the Red Sea in my time, and have a pleasant way of laying them, my darling."

And then he whispered something to the girl which made her laugh, and give him a good-humored box on the ear. In short, there was nobody knew better how to make his way among the petticoats than my grandfather.

In a little while, as was his usual way, he took complete possession of the house, swaggering all over it; into the stable to look after his horse, into the kitchen to look after his supper. He had something to say or do with every one; smoked with the Dutchmen, drank with the Germans, slapped the landlord on the shoulder, romped with his daughter and the bar-maid—never, since the days of Alley Croaker, had such a rattling blade been seen. The landlord stared at him with astonishment; the landlord's daughter hung her head and giggled whenever he came near; and as he swaggered along the corridor, with his sword trailing by his side, the maids looked after him, and whispered to one another, "What a proper man!"

At supper, my grandfather took command of the *table-d'hôte* as though he had been at home; helped everybody, not forgetting himself; talked with every one, whether he understood their language or not; and made his way into the intimacy of the rich burgher of Antwerp, who had never been known to be sociable with any one during his life. In fact, he revolutionized the whole establishment, and gave it such a rouse, that the very house reeled with it. He outsat every one at table, excepting the little fat distiller of Schiedam, who sat soaking a long time before he broke forth; but when he did, he was a very devil incarnate. He took a violent affection for my grandfather; so they sat drinking and smoking, and telling stories, and singing Dutch and Irish songs, without understanding a word each other said, until the little Hollander was fairly swamped with his own gin and water, and carried off to bed, whooping and hickuping, and trolling the burden of a Low Dutch love-song.

Well, gentlemen, my grandfather was shown to his quarters up a large staircase, composed of loads of hewn timber; and through long rigmarole passages, hung with blackened paintings of fish, and fruit, and game, and country frolics, and huge kitchens, and portly burgomasters, such as you see about old-fashioned Flemish inns, till at length he arrived at his room.

An old-times chamber it was, sure enough, and crowded with all kinds of trumpery. It looked like an infirmary for decayed and super-annuated furniture, where everything diseased or disabled was sent to nurse or to be forgotten. Or rather it might be taken for a general congress of old legitimate movables, where every kind and country had a representative. No two chairs were alike. Such high backs and low backs, and leather bottoms, and worsted bottoms, and straw bottoms, and no bottoms; and cracked marble tables with curiously carved legs, holding balls in their claws, as though they were going to play at ninepins.

My grandfather made a bow to the motley assemblage as he entered, and, having undressed himself, placed his light in the fireplace, asking pardon of the tongs, which seemed to be making love to the shovel in the chimney-corner, and whispering soft nonsense in its ear.

The rest of the guests were by this time sound asleep, for your Mynheers are huge sleepers. The housemaids, one by one, crept up yawning to their attics; and not a female head in the inn was laid on a pillow that night without dreaming of the bold dragoon.

My grandfather, for his part, got into bed, and drew over him one of those great bags of down, under which they smother a man in the Low Countries; and there he lay, melting between two feather beds, like an anchovy sandwich between two slices of toast and butter. He was a warm-complexioned man, and this smothering played the very deuce with him. So, sure enough, in a little time it seemed as if a legion of imps were twitching at him, and all the blood in his veins was in a fever-heat.

He lay still, however, until all the house was quiet excepting the snoring of the Mynheers from the different chambers; who answered one another in all kinds of tones and cadences, like so many bull-frogs in a swamp. The quieter the house became, the more unquiet became my grandfather. He waxed warmer and warmer, until at length the bed became too hot to hold him.

"Maybe the maid had warmed it too much?" said the curious gentleman, inquiringly.

"I rather think the contrary," replied the Irishman. "But, be that as it may, it grew too hot for my grandfather."

"Faith, there's no standing this any longer," says he. So he jumped out of bed, and went strolling about the house.

"What for?" said the inquisitive gentleman.

"Why, to cool himself, to be sure—or perhaps to find a more comfortable bed—or perhaps— But no matter what he went for—he never mentioned—and there's no use in taking up our time in conjecturing."

Well, my grandfather had been for some time absent from his room, and was returning, perfectly cool, when just as he reached the door, he heard a strange noise within. He paused and listened. It seemed as if some one were trying to hum a tune in defiance of the asthma. He recollected the report of the room being haunted; but he was no believer in ghosts, so he pushed the door gently open and peeped in.

Egad, gentlemen, there was a gambol carrying on within enough to have astonished St. Anthony himself. By the light of the fire he saw a pale weazen-faced fellow, in a long flannel gown and a tall white nightcap with a tassel to it, who sat by the fire with a bellows under his arm by way of bagpipe, from which he forced the asthmatical music that had bothered my grandfather. As he played, too, he kept twitching about with a thousand queer contortions, nodding his head, and bobbing about his tasselled night-cap.

My grandfather thought this very odd and mighty pre-
sumptuous, and was about to demand what business he had
to play his wind-instrument in another gentleman's quarters,
when a new cause of astonishment met his eye. From the
opposite side of the room a long-backed, bandy-legged chair,
covered with leather, and studded all over in a coxcombical
fashion with little brass nails, got suddenly into motion, thrust
out first a claw-foot, then a crooked arm, and at length, making a leg, slided gracefully up to an easy-chair of tarnished
brocade, with a hole in its bottom, and led it gallantly out in
a ghostly minuet about the floor.

The musician now played fiercer and fiercer, and bobbed
his head and his night-cap about like mad. By degrees the

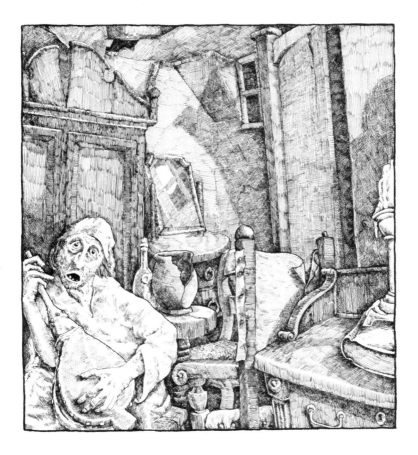

dancing mania seemed to seize upon all the other pieces of furniture. The antique, long-bodied chairs paired off in couples and led down a country-dance; a three-legged stool danced a hornpipe, though horribly puzzled by its supernumerary limb; while the amorous tongs seized the shovel round the waist, and whirled it about the room in a German waltz. In short, all the movables got in motion; pirouetting hands across, right and left, like so many devils; all except a great clothes-press, which kept courtesying and courtesying in a corner, like a dowager, in exquisite time to the music; being rather too corpulent to dance, or perhaps at a loss for a partner.

My grandfather concluded the latter to be the reason; so being, like a true Irishman, devoted to the sex, and at all times ready for a frolic, he bounced into the room, called to the musician to strike up Paddy O'Rafferty, capered up to the clothes-press, and seized upon the two handles to lead her out:—when-whirr! the whole revel was at an end. The chairs, tables, tongs and shovel, slunk in an instant as quietly into their places as if nothing had happened, and the musician vanished up the chimney, leaving the bellows behind him in his hurry. My grandfather found himself seated in the middle of the floor with the clothes-press sprawling before him, and the two handles jerked off, and in his hands.

"Then, after all, this was a mere dream," said the inquisitive gentlemen.

"The divil a bit of a dream!" replied the Irishman. "There never was a truer fact in this world. Faith, I should have liked to see any man tell my grandfather it was a dream."

Well, gentlemen, as the clothes-press was a mighty heavy body, and my grandfather likewise, particularly in rear, you may easily suppose that two such heavy bodies coming to the ground would make a bit of a noise. Faith, the old mansion shook as though it had mistaken it for an earthquake. The whole garrison was alarmed. The landlord, who slept below, hurried up with a candle to inquire the cause, but with all his haste his daughter had arrived at the scene of uproar before him. The landlord was followed by the landlady, who was followed by the bouncing bar-maid, who was followed by the simpering chambermaids, all holding together, as well as they could, such garments as they first laid hands on; but all in a terrible hurry to see what the deuce was to pay in the chamber of the bold dragoon.

My grandfather related the marvellous scene he had witnessed, and the broken handles of the prostrate clothes-press bore testimony to the fact. There was no contesting such evidence; particularly with a lad of my grandfather's complexion, who seemed able to make good every word either with sword or shillelah. So the landlord scratched his head and looked silly, as he was apt to do when puzzled. The landlady scratched—no, she did not scratch her head, but she knit her brow, and did not seem half pleased with the explanation. But the landlady's daughter corroborated it by recollecting that the last person who had dwelt in that chamber was a famous juggler who died of St. Vitus's dance, and had no doubt infected all the furniture.

This set all things to rights, particularly when the chambermaids declared that they had all witnessed strange carryings on in that room; and as they declared this "upon their honors," there could not remain a doubt upon this subject.

"And did your grandfather go to bed again in that room?" said the inquisitive gentleman.

"That's more than I can tell. Where he passed the rest of the night was a secret he never disclosed. In fact, though he had seen much service, he was but indifferently acquainted with geography, and apt to make blunders in his travels about inns at night, which it would have puzzled him sadly to account for in the morning."

"Was he ever apt to walk in his sleep?" said the knowing old gentleman.

"Never that I heard of."

There was a little pause after this rigmarole Irish romance, when the old gentleman with the haunted head observed, that the stories hitherto related had rather a burlesque tendency. "I recollect an adventure, however," added he, "which I heard of during a residence in Paris, for the truth of which I can undertake to vouch, and which is of a very grave and singular nature."

The Spectre Bridegroom

A Traveller's Tale

Shall I not take mine ease in mine inn!

Falstaff

DURING a journey that I once made through the Netherlands, I had arrived one evening at the *Pomme d' Or,* the principal inn of a small Flemish village. It was after the hour of the *table d' hôte,* so that I was obliged to make a solitary supper from the relics of its ampler board. The weather was chilly; I was seated alone in one end of a great gloomy dining-room, and, my repast being over, I had the prospect before me of a long dull evening, without any visible means of enlivening it. I summoned mine host, and requested something to read; he brought me the whole literary stock of his household, a Dutch family Bible, an almanac in the same language, and a number of old Paris newspapers. As I sat dozing over one of the latter, reading old and stale criticisms, my ear was now and then struck with bursts of laughter which seemed to proceed from the kitchen. Everyone that has travelled on the continent must know how favorite a resort the kitchen of a country inn is to the middle and inferior order of travellers; particularly in that equivocal kind of weather, when a fire becomes agreeable toward evening. I threw aside the newspaper, and explored my way to

119

the kitchen, to take a peep at the group that appeared to be so merry. It was composed partly of travellers who had arrived some hours before in a diligence, and partly of the usual attendants and hangers-on of inns. They were seated round a great burnished stove, that might have been mistaken for an altar, at which they were worshipping. It was covered with various kitchen vessels of resplendent brightness; among which steamed and hissed a huge copper tea-kettle. A large lamp threw a strong mass of light upon the group, bringing out many odd features in strong relief. Its yellow rays partially illumined the spacious kitchen, dying duskily away into remote corners, except where they settled, in mellow radiance on the broad side of a flitch of bacon, or were reflected back from well-scoured utensils, that gleamed from the midst of obscurity. A strapping Flemish lass, with long golden pendants in her ears, and a necklace with a golden heart suspended from it, was the presiding priestess of the temple.

Many of the company were furnished with pipes, and most of them with some kind of evening potation. I found their mirth was occasioned by anecdotes, which a little swarthy Frenchman, with a dry weazen face and large whiskers, was giving of his love adventures; at the end of each of which there was one of those bursts of honest unceremonious laughter, in which a man indulges in that temple of true liberty, an inn.

As I had no better mode of getting through a tedious blustering evening, I took my seat near the stove, and listened to a variety of traveller's tales, some very extravagant, and most very dull. All of them, however, have faded from my treacherous memory except one, which I will endeavor to relate. I fear, however, it derived its chief zest from the manner in which it was told, and the peculiar air and appearance of the narrator. He was a corpulent old Swiss, who had the look of a veteran traveller. He was dressed in a tarnished green travelling-jacket, with a broad belt round his waist, and a pair of overalls, with buttons from the hips to the ankles. He was of a full, rubicund countenance, with a double chin, aquiline nose and a pleasant, twinkling eye. His hair was light, and curled from under an old green velvet travelling-cap stuck on one side of his head. He was interrupted more than once by the arrival of guests, or the remarks of his auditors; and paused now and then to replenish his pipe; at which times he had generally a roguish leer, and a sly joke for the buxom kitchen-maid.

I wish my readers could imagine the old fellow lolling in a huge armchair, one arm akimbo, the other holding a curiously twisted tobacco-pipe, formed of genuine *écume de mer,* decorated with silver chain and silken tassel,—his head cocked on one side, and a whimsical cut of the eye occasionally, as he related the following story.

> He that supper for is dight,
> He lyes full cold, I trow, this night!
> Yestreen to chamber I him led,
> This night Gray-Steel has made his bed.
> SIR EGER, SIR GRAHAME, AND SIR GRAY-STEEL.

ON the summit of one of the heights of the Odenwald, a wild and romantic tract of Upper Germany, that lies not far from the confluence of the Main and the Rhine, there stood, many, many years since, the Castle of the Baron Von Landshort. It is now quite fallen to decay, and almost buried among beechtrees and dark firs; above which, however, its old watchtower may still be seen struggling, like the former possessor I have mentioned, to carry a high head, and look down upon the neighboring country.

The baron was a dry branch of the great family of Katzenellenbogen,* and inherited the relics of the property, and all the pride of his ancestors. Though the warlike disposition of his predecessors had much impaired the family possessions, yet the baron still endeavored to keep up some show of former state. The times were peaceable, and the German nobles, in general, had abandoned their inconvenient old

---

*I.e., CAT'S-ELBOW. The name of a family of those parts, very powerful in former times. The appellation, we are told, was given in compliment to a peerless dame of the family, celebrated for her fine arm.

castles, perched like eagles' nests among the mountains, and had built more convenient residences in the valleys: still the baron remained proudly drawn up in his little fortress, cherishing, with hereditary inveteracy, all the old family feuds; so that he was on ill terms with some of his nearest neighbors on account of disputes that had happened between their great-great-grandfathers.

The baron had but one child, a daughter; but nature, when she grants but one child, always compensates by making it a prodigy; and so it was with the daughter of the baron. All the nurses, gossips, and country-cousins assured her father that she had not her equal for beauty in all Germany; and who should know better than they? She had, moreover, been brought up with great care under the superintendence of two maiden aunts, who had spent some years of their early life at one of the little German courts, and were skilled in all the branches of knowledge necessary to the education of a fine lady. Under their instructions she became a miracle of accomplishments. By the time she was eighteen, she could embroider to admiration, and had worked whole histories of the saints in tapestry, with such strength of expression in their countenance, that they looked like so many souls in purgatory. She could read without great difficulty, and had spelled her way through several church legends, and almost all the chivalric wonders of the Heldenbuch. She had even made considerable proficiency in writing; could sign her own name without missing a letter, and so legibly that her aunts could read it without spectacles. She excelled in making little elegant good-for-nothing lady-like knickknacks of all kinds; was versed in the most abstruse dancing of the day; played a number of airs on the harp and guitar and knew all the tender ballads of the Minnelieders by heart.

Her aunts, too, having been great flirts and coquettes in their younger days, were admirably calculated to be vigilant guardians and strict censors of the conduct of their niece; for there is no duenna so rigidly prudent, and inexorably decorous, as a superannuated coquette. She was rarely suffered out of their sight; never went beyond the domains of the castle, unless well attended, or rather well watched; had continual lectures read to her about strict decorum and implicit obedience; and as to the men—pah!—she was taught to hold them at such a distance, and in such absolute distrust, that, unless properly authorized, she would not have cast a glance upon the handsomest cavalier in the world—no, not if he were even dying at her feet.

The good effects of this system were wonderfully apparent. The young lady was a pattern of docility and correctness. While others were wasting their sweetness in the glare of the world, and liable to be plucked and thrown aside by every hand, she was coyly blooming into fresh and lovely womanhood under the protection of those immaculate spinsters like a rose-bud blushing forth among guardian thorns. Her aunts looked upon her with pride and exultation, and vaunted that though all the other young ladies in the world might go astray, yet, thank Heaven, nothing of the kind could happen to the heiress of Katzenellenbogen.

But, however scantily the Baron Von Landshort might be provided with children, his household was by no means a small one; for Providence had enriched him with abundance of poor relations. They, one and all, possessed the affectionate disposition common to humble relatives; were wonderfully attached to the baron, and took every possible occasion to come in swarms and enliven the castle. All family festivals were commemorated by these good people at the baron's expense; and when they were filled with good cheer, they would declare that there was nothing on earth so delightful as these family meetings, these jubilees of the heart.

The baron, though a small man, had a large soul, and it swelled with satisfaction at the consciousness of being the greatest man in the little world about him. He loved to tell long stories about the dark old warriors whose portraits looked grimly down from the walls around, and he found no listeners equal to those who fed at his expense. He was much given to the marvellous, and a firm believer in all those supernatural tales with which every mountain and valley in Germany abounds. The faith of his guests exceeded even his own; they listened to every tale of wonder with open eyes and mouth, and never failed to be astonished, even though repeated for the hundredth time. Thus lived the Baron Von Landshort, the oracle of his table, the absolute monarch of his little territory, and happy, above all things, in the persuasion that he was the wisest man of the age.

At the time of which my story treats, there was a great family-gathering at the castle, on an affair of the utmost importance: it was to receive the destined bridegroom of the baron's daughter. A negotiation had been carried on between the father and an old nobleman of Bavaria, to unite the dignity of their houses by the marriage of their children. The preliminaries had been conducted with proper punctilio. The young people were betrothed without seeing each other; and the time was appointed for the marriage ceremony. The young Count Von Altenburg had been recalled from the army for the purpose, and was actually on his way to the

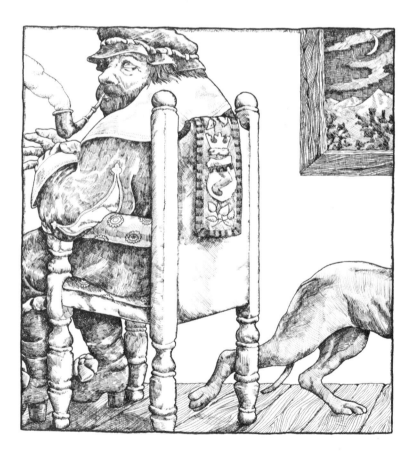

baron's to receive his bride. Missives had even been received
from him, from Würtzburg, where he was accidentally detained, mentioning the day and hour when he might be expected to arrive.

The castle was in a tumult of preparation to give him a
suitable welcome. The fair bride had been decked out with
uncommon care. The two aunts had superintended her toilet,
and quarrelled the whole morning about every article of her
dress. The young lady had taken advantage of their contest
to follow the bent of her own taste; and fortunately it was
a good one. She looked as lovely as youthful bridegroom
could desire; and the flutter of expectation heightened the
lustre of her charms.

The suffusions that mantled her face and neck, the gentle
heaving of the bosom, the eye now and then lost in reverie,
all betrayed the soft tumult that was going on in her little
heart. The aunts were continually hovering around her; for
maiden aunts are apt to take great interest in affairs of this
nature. They were giving her a world of staid counsel how
to deport herself, what to say, and in what manner to receive
the expected lover.

The baron was no less busied in preparations. He had, in
truth, nothing exactly to do; but he was naturally a fuming,
bustling little man, and could not remain passive when all the
world was in a hurry. He worried from top to bottom of the
castle with an air of infinite anxiety; he continually called the
servants from their work to exhort them to be diligent; and
buzzed about every hall and chamber, as idly restless and
importunate as a blue-bottle fly on a warm summer's day.

In the meantime the fatted calf had been killed; the forests
had rung with the clamor of the huntsmen; the kitchen was
crowded with good cheer; the cellars had yielded up whole
oceans of *Rhein-wein* and *Ferne-wein;* and even the great
Heidelberg tun had been laid under contribution. Everything
was ready to receive the distinguished guest with *Saus* and
Braus in the true spirit of German hospitality;—but the guest
delayed to make his appearance. Hour rolled after hour. The
sun, that had poured his downward rays upon the rich forest
of the Odenwald, now just gleamed along the summits of the
mountains. The baron mounted the highest tower, and

strained his eyes in the hope of catching a distant sight of the count and his attendants. Once he thought he beheld them; the sound of horns came floating from the valley, prolonged by the mountain echoes. A number of horsemen were seen far below, slowly advancing along the road; but when they had nearly reached the foot of the mountain, they suddenly struck off in a different direction. The last ray of sunshine departed—the bats began to flit by in the twilight—the road grew dimmer and dimmer to the view, and nothing appeared stirring in it but now and then a peasant lagging homeward from his labor.

While the old castle of Landshort was in this state of per-plexity, a very interesting scene was transacting in a different part of the Odenwald.

The young Count Von Altenburg was tranquilly pursuing his route in that sober jogtrot way, in which a man travels toward matrimony when his friends have taken all the trouble and uncertainty of courtship off his hands, and a bride is waiting for him, as certainly as a dinner at the end of his journey. He had encountered at Würtzburg a youthful com-panion in arms, with whom he had seen some service on the frontiers—Herman Von Starkenfaust, one of the stoutest hands and worthiest hearts of German chivalry, who was now returning from the army. His father's castle was not far distant from the old fortress of Landshort, although an hereditary feud rendered the families hostile, and strangers to each other.

In the warm-hearted moment of recognition, the young friends related all their past adventures and fortunes, and the count gave the whole history of his intended nuptials with a young lady whom he had never seen, but of whose charms he had received the most enrapturing descriptions.

As the route of the friends lay in the same direction, they agreed to perform the rest of their journey together; and, that they might do it the more leisurely, set off from Würtzburg at an early hour, the count having given directions for his retinue to follow and overtake him.

They beguiled their wayfaring with recollections of their military scenes and adventures; but the count was apt to be a little tedious, now and then, about the reputed charms of his bride, and the felicity that awaited him.

In this way they had entered among the mountains of the Odenwald, and were traversing one of its most lonely and thickly-wooded passes. It is well known that the forests of Germany have always been as much infested by robbers, as its castles by spectres; and, at this time, the former were particularly numerous, from the hordes of disbanded soldiers wandering about the country. It will not appear extraordinary, therefore, that the cavaliers were attacked by a gang of these stragglers, in the midst of the forest. They defended themselves with bravery, but were nearly overpowered, when the count's retinue arrived to their assistance. At sight of them the robbers fled, but not until the count had received a mortal wound. He was slowly and carefully conveyed back to the city of Würtzburg, and a friar summoned from a neighboring convent, who was famous for his skill in administering to both soul and body; but half of his skill was superfluous; the moments of the unfortunate count were numbered.

With his dying breath he entreated his friend to repair instantly to the castle of Landshort, and explain the fatal cause of his not keeping his appointment with his bride. Though not the most ardent of lovers, he was one of the most punctilious of men, and appeared earnestly solicitous that his mission should be speedily and courteously executed. "Unless this is done," said he, "I shall not sleep quietly in my grave!" He repeated these last words with peculiar solemnity. A request, at a moment so impressive, admitted no hesitation. Starkenfaust endeavored to soothe him to calmness; promised faithfully to execute his wish, and gave him his hand in solemn pledge. The dying man pressed it in acknowledgment, but soon lapsed into delirium—raved about his bride—his engagements—his plighted word; ordered his horse, that he might ride to the castle of Landshort; and expired in the fancied act of vaulting into the saddle.

Starkenfaust bestowed a sigh and a soldier's tear on the untimely fate of his comrade; and then pondered on the awkward mission he had undertaken. His heart was heavy, and his head perplexed; for he was to present himself an unbidden guest among hostile people, and to damp their festivity with tidings fatal to their hopes. Still there were certain whisperings of curiosity in his bosom to see this far-famed beauty of Katzenellenbogen, so cautiously shut up from the world; for he was a passionate admirer of the sex, and there was a dash of eccentricity and enterprise in his character that made him fond of all singular adventure.

Previous to his departure he made all due arrangements with the holy fraternity of the convent for the funeral solemnities of his friend, who was to be buried in the cathedral of Würtzburg, near some of his illustrious relatives; and the mourning retinue of the count took charge of his remains.

It is now high time that we should return to the ancient family of Katzenellenbogen, who were impatient for their guest, and still more for their dinner; and to the worthy little baron, whom we left airing himself on the watch-tower.

Night closed in, but still no guest arrived. The baron descended from the tower in despair. The banquet, which had been delayed from hour to hour, could no longer be postponed. The meats were already overdone; the cook in an agony; and the whole household had the look of a garrison that had been reduced by famine. The baron was obliged reluctantly to give orders for the feast without the presence of the guest. All were seated at table, and just on the point of commencing, when the sound of a horn from without the gate gave notice of the approach of a stranger. Another long blast filled the old courts of the castle with its echoes, and was answered by the warder from the walls. The baron hastened to receive his future son-in-law.

The drawbridge had been let down, and the stranger was before the gate. He was a tall, gallant cavalier, mounted on a black steed. His countenance was pale, but he had a beaming, romantic eye, and an air of stately melancholy. The baron was a little mortified that he should have come in this simple, solitary style. His dignity for a moment was ruffled, and he felt disposed to consider it a want of proper respect for the important occasion, and the important family with which he was to be connected. He pacified himself, however, with the conclusion, that it must have been youthful impatience which had induced him thus to spur on sooner than his attendants.

"I am sorry," said the stranger, "to break in upon you thus unseasonably—"

Here the baron interrupted him with a world of compliments and greetings; for, to tell the truth, he prided himself

upon his courtesy and eloquence. The stranger attempted, once or twice, to stem the torrent of words, but in vain, so he bowed his head and suffered it to flow on. By the time the baron had come to a pause, they had reached the inner court of the castle; and the stranger was again about to speak, when he was once more interrupted by the appearance of the female part of the family, leading forth the shrinking and blushing bride. He gazed on her for a moment as one entranced; it seemed as if his whole soul beamed forth in the gaze, and rested upon that lovely form. One of the maiden aunts whispered something in her ear; she made an effort to speak; her moist blue eye was timidly raised; gave a shy glance of inquiry on the stranger; and was cast again to the ground. The words died away; but there was a sweet smile playing about her lips, and a soft dimpling of the cheek that showed her glance had not been unsatisfactory. It was impossible for a girl of the fond age of eighteen, highly predisposed for love and matrimony, not to be pleased with so gallant a cavalier.

The late hour at which the guest had arrived left no time for parley. The baron was peremptory, and deferred all particular conversation until the morning, and led the way to the untasted banquet.

It was served up in the great hall of the castle. Around the walls hung the hard-favored portraits of the heroes of the house of Katzenellenbogen, and the trophies which they had gained in the field and in the chase. Hacked corselets, splintered jousting spears, and tattered banners, were mingled with the spoils of sylvan warfare; the jaws of the wolf, and the tusks of the boar, grinned horribly among cross-bows and battle-axes, and a huge pair of antlers branched immediately over the head of the youthful bridegroom.

The cavalier took but little notice of the company or the entertainment. He scarcely tasted the banquet, but seemed absorbed in admiration of his bride. He conversed in a low tone that could not be overheard—for the language of love is never loud; but where is the female ear so dull that it cannot catch the softest whisper of the lover? There was a mingled tenderness and gravity in his manner, that appeared to have a powerful effect upon the young lady. Her color came and went as she listened with deep attention. Now and then she made some blushing reply, and when his eye was turned away, she would steal a sidelong glance at his romantic countenance, and heave a gentle sigh of tender happiness. It was evident that the young couple were completely enamored. The aunts, who were deeply versed in the mysteries of the heart, declared that they had fallen in love with each other at first sight.

The feast went on merrily, or at least noisily, for the guests were all blessed with those keen appetites that attend upon light purses and mountain-air. The baron told his best and longest stories, and never had he told them so well, or with such great effect. If there was anything marvellous, his auditors were lost in astonishment; and if anything facetious, they were sure to laugh exactly in the right place. The baron, it is true, like most great men, was too dignified to utter any joke but a dull one; it was always enforced, however, by a bumper of excellent Hockheimer; and even a dull joke, at one's own table, served up with jolly old wine, is irresistible. Many good things were said by poorer and keener wits, that would not bear repeating, except on similar occasions; many sly speeches whispered in ladies' ears, that almost convulsed them with suppressed laughter; and a song or two roared out by a poor, but merry and broad-faced cousin of the baron, that absolutely made the maiden aunts hold up their fans.

Amidst all this revelry, the stranger guest maintained a most singular and unseasonable gravity. His countenance assumed a deeper caste of dejection as the evening advanced; and, strange as it may appear, even the baron's jokes seemed only to render him the more melancholy. At times he was lost in thought, and at times there was a perturbed and restless wandering of the eye that bespoke a mind but ill at ease. His conversations with the bride became more and more earnest and mysterious. Lowering clouds began to steal over the fair serenity of her brow, and tremors to run through her tender frame.

All this could not escape the notice of the company. Their gayety was chilled by the unaccountable gloom of the bridegroom; their spirits were infected; whispers and glances were interchanged, accompanied by shrugs and dubious shakes of the head. The song and the laugh grew less and less frequent;

there were dreary pauses in the conversation, which were at length succeeded by wild tales and supernatural legends. One dismal story produced another still more dismal, and the baron nearly frightened some of the ladies into hysterics with the history of the goblin horseman that carried away the fair Leonora: a dreadful story, which has since been put into excellent verse, and is read and believed by all the world.

The bridegroom listened to this tale with profound attention. He kept his eyes steadily fixed on the baron and, as the story drew to a close, began gradually to rise from his seat, growing taller and taller, until, in the baron's entranced eye, he seemed almost to tower into a giant. The moment the tale finished, he heaved a deep sigh, and took a solemn farewell of the company. They were all amazement. The baron was perfectly thunderstruck.

"What! going to leave the castle at midnight? why, everything was prepared for his reception; a chamber was ready for him if he wished to retire."

The stranger shook his head mournfully and mysteriously; "I must lay my head in a different chamber to-night!"

There was something in this reply, and the tone in which it was uttered, that made the baron's heart misgive him; but he rallied his forces, and repeated his hospitable entreaties.

The stranger shook his head silently, but positively, at every offer; and, waving his farewell to the company, stalked slowly out of the hall. The maiden aunts were absolutely petrified; the bride hung her head, and a tear stole to her eye.

The baron followed the stranger to the great court of the castle, where the black charger stood pawing the earth, and snorting with impatience. When they had reached the portal, whose deep archway was dimly lighted by a cresset, the stranger paused, and addressed the baron in a hollow tone of voice, which the vaulted roof rendered still more sepulchral.

"Now that we are alone," said he, "I will impart to you the reason of my going. I have a solemn, an indispensable engagement—"

"Why," said the baron, "cannot you send some one in your place?"

"It admits of no substitute—I must attend it in person—I must away to Würtzburg cathedral—"

"Ay," said the baron, plucking up spirit, "but not until to-morrow—tomorrow you shall take your bride there."

"No! no!" replied the stranger, with tenfold solemnity, "my engagement is with no bride—the worms! the worms expect me! I am a dead man—I have been slain by robbers—my body lies at Würtzburg—at midnight I am to be buried—the grave is waiting for me—I must keep my appointment!"

He sprang on his black charger, dashed over the draw-bridge, and the clattering of his horse's hoofs was lost in the whistling of the nightblast.

The baron returned to the hall in the utmost consternation, and related what had passed. Two ladies fainted outright, others sickened at the idea of having banqueted with a spectre. It was the opinion of some, that this might be the wild huntsman, famous in German legend. Some talked of mountain sprites, of wood-demons, and of other supernatural beings, with which the good people of Germany have been so grievously harassed since time immemorial. One of the poor relations ventured to suggest that it might be some sportive evasion of the young cavalier, and that the very gloominess of the caprice seemed to accord with so melancholy a personage. This, however, drew on him the indignation of the whole company, and especially the baron, who looked upon him as little better than an infidel; so that he was fain to abjure his heresy as speedily as possible, and come into the faith of the true believers.

But whatever may have been the doubts entertained, they were completely put to an end by the arrival, next day, of regular missives, confirming the intelligence of the young count's murder, and his interment in Würtzburg cathedral.

The dismay at the castle may well be imagined. The baron shut himself up in his chamber. The guests, who had come to rejoice with him, could not think of abandoning him in his distress. They wandered about the courts, or collected in groups in the hall, shaking their heads and shrugging their shoulders, at the troubles of so good a man; and sat longer than ever at table, and ate and drank more stoutly than ever, by way of keeping up their spirits. But the situation of the

widowed bride was the most pitiable. To have lost a husband before she had even embraced him—and such a husband! if the very spectre could be so gracious and noble, what must have been the living man. She filled the house with lamentations.

On the night of the second day of her widowhood, she had retired to her chamber, accompanied by one of her aunts, who insisted on sleeping with her. The aunt, who was one of the best tellers of ghost-stories in all Germany, had just been recounting one of her longest, and had fallen asleep in the very midst of it. The chamber was remote, and overlooked a small garden. The niece lay pensively gazing at the beams of the rising moon, as they trembled on the leaves of an aspen tree before the lattice. The castle-clock had just tolled midnight, when a soft strain of music stole up from the garden. She rose hastily from her bed, and stepped lightly to the window. A tall figure stood among the shadows of the trees. As it raised its head, a beam of moonlight fell upon the countenance. Heaven and earth! she beheld the Spectre Bridegroom! A loud shriek at that moment burst upon her ear, and her aunt, who had been awakened by the music, and had followed her silently to the window, fell into her arms. When she looked again, the spectre had disappeared.

Of the two females, the aunt now required the most soothing, for she was perfectly beside herself with terror. As to the young lady, there was something, even in the spectre of her lover, that seemed endearing. There was still the semblance of manly beauty; and though the shadow of a man is but little calculated to satisfy the affections of a lovesick girl, yet, where the substance is not to be had, even that is consoling. The aunt declared she would never sleep in that chamber again; the niece, for once, was refractory, and declared as strongly that she would sleep in no other in the castle: the consequence was, that she had to sleep in it alone; but she drew a promise from her aunt not to relate the story of the spectre, lest she should be denied the only melancholy pleasure left her on earth—that of inhabiting the chamber over which the guardian shade of her lover kept its nightly vigils.

How long the good old lady would have observed this promise is uncertain, for she dearly loved to talk of the marvellous, and there is a triumph in being the first to tell a frightful story; it is, however, still quoted in the neighborhood, as a memorable instance of female secrecy, that she kept it to herself for a whole week; when she was suddenly absolved from all further restraint, by intelligence brought to the breakfast-table one morning that the young lady was not to be found. Her room was empty—the bed had not been slept in—the window was open, and the bird had flown!

The astonishment and concern with which the intelligence was received can only be imagined by those who have witnessed the agitation which the mishaps of a great man cause among his friends. Even the poor relations paused for a moment from the indefatigable labors of the trencher; when the aunt, who had at first been struck speechless, wrung her hands, and shrieked out, "The goblin! the goblin! she's carried away by the goblin!"

In a few words she related the fearful scene in the garden, and concluded that the spectre must have carried off his bride. Two of the domestics corroborated the opinion, for they had heard the clattering of a horse's hoofs down the mountain about midnight, and had no doubt that it was the spectre on his black charger, bearing her away to the tomb. All present were struck with the direful probability; for events of the kind are extremely common in Germany, as many well-authenticated histories bear witness.

What a lamentable situation was that of the poor baron! What a heart-rending dilemma for a fond father, and a member of the great family of Katzenellenbogen! His only daughter had either been rapt away to the grave, or he was to have some wood-demon for a son-in-law, and, perchance, a troop of goblin grandchildren. As usual, he was completely bewildered, and all the castle in an uproar. The men were ordered to take horse, and scour every road and path and glen of the Odenwald. The baron himself had just drawn on his jackboots, girded on his sword, and was about to mount his steed and sally forth on a doubtful quest, when he was brought to a pause by a new apparition. A lady was seen approaching the castle, mounted on a palfrey, attended by a cavalier on horseback. She galloped up to the gate, sprang from her horse, and falling at the baron's feet, embraced his knees. It was his lost daughter, and her companion—the Spectre Bridegroom! The baron was astounded. He looked at his daughter, then at the spectre, and almost doubted the evidence of his senses. The latter, too, was wonderfully improved in his appearance since his visit to the world of spirits. His dress was splendid, and set off a noble figure of manly symmetry. He was no longer pale and melancholy. His fine countenance was flushed with the glow of youth, and joy rioted in his large dark eye.

The mystery was soon cleared up. The cavalier (for, in truth, as you must have known all the while, he was no goblin) announced himself as Sir Herman Von Starkenfaust. He related his adventure with the young count. He told how he had hastened to the castle to deliver the unwelcome tidings, but that the eloquence of the baron had interrupted him in every attempt to tell his tale. How the sight of the bride had completely captivated him, and that to pass a few hours near her, he had tacitly suffered the mistake to continue. How he had been sorely perplexed in what way to make a decent retreat, until the baron's goblin stories had suggested his eccentric exit. How, fearing the feudal hostility of the family, he had repeated his visits by stealth—had haunted the garden beneath the young lady's window—had wooed—had won— had borne away in triumph—and, in a word, had wedded the fair.

Under any other circumstances the baron would have been inflexible, for he was tenacious of paternal authority, and devoutly obstinate in all family feuds; but he loved his daughter; he had lamented her as lost; he rejoiced to find her still alive; and, though her husband was of a hostile house, yet, thank heaven, he was not a goblin. There was something, it must be acknowledged, that did not exactly accord with his notions of strict veracity, in the joke the knight had passed upon him of his being a dead man; but several old friends present, who had served in the wars, assured him that every strategem was excusable in love, and that the cavalier was entitled to especial privilege, having lately served as a trooper.

Matters, therefore, were happily arranged. The baron pardoned the young couple on the spot. The revels at the castle were resumed. The poor relations overwhelmed this new member of the family with loving-kindness; he was so gallant, so generous—and so rich. The aunts, it is true, were somewhat scandalized that their system of strict seclusion and passive obedience should be so badly exemplified, but attributed it all to their negligence in not having the windows grated. One of them was particularly mortified at having her marvellous story marred, and that the only spectre she had ever seen should turn out a counterfeit; but the niece seemed perfectly happy at having found him substantial flesh and blood—and so the story ends.

Adventure of the German Student

O N a stormy night, in the tempestuous times of the French revolution, a young German was returning to his lodgings, at a late hour, across the old part of Paris. The lightning gleamed, and the loud claps of thunder rattled through the lofty narrow streets—but I should first tell you something about this young German.

Gottfried Wolfgang was a young man of good family. He had studied for some time at Göttingen, but being of a visionary and enthusiastic character, he had wandered into those wild and speculative doctrines which have so often bewildered German students. His secluded life, his intense application, and the singular nature of his studies, had an effect on both mind and body. His health was impaired; his imagination diseased. He had been indulging in fanciful speculations on spiritual essences, until, like Swedenborg, he had an ideal world of his own around him. He took up a notion, I do not know from what cause, that there was an evil influence hanging over him; an evil genius or spirit seeking to ensnare him and ensure his perdition. Such an idea working on his melancholy temperament, produced the most gloomy effects. He became haggard and desponding. His friends discovered the mental malady preying upon him, and determined that the best cure was a change of scene; he was sent, therefore, to finish his studies amidst the splendors and gayeties of Paris.

Wolfgang arrived at Paris at the breaking out of the revolution. The popular delirium at first caught his enthusiastic mind, and he was captivated by the political and philosophical theories of the day: but the scenes of blood which followed shocked his sensitive nature, disgusted him with society and the world, and made him more than ever a recluse. He shut himself up in a solitary apartment in the *Pays Latin,* the quarter of students. There, in a gloomy street not far from the monastic walls of the Sorbonne, he pursued his favorite speculations. Sometimes he spent hours together in the great libraries of Paris, those catacombs of departed authors, rummaging among their hordes of dusty and obsolete works in quest of food for his unhealthy appetite. He was, in a manner, a literary ghoul, feeding in the charnel-house of decayed literature.

Wolfgang, though solitary and recluse, was of an ardent temperament, but for a time it operated merely upon his imagination. He was too shy and ignorant of the world to make any advances to the fair, but he was a passionate admirer of female beauty, and in his lonely chamber would often lose himself in reveries on forms and faces which he had seen, and his fancy would deck out images of loveliness far surpassing the reality.

While his mind was in this excited and sublimated state, a dream produced an extraordinary effect upon him. It was of a female face of transcendent beauty. So strong was the impression made, that he dreamt of it again and again. It haunted his thoughts by day, his slumbers by night; in fine, he became passionately enamoured of this shadow of a dream. This lasted so long that it became one of those fixed ideas which haunt the minds of melancholy men, and are at times mistaken for madness.

Such was Gottfried Wolfgang, and such his situation at the time I mentioned. He was returning home late one stormy night, through some of the old and gloomy streets of the *Marais,* the ancient part of Paris. The loud claps of thunder rattled among the high houses of the narrow streets. He came to the Place de Grève, the square where public executions are performed. The lightning quivered about the pinnacles of the ancient Hôtel de Ville, and shed flickering gleams over the open space in front. As Wolfgang was crossing the square, he shrank back with horror at finding himself close by the guillotine. It was the height of the reign of terror, when this dreadful instrument of death stood ever ready, and its scaffold was continually running with the blood of the virtuous and the brave. It had that very day been actively employed in the work of carnage, and there it stood in grim array, amidst a silent and sleeping city, waiting for fresh victims.

Wolfgang's heart sickened within him, and he was turning shuddering from the horrible engine, when he beheld a shadowy form, cowering as it were at the foot of the steps which led up to the scaffold. A succession of vivid flashes of lightning revealed it more distinctly. It was a female figure, dressed in black. She was seated on one of the lower steps of the scaffold, leaning forward, her face hid in her lap; and her long dishevelled tresses hanging to the ground, streaming with the rain which fell in torrents. Wolfgang paused. There was something awful in this solitary monument of woe. The female had the appearance of being above the common order. He knew the times to be full of vicissitude, and that many a fair head, which had once been pillowed on down, now wandered houseless. Perhaps this was some poor mourner whom the dreadful axe had rendered desolate, and who sat here heartbroken on the strand of existence, from which all that was dear to her had been launched into eternity.

He approached and addressed her in the accents of sympathy. She raised her head and gazed wildly at him. What was his astonishment at beholding, by the bright glare of the lightning, the very face which had haunted him in his dreams. It was pale and disconsolate, but ravishingly beautiful.

Trembling with violent and conflicting emotions, Wolfgang again accosted her. He spoke something of her being exposed at such an hour of the night, and to the fury of such a storm, and offered to conduct her to her friends. She pointed to the guillotine with a gesture of dreadful signification.

"I have no friend on earth!" said she.

"But you have a home," said Wolfgang.

"Yes—in the grave!"

The heart of the student melted at the words.

"If a stranger dare make an offer," said he, "without danger of being misunderstood, I would offer my humble dwelling as a shelter; myself as a devoted friend. I am friendless myself in Paris, and a stranger in the land; but if my life could be of service, it is at your disposal, and should be sacrificed before harm or indignity should come to you."

There was an honest earnestness in the young man's manner that had its effect. His foreign accent, too, was in his favor; it showed him not to be a hackneyed inhabitant of Paris. Indeed, there is an eloquence in true enthusiasm that is not to be doubted. The homeless stranger confided herself implicitly to the protection of the student.

He supported her faltering steps across the Pont Neuf, and by the place where the statue of Henry the Fourth had been overthrown by the populace. The storm had abated, and the thunder rumbled at a distance. All Paris was quiet; that great volcano of human passion slumbered for a while, to gather fresh strength for the next day's eruption. The student conducted his charge through the ancient streets of the *Pays Latin,* and by the dusky walls of the Sorbonne, to the great dingy hotel which he inhabited. The old portress who admitted them stared with surprise at the unusual sight of the melancholy Wolfgang with a female companion.

On entering his apartment, the student, for the first time, blushed at the scantiness and indifference of his dwelling. He had but one chamber—an old-fashioned saloon—heavily carved, and fantastically furnished with the remains of former magnificence, for it was one of those hotels in the quarter of the Luxembourg palace, which had once belonged to nobility. It was lumbered with books and papers, and all the usual apparatus of a student, and his bed stood in a recess at one end.

When lights were brought, and Wolfgang had a better opportunity of contemplating the stranger, he was more than ever intoxicated by her beauty. Her face was pale, but of a dazzling fairness, set off by a profusion of raven hair that hung clustering about it. Her eyes were large and brilliant, with a singular expression approaching almost to wildness.

As far as her black dress permitted her shape to be seen, it was of perfect symmetry. Her whole appearance was highly striking, though she was dressed in the simplest style. The only thing approaching to an ornament which she wore, was a broad black band round her neck, clasped by diamonds.

The perplexity now commenced with the student how to dispose of the helpless being thus thrown upon his protection. He thought of abandoning his chamber to her, and seeking shelter for himself elsewhere. Still he was so fascinated by her charms, there seemed to be such a spell upon his thoughts and senses, that he could not tear himself from her presence. Her manner, too, was singular and unaccountable. She spoke no more of the guillotine. Her grief had abated. The attentions of the student had first won her confidence, and then, apparently, her heart. She was evidently an enthusiast like himself, and enthusiasts soon understand each other.

In the infatuation of the moment, Wolfgang avowed his passion for her. He told her the story of his mysterious dream, and how she had possessed his heart before he had even seen her. She was strangely affected by his recital, and acknowledged to have felt an impulse towards him equally unaccountable. It was the time for wild theory and wild actions. Old prejudices and superstitions were done away; everything was under the sway of the "Goddess of Reason." Among other rubbish of the old times, the forms and ceremonies of marriage began to be considered superfluous bonds for honorable minds. Social compacts were the vogue. Wolfgang was too much of a theorist not to be tainted by the liberal doctrines of the day.

"Why should we separate?" said he; "our hearts are united; in the eye of reason and honor we are as one. What need is there of sordid forms to bind high souls together?"

The stranger listened with emotion: she had evidently received illumination at the same school.

"You have no home or family," continued he, "let me be everything to you, or rather let us be everything to one another. If form is necessary, form shall be observed—there is my hand. I pledge myself to you forever."

"Forever?" said the stranger, solemnly.

"Forever!" repeated Wolfgang.

The stranger clasped the hand extended to her: "Then I am yours," murmured she, and sank upon his bosom.

The next morning the student left his bride sleeping, and sallied forth at an early hour to seek more spacious apartments suitable to the change in his situation. When he returned, he found the stranger lying with her head hanging over the bed, and one arm thrown over it. He spoke to her, but received no reply. He advanced to awaken her from her uneasy posture. On taking her hand, it was cold—there was no pulsation—her face was pallid and ghastly. In a word, she was a corpse.

Horrified and frantic, he alarmed the house. A scene of confusion ensued. The police was summoned. As the officer of police entered the room, he started back on beholding the corpse.

"Great heaven!" cried he, "how did this woman come here?"

"Do you know anything about her?" said Wolfgang eagerly.

"Do I?" exclaimed the officer: "she was guillotined yesterday."

He stepped forward; undid the black collar round the neck of the corpse, and the head rolled on the floor!

The student burst into a frenzy. "The fiend! the fiend has gained possession of me!" shrieked he; "I am lost forever."

They tried to soothe him, but in vain. He was possessed with the frightful belief that an evil spirit had reanimated the dead body to ensnare him. He went distracted, and died in a mad-house.

Here the old gentleman with the haunted head finished his narrative.

"And is this really a fact?" said the inquisitive gentleman.

"A fact not to be doubted," replied the other. "I had it from the best authority. The student told it me himself. I saw him in a mad-house in Paris."

The Devil and Tom Walker

A FEW miles from Boston in Massachusetts, there is a deep inlet, winding several miles into the interior of the country from Charles Bay, and terminating in a thickly-wooded swamp or morass. On one side of this inlet is a beautiful dark grove; on the opposite side the land rises abruptly from the water's edge into a high ridge, on which grow a few scattered oaks of great age and immense size. Under one of these gigantic trees, according to old stories, there was a great amount of treasure buried by Kidd the pirate. The inlet allowed a facility to bring the money in a boat secretly and at night to the very foot of the hill; the elevation of the place permitted a good lookout to be kept that no one was at hand; while the remarkable trees formed good landmarks by which the place might easily be found again. The old stories add, moreover, that the devil presided at the hiding of the money, and took it under his guardianship; but this, it is well known, he always does with buried treasure, particularly when it has been ill-gotten. Be that as it may, Kidd never returned to recover his wealth; being shortly after seized at Boston, sent out to England, and there hanged for a pirate.

About the year 1727, just at the time that earthquakes

147

were prevalent in New England, and shook many tall sinners down upon their knees, there lived near this place a meagre, miserly fellow, of the name of Tom Walker. He had a wife as miserly as himself: they were so miserly that they even conspired to cheat each other. Whatever the woman could lay hands on, she hid away; a hen could not cackle but she was on the alert to secure the new-laid egg. Her husband was continually prying about to detect her secret hoards, and many and fierce were the conflicts that took place about what ought to have been common property. They lived in a forlorn-looking house that stood alone, and had an air of starvation. A few straggling savin-trees, emblems of sterility, grew near it; no smoke ever curled from its chimney; no traveller stopped at its door. A miserable horse, whose ribs were as articulate as the bars of a gridiron, stalked about a field, where a thin carpet of moss, scarcely covering the ragged beds of pudding-stone, tantalized and balked his hunger; and sometimes he would lean his head over the fence, look piteously at the passer-by, and seem to petition deliverance from this land of famine.

The house and its inmates had altogether a bad name. Tom's wife was a tall termagant, fierce of temper, loud of tongue, and strong of arm. Her voice was often heard in wordy warfare with her husband; and his face sometimes showed signs that their conflicts were not confined to words. No one ventured, however, to interfere between them. The lonely wayfarer shrunk within himself at the horrid clamor and clapper-clawing; eyed the den of discord askance; and hurried on his way, rejoicing, if a bachelor, in his celibacy.

One day that Tom Walker had been to a distant part of the neighborhood, he took what he considered a short cut homeward, through the swamp. Like most short cuts, it was an ill-chosen route. The swamp was thickly grown with great gloomy pines and hemlocks, some of them ninety feet high, which made it dark at noonday, and a retreat for all the owls of the neighborhood. It was full of pits and quagmires, partly covered with weeds and mosses, where the green surface often betrayed the traveller into a gulf of black, smothering mud: there were also dark and stagnant pools, the abodes of the tadpole, the bull-frog, and the water-snake; where the trunks of pines and hemlocks lay half drowned, half rotting, looking like alligators sleeping in the mire.

Tom had long been picking his way cautiously through this treacherous forest; stepping from tuft to tuft of rushes and roots, which afforded precarious footholds among deep sloughs; or pacing carefully, like a cat, along the prostrate trunks of trees; startled now and then by the sudden screaming of the bittern, or the quacking of wild duck rising on the wing from some solitary pool. At length he arrived at a firm piece of ground, which ran out like a peninsula into the deep bosom of the swamp. It had been one of the strongholds of the Indians during their wars with the first colonists. Here they had thrown up a kind of fort, which they had looked upon as almost impregnable, and had used as a place of refuge for their squaws and children. Nothing remained of the old Indian fort but a few embankments, gradually sinking to the level of the surrounding earth, and already overgrown in part by oaks and other forest trees, the foliage of which formed a contrast to the dark pines and hemlocks of the swamp.

It was late in the dusk of evening when Tom Walker reached the old fort, and he paused there awhile to rest himself. Any one but he would have felt unwilling to linger in this lonely, melancholy place, for the common people had a bad opinion of it, from the stories handed down from the time of the Indian wars; when it was asserted that the savages held incantations here, and made sacrifices to the evil spirit.

Tom Walker, however, was not a man to be troubled with any fears of the kind. He reposed himself for some time on the trunk of a fallen hemlock, listening to the boding cry of the tree-toad, and delving with his walking-staff into a mound of black mould at his feet. As he turned up the soil unconsciously, his staff struck against something hard. He raked it out of the vegetable mould, and lo! a cloven skull, with an Indian tomahawk buried deep in it, lay before him. The rust on the weapon showed the time that had elapsed since this death-blow had been given. It was a dreary memento of the fierce struggle that had taken place in this last foothold of the Indian warriors.

"Humph!" said Tom Walker, as he gave it a kick to shake the dirt from it.

"Let that skull alone!" said a gruff voice. Tom lifted up his eyes, and beheld a great black man seated directly opposite him, on the stump of a tree. He was exceedingly surprised, having neither heard nor seen any one approach; and he was still more perplexed on observing, as well as the gathering gloom would permit, that the stranger was neither negro nor Indian. It is true he was dressed in a rude half Indian garb, and had a red belt or sash swathed round his body; but his face was neither black nor copper-color, but swarthy and dingy, and begrimed with soot, as if he had been accustomed to toil among fires and forges. He had a shock of coarse black hair, that stood out from his head in all directions, and bore an axe on his shoulder.

He scowled for a moment at Tom with a pair of great red eyes.

"What are you doing on my grounds?" said the black man, with a hoarse, growling voice.

"Your grounds!" said Tom, with a sneer, "no more your grounds than mine; they belong to Deacon Peabody."

"Deacon Peabody be d——d," said the stranger, "as I flatter myself he will be, if he does not look more to his own sins and less to those of his neighbors. Look yonder, and see how Deacon Peabody is faring."

Tom looked in the direction that the stranger pointed, and beheld one of the great trees, fair and flourishing without, but rotten at the core, and saw that it had been nearly hewn through, so that the first high wind was likely to blow it down. On the bark of the tree was scored the name of Deacon Peabody, an eminent man, who had waxed wealthy by driving shrewd bargains with the Indians. He now looked around, and found most of the tall trees marked with the name of some great man of the colony, and all more or less scored by the axe. The one on which he had been seated, and which had evidently just been hewn down, bore the name of Crown-inshield; and he recollected a mighty rich man of that name, who made a vulgar display of wealth, which it was whispered he had acquired by buccaneering.

"He's just ready for burning!" said the black man, with a growl of triumph. "You see I am likely to have a good stock of firewood for winter."

"But what right have you," said Tom, "to cut down Deacon Peabody's timber?"

"The right of a prior claim," said the other. "This woodland belonged to me long before one of your white-faced race put foot upon the soil."

"And pray, who are you, if I may be so bold?" said Tom.

"Oh, I go by various names. I am the wild huntsman in some countries; the black miner in others. In this neighborhood I am known by the name of the black woodsman. I am he to whom the red men consecrated this spot, and in honor of whom they now and then roasted a white man, by way of sweet-smelling sacrifice. Since the red men have been exterminated by you white savages, I amuse myself by presiding at the persecutions of Quakers and Anabaptists; I am the great patron and prompter of slave-dealers, and the grandmaster of the Salem witches."

"The upshot of all which is, that, if I mistake not," said Tom, sturdily, "you are he commonly called Old Scratch."

"The same, at your service!" replied the black man, with a half civil nod.

Such was the opening of this interview, according to the old story; though it has almost too familiar an air to be credited. One would think that to meet with such a singular personage, in this wild, lonely place, would have shaken any man's nerves; but Tom was a hard-minded fellow, not easily daunted, and he had lived so long with a termagant wife, that he did not even fear the devil.

It is said that after this commencement they had a long and earnest conversation together, as Tom returned homeward. The black man told him of great sums of money buried by Kidd the pirate, under the oak-trees on the high ridge, not far from the morass. All these were under his command, and protected by his power, so that none could find them but such as propitiated his favor. These he offered to place within Tom Walker's reach, having conceived an especial kindness for him; but they were to be had only on certain conditions. What these conditions were may be easily surmised, though Tom never disclosed them publicly. They must have been very hard, for he required time to think of them, and he was not a man to stick at trifles when money was in view. When they had reached the edge of the swamp, the stranger paused. "What proof have I that all you have been telling me is true?" said Tom. "There's my signature," said the black man, pressing his finger on Tom's forehead. So saying, he turned off among the thickest of the swamp, and seemed, as Tom said, to go down, down, down, into the earth, until nothing but his head and shoulders could be seen, and so on, until he totally disappeared.

When Tom reached home, he found the black print of a finger burnt, as it were, into his forehead, which nothing could obliterate.

The first news his wife had to tell him was the sudden death of Absalom Crowninshield, the rich buccaneer. It was announced in the papers with the usual flourish, that "A great man had fallen in Israel."

Tom recollected the tree which his black friend had just hewn down, and which was ready for burning. "Let the freebooter roast," said Tom; "who cares!" He now felt convinced that all he had heard and seen was no illusion.

He was not prone to let his wife into his confidence; but as this was an uneasy secret, he willingly shared it with her. All her avarice was awakened at the mention of hidden gold, and she urged her husband to comply with the black man's terms, and secure what would make them wealthy for life. However Tom might have felt disposed to sell himself to the devil, he was determined not to do so to oblige his wife; so he flatly refused, out of the mere spirit of contradiction. Many and bitter were the quarrels they had on the subject; but the more she talked, the more resolute was Tom not to be damned to please her.

At length she determined to drive the bargain on her own account, and if she succeeded, to keep all the gain to herself. Being of the same fearless temper as her husband, she set off for the old Indian fort towards the close of a summer's day. She was many hours absent. When she came back, she was reserved and sullen in her replies. She spoke something of a black man, whom she met about twilight hewing at the root of a tall tree. He was sulky, however, and would not come to terms; she was to go again with a propitiatory offering, but what it was she forbore to say.

The next evening she set off again for the swamp, with her apron heavily laden. Tom waited and waited for her, but in vain; midnight came, but she did not make her appearance: morning, noon, night returned, but still she did not come. Tom now grew uneasy for her safety, especially as he found she had carried off in her apron the silver tea-pot and spoons, and every portable article of value. Another night elapsed, another morning came; but no wife. In a word, she was never heard of more.

What was her real fate nobody knows, in consequence of so many pretending to know. It is one of those facts which have become confounded by a variety of historians. Some asserted that she lost her way among the tangled mazes of the swamp, and sank into some pit or slough; others, more uncharitable, hinted that she had eloped with the household booty, and made off to some other province; while others surmised that the tempter had decoyed her into a dismal quagmire, on the top of which her hat was found lying. In confirmation of this, it was said a great black man, with an axe on his shoulder, was seen late that very evening coming out of the swamp, carrying a bundle tied in a check apron, with an air of surly triumph.

The most current and probable story, however, observes, that Tom Walker grew so anxious about the fate of his wife and his property, that he set out at length to seek them both at the Indian fort. During a long summer's afternoon he searched about the gloomy place, but no wife was to be seen. He called her name repeatedly, but she was nowhere to be heard. The bittern alone responded to his voice, as he flew screaming by; or the bull-frog croaked dolefully from a neighboring pool. At length, it is said, just in the brown hour of twilight, when the owls began to hoot, and the bats to flit about, his attention was attracted by the clamor of carrion crows hovering about a cypress tree. He looked up, and beheld a bundle tied in a check apron, and hanging in the branches of the tree, with a great vulture perched hard by, as if keeping watch upon it. He leaped with joy; for he recognized his wife's apron, and supposed it to contain the household valuables.

"Let us get hold of the property," said he, consolingly to

himself, "and we will endeavor to do without the woman."

As he scrambled up the tree, the vulture spread its wide wings, and sailed off screaming, into the deep shadows of the forest. Tom seized the checked apron, but, woful sight! found nothing but a heart and liver tied up in it!

Such, according to this most authentic old story, was all that was to be found of Tom's wife. She had probably attempted to deal with the black man as she had been accustomed to deal with her husband; but though a female scold is generally considered a match for the devil, yet in this instance she appears to have had the worst of it. She must have died game, however; for it is said Tom noticed many prints of cloven feet deeply stamped upon the tree, and found handfuls of hair, that looked as if they had been plucked from the coarse black shock of the woodman. Tom knew his wife's prowess by experience. He shrugged his shoulders, as he looked at the signs of a fierce clapper-clawing. "Egad," said he to himself, "Old Scratch must have had a tough time of it!"

Tom consoled himself for the loss of his property, with the loss of his wife, for he was a man of fortitude. He even felt something like gratitude towards the black woodman, who, he considered, had done him a kindness. He sought, therefore, to cultivate a further acquaintance with him, but for some time without success; the old black-legs played shy, for whatever people may think, he is not always to be had for calling for: he knows how to play his cards when pretty sure of his game.

At length, it is said, when delay had whetted Tom's eagerness to the quick, and prepared him to agree to anything rather than not gain the promised treasure, he met the black man one evening in his usual woodman's dress, with his axe on his shoulder, sauntering along the swamp, and humming a tune. He affected to receive Tom's advances with great indifference, made brief replies, and went on humming his tune.

By degrees, however, Tom brought him to business, and they began to haggle about the terms on which the former was to have the pirate's treasure. There was one condition which need not be mentioned, being generally understood in all cases where the devil grants favors; but there were others about which, though of less importance, he was inflexibly obstinate. He insisted that the money found through his means should be employed in his service. He proposed, therefore, that Tom should employ it in the black traffic; that is to say, that he should fit out a slave-ship. This, however, Tom resolutely refused: he was bad enough in all conscience; but the devil himself could not tempt him to turn slave-trader.

Finding Tom so squeamish on this point, he did not insist upon it, but proposed, instead, that he should turn usurer; the devil being extremely anxious for the increase of usurers, looking upon them as his peculiar people.

To this no objections were made, for it was just to Tom's taste.

"You shall open a broker's shop in Boston next month," said the black man.

"I'll do it to-morrow, if you wish," said Tom Walker.

"You shall lend money at two per cent a month."

"Egad, I'll charge four!" replied Tom Walker.

"You shall extort bonds, foreclose mortgages, drive the merchants to bankruptcy"—

"I'll drive them to the d——l," cried Tom Walker.

"You are the usurer for my money!" said black-legs with delight. "When will you want the rhino?"

"This very night."

"Done!" said the devil.

"Done!" said Tom Walker.—So they shook hands and struck a bargain.

A few days' time saw Tom Walker seated behind his desk in a counting-house in Boston.

His reputation for a ready-moneyed man, who would lend money out for a good consideration, soon spread abroad. Everybody remembers the time of Governor Belcher, when money was particularly scarce. It was a time of paper credit. The country had been deluged with government bills, the famous Land Bank had been established; there had been a rage for speculating; the people had run mad with schemes for new settlements; for building cities in the wilderness; land-jobbers went about with maps of grants, and townships, and Eldorados, lying nobody knew where, but which everybody was ready to purchase. In a word, the great speculating fever which breaks out every now and then in the country, had raged to an alarming degree, and every body was dreaming of making sudden fortunes from nothing. As usual the fever had subsided; the dream had gone off, and the imaginary fortunes with it; the patients were left in doleful plight, and the whole country resounded with the consequent cry of "hard times."

At this propitious time of public distress did Tom Walker set up as usurer in Boston. His door was soon thronged by customers. The needy and adventurous; the gambling speculator; the dreaming land-jobber; the thriftless tradesman; the merchant with cracked credit; in short, every one driven to raise money by desperate means and desperate sacrifices, hurried to Tom Walker.

Thus Tom was the universal friend of the needy, and acted like a "friend in need"; that is to say, he always exacted good pay and good security. In proportion to the distress of the applicant was the hardness of his terms. He accumulated bonds and mortgages; gradually squeezed his customers closer and closer; and sent them at length, dry as a sponge, from his door.

In this way he made money hand over hand; became a rich and mighty man, and exalted his cocked hat upon 'Change. He built himself, as usual, a vast house, out of ostentation; but left the greater part of it unfinished and unfurnished, out of parsimony. He even set up a carriage in the fulness of his vainglory, though he nearly starved the horses which drew it; and as the ungreased wheels groaned and screeched on the axle-trees, you would have thought you heard the souls of the poor debtors he was squeezing.

As Tom waxed old, however, he grew thoughtful. Having secured the good things of this world, he began to feel anxious about those of the next. He thought with regret on the bargain he had made with his black friend, and set his wits to work to cheat him out of the conditions. He became, therefore, all of a sudden, a violent church-goer. He prayed loudly and strenuously, as if heaven were to be taken by force of lungs. Indeed, one might always tell when he had sinned most during the week, by the clamor of his Sunday devotion. The quiet Christians who had been modestly and steadfastly travelling Zionward, were struck with self-reproach at seeing themselves so suddenly outstripped in their career by this new-made convert. Tom was as rigid in religious as in money matters; he was a stern supervisor and censurer of his neighbors, and seemed to think every sin entered up to their account became a credit on his own side of the page. He even talked of the expediency of reviving the persecution of Quakers and Anabaptists. In a word, Tom's zeal became as notorious as his riches.

Still, in spite of all this strenuous attention to forms, Tom had a lurking dread that the devil, after all, would have his due. That he might not be taken unawares, therefore, it is said he always carried a small Bible in his coat-pocket. He had also a great folio Bible on his counting-house desk, and would frequently be found reading it when people called on business; on such occasions he would lay his green spectacles in the book, to mark the place, while he turned round to drive some usurious bargain.

Some say that Tom grew a little crack-brained in his old days, and that, fancying his end approaching, he had his horse new shod, saddled and bridled, and buried with his feet uppermost; because he supposed that at the last day the world would be turned upside-down; in which case he should find his horse standing ready for mounting, and he was determined at the worst to give his old friend a run for it. This, however, is probably a mere old wives' fable. If he really did take such a precaution, it was totally superfluous; at least so says the authentic old legend, which closes his story in the following manner:

One hot summer afternoon in the dog-days, just as a terrible black thunder gust was coming up, Tom sat in his counting-house, in his white cap and India silk morning-gown. He was on the point of foreclosing a mortgage, by which he would complete the ruin of an unlucky land-speculator for whom he had professed the greatest friendship. The poor land-jobber begged him to grant a few months' indulgence. Tom had grown testy and irritated, and refused another day.

"My family will be ruined and brought upon the parish," said the land-jobber. "Charity begins at home," replied Tom; "I must take care of myself in these hard times."

"You have made so much money out of me," said the speculator.

Tom lost his patience and his piety. "The devil take me," said he, "if I have made a farthing!"

Just then there were three loud knocks at the street door. He stepped out to see who was there. A black man was holding a black horse, which neighed and stamped with impatience.

"Tom, you're come for," said the black fellow, gruffly. Tom shrank back, but too late. He had left his little Bible at the bottom of his coat-pocket, and his big Bible on the desk buried under the mortgage he was about to foreclose: never was sinner taken more unawares. The black man whisked him like a child into the saddle, gave the horse the lash, and away he galloped, with Tom on his back, in the midst of the thunder-storm. The clerks stuck their pens behind their ears, and stared after him from the windows. Away went Tom

Walker, dashing down the streets; his white cap bobbing up and down; his morning-gown fluttering in the wind, and his steed striking fire out of the pavement at every bound. When the clerks turned to look for the black man, he had disappeared.

Tom Walker never returned to foreclose the mortgage. A countryman, who lived on the border of the swamp, reported that in the height of the thunder-gust he had heard a great clattering of hoofs and a howling along the road, and running to the window caught sight of a figure, such as I have described, on a horse that galloped like mad across the fields, over the hills, and down into the black hemlock swamp towards the old Indian fort; and that shortly after a thunder-bolt falling in that direction seemed to set the whole forest in a blaze.

The good people of Boston shook their heads and shrugged their shoulders, but had been so much accustomed to witches and goblins, and tricks of the devil, in all kinds of shapes, from the first settlement of the colony, that they were not so much horror-struck as might have been expected. Trustees were appointed to take charge of Tom's effects. There was nothing, however, to administer upon. On searching his coffers, all his bonds and mortgages were found reduced to cinders. In place of gold and silver, his iron chest was filled with chips and shavings; two skeletons lay in his stable instead of his half-starved horses, and the very next day his great house took fire and burnt to the ground.

Such was the end of Tom Walker and his ill-gotten wealth. Let all griping money-brokers lay this story to heart. The truth of it is not to be doubted. The very hole under the oak-trees whence he dug Kidd's money is to be seen to this day; and the neighboring swamp and old Indian fort are often haunted in stormy nights by a figure on horseback, in morning-gown and white cap, which is doubtless the troubled spirit of the usurer. In fact the story has resolved itself into a proverb, and is the origin of that popular saying, so prevalent throughout New England, of "The Devil and Tom Walker."

Such, as nearly as I can recollect, was the purport of the tale told by the Cape-Cod whaler. There were divers trivial particulars which I have omitted, and which whiled away the morning very pleasantly, until the time of tide favorable to fishing being passed, it was proposed to land, and refresh ourselves under the trees, till the noontide heat should have abated.

We accordingly landed on a delectable part of the island of Manhattan, in that shady and embowered tract formerly under the domain of the ancient family of the Hardenbrooks. It was a spot well known to me in the course of the aquatic expeditions of my boyhood. Not far from where we landed there was an old Dutch family vault, constructed in the side of a bank, which had been an object of great awe and fable among my schoolboy associates. We had peered into it during one of our coasting voyages, and been startled by the sight of mouldering coffins and musty bones within; but what had given it the most fearful interest in our eyes, was its being in some way connected with the pirate wreck which lay rotting among the rocks of Hell Gate. There were stories also of smuggling connected with it, particularly relating to a time when this retired spot was owned by a noted burgher, called Ready Money Provost; a man of whom it was whispered that he had many mysterious dealings with parts beyond the seas. All these things, however, had been jumbled together in our minds in that vague way in which such themes are mingled up in the tales of boyhood.

While I was pondering upon these matters, my companions had spread a repast, from the contents of our well-stored pannier, under a broad chestnut, on the greensward which swept down to the water's edge. Here we solaced ourselves on the cool grassy carpet during the warm sunny hours of mid-day. While lolling on the grass, indulging in that kind of musing reverie of which I am fond, I summoned up the dusky recollections of my boyhood respecting this place, and repeated them like the imperfectly remembered traces of a dream, for the amusement of my companions. When I had finished, a worthy old burgher, John Josse Vandermoere, the same who once related to me the adventures of Dolph Heyliger, broke silence, and observed, that he recollected a story of money-digging, which occurred in this very neighborhood, and might account for some of the traditions which I had

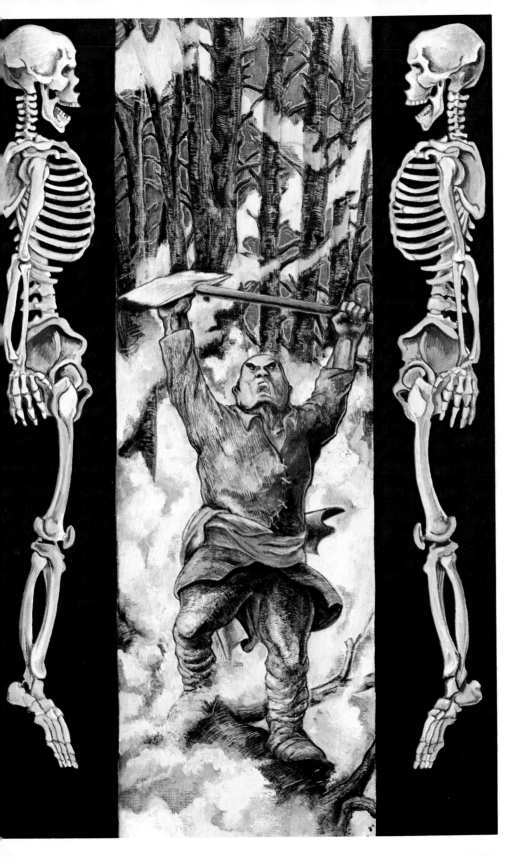

heard in my boyhood. As we knew him to be one of the most authentic narrators in the province, we begged him to let us have the particulars, and accordingly, while we solaced ourselves with a clean long pipe of Blase Moore's best tobacco, the authentic John Josse Vandermoere related the following tale.

Legend of the Arabian Astrologer

I N old times, many hundred years ago, there was a Moorish king named Aben Habuz, who reigned over the kingdom of Granada. He was a retired conqueror—that is to say, one who, having in his more youthful days led a life of constant foray and depredation, now that he was grown feeble and superannuated, "languished for repose," and desired nothing more than to live at peace with all the world, to husband his laurels, and to enjoy in quiet the possessions he had wrested from his neighbors.

It so happened, however, that this most reasonable and pacific old monarch had young rivals to deal with; princes full of his early passion for fame and fighting, and who were disposed to call him to account for the scores he had run up with their fathers. Certain distant districts of his own territories, also, which during the days of his vigor he had treated with a high hand, were prone, now that he languished for repose, to rise in rebellion and threaten to invest him in his capital. Thus he had foes on every side; and as Granada is surrounded by wild and craggy mountains, which hide the approach of an enemy, the unfortunate Aben Habuz was kept in a constant state of vigilance and alarm, not knowing in what quarter hostilities might break out.

It was in vain that he built watch-towers on the mountains, and stationed guards at every pass with orders to make fires by night and smoke by day, on the approach of an enemy. His alert foes, baffling every precaution, would break out of some unthought-of defile, ravage his lands beneath his very nose, and then make off with prisoners and booty to the mountains. Was ever peaceable and retired conqueror in a more uncomfortable predicament?

While Aben Habuz was harassed by these perplexities and molestations, an ancient Arabian physician arrived at his court. His gray beard descended to his girdle, and he had every mark of extreme age, yet he had travelled almost the whole way from Egypt on foot, with no other aid than a staff, marked with hieroglyphics. His fame had preceded him. His name was Ibrahim Ebn Abu Ayub; he was said to have lived ever since the days of Mahomet, and to be the son of Abu Ayub, the last of the companions of the Prophet. He had, when a child, followed the conquering army of Amru into Egypt, where he had remained many years studying the dark sciences, and particularly magic, among the Egyptian priests.

It was, moreover, said that he had found out the secret of prolonging life, by means of which he had arrived to the great age of upwards of two centuries, though, as he did not discover the secret until well stricken in years, he could only perpetuate his gray hairs and wrinkles.

This wonderful old man was honorably entertained by the king, who, like most superannuated monarchs, began to take physicians into great favor. He would have assigned him an apartment in his palace, but the astrologer preferred a cave in the side of the hill which rises above the city of Granada, being the same on which the Alhambra has since been built. He caused the cave to be enlarged so as to form a spacious and lofty hall, with a circular hole at the top, through which, as through a well, he could see the heavens and behold the stars even at mid-day. The walls of this hall were covered with Egyptian hieroglyphics with cabalistic symbols, and with the figures of the stars in their signs. This hall he furnished with many implements, fabricated under his directions by cunning artificers of Granada, but the occult properties of which were known only to himself.

In a little while the sage Ibrahim became the bosom coun-sellor of the king, who applied to him for advice in every emergency. Aben Habuz was once inveighing against the injustice of his neighbors, and bewailing the restless vigilance he had to observe to guard himself against their invasions; when he had finished, the astrologer remained silent for a moment, and then replied, "Know, O king, that when I was in Egypt, I beheld a great marvel devised by a pagan priestess of old. On a mountain above the city of Borsa, and over-looking the great valley of the Nile, was a figure of a ram, and above it a figure of a cock, both of molten brass, and turning upon a pivot. Whenever the country was threatened with invasion, the ram would turn in the direction of the enemy, and the cock would crow; upon this the inhabitants of the city knew of the danger, and of the quarter from which it was approaching, and could take timely means to guard against it."

"God is great!" exclaimed the pacific Aben Habuz, "what a treasure would be such a ram to keep an eye upon these mountains around me; and then such a cock, to crow in time of danger! Allah Akbar! how securely I might sleep in my palace with such sentinels on the top!"

The astrologer waited until the ecstasies of the king had subsided, and then proceeded.

"After the victorious Amru (may he rest in peace!) had finished his conquest of Egypt, I remained among the priests of the land, studying the rites and ceremonies of their idola-trous faith, and seeking to make myself master of the hidden knowledge for which they are renowned. I was one day seated on the banks of the Nile, conversing with an ancient priest, when he pointed to the mighty pyramids which rose like mountains out of the neighboring desert. 'All that we can teach thee,' said he, 'is nothing to the knowledge locked up in those mighty piles. In the centre of the central pyramid is a sepulchral chamber, in which is enclosed the mummy of the high-priest who aided in rearing that stupendous pile; and with him is buried a wondrous book of knowledge, containing all the secrets of magic and art. This book was given to Adam after his fall, and was handed down from generation to gen-eration to King Solomon the Wise, and by its aid he built the Temple of Jerusalem. How it came into the possession of the builder of the pyramids is known to Him alone who knows all things.'

"When I heard these words of the Egyptian priest, my heart burned to get possession of that book. I could command the services of many of the soldiers of our conquering army, and of a number of the native Egyptians. With these I set to work, and pierced the solid mass of the pyramid, until, after great toil, I came upon one of its interior and hidden passages. Following this up, and threading a fearful labyrinth, I penetrated into the very heart of the pyramids, even to the sepulchral chamber, where the mummy of the high-priest had lain for ages. I broke through the outer cases of the mummy; unfolded its many wrappers and bandages, and at length found the precious volume on its bosom. I seized it with a trembling hand, and groped my way out of the pyramid, leaving the mummy in its dark and silent sepulchre, there to await the final day of resurrection and judgment."

"Son of Abu Ayub," exclaimed Aben Habuz, "thou hast been a great traveller, and seen marvellous things; but of what avail to me is the secret of the pyramid, and the volume of knowledge of the wise Solomon?"

"This it is, O king! By the study of that book I am instructed in all magic arts, and can command the assistance of genii to accomplish my plans. The mystery of the Talisman of Borsa is therefore familiar to me, and such a talisman can I make, nay, one of greater virtues."

"O wise son of Abu Ayub," cried Aben Habuz, "better were such a talisman than all the watch-towers on the hills, and sentinels upon the borders. Give me such a safeguard, and the riches of my treasury are at thy command."

The astrologer immediately set to work to gratify the wishes of the monarch. He caused a great tower to be erected upon the top of the royal palace, which stood on the brow of the hill of the Albaycin. The tower was built of stones brought from Egypt, and taken, it is said, from one of the pyramids. In the upper part of the tower was a circular hall, with windows looking towards every point of the compass, and before each window was a table, on which was arranged, as on a chessboard, a mimic army of horse and foot, with the effigy of the potentate that ruled in that direction, all carved of wood. To each of these tables there was a small lance, no bigger than a bodkin, on which were engraved certain Chaldaic characters. This hall was kept constantly closed, by a gate of brass, with a great lock of steel, the key of which was in possession of the king.

On the top of the tower was a bronze figure of a Moorish horseman, fixed on a pivot, with a shield on one arm, and his lance elevated perpendicularly. The face of this horseman was towards the city, as if keeping guard over it; but if any foe were at hand, the figure would turn in that direction, and would level the lance as if for action.

When this talisman was finished, Aben Habuz was all impatient to try its virtues, and longed as ardently for an invasion as he had ever sighed after repose. His desire was soon gratified. Tidings were brought, early one morning, by the sentinel appointed to watch the tower, that the face of the bronze horseman was turned towards the mountains of Elvira, and that his lance pointed directly against the Pass of Lope.

"Let the drums and trumpets sound to arms, and all Granada be put on the alert," said Aben Habuz.

"O king," said the astrologer, "let not your city be disquieted, nor your warriors called to arms; we need no aid of force to deliver you from your enemies. Dismiss your attendants, and let us proceed alone to the secret hall of the tower."

The ancient Aben Habuz mounted the staircase of the tower, leaning on the arm of the still more ancient Ibrahim Ebn Abu Ayub. They unlocked the brazen door and entered. The window that looked towards the Pass of Lope was open. "In this direction," said the astrologer, "lies the danger; approach, O king, and behold the mystery of the table."

King Aben Habuz approached the seeming chess-board, on which were arranged the small wooden effigies, when, to his surprise, he perceived that they were all in motion. The horses pranced and curveted, the warriors brandished their weapons, and there was a faint sound of drums and trumpets, and the clang of arms, and neighing of steeds; but all no louder, nor more distinct, than the hum of the bee, or the summer-fly, in the drowsy ear of him who lies at noontide in the shade.

"Behold, O king," said the astrologer, "a proof that thy enemies are even now in the field. They must be advancing through yonder mountains, by the Pass of Lope. Would you produce a panic and confusion amongst them, and cause them to retreat without loss of life, strike these effigies with the but-end of this magic lance; would you cause bloody feud and carnage, strike with the point."

A livid streak passed across the countenance of Aben Habuz; he seized the lance with trembling eagerness; his gray beard wagged with exultation as he tottered toward the table: "Son of Abu Ayub," exclaimed he, in chuckling tone, "I think we will have a little blood!"

So saying, he thrust the magic lance into some of the pigmy effigies, and belabored others with the but-end, upon which the former fell as dead upon the board, and the rest, turning upon each other, began, pell-mell, a chance-medley fight.

It was with difficulty the astrologer could stay the hand of the most pacific of monarchs, and prevent him from absolutely exterminating his foes. At length he prevailed upon him to leave the tower, and to send out scouts to the mountains by the Pass of Lope.

They returned with the intelligence that a Christian army had advanced through the heart of the Sierra, almost within sight of Granada, where a dissension had broken out among them; they had turned their weapons against each other, and after much slaughter had retreated over the border.

Aben Habuz was transported with joy on thus proving the efficacy of the talisman. "At length," said he, "I shall lead a life of tranquillity, and have all my enemies in my power. O wise son of Abu Ayub, what can I bestow on thee in reward for such a blessing?"

"The wants of an old man and a philosopher, O king, are few and simple; grant me but the means of fitting up my cave as a suitable hermitage, and I am content."

"How noble is the moderation of the truly wise!" exclaimed Aben Habuz, secretly pleased at the cheapness of the recompense. He summoned his treasurer, and bade him dispense whatever sums might be required by Ibrahim to complete and furnish his hermitage.

The astrologer now gave orders to have various chambers hewn out of the solid rock, so as to form ranges of apartments connected with his astrological hall; these he caused to be furnished with luxurious ottomans and divans, and the walls to be hung with the richest silks of Damascus. "I am an old man," said he, "and can no longer rest my bones on stone couches, and these damp walls require covering."

He had baths too constructed, and provided with all kinds of perfumes and aromatic oils. "For a bath," said he, "is necessary to counteract the rigidity of age, and to restore freshness and suppleness to the frame withered by study."

He caused the apartments to be hung with innumerable silver and crystal lamps, which he filled with a fragrant oil prepared according to a receipt discovered by him in the tombs of Egypt. This oil was perpetual in its nature, and diffused a soft radiance like the tempered light of day. "The light of the sun," said he, "is too garish and violent for the eyes of an old man, and the light of the lamp is more congenial to the studies of a philosopher."

The treasurer of King Aben Habuz groaned at the sums daily demanded to fit up this hermitage, and he carried his complaints to the king. The royal word, however, had been given; Aben Habuz shrugged his shoulders: "We must have patience," said he; "this old man has taken his idea of a philosophic retreat from the interior of the pyramids, and of the vast ruins of Egypt; but all things have an end, and so will the furnishing of his cavern."

The king was in the right; the hermitage was at length complete, and formed a sumptuous subterranean palace. The astrologer expressed himself perfectly content, and, shutting himself up, remained for three whole days buried in study. At the end of that time he appeared again before the treasurer. "One thing more is necessary," said he, "one trifling solace for the intervals of mental labor."

"O wise Ibrahim, I am bound to furnish everything necessary for thy solitude; what more dost thou require?"

"I would fain have a few dancing-women."

"Dancing-women!" echoed the treasurer, with surprise.

"Dancing-women," replied the sage, gravely; "and let them be young and fair to look upon; for the sight of youth and beauty is refreshing. A few will suffice, for I am a philosopher of simple habits and easily satisfied."

While the philosophic Ibrahim Ebn Abu Ayub passed his time thus sagely in his hermitage, the pacific Aben Habuz carried on furious campaigns in effigy in his tower. It was a glorious thing for an old man, like himself, of quiet habits, to have war made easy, and to be enabled to amuse himself in his chamber by brushing away whole armies like so many swarms of flies.

For a time he rioted in the indulgence of his humors, and even taunted and insulted his neighbors, to induce them to make incursions; but by degrees they grew wary from repeated disasters, until no one ventured to invade his territories. For many months the bronze horseman remained on the peace establishment, with his lance elevated in the air; and the worthy old monarch began to repine at the want of his accustomed sport, and to grow peevish at his monotonous tranquillity.

At length, one day, the talismanic horseman veered suddenly round, and lowering his lance, made a dead point towards the mountains of Gaudix. Aben Habuz hastened to his tower, but the magic table in that direction remained quiet. Not a single warrior was in motion. Perplexed at the circumstance, he sent forth a troop of horse to scour the mountains and reconnoitre. They returned after three days' absence.

"We have searched every mountain pass," said they, "but not a helm or a spear was stirring. All that we have found in the course of our foray was a Christian damsel of surpassing beauty, sleeping at noontide beside a fountain, whom we have brought away captive."

"A damsel of surpassing beauty!" exclaimed Aben Habus, his eyes gleaming with animation; "let her be conducted into my presence."

The beautiful damsel was accordingly conducted into his presence. She was arrayed with all the luxury of ornament that had prevailed among the Gothic Spaniards at the time of the Arabian Conquest. Pearls of dazzling whiteness were entwined with her raven tresses; and jewels sparkled on her forehead, rivalling the lustre of her eyes. Around her neck was a golden chain, to which was suspended a silver lyre, which hung by her side.

The flashes of her dark refulgent eye were like sparks of fire on the withered, yet combustible, heart of Aben Habuz; the swimming voluptuousness of her gait made his senses reel. "Fairest of women," cried he, with rapture, "who and what art thou?"

"The daughter of one of the Gothic princes, who but lately ruled over this land. The armies of my father have been destroyed, as if by magic, among these mountains; he has been driven into exile, and his daughter is a captive."

"Beware, O king!" whispered Ibrahim Ebn Abu Ayub, "this

may be one of those northern sorceresses of whom we have heard, who assume the most seductive forms to beguile the unwary. Methinks I read witchcraft in her eye, and sorcery in every movement. Doubtless this is the enemy pointed out by the talisman."

"Son of Abu Ayub," replied the king, "thou art a wise man, I grant, a conjurer for aught I know; but thou art little versed in the ways of woman. In that knowledge will I yield to no man; no, not to the wise Solomon himself, notwithstanding the number of his wives and concubines. As to this damsel, I see no harm in her; she is fair to look upon, and finds favor in my eyes."

"Hearken, O king!" replied the astrologer. "I have given thee many victories by means of my talisman, but have never shared any of the spoil. Give me then this stray captive, to solace me in my solitude with her silver lyre. If she be indeed a sorceress, I have counter spells that set her charms at defiance."

"What! more women!" cried Aben Habuz. "Hast thou not already dancing-women enough to solace thee?"

"Dancing-women have I, it is true, but no singing-women. I would fain have a little minstrelsy to refresh my mind when weary with the toils of study."

"A truce with thy hermit cravings," said the king, impatiently. "This damsel have I marked for my own. I see much comfort in her: even such comfort as David, the father of Solomon the Wise, found in the society of Abishag the Shunamite."

Further solicitations and remonstrances of the astrologer only provoked a more peremptory reply from the monarch, and they parted in high displeasure. The sage shut himself up in his hermitage to brood over his disappointment; ere he departed, however, he gave the king one more warning to beware of his dangerous captive. But where is the old man in love that will listen to counsel? Aben Habuz resigned himself to the full sway of his passion. His only study was how to render himself amiable in the eyes of the Gothic beauty. He had not youth to recommend him, it is true, but then he had riches; and when a lover is old, he is generally generous. The Zacatin of Granada was ransacked for the most precious merchandise of the East; silks, jewels, precious gems, exquisite perfumes, all that Asia and Africa yielded of rich and rare, were lavished upon the princess. All kinds of spectacles and festivities were devised for her entertainment; minstrelsy, dancing, tournaments, bull-fights;—Granada for a time was a scene of perpetual pageant. The Gothic princess regarded all this splendor with the air of one accustomed to magnificence. She received everything as a homage due to her rank, or rather to her beauty; for beauty is more lofty in its exactions even than rank. Nay, she seemed to take a secret pleasure in exciting the monarch to expenses that made his treasury shrink, and then treating his extravagant generosity as a mere matter of course. With all his assiduity and munificence, also, the venerable lover could not flatter himself that he had made any impression on her heart. She never frowned on him, it is true, but then she never smiled. Whenever he began to plead his passion, she struck her silver lyre. There was a mystic charm in the sound. In an instant the monarch began to nod; a drowsiness stole over him, and he gradually sank into a sleep, from which he awoke wonderfully refreshed, but perfectly cooled, for the time, of his passion. This was very baffling to his suit; but then these slumbers were accompanied by agreeable dreams, which completely enthralled the senses of the drowsy lover; so he continued to dream on, while all Granada scoffed at his infatuation, and groaned at the treasures lavished for a song.

At length a danger burst on the head of Aben Habuz, against which his talisman yielded him no warning. An insurrection broke out in his very capital; his palace was surrounded by an armed rabble, who menaced his life and the life of his Christian paramour. A spark of his ancient warlike spirit was awakened in the breast of the monarch. At the head of a handful of his guards he sallied forth, put the rebels to flight, and crushed the insurrection in the bud.

When quiet was again restored, he sought the astrologer, who still remained shut up in his hermitage, chewing the bitter cud of resentment.

Aben Habuz approached him with a conciliatory tone. "O wise son of Abu Ayub," said he, "well didst thou predict dangers to me from this captive beauty; tell me then, thou who art so quick at foreseeing peril, what I should do to avert it."

"Put from thee the infidel damsel who is the cause."

"Sooner would I part with my kingdom," cried Aben Habuz.

"Thou art in danger of losing both," replied the astrologer.

"Be not harsh and angry, O most profound of philosophers; consider the double distress of a monarch and a lover, and devise some means of protecting me from the evils by which I am menaced. I care not for grandeur, I care not for power, I languish only for repose; would that I had some quiet retreat where I might take refuge from the world, and all its cares, and pomps, and troubles, and devote the remainder of my days to tranquillity and love."

The astrologer regarded him for a moment from under his bushy eyebrows.

"And what wouldst thou give, if I could provide thee such a retreat?"

"Thou shouldst name thy own reward, and whatever it might be, if within the scope of my power, as my soul liveth, it should be thine."

"Thou hast heard, O king, of the garden of Irem, one of the prodigies of Arabia the happy."

"I have heard of that garden; it is recorded in the Koran, even in the chapter entitled 'The Dawn of Day.' I have, moreover, heard marvellous things related of it by pilgrims who had been to Mecca; but I considered them wild fables, such as travellers are wont to tell who have visited remote countries."

"Discredit not, O king, the tales of travellers," rejoined the astrologer, gravely, "for they contain precious rarities of knowledge brought from the ends of the earth. As to the palace and garden of Irem, what is generally told of them is true. I have seen them with mine own eyes;—listen to my adventure, for it has a bearing upon the object of your request.

"In my younger days, when a mere Arab of the desert, I tended my father's camels. In traversing the desert of Aden, one of them strayed from the rest, and was lost. I searched after it for several days, but in vain, until, wearied and faint,

I laid myself down at noontide and slept under a palm-tree by the side of a scanty well. When I awoke I found myself at the gate of a city. I entered, and beheld noble streets, and squares, and market-places; but all were silent and without an inhabitant. I wandered on until I came to a sumptuous palace, with a garden adorned with fountains and fish-ponds, and groves and flowers, and orchards laden with delicious fruit; but still no one was to be seen. Upon which, appalled at this loneliness, I hastened to depart; and, after issuing forth at the gate of the city, I turned to look upon the place, but it was no longer to be seen; nothing but the silent desert extended before my eyes.

"In the neighborhood I met with an aged dervise, learned in the traditions and secrets of the land, and related to him what had befallen me. 'This,' said he, 'is the far-famed garden of Irem, one of the wonders of the desert. It only appears at times to some wanderer like thyself, gladdening him with the sight of towers and palaces and garden walls overhung with richly laden fruit-trees, and then vanishes, leaving nothing but a lonely desert. And this is the story of it. In old times, when this country was inhabited by the Addites, King Sheddad, the son of Ad, the great grandson of Noah, founded here a splendid city. When it was finished. and he saw its grandeur, his heart was puffed up with pride and arrogance, and he determined to build a royal palace, with gardens which should rival all related in the Koran of the celestial paradise. But the curse of heaven fell upon him for his presumption. He and his subjects were swept from the earth, and his splendid city, and palace, and gardens, were laid under a perpetual spell, which hides them from human sight, excepting that they are seen at intervals, by way of keeping his sin in perpetual remembrance.'

"This story, O king, and the wonders I had seen, ever dwelt in my mind; and in after-years, when I had been in Egypt, and was possessed of the book of knowledge of Solomon the Wise, I determined to return and revisit the garden of Irem. I did so, and found it revealed to my instructed sight. I took possession of the palace of Sheddad, and passed several days in his mock paradise. The genii who watch over the place were obedient to my magic power, and revealed to me the

spells by which the whole garden had been, as it were, conjured into existence, and by which it was rendered invisible. Such a palace and garden, O king, can I make for thee, even here, on the mountain above thy city. Do I not know all the secret spells? and am I not in possession of the book of knowledge of Solomon the Wise?"

"O wise son of Abu Ayub!" exclaimed Aben Habuz, trembling with eagerness, "thou art a traveller indeed, and hast seen and learned marvellous things! Contrive me such a paradise, and ask any reward, even to the half of my kingdom."

"Alas!" replied the other, "thou knowest I am an old man, and a philosopher, and easily satisfied; all the reward I ask is the first beast of burden, with its load, which shall enter the magic portal of the palace."

The monarch gladly agreed to so moderate a stipulation, and the astrologer began his work. On the summit of the hill, immediately above his subterranean hermitage, he caused a great gateway or barbican to be erected, opening through the centre of a strong tower.

There was an outer vestibule or porch, with a lofty arch, and within it a portal secured by massive gates. On the keystone of the portal the astrologer, with his own hand, wrought the figure of a huge key; and on the keystone of the outer arch of the vestibule, which was loftier than that of the portal, he carved a gigantic hand. These were potent talismans, over which he repeated many sentences in an unknown tongue.

When this gateway was finished, he shut himself up for two days in his astrological hall, engaged in secret incantations; on the third he ascended the hill, and passed the whole day on its summit. At a late hour of the night he came down, and presented himself before Aben Habuz. "At length, O king," said he, "my labor is accomplished. On the summit of the hill stands one of the most delectable palaces that ever the head of man devised, or the heart of man desired. It contains sumptuous halls and galleries, delicious gardens, cool fountains, and fragrant baths; in a word, the whole mountain is converted into a paradise. Like the garden of Irem, it is protected by a mighty charm, which hides it from the view and search of mortals, excepting such as possess the secret of its talismans."

"Enough!" cried Aben Habuz, joyfully, "tomorrow morning with the first light we will ascend and take possession." The happy monarch slept but little that night. Scarcely had the rays of the sun begun to play about the snowy summit of the Sierra Nevada, when he mounted his steed, and, accompanied only by a few chosen attendants, ascended a steep and narrow road leading up the hill. Beside him, on a white palfrey, rode the Gothic princess, her whole dress sparkling with jewels, while round her neck was suspended her silver lyre. The astrologer walked on the other side of the king, assisting his steps with his hieroglyphic staff, for he never mounted steed of any kind.

Aben Habuz looked to see the towers of the palace brightening above him, and the embowered terraces of its gardens stretching along the heights; but as yet nothing of the kind was to be descried. "That is the mystery and safeguard of the place," said the astrologer; "nothing can be discerned until you have passed the spell-bound gateway, and been put in possession of the place."

As they approached the gateway, the astrologer paused, and pointed out to the king the mystic hand and key carved upon the portal of the arch. "These," said he, "are the talismans which guard the entrance to this paradise. Until yonder hand shall reach down and seize that key, neither mortal power nor magic artifice can prevail against the lord of this mountain."

While Aben Habuz was gazing, with open mouth and silent wonder, at these mystic talismans, the palfrey of the princess proceeded, and bore her in at the portal, to the very centre of the barbican.

"Behold," cried the astrologer, "my promised reward; the first animal with its burden which should enter the magic gateway."

Aben Habuz smiled at what he considered a pleasantry of the ancient man; but when he found him to be in earnest, his gray beard trembled with indignation.

"Son of Abu Ayub," said he, sternly, "what equivocation is this? Thou knowest the meaning of my promise: the first beast of burden with its load, that should enter this portal. Take the strongest mule in my stables, load it with the most precious things of my treasury, and it is thine; but dare not raise thy thoughts to her who is the delight of my heart."

"What need I of wealth?" cried the astrologer, scornfully; "have I not the book of knowledge of Solomon the Wise, and through it the command of the secret treasures of the earth? The princess is mine by right; thy royal word is pledged; I claim her as my own."

The princess looked down haughtily from her palfrey, and a light smile of scorn curled her rosy lip at this dispute between two gray-beards for the possession of youth and beauty. The wrath of the monarch got the better of his discretion. "Base son of the desert," cried he, "thou mayst be master of many arts, but know me for thy master, and presume not to juggle with thy king."

"My master! my king!" echoed the astrologer,—"the monarch of a mole-hill to claim sway over him who possesses the talismans of Solomon! Farewell, Aben Habuz; reign over thy petty kingdom, and revel in thy paradise of fools; for me, I will laugh at thee in my philosophic retirement."

So saying, he seized the bridle of the palfrey, smote the earth with his staff, and sank with the Gothic princess through the centre of the barbican. The earth closed over them, and no trace remained of the opening by which they had descended.

Aben Habuz was struck dumb for a time with astonishment. Recovering himself, he ordered a thousand workmen to dig, with pickaxe and spade, into the ground where the astrologer had disappeared. They digged and digged, but in vain; the flinty bosom of the hill resisted their implements; or if they did penetrate a little way, the earth filled in again as fast as they threw it out. Aben Habuz sought the mouth of the cavern at the foot of the hill, leading to the subterranean palace of the astrologer; but it was nowhere to be found. Where once had been an entrance, was now a solid surface of primeval rock. With the disappearance of Ibrahim Ebn Abu Ayub ceased the benefit of his talismans. The bronze horseman remained fixed, with his face turned toward the hill, and his spear pointed to the spot where the astrologer had descended, as if there still lurked the deadliest foe of Aben Habuz.

From time to time the sound of music, and the tones of a female voice, could be faintly heard from the bosom of the hill; and a peasant one day brought word to the king, that in the preceding night he had found a fissure in the rock, by which he had crept in, until he looked down into a subterranean hall, in which sat the astrologer, on a magnificent divan, slumbering and nodding to the silver lyre of the princess, which seemed to hold a magic sway over his senses.

Aben Habuz sought the fissure in the rock, but it was again closed. He renewed the attempt to unearth his rival, but all in vain. The spell of the hand and key was too potent to be counteracted by human power. As to the summit of the mountain, the site of the promised palace and garden, it remained a naked waste; either the boasted elysium was hidden from sight by enchantment, or was a mere fable of the astrologer. The world charitably supposed the latter, and some used to call the place "The King's Folly"; while others named it "The Fool's Paradise."

To add to the chagrin of Aben Habuz, the neighbors whom he had defied and taunted, and cut up at his leisure while master of the talismanic horseman, finding him no longer protected by magic spell, made inroads into his territories from all sides, and the remainder of the life of the most pacific of monarchs was a tissue of turmoils.

At length Aben Habuz died, and was buried. Ages have since rolled away. The Alhambra has been built on the eventful mountain, and in some measure realizes the fabled delights of the garden of Irem. The spellbound gateway still exists entire, protected no doubt by the mystic hand and key, and now forms the Gate of Justice, the grand entrance to the fortress. Under the gateway, it is said, the old astrologer remains in his subterranean hall, nodding on his divan, lulled by the silver lyre of the princess.

The old invalid sentinels who mount guard at the gate hear the strains occasionally in the summer nights; and, yielding to their soporific power, doze quietly at their posts. Nay, so drowsy an influence pervades the place, that even those who watch by day may generally be seen nodding on the stone benches of the barbican, or sleeping under the neighboring trees; so that in fact it is the drowsiest military post in all Christendom. All this, say the ancient legends, will endure from age to age. The princess will remain captive to the astrologer; and the astrologer, bound up in magic slumber by the princess, until the last day, unless the mystic hand shall grasp the fated key, and dispel the whole charm of this enchanted mountain.

NOTE TO THE ARABIAN ASTROLOGER

Al Makkari, in his "History of the Mohammedan Dynasties in Spain," cites from another Arabian writer an account of a talismanic effigy somewhat similar to the one in the foregoing legend.

In Cadiz, says he, there formerly stood a square tower upwards of one hundred cubits high, built of huge blocks of stone, fastened together with clamps of brass. On the top was the figure of a man, holding a staff in his right hand, his face turned to the Atlantic, and pointing with the forefinger of his left hand to the Straits of Gibraltar. It was said to have been set up in ancient times by the Gothic kings of Andalus, as a beacon or guide to navigators. The Moslems of Barbary and Andalus considered it a talisman which exercised a spell over the seas. Under its guidance, swarms of piratical people of a nation called Majus, appeared on the coast in large vessels with a square sail in the bow, and another in the stern. They came every six or seven years; captured everything they met with on the sea;—guided by the statue, they passed through the Straits into the Mediterranean, landed on the coasts of Andalus, laid everything waste with fire and sword; and sometimes carried their depredations on the opposite coasts even as far as Syria.

At length it came to pass in the time of the civil wars, a Moslem admiral who had taken possession of Cadiz, hearing that the statue on top of the tower was of pure gold, had it lowered to the ground and broken to pieces, when it proved to be of gilded brass. With the destruction of the idol, the spell over the sea was at an end. From that time forward nothing more was seen of the piratical people of the ocean, excepting that two of their barks were wrecked on the coast, one at Marsu-l-Majus (the port of the Majus), the other close to the promontory of Al-Aghan.

The maritime invaders above mentioned by Al Makkari must have been the Northmen.

Legend of Prince Ahmed Al Kamel

or *The Pilgrim of Love*

THERE was once a Moorish king of Granada, who had but one son, whom he named Ahmed, to which his courtiers added the surname of Al Kamel, or The Perfect, from the indubitable signs of superexcellence which they perceived in him in his very infancy. The astrologers countenanced them in their foresight, predicting everything in his favor that could make a perfect prince and a prosperous sovereign. One cloud only rested upon his destiny, and even that was of a roseate hue: he would be of an amorous temperament, and run great perils from the tender passion. If, however, he could be kept from the allurements of love until of mature age, these dangers would be averted, and his life thereafter be one uninterrupted course of felicity.

To prevent all danger of the kind, the king wisely determined to rear the prince in a seclusion where he would never see a female face, nor hear even the name of love. For this purpose he built a beautiful palace on the brow of the hill above the Alhambra, in the midst of delightful gardens, but surrounded by lofty walls, being, in fact, the same palace known at the present day by the name of the Generalife. In this palace the youthful prince was shut up, and intrusted to the guardianship and instruction of Eben Bonabben, one of the wisest and dryest of Arabian sages, who had passed the greatest part of his life in Egypt, studying hieroglyphics, and making researches among the tombs and pyramids, and who saw more charms in an Egyptian mummy than in the most tempting of living beauties. The sage was ordered to instruct the prince in all kinds of knowledge but one—he was to be kept utterly ignorant of love. "Use every precaution for the purpose you may think proper," said the king, "but remember, O Eben Bonabben, if my son learns aught of that forbidden knowledge while under your care, your head shall answer for it." A withered smile came over the dry visage of the wise Bonabben at the menace. "Let your majesty's heart be as easy about your son, as mine is about my head: am I a man likely to give lessons in the idle passion?"

Under the vigilant care of the philosopher, the prince grew up in the seclusion of the palace and its gardens. He had black slaves to attend upon him—hideous mutes who knew nothing of love, or if they did, had not words to communicate it. His mental endowments were the peculiar care of Eben Bonabben, who sought to initiate him into the abstruse lore of Egypt; but in this the prince made little progress, and it was soon evident that he had no turn for philosophy.

He was, however, amazingly ductile for a youthful prince, ready to follow any advice, and always guided by the last counsellor. He suppressed his yawns, and listened patiently to the long and learned discourses of Eben Bonabben, from which he imbibed a smattering of various kinds of knowledge, and thus happily attained his twentieth year, a miracle of princely wisdom—but totally ignorant of love.

About this time, however, a change came over the conduct of the prince. He completely abandoned his studies, and took to strolling about the gardens, and musing by the side of the fountains. He had been taught a little music among his various accomplishments; it now engrossed a great part of his time, and a turn for poetry became apparent. The sage Eben Bonabben took the alarm, and endeavored to work these idle humors out of him by a severe course of algebra; but the prince turned from it with distaste. "I cannot endure algebra," said he; "it is an abomination to me. I want something that speaks more to the heart."

The sage Eben Bonabben shook his dry head at the words. "Here is an end to philosophy," thought he. "The prince has discovered he has a heart!" He now kept anxious watch upon his pupil, and saw that the latent tenderness of his nature was in activity, and only wanted an object. He wandered about the gardens of the Generalife in an intoxication of feelings of which he knew not the cause. Sometimes he would sit plunged in a delicious reverie; then he would seize his lute and draw from it the most touching notes, and then throw it aside, and break forth into sighs and ejaculations.

By degrees this loving disposition began to extend to inanimate objects; he had his favorite flowers, which he cherished with tender assiduity; then he became attached to various trees, and there was one in particular, of a graceful form and drooping foliage, on which he lavished his amorous devotion, carving his name on its bark, hanging garlands on its branches, and singing couplets in its praise, to the accompaniment of his lute.

Eben Bonabben was alarmed at this excited state of his pupil. He saw him on the very brink of forbidden knowledge—the least hint might reveal to him the fatal secret. Trembling for the safety of the prince and the security of his own head, he hastened to draw him from the seductions of the garden, and shut him up in the highest tower of the Generalife. It contained beautiful apartments, and commanded an almost boundless prospect, but was elevated far above the atmosphere of sweets and those witching bowers so dangerous to the feelings of the too susceptible Ahmed.

What was to be done, however, to reconcile him to this restraint and to beguile the tedious hours? He had exhausted almost all kinds of agreeable knowledge; and algebra was not to be mentioned. Fortunately Eben Bonabben had been instructed, when in Egypt, in the language of birds by a Jewish Rabbin, who had received it in lineal transmission from Solomon the Wise, who had been taught it by the Queen of

Sheba. At the very mention of such a study, the eyes of the prince sparkled with animation, and he applied himself to it with such avidity, that he soon became as great an adept as his master.

The tower of the Generalife was no longer a solitude; he had companions at hand with whom he could converse. The first acquaintance he formed was with a hawk, who built his nest in a crevice of the lofty battlements, whence he soared far and wide in quest of prey. The prince, however, found little to like or esteem in him. He was a mere pirate of the air, swaggering and boastful, whose talk was all about rapine and carnage, and desperate exploits.

His next acquaintance was an owl, a mighty wise-looking bird, with a huge head and staring eyes, who sat blinking and goggling all day in a hole in the wall, but roamed forth at night. He had great pretensions to wisdom, talked something of astrology and the moon, and hinted at the dark sciences; he was grievously given to metaphysics, and the prince found his prosings even more ponderous than those of the sage Eben Bonabben.

Then there was a bat, that hung all day by his heels in the dark corner of a vault, but sallied out in slipshod style at twilight. He, however, had but twilight ideas on all subjects, derided things of which he had taken but an imperfect view, and seemed to take delight in nothing.

Besides these there was a swallow, with whom the prince was at first much taken. He was a smart talker, but restless, bustling, and forever on the wing; seldom remaining long enough for any continued conversation. He turned out in the end to be a mere smatterer, who did but skim over the surface of things, pretending to know everything, but knowing nothing thoroughly.

These were the only feathered associates with whom the prince had any opportunity of exercising his newly acquired language; the tower was too high for any other birds to frequent it. He soon grew weary of his new acquaintances, whose conversation spoke so little to the head and nothing to the heart, and gradually relapsed into his loneliness. A winter passed away, spring opened with all its bloom and verdure and breathing sweetness, and the happy time arrived for birds to pair and build their nests. Suddenly, as it were, a universal burst of song and melody broke forth from the groves and gardens of the Generalife, and reached the prince in the solitude of his tower. From every side he heard the same universal theme—love—love—love—chanted forth, and responded to in every variety of note and tone. The prince listened in silence and perplexity. "What can be this love," thought he, "of which the world seems so full, and of which I know nothing?" He applied for information to his friend the hawk. The ruffian bird answered in a tone of scorn: "You must apply," said he, "to the vulgar peaceable birds of earth, who are made for the prey of us princes of the air. My trade is war, and fighting my delight. I am a warrior, and know nothing of this thing called love."

The prince turned from him with disgust, and sought the owl in his retreat. "This is a bird," said he, "of peaceful habits, and may be able to solve my question." So he asked the owl to tell him what was this love about which all the birds in the groves below were singing.

Upon this the owl put on a look of offended dignity. "My nights," said he, "are taken up in study and research, and my days in ruminating in my cell upon all that I have learnt. As to these singing birds of whom you talk, I never listen to them—I despise them and their themes. Allah be praised, I cannot sing; I am a philosopher, and know nothing of this thing called love."

The prince now repaired to the vault, where his friend the bat was hanging by the heels, and propounded the same question. The bat wrinkled up his nose into a most snappish expression. "Why do you disturb me in my morning's nap with such an idle question?" said he, peevishly. "I only fly by twilight, when all birds are asleep, and never trouble myself with their concerns. I am neither bird nor beast, and I thank heaven for it. I have found out the villany of the whole of them, and hate them one and all. In a word, I am a misanthrope—and know nothing of this thing called love."

As a last resort, the prince now sought the swallow, and stopped him just as he was circling about the summit of the tower. The swallow, as usual, was in a prodigious hurry, and had scarce time to make a reply. "Upon my word," said he,

"I have so much public business to attend to, and so many pursuits to follow, that I have had no time to think on the subject. I have every day a thousand visits to pay; a thousand affairs of importance to examine into, that leave me not a moment of leisure for these little sing-song matters. In a word, I am a citizen of the world—I know nothing of this thing called love." So saying, the swallow dived into the valley, and was out of sight in a moment.

The prince remained disappointed and perplexed, but with his curiosity still more piqued by the difficulty of gratifying it. While in this mood, his ancient guardian entered the tower. The prince advanced eagerly to meet him. "O Eben Bonabben," cried he, "thou hast revealed to me much of the wisdom of the earth; but there is one thing of which I remain in utter ignorance, and would fain be informed."

"My prince has but to make the inquiry, and everything within the limited range of his servant's intellect is at his command."

"Tell me, then, O most profound of sages, what is the nature of this thing called love?"

Eben Bonabben was struck as with a thunderbolt. He trembled and turned pale, and felt as if his head sat but loosely on his shoulders.

"What could suggest such a question to my prince,—where could he have learnt so idle a word?"

The prince led him to the window of the tower. "Listen, Eben Bonabben," said he. The sage listened. The nightingale sat in a thicket below the tower, singing to his paramour, the rose; from every blossomed spray and tufted grove rose a strain of melody; and love—love—love—was still the unvarying strain.

"Allah Akbar! God is great!" exclaimed the wise Bonabben. "Who shall pretend to keep this secret from the heart of man, when even the birds of the air conspire to betray it?"

Then turning to Ahmed—"O my prince," cried he, "shut thine ears to these seductive strains. Close thy mind against this dangerous knowledge. Know that this love is the cause of half the ills of wretched mortality. It is this which produces bitterness and strife between brethren and friends; which causes treacherous murder and desolating war. Care and sorrow, weary days and sleepless nights, are its attendants. It withers the bloom and blights the joy of youth, and brings on the ills and griefs of premature old age. Allah preserve thee, my prince, in total ignorance of this thing called love!"

The sage Eben Bonabben hastily retired, leaving the prince plunged in still deeper perplexity. It was in vain he attempted to dismiss the subject from his mind; it still continued uppermost in his thoughts, and teased and exhausted him with vain conjectures. Surely, said he to himself, as he listened to the tuneful strains of the birds, there is no sorrow in those notes; everything seems tenderness and joy. If love be a cause of such wretchedness and strife, why are not these birds drooping in solitude, or tearing each other in pieces, instead of fluttering cheerfully about the groves, or sporting with each other among the flowers?

He lay one morning on his couch, meditating on this inexplicable matter. The window of his chamber was open to admit the soft morning breeze, which came laden with the perfume of orange-blossoms from the valley of the Darro. The voice of the nightingale was faintly heard, still chanting the wonted theme. As the prince was listening and sighing, there was a sudden rushing noise in the air; a beautiful dove, pursued by a hawk, darted in at the window, and fell panting on the floor, while the pursuer, balked of his prey, soared off to the mountains.

The prince took up the gasping bird, smoothed its feathers, and nestled it in his bosom. When he had soothed it by his caresses, he put it in a golden cage, and offered it, with his own hands, the whitest and finest of wheat and the purest of water. The bird, however, refused food, and sat drooping and pining, and uttering piteous moans.

"What aileth thee?" said Ahmed. "Hast thou not everything thy heart can wish?"

"Alas, no!" replied the dove; "am I not separated from the partner of my heart, and that too in the happy spring-time, the very season of love!"

"Of love!" echoed Ahmed. "I pray thee, my pretty bird, canst thou then tell me what is love?"

"Too well can I, my prince. It is the torment of one, the felicity of two, the strife and enmity of three. It is a charm which draws two beings together, and unites them by delicious sympathies, making it happiness to be with each other, but misery to be apart. Is there no being to whom you are drawn by these ties of tender affection?"

"I like my old teacher Eben Bonabben better than any other being; but he is often tedious, and I occasionally feel myself happier without his society."

"That is not the sympathy I mean. I speak of love, the great mystery and principle of life: the intoxicating revel of youth; the sober delight of age. Look forth, my prince, and behold how at this blest season all nature is full of love. Every created being has its mate; the most insignificant bird sings to its paramour; the very beetle wooes its lady-beetle in the dust, and yon butterflies which you see fluttering high above the tower and toying in the air, are happy in each other's loves. Alas, my prince! hast thou spent so many of the precious days of youth without knowing anything of love? Is there no gentle being of another sex—no beautiful princess nor lovely damsel who has ensnared your heart, and filled your bosom with a soft tumult of pleasing pains and tender wishes?"

"I begin to understand," said the prince, sighing; "such a tumult I have more than once experienced, without knowing the cause; and where should I seek for an object such as you describe in this dismal solitude?"

A little further conversation ensued, and the first amatory lesson of the prince was complete.

"Alas!" said he, "if love be indeed such a delight, and its interruption such a misery, Allah forbid that I should mar the joy of any of its votaries." He opened the cage, took out the dove, and having fondly kissed it, carried it to the window. "Go, happy bird," said he, "rejoice with the partner of thy heart in the days of youth and spring-time. Why should I make thee a fellow-prisoner in this dreary tower, where love can never enter?"

The dove flapped its wings in rapture, gave one vault into the air, and then swooped downward on whistling wings to the blooming bowers of the Darro.

The prince followed him with his eyes, and then gave way to bitter repining. The singing of the birds, which once delighted him, now added to his bitterness. Love! love! love!

Alas, poor youth! he now understood the strain.

His eyes flashed fire when next he beheld the sage Bonabben. "Why has thou kept me in this abject ignorance?" cried he. "Why has the great mystery and principle of life been withheld from me, in which I find the meanest insect is so learned? Behold all nature is in a revel of delight. Every created being rejoices with its mate. This—this is the love about which I have sought instruction. Why am I alone debarred its enjoyment? Why has so much of my youth been wasted without a knowledge of its raptures?"

The sage Bonabben saw that all further reserve was useless; for the prince had acquired the dangerous and forbidden knowledge. He revealed to him, therefore, the predictions of the astrologers and the precautions that had been taken in his education to avert the threatened evils. "And now, my prince," added he, "my life is in your hands. Let the king, your father, discover that you have learned the passion of love while under my guardianship, and my head must answer for it."

The prince was as reasonable as most young men of his age, and easily listened to the remonstrances of his tutor, since nothing pleaded against them. Besides, he really was attached to Eben Bonabben, and being as yet but theoretically acquainted with the passion of love, he consented to confine his knowledge of it to his own bosom, rather than endanger the head of the philosopher.

His discretion was doomed, however, to be put to still further proofs. A few mornings afterward, as he was ruminating on the battlements of the tower, the dove which had been released by him came hovering in the air, and alighted fearlessly upon his shoulder.

The prince fondled it to his heart. "Happy bird," said he, "who can fly, as it were, with the wings of the morning to the uttermost parts of the earth. Where hast thou been since we parted?"

"In a far country, my prince, whence I bring you tidings in reward for my liberty. In the wild compass of my flight, which extends over plain and mountain, as I was soaring in the air, I beheld below me a delightful garden with all kinds of fruits and flowers. It was in a green meadow, on the banks of a wandering stream, and in the centre of the garden was a stately palace. I alighted in one of the bowers to repose after my weary flight. On the green bank below me was a youthful princess, in the very sweetness and bloom of her years. She was surrounded by female attendants; young like herself, who decked her with garlands and coronets of flowers; but no flower of field or garden could compare with her for loveliness. Here, however, she bloomed in secret, for the garden was surrounded by high walls, and no mortal man was permitted to enter. When I beheld this beauteous maid, thus young and innocent and unspotted by the world, I thought, here is the being formed by heaven to inspire my prince with love."

The description was a spark of fire to the combustible heart of Ahmed; all the latent amorousness of his temperament had at once found an object, and he conceived an immeasurable passion for the princess. He wrote a letter, couched in the most impassioned language, breathing his fervent devotion, but bewailing the unhappy thraldom of his person, which prevented him from seeking her out and throwing himself at her feet. He added couplets of the most tender and moving eloquence, for he was a poet by nature, and inspired by love. He addressed his letter—"To the Unknown Beauty, from the captive Prince Ahmed"; then perfuming it with musk and roses, he gave it to the dove.

"Away, trustiest of messengers!" said he. "Fly over mountain, and valley, and river, and plain; rest not in bower, nor set foot on earth, until thou hast given this letter to the mistress of my heart."

The dove soared high in air, and taking his course darted away in one undeviating direction. The prince followed him with his eye until he was a mere speck on a cloud, and gradually disappeared behind a mountain.

Day after day he watched for the return of the messenger of love, but he watched in vain. He began to accuse him of forgetfulness, when towards sunset one evening the faithful bird fluttered into his apartment, and falling at his feet expired. The arrow of some wanton archer had pierced his breast, yet he had struggled with the lingerings of life to execute his mission. As the prince bent with grief over this gentle martyr to fidelity, he beheld a chain of pearls round his neck, attached to which, beneath his wing, was a small enameled picture. It represented a lovely princess in the very flower of her years. It was doubtless the unknown beauty of the garden; but who and where was she?—how had she received his letter? and was this picture sent as a token of her approval of his passion? Unfortunately the death of the faithful dove left everything in mystery and doubt.

The prince gazed on the picture till his eyes swam with tears. He pressed it to his lips and to his heart; he sat for hours contemplating it almost in an agony of tenderness. "Beautiful image!" said he, "alas, thou art but an image! Yet thy dewy eyes beam tenderly upon me; those rosy lips look as though they would speak encouragement: vain fancies! Have they not looked the same on some more happy rival? But where in this wide world shall I hope to find the original? Who knows what mountains, what realms may separate us; what adverse chances may intervene? Perhaps now, even now, lovers may be crowding around her, while I sit here a prisoner in a tower, wasting my time in adoration of a painted shadow."

The resolution of Prince Ahmed was taken. "I will fly from this palace," said he, "which has become an odious prison; and, a pilgrim of love, will seek this unknown princess throughout the world." To escape from the tower in the day, when every one was awake, might be a difficult matter; but at night the palace was slightly guarded; for no one apprehended any attempt of the kind from the prince, who had always been so passive in his captivity. How was he to guide himself, however, in his darkling flight, being ignorant of the country? He bethought him of the owl, who was accustomed to roam at night, and must know every by-lane and secret pass. Seeking him in his hermitage, he questioned him touching his knowledge of the land. Upon this the owl put on a mighty self-important look. "You must know, O prince," said he, "that we owls are of a very ancient and extensive family, though rather fallen to decay, and possess ruinous castles and palaces in all parts of Spain. There is scarcely a tower of the mountains, or a fortress of the plains, or an old citadel of a city, but has some brother, or uncle, or cousin quartered in it; and in going the rounds to visit this my numerous kindred, I have pried into every nook and corner, and made myself acquainted with every secret of the land."

The prince was overjoyed to find the owl so deeply versed in topography, and now informed him, in confidence, of his tender passion and his intended elopement, urging him to be his companion and counsellor.

"Go to!" said the owl, with a look of displeasure; "am I a bird to engage in a love-affair?—I, whose whole time is devoted to meditation and the moon?"

"Be not offended, most solemn owl," replied the prince; "abstract thyself for a time from meditation and the moon, and aid me in my flight, and thou shalt have whatever heart can wish."

"I have that already," said the owl; "a few mice are sufficient for my frugal table, and this hole in the wall is spacious enough for my studies; and what more does a philosopher like myself desire?"

"Bethink thee, most wise owl, that while moping in thy cell and gazing at the moon, all thy talents are lost to the world. I shall one day be a sovereign prince, and may advance thee to some post of honor and dignity."

The owl, though a philosopher and above the ordinary wants of life, was not above ambition, so he was finally prevailed on to elope with the prince, and be his guide and mentor in his pilgrimage.

The plans of a lover are promptly executed. The prince collected all his jewels, and concealed them about his person as travelling funds. That very night he lowered himself by his scarf from a balcony of the tower, clambered over the outer walls of the Generalife, and, guided by the owl, made good his escape before morning to the mountains.

He now held a council with his mentor as to his future course.

"Might I advise," said the owl, "I would recommend you to repair to Seville. You must know that many years since I was on a visit to an uncle, an owl of great dignity and power, who lived in a ruined wing of the Alcazar of that place. In my hoverings at night over the city I frequently remarked a light burning in a lonely tower. At length I alighted on the battlements, and found it to proceed from the lamp of an Arabian magician: he was surrounded by his magic books, and on his shoulder was perched his familiar, an ancient raven who had come with him from Egypt. I am acquainted with that raven, and owe to him a great part of the knowledge I possess. The magician is since dead, but the raven still inhabits the tower, for these birds are of wonderful long life. I would advise you, O prince, to seek that raven, for he is a soothsayer and a conjurer, and deals in the black art, for which all ravens, and especially those of Egypt, are renowned."

The prince was struck with the wisdom of this advice, and accordingly bent his course towards Seville. He travelled only in the night to accommodate his companion, and lay by during the day in some dark cavern or mouldering watch-tower, for the owl knew every hiding-hole of the kind, and had a most antiquarian taste for ruins.

At length one morning at breakfast they reached the city of Seville, where the owl, who hated the glare and bustle of crowded streets, halted without the gate, and took up his quarters in a hollow tree.

The prince entered the gate, and readily found the magic tower, which rose above the houses of the city, as a palm-tree rises above the shrubs of the desert; it was in fact the same tower standing at the present day, and known as the Giralda, the famous Moorish tower of Seville.

The prince ascended by a great winding staircase to the summit of the tower, where he found the cabalistic raven— an old, mysterious, gray-headed bird, ragged in feather, with a film over one eye that gave him the glare of a spectre. He was perched on one leg, with his head turned on one side, poring with his remaining eye on a diagram described on the pavement.

The prince approached him with the awe and reverence naturally inspired by his venerable appearance and super-natural wisdom. "Pardon me, most ancient and darkly wise raven," exclaimed he, "if for a moment I interrupt those studies which are the wonder of the world. You behold before you a votary of love, who would fain seek your counsel how to obtain the object of his passion."

"In other words," said the raven, with a significant look,

"you seek to try my skill in palmistry. Come, show me your hand, and let me decipher the mysterious lines of fortune."

"Excuse me," said the prince, "I come not to pry into the decrees of fate, which are hidden by Allah from the eyes of mortals; I am a pilgrim of love, and seek but to find a clue to the object of my pilgrimage."

"And can you be at any loss for an object in amorous Andalusia?" said the old raven, leering upon him with his single eye; "above all, can you be at a loss in wanton Seville, where black-eyed damsels dance the *zambra* under every orange grove?"

The prince blushed, and was somewhat shocked at hearing an old bird with one foot in the grave talk thus loosely. "Believe me," said he, gravely, "I am on none such light and vagrant errand as thou dost insinuate. The black-eyed damsels of Andalusia who dance among the orange groves of the Guadalquivir are as naught to me. I seek one unknown but immaculate beauty, the original of this picture; and I beseech thee, most potent raven, if it be within the scope of thy knowledge or the reach of thy art, inform me where she may be found?"

The gray-headed raven was rebuked by the gravity of the prince.

"What know I," replied he, dryly, "of youth and beauty? My visits are to the old and withered, not to the fresh and fair; the harbinger of fate am I, who croak bodings of death from the chimney-top, and flap my wings at the sick man's window. You must seek elsewhere for tidings of your unknown beauty."

"And where can I seek if not among the sons of wisdom, versed in the book of destiny? Know that I am a royal prince, fated by the stars, and sent on a mysterious enterprise on which may hang the destiny of empires."

When the raven heard that it was a matter of vast moment, in which the stars took interest, he changed his tone and manner, and listened with profound attention to the story of the prince. When it was concluded, he replied: "Touching this princess, I can give thee no information of myself, for my flight is not among gardens, or around ladies' bowers; but hie thee to Cordova, seek the palm-tree of the great Abderahman, which stands in the court of the principal mosque; at the foot of it thou wilt find a great traveller who has visited all countries and courts, and been a favorite with queens and princesses. He will give thee tidings of the object of thy search."

"Many thanks for this precious information," said the prince. "Farewell, most venerable conjurer."

"Farewell, pilgrim of love," said the raven, dryly, and again fell to pondering on the diagram.

The prince sallied forth from Seville, sought his fellow-traveller the owl, who was still dozing in the hollow tree, and set off for Cordova.

He approached it along hanging gardens and orange and citron groves, overlooking the fair valley of the Guadalquivir. When arrived at its gates the owl flew up to a dark hole in the wall, and the prince proceeded in quest of the palm-tree planted in days of yore by the great Abderahman. It stood in the midst of the great court of the mosque, towering from amidst orange and cypress trees. Dervises and faquirs were seated in groups under the cloisters of the court, and many of the faithful were performing their ablutions at the fountains before entering the mosque.

At the foot of the palm tree was a crowd listening to the words of one who appeared to be talking with great volubility. "This," said the prince to himself, "must be the great traveller who is to give me tidings of the unknown princess." He mingled in the crowd, but was astonished to perceive that they were all listening to a parrot, who, with his bright-green coat, pragmatical eye, and consequential top-knot, had the air of a bird on excellent terms with himself.

"How is this," said the prince to one of the bystanders, "that so many grave persons can be delighted with the garrulity of a chattering bird?"

"You know not whom you speak of," said the other; "this parrot is a descendant of the famous parrot of Persia, renowned for his story-telling talent. He has all the learning of the East at the tip of his tongue, and can quote poetry as fast as he can talk. He has visited various foreign courts, where he has been considered an oracle of erudition. He has been a universal favorite also with the fair sex, who have a vast admiration for erudite parrots that can quote poetry."

"Enough," said the prince, "I will have some private talk with this distinguished traveller."

He sought a private interview, and expounded the nature of his errand. He had scarcely mentioned it when the parrot burst into a fit of dry rickety laughter, that absolutely brought tears into his eyes. "Excuse my merriment," said he, "but the mere mention of love always sets me laughing."

The prince was shocked at this ill-timed mirth. "Is not love," said he, "the great mystery of nature, the secret principle of life, the universal bond of sympathy?"

"A fig's end!" cried the parrot, interrupting him; "prithee where hast thou learned this sentimental jargon? Trust me, love is quite out of vogue; one never hears of it in the company of wits and people of refinement."

The prince sighed as he recalled the different language of his friend the dove. But this parrot, thought he, has lived about the court, he affects the wit and the fine gentleman, he knows nothing of the thing called love. Unwilling to provoke any more ridicule of the sentiment which filled his heart, he now directed his inquiries to the immediate purport of his visit.

"Tell me," said he, "most accomplished parrot, thou who hast everywhere been admitted to the most secret bowers of beauty, hast thou in the course of thy travels met with the original of this portrait?"

The parrot took the picture in his claw, turned his head from side to side, and examined it curiously with either eye. "Upon my honor," said he, "a very pretty face, very pretty; but then one sees so many pretty women in one's travels that one can hardly—but hold—bless me! now I look at it again— sure enough, this is the Princess Aldegonda: how could I forget one that is so prodigious a favorite with me!"

"The Princess Aldegonda!" echoed the prince; "and where is she to be found?"

"Softly, softly," said the parrot, "easier to be found than gained. She is the only daughter of the Christian king who reigns at Toledo, and is shut up from the world until her seventeenth birthday, on account of some prediction of those meddlesome fellows the astrologers. You'll not get a sight of her; no mortal man can see her. I was admitted to her presence to entertain her, and I assure you, on the word of a parrot who has seen the world, I have conversed with much sillier princesses in my time."

"A word in confidence, my dear parrot," said the prince. "I am heir to a kingdom, and shall one day sit upon a throne. I see that you are a bird of parts, and understand the world. Help me to gain possession of this princess, and I will advance you to some distinguished place about court."

"With all my heart," said the parrot; "but let it be a sinecure if possible, for we wits have a great dislike to labor."

Arrangements were promptly made: the prince sallied forth from Cordova through the same gate by which he had entered; called the owl down from the hole in the wall, introduced him to his new travelling companion as a brother savant, and away they set off on their journey.

They travelled much more slowly than accorded with the impatience of the prince; but the parrot was accustomed to high life, and did not like to be disturbed early in the morning. The owl, on the other hand, was for sleeping at mid-day, and lost a great deal of time by his long siestas. His antiquarian taste also was in the way; for he insisted on pausing and inspecting every ruin, and had long legendary tales to tell about every old tower and castle in the country. The prince had supposed that he and the parrot, being both birds of learning, would delight in each other's society, but never had he been more mistaken. They were eternally bickering. The one was a wit, the other a philosopher. The parrot quoted poetry, was critical on new readings and eloquent on small points of erudition, the owl treated all such knowledge as trifling, and relished nothing but metaphysics. Then the parrot would sing songs and repeat *bon mots* and crack jokes upon his solemn neighbor, and laugh outrageously at his own wit; all which proceedings the owl considered as a grievous invasion of his dignity, and would scowl and sulk and swell, and be silent for a whole day together.

The prince heeded not the wranglings of his companions, being wrapped up in the dreams of his own fancy and the contemplation of the portrait of the beautiful princess. In this way they journeyed through the stern passes of the Sierra

Morena, across the sunburnt plains of La Mancha and Castile, and along the banks of the "Golden Tagus," which winds its wizard mazes over one half of Spain and Portugal. At length they came in sight of a strong city with walls and towers built on a rocky promontory, round the foot of which the Tagus circled with brawling violence.

"Behold," exclaimed the owl, "the ancient and renowned city of Toledo; a city famous for its antiquities. Behold those venerable domes and towers, hoary with time and clothed with legendary grandeur, in which so many of my ancestors have meditated."

"Pish!" cried the parrot, interrupting his solemn antiquarian rapture, "what have we to do with antiquities, and legends, and your ancestry? Behold what is more to the purpose—behold the abode of youth and beauty—behold at length, O prince, the abode of your long-sought princess."

The prince looked in the direction indicated by the parrot, and beheld, in a delightful green meadow on the banks of the Tagus, a stately palace rising from amidst the bowers of a delicious garden. It was just such a place as had been described by the dove as the residence of the original of the picture. He gazed at it with a throbbing heart; "perhaps at this moment," thought he, "the beautiful princess is sporting beneath those shady bowers, or pacing with delicate step those stately terraces, or reposing beneath those lofty roofs!" As he looked more narrowly, he perceived that the walls of the garden were of great height, so as to defy access, while numbers of armed guards patrolled around them.

The prince turned to the parrot. "O most accomplished of birds," said he, "thou hast the gift of human speech. Hie thee to yon garden; seek the idol of my soul, and tell her that Prince Ahmed, a pilgrim of love, and guided by the stars, has arrived in quest of her on the flowery banks of the Tagus."

The parrot, proud of his embassy, flew away to the garden, mounted above its lofty walls, and after soaring for a time over the lawns and groves, alighted on the balcony of a pavilion that overhung the river. Here, looking in at the casement, he beheld the princess reclining on a couch, with her eyes fixed on a paper, while tears gently stole after each other down her pallid cheek.

Pluming his wings for a moment, adjusting his bright-green coat, and elevating his top-knot, the parrot perched himself beside her with a gallant air; then assuming a tenderness of tone, "Dry thy tears, most beautiful of princesses," said he; "I come to bring solace to thy heart."

The princess was startled on hearing a voice, but turning, and seeing nothing but a little green-coated bird bobbing and bowing before her, "Alas! what solace canst thou yield," said she, "seeing thou art but a parrot?"

The parrot was nettled at the question. "I have consoled many beautiful ladies in my time," said he; "but let that pass. At present I come ambassador from a royal prince. Know that Ahmed, the Prince of Granada, has arrived in quest of thee, and is encamped even now on the flowery banks of the Tagus."

The eyes of the beautiful princess sparkled at these words, even brighter than the diamonds in her coronet. "O sweetest of parrots," cried she, "joyful indeed are thy tidings, for I was faint and weary, and sick almost unto death with doubt of the constancy of Ahmed. Hie thee back, and tell him that the words of his letter are engraven in my heart, and his poetry has been the food of my soul. Tell him, however, that he must prepare to prove his love by force of arms; to-morrow is my seventeenth birthday, when the king, my father, holds a great tournament; several princes are to enter the lists, and my hand is to be the prize of the victor."

The parrot again took wing, and rustling through the groves, flew back to where the prince awaited his return. The rapture of Ahmed on finding the original of his adored portrait, and finding her kind and true, can only be conceived by those favored mortals who have had the good fortune to realize daydreams and turn a shadow into substance; still there was one thing that alloyed his transport—this impending tournament. In fact, the banks of the Tagus were already glittering with arms, and resounding with trumpets of the various knights, who, with proud retinues, were prancing on towards Toledo to attend the ceremonial. The same star that had controlled the destiny of the prince had governed that of the princess, and until her seventeenth birthday she had been shut up from the world, to guard her from the tender passion. The fame of her charms, however, had been enhanced rather than obscured by this seclusion. Several powerful princes had contended for her hand; and her father, who was a king of wondrous shrewdness, to avoid making enemies by showing partiality, had referred them to the arbitrament of arms. Among the rival candidates were several renowned for strength and prowess. What a predicament for the unfortunate Ahmed, unprovided as he was with weapons, and unskilled in the exercise of chivalry! "Luckless prince that I am!" said he, "to have been brought up in seclusion under the eye of a philosopher! Of what avail are algebra and philosophy in affairs of love? Alas, Eben Bonabben! why hast thou neglected to instruct me in the management of arms?" Upon this the owl broke silence, precluding his harangue with a pious ejaculation, for he was a devout Mussulman.

"Allah Akbar! God is great!" exclaimed he; "in his hands are all secret things—he alone governs the destiny of princes! Know, O prince, that this land is full of mysteries, hidden from all but those who, like myself, can grope after knowledge in the dark. Know that in the neighboring mountains there is a cave, and in that cave there is an iron table, and on that table there lies a suit of magic armor, and beside that table there stands a spell-bound steed, which have been shut up there for many generations."

The prince stared with wonder, while the owl, blinking his huge round eyes, and erecting his horns, proceeded.

"Many years since I accompanied my father to these parts on a tour of his estates, and we sojourned in that cave; and thus became I acquainted with the mystery. It is a tradition in our family which I have heard from my grandfather, when I was yet but a very little owlet, that this armor belonged to a Moorish magician, who took refuge in this cavern when Toledo was captured by the Christians, and died here, leaving his steed and weapons under a mystic spell, never to be used but by a Moslem, and by him only from sunrise to mid-day. In that interval, whoever uses them will overthrow every opponent."

"Enough: let us seek this cave!" exclaimed Ahmed.

Guided by his legendary mentor, the prince found the cavern, which was in one of the wildest recesses of those rocky cliffs which rise around Toledo; none but the mousing eye of an owl or an antiquary could have discovered the entrance to it. A sepulchral lamp of everlasting oil shed a solemn light through the place. On an iron table in the centre of the cavern lay the magic armor, against it leaned the lance, and beside it stood an Arabian steed, caparisoned for the field, but motionless as a statue. The armor was bright and unsullied as it had gleamed in days of old, the steed in as good condition as if just from the pasture, and when Ahmed laid his hand upon his neck, he pawed the ground and gave a loud neigh of joy that shook the walls of the cavern. Thus amply provided with "horse and rider and weapon to wear," the prince determined to defy the field in the impending tourney.

The eventful morning arrived. The lists for the combat were prepared in the *vega,* or plain, just before the cliff-built walls of Toledo, where stages and galleries were erected for the spectators, covered with rich tapestry, and sheltered from the sun by silken awnings. All the beauties of the land were

assembled in those galleries, while below pranced plumed knights with their pages and esquires, among whom figured conspicuously the princes who were to contend in the tourney. All the beauties of the land, however, were eclipsed when the Princess Aldegonda appeared in the royal pavilion, and for the first time broke forth upon the gaze of an admiring world. A murmur of wonder ran through the crowd at her transcendent loveliness; and the princes who were candidates for her hand, merely on the faith of her reported charms, now felt tenfold ardor for the conflict.

The princess, however, had a troubled look. The color came and went from her cheek, and her eye wandered with a restless and unsatisfied expression over the plumed throng of knights. The trumpets were about sounding for the encounter, when the herald announced the arrival of a strange knight, and Ahmed rode into the field. A steel helmet studded with gems rose above his turban, his cuirass was embossed with gold, his cimeter and dagger were of the workmanship of Fez, and flamed with precious stones. A round shield was at his shoulder, and in his hand he bore the lance of charmed virtue. The caparison of his Arabian steed was richly embroidered and swept the ground, and the proud animal pranced and snuffed the air, and neighed with joy at once more beholding the array of arms. The lofty and graceful demeanor of the prince struck every eye, and when his appellation was announced, "The Pilgrim of Love," a universal flutter and agitation prevailed among the fair dames in the galleries.

When Ahmed presented himself at the lists, however, they were closed against him, none but princes, he was told, were admitted to the contest. He declared his name and rank. Still worse!—he was a Moslem, and could not engage in a tourney where the hand of a Christian princess was the prize.

The rival princes surrounded him with haughty and menacing aspects, and one of insolent demeanor and herculean frame sneered at his light and youthful form, and scoffed at his amorous appellation. The ire of the prince was roused. He defied his rival to the encounter. They took distance, wheeled, and charged: and at the first touch of the magic lance, the brawny scoffer was tilted from his saddle. Here the

prince would have paused, but, alas! he had to deal with a demoniac horse and armor; once in action, nothing could control them. The Arabian steed charged into the thickest of the throng; the lance overturned everything that presented; the gentle prince was carried pell-mell about the field, strewing it with high and low, gentle and simple, and grieving at his own involuntary exploits. The king stormed and raged at this outrage on his subjects and his guests. He ordered out all his guards—they were unhorsed as fast as they came up. The king threw off his robes, grasped buckler and lance, and rode forth to awe the stranger with the presence of majesty itself. Alas! majesty fared no better than the vulgar; the steel and lance were no respecters of presons; to the dismay of Ahmed, he was borne full tilt against the king, and in a moment the royal heels were in the air, and the crown was rolling in the dust.

At this moment the sun reached the meridian; the magic spell resumed its power; the Arabian steed scoured across the plain, leaped the barrier, plunged into the Tagus, swam its raging current, bore the prince breathless and amazed to the cavern, and resumed his station, like a statue, beside the iron table. The prince dismounted right gladly, and replaced the armor, to abide the further decrees of fate. Then seating himself in the cavern, he ruminated on the desperate state to which this demoniac steed and armor had reduced him. Never should he dare to show his face at Toledo after inflicting such disgrace upon its chivalry, and such an outrage on its king. What, too, would the princess think of so rude and riotous an achievement? Full of anxiety, he sent forth his winged messengers to gather tidings. The parrot resorted to all the public places and crowded resorts of the city, and soon returned with a world of gossip. All Toledo was in consternation. The princess had been borne off senseless to the palace; the tournament had ended in confusion; every one was talking of the sudden apparition, prodigious exploits, and strange disappearance of the Moslem knight. Some pronounced him a Moorish magician, others thought him a demon who had assumed a human shape, while others related traditions of enchanted warriors hidden in the caves of the mountains, and thought it might be one of these, who had made a sudden irruption from his den. All agreed that no mere ordinary mortal could have wrought such wonders, or unhorsed such accomplished and stalwart Christian warriors.

The owl flew forth at night and hovered about the dusky city, perching on the roofs and chimneys. He then wheeled his flight up to the royal palace, which stood on a rocky summit of Toledo, and went prowling about its terraces and battlements, eavesdropping at every cranny, and glaring in with his big goggling eyes at every window where there was a light, so as to throw two or three maids of honor into fits. It was not until the gray dawn began to peer above the mountains that he returned from his mousing expedition, and related to the prince what he had seen.

"As I was prying about one of the loftiest towers of the palace," said he, "I beheld through a casement a beautiful princess. She was reclining on a couch with attendants and physicians around her, but she would none of their ministry and relief. When they retired, I beheld her draw forth a letter from her bosom, and read and kiss it, and give way to loud lamentations; at which, philosopher as I am, I could but be greatly moved."

The tender heart of Ahmed was distressed at these tidings. "Too true were thy words, O sage Eben Bonabben," cried he; "care and sorrow and sleepless nights are the lot of lovers. Allah preserve the princess from the blighting influence of this thing called love!"

Further intelligence from Toledo corroborated the report of the owl. The city was a prey to uneasiness and alarm. The princess was conveyed to the highest tower of the palace, every avenue to which was strongly guarded. In the meantime a devouring melancholy had seized upon her, of which no one could divine the cause—she refused food and turned a deaf ear to every consolation. The most skilful physicians had essayed their art in vain; it was thought some magic spell had been practised upon her, and the king made proclamation, declaring that whoever should effect her cure should receive the richest jewel in the royal treasury.

When the owl, who was dozing in a corner, heard of this proclamation, he rolled his large eyes and looked more mysterious than ever.

"Allah Akbar!" exclaimed he, "happy the man that shall effect that cure, should he but know what to choose from the royal treasury."

"What mean you, most reverend owl?" said Ahmed.

"Hearken, O prince, to what I shall relate. We owls, you must know, are a learned body, and much given to dark and dusty research. During my late prowling at night about the domes and turrets of Toledo, I discovered a college of antiquarian owls, who hold their meetings in a great vaulted tower where the royal treasury is deposited. Here they were discussing the forms and inscriptions and designs of ancient gems and jewels, and of golden and silver vessels, heaped up in the treasury, the fashion of every country and age; but mostly they were interested about certain relics and talismans that have remained in the treasury since the time of Roderick the Goth. Among these was a box of sandal-wood secured by bands of steel of Oriental workmanship, and inscribed with mystic characters known only to the learned few. This box and its inscription had occupied the college for several sessions, and had caused much long and grave dispute. At the time of my visit a very ancient owl, who had recently arrived from Egypt, was seated on the lid of the box, lecturing upon the inscription, and he proved from it that the coffer contained the silken carpet of the throne of Solomon the Wise; which doubtless had been brought to Toledo by the Jews who took refuge there after the downfall of Jerusalem."

When the owl had concluded his antiquarian harangue, the prince remained for a time absorbed in thought. "I have heard," said he, "from the sage Eben Bonabben, of the wonderful properties of that talisman, which disappeared at the fall of Jerusalem, and was supposed to be lost to mankind. Doubtless it remains a sealed mystery to the Christians of Toledo. If I can get possession of that carpet, my fortune is secure."

The next day the prince laid aside his rich attire, and arrayed himself in the simple garb of an Arab of the desert. He dyed his complexion to a tawny hue, and no one could have recognized in him the splendid warrior who had caused such admiration and dismay at the tournament. With staff in hand, and scrip by his side, and a small pastoral reed, he repaired to Toledo, and presenting himself at the gate of the royal palace, announced himself as a candidate for the reward offered for the cure of the princess. The guards would have driven him away with blows. "What can a vagrant Arab like thyself pretend to do," said they, "in a case where the most learned of the land have failed?" The king, however, overheard the tumult, and ordered the Arab to be brought into his presence.

"Most potent king," said Ahmed, "you behold before you a Bedouin Arab, the greater part of whose life has been passed in the solitudes of the desert. These solitudes, it is well known, are the haunts of demons and evil spirits, who beset us poor shepherds in our lonely watchings, enter into and possess our flocks and herds, and sometimes render even the patient camel furious; against these, our counter charm is music; and we have legendary airs handed down from generation to generation, that we chant and pipe, to cast forth these evil spirits. I am of a gifted line, and possess this power in its fullest force. If it be any evil influence of the kind that holds a spell over thy daughter, I pledge my head to free her from its sway."

The king, who was a man of understanding, and knew the wonderful secrets possessed by the Arabs, was inspired with hope by the confident language of the prince. He conducted him immediately to the lofty tower, secured by several doors, in the summit of which was the chamber of the princess. The windows opened upon a terrace with balustrades, commanding a view over Toledo and all the surrounding country. The windows were darkened, for the princess lay within, a prey to a devouring grief that refused all alleviation.

The prince seated himself on the terrace, and performed several wild Arabian airs on his pastoral pipe, which he had learnt from his attendants in the Generalife at Granada. The princess continued insensible, and the doctors who were present shook their heads and smiled with incredulity and contempt: at length the prince laid aside the reed, and, to a simple melody, chanted the amatory verses of the letter which had declared his passion.

The princess recognized the strain—a fluttering joy stole to her heart; she raised her head and listened; tears rushed to her eyes and streamed down her cheeks; her bosom rose and fell with a tumult of emotions. She would have asked for the minstrel to be brought into her presence, but maiden coyness held her silent. The king read her wishes, and at his command Ahmed was conducted into the chamber. The lovers were discreet: they but exchanged glances, yet those glances spoke volumes. Never was triumph of music more complete. The rose had returned to the soft cheek of the princess, the freshness to her lip, and the dewy light to her languishing eyes.

All the physicians present stared at each other with astonishment. The king regarded the Arab minstrel with admiration mixed with awe. "Wonderful youth!" exclaimed he, "thou shalt henceforth be the first physician of my court, and no other prescription will I take but thy melody. For the present receive thy reward, the most precious jewel in my treasury."

"O king," replied Ahmed, "I care not for silver or gold or precious stones. One relic hast thou in thy treasury, handed down from the Moslems who once owned Toledo—a box of sandal-wood containing a silken carpet: give me that box, and I am content."

All present were surprised at the moderation of the Arab, and still more when the box of sandal-wood was brought and the carpet drawn forth. It was of fine green silk, covered with Hebrew and Chaldaic characters. The court physicians looked at each other, shrugged their shoulders, and smiled at the simplicity of this new practitioner, who could be content with so paltry a fee.

"This carpet," said the prince, "once covered the throne of Solomon the Wise; it is worthy of being placed beneath the feet of beauty."

So saying, he spread it on the terrace beneath an ottoman that had been brought forth for the princess; then seating himself at her feet—

"Who," said he, "shall counteract what is written in the book of fate? Behold the prediction of the astrologers verified. Know, O king, that your daughter and I have long loved each other in secret. Behold in me the Pilgrim of Love!"

These words were scarcely from his lips when the carpet

rose in the air, bearing off the prince and the princess. The king and the physicians gazed after it with open mouths and straining eyes until it became a little speck on the white bosom of a cloud, and then disappeared in the blue vault of heaven.

The king in a rage summoned his treasurer. "How is this," said he, "that thou hast suffered an infidel to get possession of such a talisman?"

"Alas, sir, we knew not its nature, nor could we decipher the inscription of the box. If it be indeed the carpet of the throne of the wise Solomon, it is possessed of magic power, and can transport its owner from place to place through the air."

The king assembled a mighty army, and set off for Granada in pursuit of the fugitives. His march was long and toilsome. Encamping in the Vega, he sent a herald to demand restitution of his daughter. The king himself came forth with all his court to meet him. In the king he beheld the real minstrel, for Ahmed had succeeded to the throne on the death of his father, and the beautiful Aldegonda was his sultana.

The Christian king was easily pacified when he found that his daughter was suffered to continue in her faith; not that he was particularly pious, but religion is always a point of pride and etiquette with princes. Instead of bloody battles, there was a succession of feasts and rejoicings, after which the king returned well pleased to Toledo, and the youthful couple continued to reign, as happily as wisely, in the Alhambra.

It is proper to add that the owl and the parrot had severally followed the prince by easy stages to Granada; the former travelling by night, and stopping at the various hereditary possessions of his family; the latter figuring in gay circles of every town and city on his route.

Ahmed gratefully requited the services which they had rendered on his pilgrimage. He appointed the owl his prime-minister, the parrot his master of ceremonies. It is needless to say that never was a realm more sagely administered, nor a court conducted with more exact punctilio.

Legend of the Moor's Legacy

JUST within the fortress of the Alhambra, in front of the royal palace, is a broad open esplanade, called the Place or Square of the Cisterns (La Plaza de los Algibes), so called from being undermined by reservoirs of water, hidden from sight, and which have existed from the time of the Moors. At one corner of this esplanade is a Moorish well, cut through the living rock to a great depth, the water of which is cold as ice and clear as crystal. The wells made by the Moors are always in repute, for it is well known what pains they took to penetrate to the purest and sweetest springs and fountains. The one of which we now speak is famous throughout Granada, insomuch that water-carriers, some bearing great water-jars on their shoulders, others driving asses before them laden with earthen vessels, are ascending and descending the steep woody avenues of the Alhambra, from early dawn until a late hour of the night.

Fountains and wells, ever since the scriptural days, have been noted gossiping-places in hot climates; and at the well in question there is a kind of perpetual club kept up during the livelong day, by the invalids, old women, and other curious do-nothing folk of the fortress, who sit here on the stone benches, under an awning spread over the well to shelter the toll-gatherer from the sun, and dawdle over the gossip

214

of the fortress, and question every water-carrier that arrives about the news of the city, and make long comments on everything they hear and see. Not an hour of the day but loitering housewives and idle maid-servants may be seen, lingering, with pitcher on head or in hand, to hear the last of the endless tattle of these worthies.

Among the water-carriers who once resorted to this well, there was a sturdy, strong-backed, bandy-legged little fellow, named Pedro Gil, but called Peregil for shortness. Being a water-carrier, he was a Gallego, or native of Galicia, of course. Nature seems to have formed races of men, as she has of animals, for different kinds of drudgery. In France the shoe-blacks are all Savoyards, the porters of hotels all Swiss, and in the days of hoops and hair-powder in England, no man could give the regular swing to a sedan-chair but a bog-trot-ting Irishman. So in Spain, the carriers of water and bearers of burdens are all sturdy little natives of Galicia. No man says, "Get me a porter," but, "Call a Gallego."

To return from this digression, Peregil the Gallego had begun business with merely a great earthen jar which he carried upon his shoulder; by degrees he rose in the world, and was enabled to purchase an assistant of a correspondent class of animals, being a stout shaggy-haired donkey. On each side of this his long-eared aide-de-camp, in a kind of pannier, were slung his water-jars, covered with fig-leaves to protect them from the sun. There was not a more industrious water-carrier in all Granada, nor one more merry withal. The streets rang with his cheerful voice as he trudged after his donkey, singing forth the usual summer note that resounds through the Spanish towns: *"Quien quiere agua—agua mas fria que la nieve?"*—"Who wants water—water colder than snow? Who wants water from the well of the Alhambra, cold as ice and clear as crystal?" When he served a customer with a sparkling glass, it was always with a pleasant word that caused a smile; and if, perchance it was a comely dame or dimpling damsel, it was always with a sly leer and a compliment to her beauty that was irresistible. Thus Peregil the Gallego was noted throughout all Granada for being one of the civilest, pleas-antest, and happiest of mortals. Yet it is not he who sings loudest and jokes most that has the lightest heart. Under all this air of merriment, honest Peregil had his cares and troubles. He had a large family of ragged children to support, who were hungry and clamorous as a nest of young swallows, and beset him with their outcries for food whenever he came home of an evening. He had a helpmate, too, who was anything but a help to him. She had been a village beauty before marriage, noted for her skill at dancing the *bolero* and rattling the castanets; and she still retained her early propensities, spending the hard earnings of honest Peregil in frippery, and laying the very donkey under requisition for junketing parties into the country on Sundays and saints' days, and those innumerable holidays, which are rather more numerous in Spain than the days of the week. With all this she was a little of a slattern, something more of a lie-abed, and, above all, a gossip of the first water; neglecting house, household, and everything else, to loiter slipshod in the houses of her gossip neighbors.

He, however, who tempers the wind to the shorn lamb, accommodates the yoke of matrimony to the submissive neck. Peregil bore all the heavy dispensations of wife and children with as meek a spirit as his donkey bore the water-jars; and, however he might shake his ears in private, never ventured to question the household virtues of his slattern spouse.

He loved his children, too, even as an owl loves it owlets, seeing in them his own image multiplied and perpetuated; for they were a sturdy, long-backed, bandy-legged little brood. The great pleasure of honest Peregil was, whenever he could afford himself a scanty holiday, and had a handful of *maravedis* to spare, to take the whole litter forth with him, some in his arms, some tugging at his skirts, and some trudging at his heels, and to treat them to a gambol among the orchards of the Vega, while his wife was dancing with her holiday friends in the Angosturas of the Darro.

It was a late hour one summer night, and most of the water-carriers had desisted from their toils. The day had been commonly sultry; the night was one of those delicious moonlights which tempt the inhabitants of southern climes to indemnify themselves for the heat and inaction of the day, by lingering in the open air, and enjoying its tempered sweetness until after midnight. Customers for water were therefore still abroad. Peregil, like a considerate, painstaking father, thought of his hungry children. "One more journey to the well," said he to himself, "to earn a Sunday's *puchero* for the little ones." So saying, he trudged manfully up the steep avenue of the Alhambra, singing as he went, and now and then bestowing a hearty thwack with a cudgel on the flanks of his donkey, either by way of cadence to the song, or refreshment to the animal; for dry blows serve in lieu of provender in Spain for all beasts of burden.

When arrived at the well, he found it deserted by every one except a solitary stranger in Moorish garb, seated on a stone bench in the moonlight. Peregil paused at first and regarded him with surprise, not unmixed with awe, but the Moor feebly beckoned him to approach. "I am faint and ill," said he; "aid me to return to the city, and I will pay thee double what thou couldst gain by the jars of water."

The honest heart of the little water-carrier was touched with compassion at the appeal of the stranger. "God forbid," said he, "that I should ask fee or reward for doing a common act of humanity." He accordingly helped the Moor on his donkey, and set off slowly for Granada, the poor Moslem being so weak that it was necessary to hold him on the animal to keep him from falling to the earth.

When they entered the city the water-carrier demanded whither he should conduct him. "Alas!" said the Moor, faintly, "I have neither home nor habitation; I am a stranger in the land. Suffer me to lay my head this night beneath thy roof, and thou shalt be amply repaid."

Honest Peregil thus saw himself unexpectedly saddled with an infidel guest, but he was too humane to refuse a night's shelter to a fellow-being in so forlorn a plight; so he conducted the Moor to his dwelling. The children, who had sallied forth open-mouthed as usual on hearing the tramp of the donkey, ran back with affright when they beheld the turbaned stranger, and hid themselves behind their mother. The latter stepped forth intrepidly, like a ruffling hen before her brood when a vagrant dog approaches.

"What infidel companion," cried she, "is this you have brought home at this late hour to draw upon us the eyes of the inquisition?"

"Be quiet, wife," replied the Gallego; "here is a poor sick

stranger, without friend or home; wouldst thou turn him forth to perish in the streets?"

The wife would still have remonstrated, for although she lived in a hovel, she was a furious stickler for the credit of her house; the little water-carrier, however, for once was stiffnecked, and refused to bend beneath the yoke. He assisted the poor Moslem to alight, and spread a mat and a sheep-skin for him, on the ground, in the coolest part of the house; being the only kind of bed that his poverty afforded.

In a little while the Moor was seized with violent convulsions, which defied all the ministering skill of the simple water-carrier. The eye of the poor patient acknowledged his kindness. During an interval of his fits he called him to his side, and addressing him in a low voice: "My end," said he, "I fear is at hand. If I die, I bequeath you this box as a reward for your charity"; so saying, he opened his *albornoz*, or cloak, and showed a small box of sandal-wood, strapped round his body. "God grant, my friend," replied the worthy little Gallego, "that you may live many years to enjoy your treasure, whatever it may be." The Moor shook his head; he laid his hand upon the box, and would have said something more concerning it, but his convulsions returned with increasing violence, and in a little while he expired.

The water-carrier's wife was now as one distracted. "This comes," said she, "of your foolish good-nature, always running into scrapes to oblige others. What will become of us when this corpse is found in our house? We shall be sent to prison as murderers; and if we escape with our lives, we shall be ruined by notaries and *alguazils*."

Poor Peregil was in equal tribulation, and almost repented himself of having done a good deed. At length a thought struck him. "It is not yet day," said he; "I can convey the dead body out of the city, and bury it in the sands on the banks of the Xenil. No one saw the Moor enter our dwelling, and no one will know anything of his death."

So said, so done. The wife aided him; they rolled the body of the unfortunate Moslem in the mat on which he had expired, laid it across the ass, and Peregil set out with it for the banks of the river.

As ill-luck would have it, there lived opposite to the water-carrier a barber named Pedrillo Pedrugo, one of the most prying, tattling, and mischief-making of his gossip tribe. He was a weasel-faced, spider-legged varlet, supple and insinuating; the famous barber of Seville could not surpass him for his universal knowledge of the affairs of others, and he had no more power of retention than a sieve. It was said that he slept but with one eye at a time, and kept one ear uncovered, so that even in his sleep he might see and hear all that was going on. Certain it is, he was a sort of scandalous chronicle for the quidnuncs of Granada, and had more customers than all the rest of his fraternity.

This meddlesome barber heard Peregil arrive at an unusual hour at night, and the exclamations of his wife and children. His head was instantly popped out of a little window which served him as a look-out, and he saw his neighbor assist a man in Moorish garb into his dwelling. This was so strange an occurrence that Pedrillo Pedrugo slept not a wink that night. Every five minutes he was at his loophole, watching the lights that gleamed through the chinks of his neighbor's door, and before daylight he beheld Peregil sally forth with his donkey unusually laden.

The inquisitive barber was in a fidget; he slipped on his clothes, and, stealing forth silently, followed the water-carrier at a distance, until he saw him dig a hole in the sandy bank of the Xenil, and bury something that had the appearance of a dead body.

The barber hied him home, and fidgeted about his shop, setting everything upside down, until sunrise. He then took a basin under his arm, and sallied forth to the house of his daily customer the Alcalde.

The Alcalde had just risen. Pedrillo Pedrugo seated him in a chair, threw a napkin round his neck, put a basin of hot water under his chin, and began to mollify his beard with his fingers.

"Strange doings!" said Pedrugo, who played barber and newsmonger at the same time, "strange doings! Robbery, and murder, and burial all in one night!"

"Hey!—how!—what is that you say," cried the Alcalde.

"I say," replied the barber, rubbing a piece of soap over

the nose and mouth of the dignitary, for a Spanish barber disdains to employ a brush,—"I say that Peregil the Gallego has robbed and murdered a Moorish Mussulman, and buried him, this blessed night. *Maldita sea la noche;*—Accursed be the night for the same!"

"But how do you know all this?" demanded the Alcalde.

"Be patient, Señor, and you shall hear all about it," replied Pedrillo, taking him by the nose and sliding a razor over his cheek. He then recounted all that he had seen, going through both operations at the same time, shaving his beard, washing his chin, and wiping him dry with a dirty napkin, while he was robbing, murdering, and burying the Moslem.

Now it so happened that this Alcalde was one of the most overbearing and at the same time most griping and corrupt curmudgeons in all Granada. It could not be denied, however, that he set a high value upon justice, for he sold it at its weight in gold. He presumed the case in point to be one of murder and robbery; doubtless there must be a rich spoil; how was it to be secured into the legitimate hands of the law? for as to merely entrapping the delinquent—that would be feeding the gallows; but entrapping the booty—that would be enriching the judge, and such, according to his creed, was the great end of justice. So thinking, he summoned to his presence his trustiest *alguazil*—a gaunt, hungry-looking varlet, clad, according to the custom of his order, in the ancient Spanish garb, a broad black beaver turned up at its sides; a quaint ruff; a small black cloak dangling from his shoulders; rusty black under-clothes that set off his spare wiry frame, while in his hand he bore a slender white wand, the dreaded insignia of his office. Such was the legal bloodhound of the ancient Spanish breed, that he put upon the traces of the unlucky water-carrier, and such was his speed and certainty, that he was upon the haunches of poor Peregil before he had returned to his dwelling, and brought both him and his donkey before the dispenser of justice.

The Alcalde bent upon him one of the most terrific frowns. "Hark ye, culprit!" roared he, in a voice that made the knees of the little Gallego smite together, "hark ye, culprit! there is no need of denying thy guilt, everything is known to me. A gallows is the proper reward for the crime thou hast com-

mitted, but I am merciful, and readily listen to reason. The
man that has been murdered in thy house was a Moor, an
infidel, the enemy of our faith. It was doubtless in a fit of
religious zeal that thou hast slain him. I will be indulgent,
therefore; render up the property of which thou hast robbed
him, and we will hush the matter up."

The poor water-carrier called upon all the saints to witness
his innocence; alas! not one of them appeared; and if they
had the Alcalde would have disbelieved the whole calendar.
The water-carrier related the whole story of the dying Moor
with the straightforward simplicity of truth, but it was all in
vain. "Wilt thou persist in saying," demanded the judge, "that
this Moslem had neither gold nor jewels, which were the
object of thy cupidity?"

"As I hope to be saved, your worship," replied the water-
carrier, "he had nothing but a small box of sandal-wood,
which he bequeathed to me in reward for my services."

"A box of sandal-wood! a box of sandal-wood!" exclaimed
the Alcalde, his eyes sparkling at the idea of precious jewels.
"And where is this box? where have you concealed it?"

"An' it please your grace," replied the water-carrier, "it is
in one of the panniers of my mule, and heartily at the service
of your worship."

He had hardly spoken the words, when the keen *alguazil*
darted off, and reappeared in an instant with the mysterious
box of sandal-wood. The Alcalde opened it with an eager and
trembling hand; all pressed forward to gaze upon the treasure
it was expected to contain; when, to their disappointment,
nothing appeared within, but a parchment scroll, covered
with Arabic characters, and an end of a waxen taper.

When there is nothing to be gained by the conviction of
a prisoner, justice, even in Spain, is apt to be impartial. The
Alcalde, having recovered from his disappointment, and
found that there was really no booty in the case, now listened
dispassionately to the explanation of the water-carrier, which
was corroborated by the testimony of his wife. Being convinced, therefore, of his innocence, he discharged him from
arrest; nay, more, he permitted him to carry off the Moor's
legacy, the box of sandal-wood and its contents, as the well-

merited reward of his humanity; but he retained his donkey in payment of costs and charges.

Behold the unfortunate little Gallego reduced once more to the necessity of being his own water-carrier, and trudging up to the well of the Alhambra with a great earthen jar upon his shoulder.

As he toiled up the hill in the heat of a summer noon, his usual good-humor forsook him. "Dog of an Alcalde!" would he cry, "to rob a poor man of the means of his subsistence, of the best friend he had in the world!" And then at the remembrance of the beloved companion of his labors, all the kindness of his nature would break forth. "Ah, donkey of my heart!" would he exclaim, resting his burden on a stone, and wiping the sweat from his brow—"ah, donkey of my heart! I warrant me thou thinkest of thy old master! I warrant me thou missest the water-jars—poor beast!"

To add to his afflictions, his wife received him, on his return home, with whimperings and repinings; she had clearly the vantage-ground of him, having warned him not to commit the egregious act of hospitality which had brought on him all these misfortunes; and, like a knowing woman, she took every occasion to throw her superior sagacity in his teeth. If her children lacked food, or needed a new garment, she could answer with a sneer, "Go to your father—he is heir to King Chico of the Alhambra: ask him to help you out of the Moor's strong box."

Was ever poor mortal so soundly punished for having done a good action? The unlucky Peregil was grieved in flesh and spirit, but still he bore meekly with the railings of his spouse. At length, one evening, when, after a hot day's toil, she taunted him in the usual manner, he lost all patience. He did not venture to retort upon her, but his eye rested upon the box of sandal-wood, which lay on a shelf with lid half open, as if laughing in mockery at his vexation. Seizing it up, he dashed it with indignation to the floor. "Unlucky was the day that I ever set eyes on thee," he cried, "or sheltered thy master beneath my roof!"

As the box struck the floor, the lid flew wide open, and the parchment scroll rolled forth.

Peregil sat regarding the scroll for some time in moody silence. At length rallying his ideas, "Who knows," thought he, "but this writing may be of some importance, as the Moor seems to have guarded it with such care?" Picking it up therefore, he put it in his bosom, and the next morning, as he was crying water through the streets, he stopped at the shop of a Moor, a native of Tangiers, who sold trinkets and perfumery in the Zacatin, and asked him to explain the contents.

The Moor read the scroll attentively, then stroked his beard and smiled. "This manuscript," said he, "is a form of incantation for the recovery of hidden treasure that is under the power of enchantment. It is said to have such virtue that the strongest bolts and bars, nay the adamantine rock itself, will yield before it!"

"Bah!" cried the little Gallego, "what is all that to me? I am no enchanter, and know nothing of buried treasure." So saying, he shouldered his water-jar, left the scroll in the hands of the Moor, and trudged forward on his daily rounds.

That evening, however, as he rested himself about twilight at the well of the Alhambra, he found a number of gossips assembled at the place, and their conversation, as is not unusual at that shadowy hour, turned upon old tales and traditions of a supernatural nature. Being all poor as rats, they dwelt with peculiar fondness upon the popular theme of enchanted riches left by the Moors in various parts of the Alhambra. Above all, they concurred in the belief that there were great treasures buried deep in the earth under the Tower of the Seven Floors.

These stories made an unusual impression on the mind of the honest Peregil, and they sank deeper and deeper into his thoughts as he returned alone down the darkling avenues. "If, after all, there should be treasure hid beneath that tower; and if the scroll I left with the Moor should enable me to get at it!" In the sudden ecstasy of the thought he had well-nigh let fall his water-jar.

That night he tumbled and tossed, and could scarcely get a wink of sleep for the thoughts that were bewildering his brain. Bright and early he repaired to the shop of the Moor, and told him all that was passing in his mind. "You can read Arabic," said he; "suppose we go together to the tower, and

try the effect of the charm; if it fails, we are no worse off than before; but if it succeeds, we will share equally all the treasure we may discover."

"Hold," replied the Moslem; "this writing is not sufficient of itself; it must be read at midnight, by the light of a taper singularly compounded and prepared, the ingredients of which are not within my reach. Without such a taper the scroll is of no avail."

"Say no more!" cried the little Gallego; "I have such a taper at hand, and will bring it here in a moment." So saying, he hastened home, and soon returned with the end of yellow wax taper that he had found in the box of sandal-wood.

The Moor felt it and smelled of it. "Here are rare and costly perfumes," said he, "combined with this yellow wax. This is the kind of taper specified in the scroll. While this burns, the strongest walls and most secret caverns will remain open. Woe to him, however, who lingers within until it be extinguished. He will remain enchanted with the treasure."

It was now agreed between them to try the charm that very night. At a late hour, therefore, when nothing was stirring but bats and owls, they ascended the woody hill of the Alhambra, and approached that awful tower, shrouded by trees and rendered formidable by so many traditionary tales. By the light of a lantern they groped their way through bushes, and over fallen stones, to the door of a vault beneath the tower. With fear and trembling they descended a flight of steps cut into the rock. It led to an empty chamber, damp and drear, from which another flight of steps led to a deeper vault. In this way they descended four several flights, leading into as many vaults, one below the other, but the floor of the fourth was solid; and though, according to tradition, there remained three vaults still below, it was said to be impossible to penetrate farther, the residue being shut up by strong enchantment. The air of this vault was damp and chilly, and had an earthy smell, and the light scarce cast forth any rays. They paused here for a time, in breathless suspense, until they faintly heard the clock of the watchtower strike midnight; upon this they lit the waxen taper, which diffused an odor of myrrh and frankincense and storax.

The Moor began to read in a hurried voice. He had scarce

finished when there was a noise as of subterraneous thunder. The earth shook, and the floor, yawning open, disclosed a flight of steps. Trembling with awe, they descended, and by the light of the lantern found themselves in another vault covered with Arabic inscriptions. In the centre stood a great chest, secured with seven bands of steel, at each end of which sat an enchanted Moor in armor, but motionless as a statue, being controlled by the power of the incantation. Before the chest were several jars filled with gold and silver and precious stones. In the largest of these they thrust their arms up to the elbow, and at every dip hauled forth handfuls of broad yellow pieces of Moorish gold, or bracelets and ornaments of the same precious metal, while occasionally a necklace of Oriental pearl would stick to their fingers. Still they trembled and breathed short while cramming their pockets with the spoils; and cast many a fearful glance at the two enchanted Moors, who sat grim and motionless, glaring upon them with unwinking eyes. At length, struck with a sudden panic at some fancied noise, they both rushed up the staircase, tumbled over one another into the upper apartment, overturned and extinguished the waxen taper, and the pavement again closed with a thundering sound.

Filled with dismay, they did not pause until they had groped their way out of the tower, and beheld the stars shining through the trees. Then, seating themselves upon the grass, they divided the spoil, determining to content themselves for the present with this mere skimming of the jars, but to return on some future night and drain them to the bottom. To make sure of each other's good faith, also, they divided the talismans between them, one retaining the scroll and the other the taper; this done, they set off with light hearts and well-lined pockets for Granada.

As they wended their way down the hill, the shrewd Moor whispered a word of counsel in the ear of the simple little water-carrier.

"Friend Peregil," said he, "all this affair must be kept a profound secret until we have secured the treasure, and conveyed it out of harm's way. If a whisper of it gets to the ear of the Alcalde, we are undone!"

"Certainly," replied the Gallego, "nothing can be more true."

"Friend Peregil," said the Moor, "you are a discreet man, and I make no doubt can keep a secret; but you have a wife."

"She shall not know a word of it," replied the little water-carrier sturdily.

"Enough," said the Moor, "I depend upon thy discretion and thy promise."

Never was promise more positive and sincere; but alas! what man can keep a secret from his wife? Certainly not such a one as Peregil the water-carrier, who was one of the most loving and tractable of husbands. On his return home, he found his wife moping in a corner. "Mighty well," cried she as he entered, "you've come at last, after rambling about until this hour of the night. I wonder you have not brought home another Moor as a house-mate." Then bursting into tears, she

began to wring her hands and smite her breast. "Unhappy woman that I am!" exclaimed she, "what will become of me? My house stripped and plundered by lawyers and *alguazils;* my husband a do-no-good, that no longer brings home bread to his family, but goes rambling about day and night, with infidel Moors! O my children! my children! what what will become of us? We shall all have to beg in the streets!"

Honest Peregil was so moved by the distress of his spouse that he could not help whimpering also. His heart was as full as his pocket, and not to be restrained. Thrusting his hand into the latter he hauled forth three or four broad gold-pieces, and slipped them into her bosom. The poor woman stared with astonishment, and could not understand the meaning of this golden shower. Before she could recover her surprise, the little Gallego drew forth a chain of gold and dangled it before her, capering with exultation, his mouth distended from ear to ear.

"Holy Virgin protect us!" exclaimed the wife. "What hast thou been doing, Peregil? surely thou hast not been committing murder and robbery!"

The idea scarce entered the brain of the poor woman than it became a certainty with her. She saw a prison and a gallows in the distance, and a littly bandy-legged Gallego hanging pendent from it; and, overcome by the horrors conjured up by imagination, fell into violent hysterics.

What could the poor man do? He had no other means of pacifying his wife, and dispelling the phantoms of her fancy, than by relating the whole story of his good fortune. This, however, he did not do until he had exacted from her the most solemn promise to keep it a profound secret from every living being.

To describe her joy would be impossible. She flung her arms round the neck of her husband, and almost strangled him with her caresses.

"Now, wife," exclaimed the little man, with honest exultation, "what say you now to the Moor's legacy? Henceforth never abuse me for helping a fellow-creature in distress."

The honest Gallego retired to his sheep-skin mat, and slept as soundly as if on a bed of down. Not so his wife. She emptied the whole contents of his pockets upon the mat, and sat counting gold pieces of Arabic coin, trying on necklaces and earrings, and fancying the figure she should one day make when permitted to enjoy her riches.

On the following morning the honest Gallego took a broad golden coin, and repaired with it to a jeweller's shop in the Zacatin to offer it for sale, pretending to have found it among the ruins of the Alhambra. The jeweller saw that it had an Arabic inscription, and was of the purest gold; he offered, however, but a third of its value, with which the water-carrier was perfectly content. Peregil now bought new clothes for his little flock, and all kinds of toys, together with ample provisions for a hearty meal, and returning to his dwelling, set all his children dancing around him, while he capered in the midst, the happiest of fathers.

The wife of the water-carrier kept her promise of secrecy with surprising strictness. For a whole day and a half she went about, with a look of mystery and a heart swelling almost to bursting; yet she held her peace, though surrounded by her gossips. It is true she could not help giving herself a few airs, apologized for her ragged dress, and talked of ordering a new *basquiña*, all trimmed with gold lace and bugles, and a new lace *mantilla*. She threw out hints of her husband's intention of leaving off his trade of water-carrying, as it did not altogether agree with his health. In fact, she thought they should all retire to the country for the summer, that the children might have the benefit of the mountain air, for there was no living in the city in this sultry season.

The neighbors stared at each other, and thought the poor woman had lost her wits; and her airs and graces and elegant pretensions were the theme of universal scoffing and merriment among her friends the moment her back was turned.

If she restrained herself abroad, however, she indemnified herself at home, and putting a string of rich Oriental pearls round her neck, Moorish bracelets on her arms, and an *aigrette* of diamonds on her head, sailed backwards and forwards in her slattern rags about the room, now and then stopping to admire herself in a broken mirror. Nay, in the impulse of her simple vanity, she could not resist, on one occasion, showing herself at the window, to enjoy the effect of her finery on the passers by.

As the fates would have it, Pedrillo Pedrugo, the meddle-some barber, was at this moment sitting idly in his shop on the opposite side of the street, when his ever-watchful eye caught the sparkle of a diamond. In an instant he was at his loophole reconnoitring the slattern spouse of the water-carrier, decorated with the splendor of an Eastern bride. No sooner had he taken an accurate inventory of her ornaments, than he posted off with all speed to the Alcalde. In a little while the hungry *alguazil* was again on the scent, and before the day was over the unfortunate Peregil was once more dragged into the presence of the judge.

"How is this, villain!" cried the Alcalde, in a furious voice. "You told me that the infidel who died in your house left nothing behind but an empty coffer, and now I hear of your wife flaunting in her rags decked out with pearls and dia-monds. Wretch that thou art! prepare to render up the spoils of thy miserable victim, and to swing on the gallows that is already tired of waiting for thee."

The terrified water-carrier fell on his knees, and made a full relation of the marvellous manner in which he had gained his wealth. The Alcalde, the *alguazil,* and the inquisitive bar-ber listened with greedy ears to this Arabian tale of enchanted treasure. The *alguazil* was despatched to bring the Moor who had assisted in the incantation. The Moslem entered, half frightened out of his wits at finding himself in the hands of the harpies of the law. When he beheld the water-carrier standing with sheepish looks and downcast countenance, he comprehended the whole matter. "Miserable animal," said he, as he passed near him, "did I not warn thee against bab-bling to thy wife?"

The story of the Moor coincided exactly with that of his colleague; but the Alcalde affected to be slow of belief, and threw out menaces of imprisonment and rigorous investiga-tion.

"Softly, good Señor Alcalde," said the Mussulman, who by this time had recovered his usual shrewdness and self-pos-session. "Let us not mar fortune's favors in the scramble for them. Nobody knows anything of this matter but ourselves; let us keep the secret. There is wealth enough in the cave to enrich us all. Promise a fair division, and all shall be produced; refuse, and the cave shall remain forever closed."

The Alcalde consulted apart with the *alguazil*. The latter was an old fox in his profession. "Promise anything," said he, "until you get possession of the treasure. You may then seize upon the whole, and if he and his accomplice dare to murmur, threaten them with the fagot and the stake as infidels and sorcerers."

The Alcalde relished the advice. Smoothing his brow and turning to the Moor: "This is a strange story," said he, "and may be true; but I must have ocular proof of it. This very night you must repeat the incantation in my presence. If there be really such treasure, we will share it amicably between us, and say nothing further of the matter; if ye have deceived me, expect no mercy at my hands. In the meantime you must remain in custody."

The Moor and the water-carrier cheerfully agreed to these conditions, satisfied that the event would prove the truth of their words.

Towards midnight the Alcalde sallied forth secretly, attended by the *alguazil* and the meddlesome barber, all strongly armed. They conducted the Moor and the water-carrier as prisoners, and were provided with the stout donkey of the latter to bear off the expected treasure. They arrived at the tower without being observed, and tying the donkey to a fig-tree, descended into the fourth vault of the tower.

The scroll was produced, the yellow waxen taper lighted, and the Moor read the form of incantation. The earth trembled as before, and the pavement opened with a thundering sound, disclosing the narrow flight of steps. The Alcalde, the *alguazil,* and the barber were struck aghast, and could not summon courage to descend. The Moor and the water-carrier entered the lower vault, and found the two Moors seated as before, silent and motionless. They removed two of the great jars, filled with golden coins and precious stones. The water-carrier bore them up one by one upon his shoulders, but though a strong-backed little man, and accustomed to carry burdens, he staggered beneath their weight, and found, when slung on each side of his donkey, they were as much as the animal could bear.

"Let us be content for the present," said the Moor; "here is as much treasure as we can carry off without being perceived, and enough to make us all wealthy to our heart's desire."

"Is there more treasure remaining behind?" demanded the Alcalde.

"The greatest prize of all," said the Moor, "a huge coffer bound with bands of steel, and filled with pearls and precious stones."

"Let us have up the coffer by all means," cried the grasping Alcalde.

"I will descend for no more," said the Moor, doggedly; "enough is enough for a reasonable man—more is superfluous."

"And I," said the water-carrier, "will bring up no further burden to break the back of my poor donkey."

Finding commands, threats, and entreaties equally vain, the Alcalde turned to his two adherents. "Aid me," said he, "to bring up the coffer, and its contents shall be divided between us." So saying, he descended the steps, followed with trembling reluctance by the *alguazil* and the barber.

No sooner did the Moor behold them fairly earthed than he extinguished the yellow taper; the pavement closed with its usual crash, and the three worthies remained buried in its womb.

He then hastened up the different flights of steps, nor stopped until in the open air. The little water-carrier followed him as fast as his short legs would permit.

"What hast thou done?" cried Peregil, as soon as he could recover breath. "The Alcalde and the other two are shut up in the vault."

"It is the will of Allah!" said the Moor, devoutly.

"And will you not release them?" demanded the Gallego.

"Allah forbid!" replied the Moor, smoothing his beard. "It is written in the book of fate that they shall remain enchanted until some future adventurer arrive to break the charm. The will of God be done!" so saying, he hurled the end of the waxen taper far among the gloomy thickets of the glen.

There was now no remedy; so the Moor and the water-carrier proceeded with the richly laden donkey toward the city, nor could honest Peregil refrain from hugging and kissing his long-eared fellow-laborer, thus restored to him from the clutches of the law; and, in fact, it is doubtful which gave the simple-hearted little man most joy at the moment, the gaining of the treasure, or the recovery of the donkey.

The two partners in good luck divided their spoil amicably and fairly, except that the Moor, who had a little taste for trinketry, made out to get into his heap the most of the pearls and precious stones and other baubles, but then he always gave the water-carrier in lieu magnificent jewels of massy gold, of five times the size, with which the latter was heartily content. They took care not to linger within reach of accidents, but made off to enjoy their wealth undisturbed in other countries. The Moor returned to Africa, to his native city of Tangiers, and the Gallego, with his wife, his children, and his donkey, made the best of his way to Portugal. Here, under the admonition and tuition of his wife, he became a personage of some consequence, for she made the worthy little man array his long body and short legs in doublet and hose, with a feather in his hat and a sword by his side, and laying aside his familiar appellation of Peregil, assume the more sonorous title of Don Pedro Gil: his progeny grew up a thriving and merry-hearted, though short and bandy-legged generation, while Señora Gil, befringed, belaced, and betasselled from her head to her heels, with glittering rings on every finger, became a model of slattern fashion and finery.

As to the Alcalde and his adjuncts, they remained shut up under the great Tower of the Seven Floors, and there they remain spellbound at the present day. Whenever there shall be a lack in Spain of pimping barbers, sharking *alguazils,* and corrupt *alcaldes,* they may be sought after; but if they have to wait until such time for their deliverance, there is danger of their enchantment enduring until doomsday.

Legend of the Rose of the Alhambra

FOR some time after the surrender of Granada by the Moors, that delightful city was a frequent and favorite residence of the Spanish sovereigns, until they were frightened away by successive shocks of earthquakes, which toppled down various houses, and made the old Moslem towers rock to their foundation.

Many, many years then rolled away, during which Granada was rarely honored by a royal guest. The palaces of the nobility remained silent and shut up; and the Alhambra, like a slighted beauty, sat in mournful desolation among her neglected gardens. The Tower of the Infantas, once the residence of the three beautiful Moorish princesses, partook of the general desolation; the spider spun her web athwart the gilded vault, and bats and owls nestled in those chambers that had been graced by the presence of Zayda, Zorayda, and Zorahayda. The neglect of this tower may have been partly owing to some superstitious notions of the neighbors. It was rumored that the spirit of the youthful Zorahayda, who had perished in that tower, was often seen by moonlight seated beside the fountain in the hall, or moaning about the battlements, and that the notes of her silver lute would be heard at midnight by wayfarers passing along the glen.

At length the city of Granada was once more welcomed

by the royal presence. All the world knows that Philip V was the first Bourbon that swayed the Spanish sceptre. All the world knows that he married, in second nuptials, Elizabetta or Isabella (for they are the same), the beautiful princess of Parma; and all the world knows that by this chain of contingencies a French prince and an Italian princess were seated together on the Spanish throne. For a visit of this illustrious pair, the Alhambra was repaired and fitted up with all possible expedition. The arrival of the court changed the whole aspect of the lately deserted palace. The clangor of drum and trumpet, the tramp of steed about the avenues and outer court, the glitter of arms and display of banners about barbican and battlement, recalled the ancient and war-like glories of the fortress. A softer spirit, however, reigned within the royal palace. There was the rustling of robes and the cautious tread and murmuring voice of reverential courtiers about the antechambers, a loitering of pages and maids of honor about the gardens, and the sound of music stealing from open casements.

Among those who attended in the train of the monarchs was a favorite page of the queen, named Ruyz de Alarcon. To say that he was a favorite page of the queen was at once to speak his eulogium, for every one in the suite of the stately Elizabetta was chosen for grace, and beauty, and accomplishments. He was just turned of eighteen, light and lithe of form, and graceful as a young Antinous. To the queen he was all deference and respect, yet he was at heart a roguish stripling, petted and spoiled by the ladies about the court, and experienced in the ways of women far beyond his years.

This loitering page was one morning rambling about the groves of the Generalife, which overlook the grounds of the Alhambra. He had taken with him for his amusement a favorite gerfalcon of the queen. In the course of his rambles, seeing a bird rising from a thicket, he unhooded the hawk and let him fly. The falcon towered high in the air, made a swoop at his quarry, but missing it, soared away, regardless of the calls of the page. The latter followed the truant bird with his eye, in its capricious flight, until he saw it alight upon the battlements of a remote and lonely tower, in the outer wall of the Alhambra, built on the edge of a ravine that separated the royal fortress from the grounds of the Generalife. It was in fact the "Tower of the Princesses."

The page descended into the ravine and approached the tower, but it had no entrance from the glen, and its lofty height rendered any attempt to scale it fruitless. Seeking one of the gates of the fortress, therefore, he made a wide circuit to that side of the tower facing within the walls.

A small garden, enclosed by a trellis-work of reeds overhung with myrtle, lay before the tower. Opening a wicket, the page passed between beds of flowers and thickets of roses to the door. It was closed and bolted. A crevice in the door gave him a peep into the interior. There was a small Moorish hall with fretted walls, light marble columns, and an alabaster fountain surrounded with flowers. In the centre hung a gilt cage containing a singing-bird; beneath it, on a chair, lay a tortoise-shell cat among reels of silk and other articles of female labor, and a guitar decorated with ribbons leaned against the fountain.

Ruyz de Alarcon was struck with these traces of female taste and elegance in a lonely and, as he had supposed, deserted tower. They reminded him of the tales of enchanted halls current in the Alhambra; and the tortoise-shell cat might be some spell-bound princess.

He knocked gently at the door. A beautiful face peeped out from a little window above, but was instantly withdrawn. He waited, expecting that the door would be opened, but he waited in vain; no footstep was to be heard within—all was silent. Had his senses deceived him, or was this beautiful apparition the fairy of the tower? He knocked again, and more loudly. After a little while the beaming face once more peeped forth; it was that of a blooming damsel of fifteen.

The page immediately doffed his plumed bonnet, and entreated in the most courteous accents to be permitted to ascend the tower in pursuit of his falcon.

"I dare not open the door, Señor," replied the little damsel, blushing, "my aunt has forbidden it."

"I do beseech you, fair maid—it is the favorite falcon of the queen. I dare not return to the palace without it."

"Are you then one of the cavaliers of the court?"

"I am, fair maid; but I shall lose the queen's favor and my place, if I lose this hawk."

"*Santa Maria!* It is against you cavaliers of the court my aunt has charged me especially to bar the door."

"Against wicked cavaliers doubtless, but I am none of these, but a simple, harmless page, who will be ruined and undone if you deny me this small request."

The heart of the little damsel was touched by the distress of the page. It was a thousand pities he should be ruined for the want of so trifling a boon. Surely too he could not be one of those dangerous beings whom her aunt had described as a species of cannibal, ever on the prowl to make prey of thoughtless damsels; he was gentle and modest, and stood so entreatingly with cap in hand, and looked so charming.

The sly page saw that the garrison began to waver, and redoubled his entreaties in such moving terms that it was not in the nature of mortal maiden to deny him; so the blushing little warden of the tower descended, and opened the door with a trembling hand, and if the page had been charmed by a mere glimpse of her countenance from the window, he was ravished by the full-length portrait now revealed to him.

Her Andalusian bodice and trim *basquiña* set off the round but delicate symmetry of her form, which was as yet scarce verging into womanhood. Her glossy hair was parted on her forehead with scrupulous exactness, and decorated with a fresh-plucked rose, according to the universal custom of the country. It is true her complexion was tinged by the ardor of a southern sun, but it served to give richness to the mantling bloom of her cheek, and to heighten the lustre of her melting eyes.

Ruyz de Alarcon beheld all this with a single glance, for it became him not to tarry; he merely murmured his acknowledgments, and then bounded lightly up the spiral staircase in quest of his falcon.

He soon returned with the truant bird upon his fist. The damsel, in the meantime, had seated herself by the fountain in the hall, and was winding silk; but in her agitation she let fall the reel upon the pavement. The page sprang and picked it up, then dropping gracefully on one knee, presented it to her; but, seizing the hand extended to receive it, imprinted on it a kiss more fervent and devout than he had ever imprinted on the fair hand of his sovereign.

"*Ave Maria, Señor!*" exclaimed the damsel, blushing still

deeper with confusion and surprise, for never before had she
received such a salutation.

The modest page made a thousand apologies, assuring her
it was the way at court of expressing the most profound
homage and respect.

Her anger, if anger she felt, was easily pacified, but her
agitation and embarrassment continued, and she sat blushing
deeper and deeper, with her eyes cast down upon her work,
entangling the silk which she attempted to wind.

The cunning page saw the confusion in the opposite camp,
and would fain have profited by it, but the fine speeches he
would have uttered died upon his lips; his attempts at gal-
lantry were awkward and ineffectual; and to his surprise, the
adroit page, who had figured with such grace and effrontery
among the most knowing and experienced ladies of the court,
found himself awed and abashed in the presence of a simple
damsel of fifteen.

In fact, the artless maiden, in her own modesty and innocence, had guardians more effectual than the bolts and bars
prescribed by her vigilant aunt. Still, where is the female
bosom proof against the first whisperings of love? The little
damsel, with all her artlessness, instinctively comprehended
all that the faltering tongue of the page failed to express, and
her heart was fluttered at beholding, for the first time, a lover
at her feet—and such a lover!

The diffidence of the page, though genuine, was short-
lived, and he was recovering his usual ease and confidence,
when a shrill voice was heard at a distance.

"My aunt is returning from mass!" cried the damsel in
affright; "I pray you, Señor, depart."

"Not until you grant me that rose from your hair as a
remembrance."

She hastily untwisted the rose from her raven locks. "Take
it," cried she, agitated and blushing, "but pray begone."

The page took the rose, and at the same time covered with
kisses the fair hand that gave it. Then, placing the flower in
his bonnet, and taking the falcon upon his fist, he bounded
off through the garden, bearing away with him the heart of
the gentle Jacinta.

When the vigilant aunt arrived at the tower, she remarked

the agitation of her niece, and an air of confusion in the hall; but a word of explanation sufficed. "A gerfalcon had pursued his prey into the hall."

"Mercy on us! to think of a falcon flying into the tower. Did ever one hear of so saucy a hawk? Why, the very bird in the cage is not safe!"

The vigilant Fredegonda was one of the most wary of ancient spinsters. She had a becoming terror and distrust of what she denominated "the opposite sex," which had gradually increased through a long life of celibacy. Not that the good lady had ever suffered from their wiles, nature having set up a safeguard in her face that forbade all trespass upon her premises; but ladies who have least cause to fear for themselves are most ready to keep a watch over their more tempting neighbors.

The niece was the orphan of an officer who had fallen in the wars. She had been educated in a convent, and had recently been transferred from her sacred asylum to the immediate guardianship of her aunt, under whose overshadowing care she vegetated in obscurity, like an opening rose blooming beneath a brier. Nor indeed is this comparison entirely accidental; for, to tell the truth, her fresh and dawning beauty had caught the public eye, even in her seclusion, and, with that poetical turn common to the people of Andalusia, the peasantry of the neighborhood had given her the appellation of "the Rose of the Alhambra."

The wary aunt continued to keep a faithful watch over her tempting little niece as long as the court continued at Granada, and flattered herself that her vigilance had been successful. It is true the good lady was now and then discomposed by the tinkling of guitars and chanting of love-ditties from the moonlit groves beneath the tower; but she would exhort her niece to shut her ears against such idle minstrelsy, assuring her that it was one of the arts of the opposite sex, by which simple maids were often lured to their undoing. Alas! what chance with a simple maid has a dry lecture against a moonlight serenade?

At length King Philip cut short his sojourn at Granada, and suddenly departed with all his train. The vigilant Fredegonda watched the royal pageant as it issued forth from the Gate of Justice and descended the great avenue leading to the city. When the last banner disappeared from her sight, she returned exulting to her tower, for all her cares were over. To her surprise, a light Arabian steed pawed the ground at the wicket-gate of the garden—to her horror she saw through the thickets of roses a youth in gayly embroidered dress, at the feet of her niece. At the sounds of her footsteps he gave a tender adieu, bounded lightly over the barrier of reeds and myrtles, sprang upon his horse, and was out of sight in an instant.

The tender Jacinta, in the agony of her grief, lost all thought of her aunt's displeasure. Throwing herself into her arms, she broke forth into sobs and tears.

"*Ay de mi!*" cried she; "he's gone! he's gone! and I shall never see him more!"

"Gone!—who is gone?—what youth is that I saw at your feet?"

"A queen's page, aunt, who came to bid me farewell."

"A queen's page, child!" echoed the vigilant Fredegonda, faintly, "and when did you become acquainted with the queen's page?"

"The morning that the gerfalcon came into the tower. It was the queen's gerfalcon, and he came in pursuit of it."

"Ah silly, silly girl! know that there are no gerfalcons half so dangerous as these young prankling pages, and it is precisely such simple birds as thee that they pounce upon."

The aunt was at first indignant at learning that in despite of her boasted vigilance, a tender intercourse had been carried on by the youthful lovers, almost beneath her eye; but when she found that her simple-hearted niece, though thus exposed, without the protection of bolt or bar, to all the machinations of the opposite sex, had come forth unsinged from the fiery ordeal, she consoled herself with the persuasion that it was owing to the chaste and cautious maxims in which she had, as it were, steeped her to the very lips.

While the aunt laid this soothing unction to her pride, the niece treasured up the oft-repeated vows of fidelity of the page. But what is the love of restless, roving man? A vagrant stream that dallies for a time with each flower upon its bank, then passes on, and leaves them all in tears.

Days, weeks, months elapsed, and nothing more was heard of the page. The pomegranate ripened, the vine yielded up its fruit, the autumnal rains descended in torrents from the mountains; the Sierra Nevada became covered with a snowy mantle, and wintry blasts howled through the halls of the Alhambra—still he came not. The winter passed away. Again the genial spring burst forth with song and blossom and balmy zephyr; the snows melted from the mountains, until none remained but on the lofty summit of Nevada, glistening through the sultry summer air. Still nothing was heard of the forgetful page.

In the meantime the poor little Jacinta grew pale and thoughtful. Her former occupations and amusements were abandoned, her silk lay entangled, her guitar unstrung, her flowers were neglected, the notes of her bird unheeded, and her eyes, once so bright, were dimmed with secret weeping. If any solitude could be devised to foster the passion of a love-lorn damsel it would be such a place as the Alhambra, where everything seems disposed to produce tender and romantic reveries. It is a very paradise for lovers; how hard then to be alone in such a paradise—and not merely alone, but forsaken!

"Alas, silly child!" would the staid and immaculate Fredegonda say, when she found her niece in one of her desponding moods—"did I not warn thee against the wiles and deceptions of these men? What couldst thou expect, too, from one of a haughty and aspiring family—thou an orphan, the descendant of a fallen and impoverished line? Be assured, if the youth were true, his father, who is one of the proudest nobles about the court, would prohibit his union with one so humble and portionless as thou. Pluck up thy resolution therefore, and drive these idle notions from thy mind."

The words of the immaculate Fredegonda only served to increase the melancholy of her niece, but she sought to indulge it in private. At a late hour one midsummer night, after her aunt had retired to rest, she remained alone in the hall of the tower, seated beside the alabaster fountain. It was here that the faithless page had first knelt and kissed her hand; it was here that he had often vowed eternal fidelity. The poor little damsel's heart was overladen with sad and tender recollections, her tears began to flow, and slowly fell drop by drop into the fountain. By degrees the crystal water became agitated, and—bubble—bubble—bubble—boiled up and was tossed about, until a female figure, richly clad in Moorish robes, slowly rose to view.

Jacinta was so frightened that she fled from the hall and did not venture to return. The next morning she related what she had seen to her aunt, but the good lady treated it as a fantasy of her troubled mind, or supposed she had fallen asleep and dreamt beside the fountain. "Thou hast been thinking of the story of the three Moorish princesses that once inhabited this tower," continued she, "and it has entered into thy dreams."

"What story, aunt? I know nothing of it."

"Thou hast certainly heard of the three princesses, Zayda, Zorayda, and Zorahayda, who were confined in this tower by the king their father, and agreed to fly with three Christian cavaliers. The two first accomplished their escape, but the third failed in her resolution, and, it is said, died in this tower."

"I now recollect to have heard of it," said Jacinta, "and to have wept over the fate of the gentle Zorahayda."

"Thou mayest well weep over her fate," continued the aunt, "for the lover of Zorahayda was thy ancestor. He long bemoaned his Moorish love; but time cured him of his grief, and he married a Spanish lady, from whom thou art descended."

Jacinta ruminated over these words. "That which I have seen is no fantasy of the brain," said she to herself, "I am confident. If indeed it be the spirit of the gentle Zorahayda, which I have heard lingers about this tower, of what should I be afraid? I'll watch by the fountain to-night—perhaps the visit will be repeated."

Towards midnight, when everything was quiet, she again took her seat in the hall. As the bell in the distant watchtower of the Alhambra struck the midnight hour, the fountain was again agitated; and bubble—bubble—bubble—it tossed about the waters until the Moorish female again rose to view. She was young and beautiful; her dress was rich with jewels, and in her hand she held a silver lute. Jacinta trembled and was faint, but was reassured by the soft and plaintive voice of the apparition, and the sweet expression of her pale, melancholy countenance.

"Daughter of mortality," said she, "what aileth thee? Why do thy tears trouble my fountain, and thy sighs and plaints disturb the quiet watches of the night?"

"I weep because of the faithlessness of man, and I bemoan my solitary and forsaken state."

"Take comfort; thy sorrows may yet have an end. Thou beholdest a Moorish princess, who, like thee, was unhappy in her love. A Christian knight, thy ancestor, won my heart, and would have borne me to his native land and to the bosom of his church. I was a convert in my heart, but I lacked courage equal to my faith, and lingered till too late. For this the evil genii are permitted to have power over me, and I remain enchanted in this tower until some pure Christian will deign to break the magic spell. Wilt thou undertake the task?"

"I will," replied the damsel, trembling.

"Come hither, then, and fear not; dip thy hand in the fountain, sprinkle the water over me, and baptize me after the manner of thy faith; so shall the enchantment be dispelled, and my troubled spirit have repose."

The damsel advanced with faltering steps, dipped her hand in the fountain, collected water in the palm, and sprinkled it over the pale face of the phantom.

The latter smiled with ineffable benignity. She dropped her silver lute at the feet of Jacinta, crossed her white arms upon her bosom, and melted from sight, so that it seemed merely as if a shower of dewdrops had fallen into the fountain.

Jacinta retired from the hall filled with awe and wonder. She scarcely closed her eyes that night; but when she awoke at daybreak out of a troubled slumber, the whole appeared to her like a distempered dream. On descending into the hall, however, the truth of the vision was established, for beside the fountain she beheld the silver lute glittering in the morning sunshine.

She hastened to her aunt, to relate all that had befallen her, and called her to behold the lute as a testimonial of the reality of her story. If the good lady had any lingering doubts, they were removed when Jacinta touched the instrument, for she drew forth such ravishing tones as to thaw even the frigid bosom of the immaculate Fredegonda, that region of eternal winter, into a genial flow. Nothing but supernatural melody could have produced such an effect.

The extraordinary power of the lute became every day more and more apparent. The wayfarer passing by the tower was detained, and, as it were, spellbound in breathless ecstasy. The very birds gathered in the neighboring trees, and hushing their own strains, listened in charmed silence.

Rumor soon spread the news abroad. The inhabitants of Granada thronged to the Alhambra to catch a few notes of the transcendent music that floated about the Tower of Las Infantas.

The lovely little minstrel was at length drawn forth from her retreat. The rich and powerful of the land contended who should entertain and do honor to her; or rather, who should secure the charms of her lute to draw fashionable throngs to their saloons. Wherever she went her vigilant aunt kept a dragon watch at her elbow, awing the throngs of impassioned admirers who hung in raptures on her strains. The report of her wonderful powers spread from city to city. Malaga, Seville, Cordova, all became successively mad on the theme; nothing was talked of throughout Andalusia but the beautiful minstrel of the Alhambra. How could it be otherwise among a people so musical and gallant as the Andalusians, when the lute was magical in its powers, and the minstrel inspired by love!

While all Andalusia was thus music mad, a different mood prevailed at the court of Spain. Philip V, as is well known, was a miserable hypochondriac, and subject to all kinds of fancies. Sometimes he would keep to his bed for weeks together, groaning under imaginary complaints. At other times he would insist upon abdicating his throne, to the great annoyance of his royal spouse, who had a strong relish for the splendors of a court and the glories of a crown, and guided the sceptre of her imbecile lord with an expert and steady hand.

Nothing was found to be so efficacious in dispelling the royal megrims as the power of music; the queen took care, therefore, to have the best performers, both vocal and instrumental, at hand, and retained the famous Italian singer Farinelli about the court as a kind of royal physician.

At the moment we treat of, however, a freak had come over the mind of this sapient and illustrious Bourbon that surpassed all former vagaries. After a long spell of imaginary illness, which set all the strains of Farinelli and the consultations of a whole orchestra of court fiddlers at defiance, the monarch fairly, in idea, gave up the ghost, and considered himself absolutely dead.

This would have been harmless enough, and even convenient both to his queen and courtiers, had he been content to remain in the quietude befitting a dead man; but to their annoyance he insisted upon having the funeral ceremonies performed over him, and, to their inexpressible perplexity, began to grow impatient, and to revile bitterly at them for negligence and disrespect, in leaving him unburied. What was to be done? To disobey the king's positive commands was monstrous in the eyes of the obsequious courtiers of a punctilious court—but to obey him, and bury him alive, would be downright regicide!

In the midst of this fearful dilemma a rumor reached the court of the female minstrel who was turning the brains of all Andalusia. The queen despatched missions in all haste to summon her to St. Ildefonso, where the court at that time resided.

Within a few days, as the queen with her maids of honor was walking in those stately gardens, intended, with their avenues and terraces and fountains, to eclipse the glories of Versailles, the far-famed minstrel was conducted into her presence. The imperial Elizabetta gazed with surprise at the youthful and unpretending appearance of the little being that had set the world madding. She was in her picturesque Andalusian dress, her silver lute in hand, and stood with modest and downcast eyes, but with a simplicity and freshness of beauty that still bespoke her "the Rose of the Alhambra."

As usual she was accompanied by the ever-vigilant Fredegonda, who gave the whole history of her parentage and descent to the inquiring queen. If the stately Elizabetta had been interested by the appearance of Jacinta, she was still more pleased when she learnt that she was of a meritorious though impoverished line, and that her father had bravely fallen in the service of the crown. "If thy powers equal thy renown," said she, "and thou canst cast forth this evil spirit that possesses thy sovereign, thy fortunes shall henceforth be my care, and honors and wealth attend thee."

Impatient to make trial of her skill, she led the way at once to the apartment of the moody monarch.

Jacinta followed with downcast eyes through files of guards and crowds of courtiers. They arrived at length at a great chamber hung with black. The windows were closed to exclude the light of day; a number of yellow wax tapers in silver sconces diffused a lugubrious light, and dimly revealed the figures of mutes in mourning dresses, and courtiers who glided about with noiseless step and woebegone visage. In the midst of a funeral bed or bier, his hands folded on his breast, and the tip of his nose just visible, lay extended this would-be-buried monarch.

The queen entered the chamber in silence, and pointing to a footstool in an obscure corner, beckoned to Jacinta to sit down and commence.

At first she touched her lute with a faltering hand, but gathering confidence and animation as she proceeded, drew forth such soft aërial harmony, that all present could scarce believe it mortal. As to the monarch, who had already considered himself in the world of spirits, he set it down for some angelic melody or the music of the spheres. By degrees the theme was varied, and the voice of the minstrel accompanied the instrument. She poured forth one of the legendary ballads treating of the ancient glories of the Alhambra and the achievements of the Moors. Her whole soul entered into the theme, for with the recollections of the Alhambra was associated the story of her love. The funeral-chamber resounded with the animating strain. It entered into the gloomy heart of the monarch. He raised his head and gazed around: he sat up on his couch, his eye began to kindle—at length, leaping upon the floor, he called for sword and buckler.

The triumph of music, or rather of the enchanted lute, was complete; the demon of melancholy was cast forth; and, as it were, a dead man brought to life. The windows of the apartment were thrown open; the glorious effulgence of

Spanish sunshine burst into the late lugubrious chamber; all eyes sought the lovely enchantress, but the lute had fallen from her hand, she had sunk upon the earth, and the next moment was clasped to the bosom of Ruyz de Alarcon.

The nuptials of the happy couple were celebrated soon afterwards with great splendor, and the Rose of the Alhambra became the ornament and delight of the court. "But hold— not so fast"—I hear the reader exclaim; "this is jumping to the end of a story at a furious rate! First let us know how Ruyz de Alarcon managed to account to Jacinta for his long neglect?" Nothing more easy; the venerable, time-honored excuse, the opposition to his wishes by a proud, pragmatical old father; besides, young people who really like one another soon come to an amicable understanding, and bury all past grievances when once they meet.

But how was the proud, pragmatical old father reconciled to the match?

Oh! as to that, his scruples were easily overcome by a word or two from the queen; especially as dignities and rewards were showered upon the blooming favorite of royalty. Besides, the lute of Jacinta, you know, possessed a magic power, and could control the most stubborn head and hardest breast.

And what came of the enchanted lute?

Oh, that is the most curious matter of all, and plainly proves the truth of the whole story. That lute remained for some time in the family, but was purloined and carried off, as was supposed, by the great singer Farinelli, in pure jealousy. At his death it passed into other hands in Italy, who were ignorant of its mystic powers, and melting down the silver, transferred the strings to an old Cremona fiddle. The strings still retain something of their magic virtues. A word in the reader's ear, but let it go no further: that fiddle is now bewitching the whole world—it is the fiddle of Paganini!

The Legend of the
Enchanted Soldier

EVERYBODY has heard of the Cave of St. Cyprian at
Salamanca, where in old times judicial astronomy, necromancy, chiromancy, and other dark and damnable
arts were secretly taught by an ancient sacristan; or, as some
will have it, by the Devil himself, in that disguise. The cave
has long been shut up and the very site of it forgotten; though,
according to tradition, the entrance was somewhere about
where the stone cross stands in the small square of the seminary of Carvajal; and this tradition appears in some degree
corroborated by the circumstances of the following story.

There was at one time a student of Salamanca, Don Vicente
by name, of that merry but mendicant class, who set out on
the road to learning without a penny in pouch for the journey,
and who, during college vacations, beg from town to town
and village to village to raise funds to enable them to pursue
their studies through the ensuing term. He was now about
to set forth on his wanderings; and being somewhat musical,
slung on his back a guitar with which to amuse the villagers,
and pay for a meal or a night's lodging.

As he passed by the stone cross in the seminary square,
he pulled off his hat and made a short invocation to St. Cyprian, for good luck; when casting his eyes upon the earth,

he perceived something glitter at the foot of the cross. On picking it up, it proved to be a seal-ring of mixed metal, in which gold and silver appeared to be blended. The seal bore as a device two triangles crossing each other, so as to form a star. This device is said to be a cabalistic sign, invented by King Solomon the Wise, and of mighty power in all cases of enchantment; but the honest student, being neither sage nor conjurer, knew nothing of the matter. He took the ring as a present from St. Cyprian in reward of his prayer; slipped it on his finger, made a bow to the cross, and strumming his guitar, set off merrily on his wandering.

The life of a mendicant student in Spain is not the most miserable in the world, especially if he has any talent at making himself agreeable. He rambles at large from village to village, and city to city, wherever curiosity or caprice may conduct him. The country curates, who, for the most part, have been mendicant students in their time, give him shelter for the night, and a comfortable meal, and often enrich him with several *quartos* or half-pence in the morning. As he presents himself from door to door in the streets of the cities, he meets with no harsh rebuff, no chilling contempt, for there is no disgrace attending his mendacity, many of the most learned men in Spain having commenced their career in this manner; but if, like the student in question, he is a good-looking varlet and a merry companion, and, above all, if he can play the guitar, he is sure of a hearty welcome among the peasants, and smiles and favors from their wives and daughters.

In this way, then, did our ragged and musical son of learning make his way over half the kingdom; with the fixed determination to visit the famous city of Granada before his return. Sometimes he was gathered for the night into the fold of some village pastor; sometimes he was sheltered under the humble but hospitable roof of the peasant. Seated at the cottage-door with his guitar, he delighted the simple folk with his ditties; or striking up a *fandango* or *bolero,* set the brown country lads and lasses dancing in the mellow twilight. In the morning he departed with kind words from host and hostess, and kind looks and, peradventure, a squeeze of the hand from the daughter.

At length he arrived at the great object of his musical vagabondizing, the far-famed city of Granada, and hailed with wonder and delight its Moorish towers, its lovely *vega,* and its snowy mountains glistening through a summer atmosphere. It is needless to say with what eager curiosity he entered its gates and wandered through its streets, and gazed upon its Oriental monuments. Every female face peering through a window or beaming from a balcony was to him a Zorayda or a Zelinda, nor could he meet a stately dame on the Alameda but he was ready to fancy her a Moorish princess, and to spread his student's robe beneath her feet.

His musical talent, his happy humor, his youth, and his good looks won him a universal welcome in spite of his ragged robes, and for several days he led a gay life in the old Moorish capital and its environs. One of his occasional haunts was the fountain of Avellanos, in the valley of Darro. It is one of the popular resorts of Granada, and has been so since the days of the Moors; and here the student had an opportunity of pursuing his studies of female beauty; a branch of study to which he was a little prone.

Here he would take his seat with his guitar, improvise love-ditties to admiring groups of *majos* and *majas,* or prompt with his music the ever-ready dance. He was thus engaged one evening when he beheld a padre of the church advancing, at whose approach every one touched the hat. He was evidently a man of consequence; he certainly was a mirror of good if not of holy living; robust and rosy-faced, and breathing at every pore with the warmth of the weather and the exercise of the walk. As he passed along he would every now and then draw a *maravedi* out of his pocket and bestow it on a beggar with an air of signal beneficence. "Ah, the blessed father!" would be the cry; "long life to him, and may he soon be a bishop!"

To aid his steps in ascending the hill he leaned gently now and then on the arm of a handmaid, evidently the pet-lamb of this kindest of pastors. Ah, such a damsel! Andalus from head to foot; from the rose in her hair, to the fairy shoe and lacework stocking; Andalus in every movement; in every undulation of the body:—ripe, melting Andalus!—But then so modest!—so shy!—ever, with downcast eyes, listening to the words of the padre; or, if by chance she let flash a side glance, it was suddenly checked and her eyes once more cast to the ground.

The good padre looked benignantly on the company about the fountain, and took his seat with some emphasis on a stone bench, while the handmaid hastened to bring him a glass of sparkling water. He sipped it deliberately and with a relish, tempering it with one of those spongy pieces of frosted eggs and sugar so dear to Spanish epicures, and on returning the glass to the hand of the damsel pinched her cheek with infinite loving-kindness.

"Ah, the good pastor!" whispered the student to himself; "what a happiness would it be to be gathered into his fold with such a pet-lamb for a companion!"

But no such good fare was likely to befall him. In vain he

essayed those powers of pleasing which he had found so irresistible with country curates and country lasses. Never had he touched his guitar with such skill; never had he poured forth more soul-moving ditties, but he had no longer a country curate or country lass to deal with. The worthy priest evidently did not relish music, and the modest damsel never raised her eyes from the ground. They remained but a short time at the fountain; the good padre hastened their return to Granada. The damsel gave the student one shy glance in retiring; but it plucked the heart out of his bosom!

He inquired about them after they had gone. Padre Tomás was one of the saints of Granada, a model of regularity; punctual in his hour of rising; his hour of taking a *paseo* for an appetite; his hours of eating; his hour of taking his *siesta*; his hour of playing his game of *tresillo,* of an evening, with some of the dames of the cathedral circle; his hour of supping, and his hour of retiring to rest, to gather fresh strength for another day's round of similar duties. He had an easy sleek mule for his riding; a matronly housekeeper skilled in preparing tidbits for his table; and the pet-lamb, to smooth his pillow at night and bring him his chocolate in the morning.

Adieu now to the gay, thoughtless life of the student; the side-glance of the bright eye had been the undoing of him. Day and night he could not get the image of this most modest damsel out of his mind. He sought the mansion of the padre. Alas! it was above the class of houses accessible to a strolling student like himself. The worthy padre had no sympathy with him; he had never been *estudiante sopista,* obliged to sing for his supper. He blockaded the house by day, catching a glance of the damsel now and then as she appeared at a casement; but these glances only fed his flame without encouraging his hope. He serenaded her balcony at night, and at one time was flattered by the appearance of something white at a window. Alas, it was only the night cap of the padre.

Never was lover more devoted; never damsel more shy; the poor student was reduced to despair. At length arrived the eve of St. John, when the lower classes of Granada swarm into the country, dance away the afternoon, and pass midsummer's night on the banks of the Darro and the Xenil. Happy are they who on this eventful night can wash their faces in those waters just as the cathedral bell tells midnight, for at that precise moment they have a beautifying power. The student, having nothing to do, suffered himself to be carried away by the holiday-seeking throng until he found himself in the narrow valley of the Darro, below the lofty hill and ruddy towers of the Alhambra. The dry bed of the river; the rocks which border it; the terraced gardens which overhang it, were alive with variegated groups, dancing under the vines and fig-trees to the sound of the guitar and castanets.

The student remained for some time in doleful dumps, leaning against one of the huge misshapen stone pomegranates which adorn the ends of the little bridge over the Darro. He cast a wistful glance upon the merry scene, where every cavalier had his dame; or, to speak more appropriately, every Jack his Jill; sighed at his own solitary state, a victim to the black eye of the most unapproachable of damsels, and repined at his ragged garb, which seemed to shut the gate of hope against him.

By degrees his attention was attracted to a neighbor equally solitary with himself. This was a tall soldier, of a stern aspect and grizzled beard, who seemed posted as a sentry at the opposite pomegranate. His face was bronzed by time; he was arrayed in ancient Spanish armor, with buckler and lance, and stood immovable as a statue. What surprised the student was, that though thus strangely equipped, he was totally unnoticed by the passing throng, albeit that many almost brushed against him.

"This is a city of old time peculiarities," thought the student, "and doubtless this is one of them with which the inhabitants are too familiar to be surprised." His own curiosity, however, was awakened, and being of a social disposition, he accosted the soldier.

"A rare old suit of armor that which you wear, comrade. May I ask what corps you belong to?"

The soldier gasped out a reply from a pair of jaws which seemed to have rusted on their hinges.

"The royal guard of Ferdinand and Isabella."

"*Santa Maria!* Why, it is three centuries since that corps was in service."

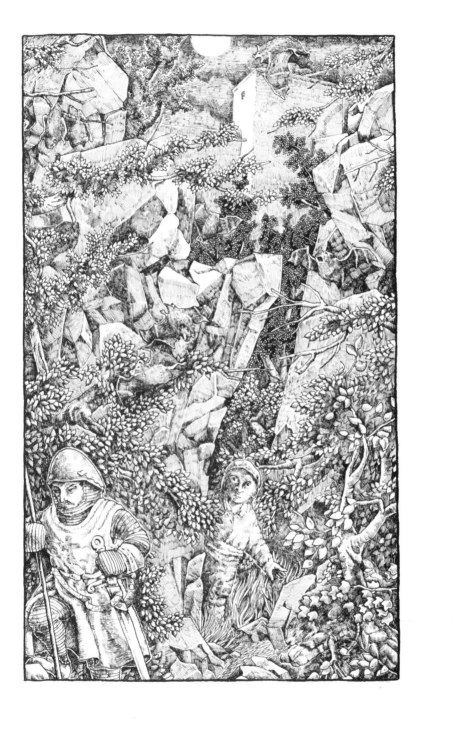

"And for three centuries have I been mounting guard. Now I trust my tour of duty draws to a close. Dost thou desire fortune?"

The student held up his tattered cloak in reply.

"I understand thee. If thou hast faith and courage, follow me, and thy fortune is made."

"Softly, comrade, to follow thee would require small courage in one who has nothing to lose but life and an old guitar, neither of much value; but my faith is of a different matter, and not to be put in temptation. If it be any criminal act by which I am to mend my fortune, think not my ragged coat will make me undertake it."

The soldier turned on him a look of high displeasure. "My sword," said he, "has never been drawn but in the cause of the faith and the throne. I am a *Cristiano viejo*; trust in me and fear no evil."

The student followed him wondering. He observed that no one heeded their conversation, and that the soldier made his way through the various groups of idlers unnoticed, as if invisible.

Crossing the bridge, the soldier led the way by a narrow and steep path past a Moorish mill and aqueduct, and up the ravine which separates the domains of the Generalife from those of the Alhambra. The last ray of the sun shone upon the red battlements of the latter, which beetled far above; and the convent bells were proclaiming the festival of the ensuing day. The ravine was overshadowed by fig-trees, vines, and myrtles, and the outer towers and walls of the fortress. It was dark and lonely, and the twilight-loving bats began to flit about. At length the soldier halted at a remote and ruined tower, apparently intended to guard a Moorish aqueduct. He struck the foundation with the but-end of his spear. A rumbling sound was heard, and the solid stones yawned apart, leaving an opening as wide as a door.

"Enter in the name of the Holy Trinity," said the soldier, "and fear nothing." The student's heart quaked, but he made the sign of the cross, muttered his *Ave Maria,* and followed his mysterious guide into a deep vault cut out of the solid rock under the tower, and covered with Arabic inscriptions. The soldier pointed to a stone seat hewn along one side of the vault. "Behold," said he, "my couch for three hundred years." The bewildered student tried to force a joke. "By the blessed St. Anthony," said he, "but you must have slept soundly, considering the hardness of your couch."

"On the contrary, sleep has been a stranger to these eyes, incessant watchfulness has been my doom. Listen to my lot. I was one of the royal guards of Ferdinand and Isabella; but was taken prisoner by the Moors in one of their sorties, and confined a captive in this tower. When preparations were made to surrender the fortress to the Christian sovereigns, I was prevailed upon by an Alfaqui, a Moorish priest, to aid him in secreting some of the treasures of Boabdil in this vault. I was justly punished for my fault. The Alfaqui was an African necromancer, and by his infernal arts, cast a spell upon me—to guard his treasures. Something must have happened to him, for he never returned, and here have I remained ever since, buried alive. Years and years have rolled away; earthquakes have shaken this hill; I have heard stone by stone of the tower above tumbling to the ground, in the natural operation of time; but the spellbound walls of this vault set both time and earthquakes at defiance.

"Once every hundred years, on the festival of St. John, the enchantment ceases to have thorough sway; I am permitted to go forth and post myself upon the bridge of the Darro, where you met me, waiting until some one shall arrive who may have power to break this magic spell. I have hitherto mounted guard there in vain. I walk as in a cloud, concealed from mortal sight. You are the first to accost me for now three hundred years. I behold the reason. I see on your finger the seal-ring of Solomon the Wise, which is proof against all enchantment. With you it remains to deliver me from this awful dungeon, or to leave me to keep guard for another hundred years."

The student listened to this tale in mute wonderment. He had heard many tales of treasures shut up under strong enchantment in the vaults of the Alhambra, but had treated them as fables. He now felt the value of the seal-ring, which had, in a manner, been given to him by St. Cyprian. Still, though armed by so potent a talisman, it was an awful thing to find himself *tête-à-tête* in such a place wtih an enchanted soldier, who, according to the laws of nature, ought to have been quietly in his grave for nearly three centuries.

A personage of this kind, however, was quite out of the ordinary run, and not to be trifled with, and he assured him he might rely upon his friendship and good-will to do everything in his power for his deliverance.

"I trust to a motive more powerful than friendship," said the soldier.

He pointed to a ponderous iron coffer, secured by locks inscribed with Arabic characters. "That coffer," said he, "contains countless treasure in gold and jewels and precious stones. Break the magic spell by which I am enthralled, and one half of this treasure shall be thine."

"But how am I to do it?"

"The aid of a Christian priest and a Christian maid is necessary. The priest to exorcise the powers of darkness; the damsel to touch this chest with the seal of Solomon. This must be done at night. But have a care. This is solemn work, and not to be effected by the carnal-minded. The priest must be a *Cristiano viejo,* a model of sanctity; and must mortify the flesh, before he comes here, by a rigorous fast of four-and-twenty hours: and as to the maiden, she must be above reproach, and proof against temptation. Linger not in finding such aid. In three days my furlough is at an end; if not delivered before midnight of the third, I shall have to mount guard for another century."

"Fear not," said the student, "I have in my eye the very priest and damsel you describe; but how am I to regain admission to this tower?"

"The seal of Solomon will open the way for thee."

The student issued forth from the tower much more gayly than he had entered. The wall closed behind him, and remained solid as before.

The next morning he repaired boldly to the mansion of the priest, no longer a poor strolling student, thrumming his way with a guitar; but an ambassador from the shadowy world, with enchanted treasures to bestow. No particulars are told of his negotiation, excepting that the zeal of the worthy priest was easily kindled at the idea of rescuing an old soldier of the faith and a strong-box of King Chico from the very clutches of Satan; and then what alms might be dispensed, what churches built, and how many poor relatives enriched with the Moorish treasure!

As to the immaculate handmaid, she was ready to lend her hand, which was all that was required, to the pious work; and if a shy glance now and then might be believed, the ambassador began to find favor in her modest eyes.

The greatest difficulty, however, was the fast to which the good padre had to subject himself. Twice he attempted it, and twice the flesh was too strong for the spirit. It was only on the third day that he was enabled to withstand the temptations of the cupboard; but it was still a question whether he would hold out until the spell was broken.

At a late hour of the night the party groped their way up the ravine by the light of a lantern, and bearing a basket with provisions for exorcising the demon of hunger so soon as the other demons should be laid in the Red Sea.

The seal of Solomon opened their way into the tower. They found the soldier seated on the enchanted strong-box, awaiting their arrival. The exorcism was performed in due style. The damsel advanced and touched the locks of the coffer with the seal of Solomon. The lid flew open; and such treasures of gold and jewels and precious stones as flashed upon the eye!

"Here's cut and come again!" cried the student, exultingly, as he proceeded to cram his pockets.

"Fairly and softly," exclaimed the soldier. "Let us get the coffer out entire, and then divide."

They accordingly went to work with might and main; but it was a difficult task; the chest was enormously heavy, and had been imbedded there for centuries. While they were thus employed the good dominie drew on one side and made a vigorous onslaught on the basket, by way of exorcising the demon of hunger which was raging in his entrails. In a little while a fat capon was devoured, and washed down by a deep potation of Val de peñas; and, by way of grace after meat, he gave a kind-hearted kiss to the pet-lamb who waited on him. It was quietly done in a corner, but the tell-tale walls babbled it forth as if in triumph. Never was chaste salute more awful in its effects. At the sound the soldier gave a great cry of despair; the coffer, which was half raised, fell back in its place and was locked once more. Priest, student, and damsel found themselves outside of the tower, the wall of which closed with a thundering jar. Alas! the good padre had broken his fast too soon!

When recovered from his surprise, the student would have re-entered the tower, but learnt to his dismay that the damsel, in her fright, had let fall the seal of Solomon; it remained within the vault.

In a word, the cathedral bell tolled midnight; the spell was renewed; the soldier was doomed to mount guard for another hundred years, and there he and the treasure remain to this day—and all because the kind-hearted padre kissed his hand-maid. "Ah, father! father!" said the student, shaking his head ruefully, as they returned down the ravine, "I fear there was less of the saint than the sinner in that kiss!"

Thus ends the legend as far as it has been authenticated. There is a tradition, however, that the student had brought off treasure enough in his pocket to set him up in the world; that he prospered in his affairs, that the worthy padre gave him the pet-lamb in marriage, by way of amends for the blunder in the vault; that the immaculate damsel proved a pattern for wives as she had been for handmaids, and bore her husband a numerous progeny; that the first was a wonder; it was born seven months after her marriage, and though a seven-months' boy, was the sturdiest of the flock. The rest were all born in the ordinary course of time.

The story of the enchanted soldier remains one of the popular traditions of Granada, though told in a variety of ways; the common people affirm that he still mounts guard on midsummer eve, beside the gigantic stone pomegranate on the bridge of the Darro; but remains invisible excepting to such lucky mortal as may possess the seal of Solomon.

NOTES TO THE ENCHANTED SOLDIER

Among the ancient superstitions of Spain, were those of the existence of profound caverns in which the magic arts were taught, either by the Devil in person, or some sage devoted to his service. One of the most famous of these caves was at Salamanca. Don Francisco de Torreblanca makes mention of it in the first book of his work on magic, C. 2, No. 4. The Devil was said to play the part of oracle there; giving replies to those who repaired thither to propound fateful questions, as in the celebrated cave of Trophonius. Don Francisco, though he records this story, does not put faith in it; he gives it however as certain, that a sacristan, named Clement Potosi, taught secretly the magic arts in that cave. Padre Feyjoo, who inquired into the matter, reports it as a vulgar belief, that the Devil himself taught those arts there; admitting only seven disciples at a time, one of whom, to be determined by lot, was to be devoted to him body and soul forever. Among one of these sets of students was a young man, son of the Marquis de Villena, on whom, after having accomplished his studies, the lot fell. He succeeded, however, in cheating the Devil, leaving him his shadow instead of his body.

Don Juan de Dios, Professor of Humanities in the university, in the early part of the last century, gives the following version of the story, extracted, as he says, from an ancient manuscript. It will be perceived he has marred the supernatural part of the tale, and ejected the Devil from it altogether.

As to the fable of the cave of San Cyprian, says he, all that we have been able to verify is, that where the stone cross stands, in the small square or place called by the name of the Seminary of Carvajal, there was the parochial church of San Cyprian. A descent of twenty steps led down to a subterranean sacristy, spacious and vaulted like a cave. Here a sacristan once taught magic, judicial astrology, geomancy, hydromancy, pyromancy, acromancy, chiromancy, necromancy, etc.

The extract goes on to state that seven students engaged at a time with the sacristan, at a fixed stipend. Lots were cast among them which one of their number should pay for the whole, with the understanding that he on whom the lot fell, if he did not pay promptly, should be detained in a chamber of the sacristy until the funds were forthcoming. This became thenceforth the usual practice.

On one occasion the lot fell on Henry de Villena, son of the marquis of the same name. He having perceived that there had been trick and shuffling in the casting of the lot, and suspecting the sacristan to be cognizant thereof, refused to pay. He was forthwith left in limbo. It so happened, that in a dark corner of the sacristy was a huge jar or earthen reservoir for water, which was cracked and empty. In this the youth contrived to conceal himself. The sacristan returned at night with a servant, bringing lights and a supper. Unlocking the door, they found no one in the vault, and a book of magic lying open on the table. They retreated in dismay, leaving the door open, by which Villena made his escape. The story went about that through magic he had made himself invisible. The reader has now both versions of the story, and may make his choice. I will only observe that the sages of the Alhambra incline to the diabolical one.

This Henry de Villena flourished in the time of Juan II, King of Castile, of whom he was uncle. He became famous for his knowledge of the natural sciences; and hence in that ignorant age was stigmatized as a necromancer. Fernan Perez de Guzman, in his account of distinguished men, gives him credit for great learning, but says he devoted himself to the arts of divination, the interpretation of dreams, of signs, and portents.

At the death of Villena, his library fell into the hands of the king, who was warned that it contained books treating of magic, and not proper to be read. King Juan ordered that they should be transported in carts to the residence of a reverend prelate to be examined. The prelate was less learned than devout. Some of the books treated of mathematics, others of astronomy, with figures and diagrams, and planetary signs; others of chemistry or alchemy, with foreign and mystic words. All these were necromancy in the eyes of the pious prelate, and the books were consigned to the flames, like the library of Don Quixote.

THE SEAL OF SOLOMON—The device consists of two equilateral triangles, interlaced so as to form a star, and surrounded by a circle. According to Arab tradition, when the Most High gave Solomon the choice of blessings, and he chose wisdom, there came from heaven a ring, on which this device was engraven. This mystic talisman was the arcanum of his wisdom, felicity, and grandeur; by this he governed and prospered. In consequence of a temporary lapse from virtue he lost the ring in the sea, and was at once reduced to the level of ordinary men. By penitence and prayer he made his peace with the Deity, was permitted to find his ring again in the belly of a fish, and thus recovered his celestial gifts. That he might not utterly lose them again, he communicated to others the secret of the marvellous ring.

This symbolical seal we are told was sacrilegiously used by the Mohammedan infidels; and before them by the Arabian idolaters, and before them by the Hebrews, for "diabolical enterprises and abominable superstitions." Those who wish to be more thoroughly informed on the subject, will do well to consult the learned Father Athanasius Kirker's treatise on the *Cabala Sarracenica.*

A word more to the curious reader. There are many persons in these sceptical times who affect to deride everything connected with the occult sciences, or black art; who have no faith in the efficacy of conjurations, incantations, or divinations; and who stoutly contend that such things never had existence. To such determined unbelievers the testimony of past ages is as nothing; they require the evidence of their own senses, and deny that such arts and practices have prevailed in days of yore, simply because they meet with no instance of them in the present day. They cannot perceive that, as the world became versed in the natural sciences, the supernatural became superfluous and fell into disuse; and that the hardy inventions of art superseded the mysteries of magic. Still, say the enlightened few, those mystic powers exist, though in a latent state, and untasked by the ingenuity of men. A talisman is still a talisman, possessing all its indwelling and awful properties; though it may have lain dormant for ages at the bottom of the sea, or in the dusty cabinet of the antiquary.

The signet of Solomon the Wise, for instance, is well known to have held potent control over genii, demons, and enchantments; now who will positively assert that the same mystic signet, wherever it may exist, does not at the present moment possess the same marvellous virtues which distinguished it in the olden time? Let those who doubt repair to Salamanca, delve into the cave of San Cyprian, explore its hidden secrets, and decide. As to those who will not be at the pains of such investigation, let them substitute faith for incredulity, and receive with honest credence the foregoing legend.

Legend of Don Munio
Sancho de Hinojosa

IN the cloisters of the ancient Benedictine convent of San Domingo, at Silos, in Castile, are the mouldering yet magnificent monuments of the once powerful and chivalrous family of Hinojosa. Among these reclines the marble figure of a knight, in complete armor, with the hands pressed together, as if in prayer. On one side of his tomb is sculptured in relief a band of Christian cavaliers, capturing a cavalcade of male and female Moors; on the other side, the same cavaliers are represented kneeling before an altar. The tomb, like most of the neighboring monuments, is almost in ruins, and the sculpture is nearly unintelligible, excepting to the keen eye of the antiquary. The story connected with the sepulchre, however, is still preserved in the old Spanish chronicles, and is to the following purport.

In old times, several hundred years ago, there was a noble Castilian cavalier, named Don Munio Sancho de Hinojosa, lord of a border castle, which had stood the brunt of many a Moorish foray. He had seventy horsemen as his household troops, all of the ancient Castilian proof; stark warriors, hard riders, and men of iron; with these he scoured the Moorish lands, and made his name terrible throughout the borders. His castle-hall was covered with banners, cimeters, and Moslem helms, the trophies of his prowess. Don Munio was, moreover, a keen huntsman; and rejoiced in hounds of all kinds, steeds for the chase, and hawks for the towering sport of falconry. When not engaged in warfare his delight was to beat up the neighboring forests; and scarcely ever did he ride forth without hound and horn, a boar-spear in his hand, or hawk upon his fist, and an attendant train of huntsmen.

His wife, Doña Maria Palacin, was of a gentle and timid nature, little fitted to be the spouse of so hardy and adventurous a knight; and many a tear did the poor lady shed, when he sallied forth upon his daring enterprises, and many a prayer did she offer up for his safety.

As this doughty cavalier was one day hunting, he stationed himself in a thicket, on the borders of a green glade of the forest, and dispersed his followers to rouse the game, and drive it toward his stand. He had not been here long, when a cavalcade of Moors, of both sexes, came prankling over the forest-lawn. They were unarmed, and magnificently dressed in robes of tissue and embroidery, rich shawls of India, bracelets and anklets of gold, and jewels that sparkled in the sun.

At the head of this gay cavalcade rode a youthful cavalier,

superior to the rest in dignity and loftiness of demeanor, and in splendor of attire; beside him was a damsel, whose veil, blown aside by the breeze, displayed a face of surpassing beauty, and eyes cast down in maiden modesty, yet beaming with tenderness and joy.

Don Munio thanked his stars for sending him such a prize, and exulted at the thought of bearing home to his wife the glittering spoils of these infidels. Putting his hunting-horn to his lips, he gave a blast that wrung through the forest. His huntsmen came running from all quarters, and the astonished Moors were surrounded and made captives.

The beautiful Moor wrung her hands in despair, and her female attendants uttered the most piercing cries. The young Moorish cavalier alone retained self-possession. He inquired the name of the Christian knight who commanded this troop of horsemen. When told that it was Don Munio Sancho de Hinojosa, his countenance lighted up. Approaching that cavalier, and kissing his hand, "Don Munio Sancho," said he, "I have heard of your fame as a true and valiant knight, terrible in arms, but schooled in the noble virtues of chivalry. Such do I trust to find you. In me you behold Abadil, son of a Moorish Alcalde. I am on the way to celebrate my nuptials with this lady; chance has thrown us in your power, but I confide in your magnanimity. Take all our treasure and jewels; demand what ransom you think proper for our persons, but suffer us not to be insulted nor dishonored."

When the good knight heard this appeal, and beheld the beauty of the youthful pair, his heart was touched with tenderness and courtesy. "God forbid," said he, "that I should disturb such happy nuptials. My prisoners in troth shall ye be, for fifteen days, and immured within my castle, where I claim, as conqueror, the right of celebrating your espousals."

So saying, he despatched one of his fleetest horsemen in advance, to notify Doña Maria Palacin of the coming of this bridal party; while he and his huntsmen escorted the cavalcade, not as captors, but as a guard of honor. As they drew near to the castle, the banners were hung out, and the trumpets sounded from the battlements; and on their nearer approach, the drawbridge was lowered, and Doña Maria came forth to meet them, attended by her ladies and knights, her pages and her minstrels. She took the young bride, Allifra, in her arms, kissed her with the tenderness of a sister, and conducted her into the castle. In the meantime, Don Munio sent forth missives in every direction, and had viands and dainties of all kinds collected from the country round; and the wedding of the Moorish lovers was celebrated with all possible state and festivity. For fifteen days the castle was given up to joy and revelry. There were tiltings and jousts at the ring, and bull-fights, and banquets, and dances to the sound of minstrelsy. When the fifteen days were at an end, he made the bride and bridegroom magnificent presents, and conducted them and their attendants safely beyond the borders. Such, in old times, were the courtesy and generosity of a Spanish cavalier.

Several years after this event, the king of Castile summoned his nobles to assist him in a campaign against the Moors. Don Munio Sancho was among the first to answer to the call, with seventy horsemen, all stanch and well-tried warriors. His wife, Doña Maria, hung about his neck. "Alas, my lord!" exclaimed she, "how often wilt thou tempt thy fate, and when will thy thirst for glory be appeased!"

"One battle more," replied Don Munio, "one battle more, for the honor of Castile, and I here make a vow that, when this is over, I will lay by my sword, and repair with my cavaliers in pilgrimage to the sepulchre of our Lord at Jerusalem." The cavaliers all joined with him in the vow, and Doña Maria felt in some degree soothed in spirit; still, she saw with a heavy heart the departure of her husband, and watched his banner with wistful eyes, until it disappeared among the trees of the forest.

The king of Castile led his army to the plains of Salmanara, where they encountered the Moorish host, near to Ucles. The battle was long and bloody; the Christians repeatedly wavered and were as often rallied by the energy of their commanders. Don Munio was covered with wounds, but refused to leave the field. The Christians at length gave way, and the king was hardly pressed, and in danger of being captured.

Don Munio called upon his cavaliers to follow him to the rescue. "Now is the time," cried he, "to prove your loyalty.

Fall to, like brave men! We fight for the true faith, and if we lose our lives here, we gain a better life hereafter."

Rushing with his men between the king and his pursuers, they checked the latter in their career, and gave time for their monarch to escape; but they fell victims to their loyalty. They fought to the last gasp. Don Munio was singled out by a powerful Moorish knight, but having been wounded in the right arm, he fought to disadvantage, and was slain. The battle being over, the Moor paused to possess himself of the spoils of this redoubtable Christian warrior. When he unlaced the helmet, however, and beheld the countenance of Don Munio, he gave a great cry and smote his breast. "Woe is me!" cried he, "I have slain my benefactor! The flower of knightly virtue! the most magnanimous of cavaliers!"

While the battle had been raging on the plain of Salmanara, Doña Maria Palacin remained in her castle, a prey to the keenest anxiety. Her eyes were ever fixed on the road that led from the country of the Moors, and often she asked the watchman of the tower, "What seest thou?"

One evening, at the shadowy hour of twilight, the warden sounded his horn. "I see," cried he, "a numerous train winding up the valley. There are mingled Moors and Christians. The banner of my lord is in the advance. Joyful tidings!" exclaimed the old seneschal; "my lord returns in triumph, and brings captives!" Then the castle courts rang with shouts of joy; and the standard was displayed, and the trumpets were sounded, and the drawbridge was lowered, and Doña Maria went forth wtih her ladies, and her knights, and her pages, and her minstrels, to welcome her lord from the wars. But as the train drew nigh, she beheld a sumptuous bier, covered with black velvet, and on it lay a warrior, as if taking his repose: he lay in his armor, with his helmet on his head, and his sword in his hand, as one who had never been conquered, and around the bier were the escutcheons of the house of Hinojosa.

A number of Moorish cavaliers attended the bier, with emblems of mourning, and with dejected countenances; and their leader cast himself at the feet of Doña Maria, and hid his face in his hands. She beheld in him the gallant Abadil, whom she had once welcomed with his bride to her castle;

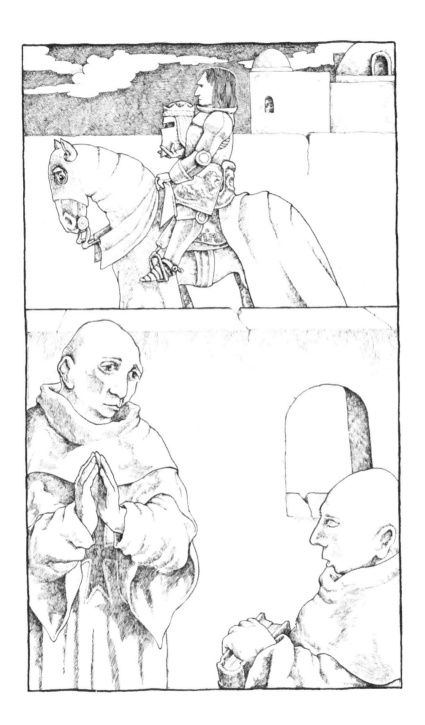

but who now came with the body of her lord, whom he had unknowingly slain in battle!

The sepulchre erected in the cloisters of the convent of San Domingo was achieved at the expense of the Moor Abadil, as a feeble testimony of his grief for the death of the good knight Don Munio, and his reverence for his memory. The tender and faithful Doña Maria soon followed her lord to the tomb. On one of the stones of a small arch, beside his sepulchre, is the following simple inscription: *"Hic jacet Maria Palacin, uxor Munonis Sancij De Finojosa"*—Here lies Maria Palacin, wife of Munio Sancho de Hinojosa.

The legend of Don Munio Sancho does not conclude with his death. On the same day on which the battle took place on the plain of Salmanara, a chaplain of the Holy Temple at Jerusalem, while standing at the outer gate, beheld a train of Christian cavaliers advancing, as if in pilgrimage. The chaplain was a native of Spain, and as the pilgrims approached, he knew the foremost to be Don Munio Sancho de Hinojosa, with whom he had been well acquainted in former times. Hastening to the patriarch, he told him of the honorable rank of the pilgrims at the gate. The patriarch, therefore, went forth with a grand procession of priests and monks, and received the pilgrims with all due honor. There were seventy cavaliers beside their leader—all stark and lofty warriors. They carried their helmets in their hands, and their faces were deadly pale. They greeted no one, nor looked either to the right or to the left, but entered the chapel, and kneeling before the sepulchre of our Saviour, performed their orisons in silence. When they had concluded, they rose as if to depart, and the patriarch and his attendants advanced to speak to them, but they were no more to be seen. Every one marvelled what could be the meaning of this prodigy. The patriarch carefully noted down the day, and sent to Castile to learn tidings of Don Munio Sancho de Hinojosa. He received the reply, that, on the very day specified, that worthy knight, with seventy of his followers, had been slain in battle. These, therefore, must have been the blessed spirits of those Christian warriors, come to fulfil their vow of pilgrimage to the Holy Sepulchre at Jerusalem. Such was Castilian faith in the olden time, which kept its word, even beyond the grave.

If any one should doubt of the miraculous apparition of these phantom knights, let him consult the "History of the Kings of Castile and Leon," by the learned and pious Fray Prudencio de Sandoval, Bishop of Pamplona, where he will find it recorded in the "History of King Don Alonzo VI," on the hundred and second page. It is too precious a legend to be lightly abandoned to the doubter.

Legend of the Two Discreet Statues

THERE lived once in a waste apartment of the Alhambra a merry little fellow, named Lope Sanchez, who worked in the gardens, and was as brisk and as blithe as a grasshopper, singing all day long. He was the life and soul of the fortress; when his work was over, he would sit on one of the stone benches of the esplanade, strum his guitar, and sing long ditties about the Cid, and Barnardo del Carpio, and Fernando del Pulgar, and other Spanish heroes, for the amusement of the old soldiers of the fortress; or would strike up a merrier tune, and set the girls dancing *boleros* and *fandangos*.

Like most little men, Lope Sanchez had a strapping buxom dame for a wife, who could almost have put him in her pocket; but he lacked the usual poor man's lot—instead of ten children he had but one. This was a little black-eyed girl about twelve years of age, named Sanchica, who was as merry as himself, and the delight of his heart. She played about him as he worked in the gardens, danced to his guitar as he sat in the shade, and ran as wild as a young fawn about the groves and alleys and ruined halls of the Alhambra.

It was now the eve of the blessed St. John, and the holiday-loving gossips of the Alhambra, men, women, and children, went up at night to the Mountain of the Sun, which rises above the Generalife, to keep their midsummer vigil on its level summit. It was a bright moonlight night, and all the mountains were gray and silvery, and the city, with its domes and spires, lay in shadows below, and the Vega was like a fairy land, with haunted streams gleaming among its dusky groves. On the highest part of the mountain they lit up a bonfire, according to an old custom of the country handed down from the Moors. The inhabitants of the surrounding country were keeping a similar vigil, and bonfires, here and there in the Vega, and along the folds of the mountains, blazed up palely in the moonlight.

The evening was gayly passed in dancing to the guitar of Lope Sanchez, who was never so joyous as when on a holiday revel of the kind. While the dance was going on, the little Sanchica with some of her playmates sported among the ruins of an old Moorish fort that crowns the mountain, when, in gathering pebbles in the fosse, she found a small hand curiously carved of jet, the fingers closed, and the thumb firmly clasped upon them. Overjoyed with her good fortune, she ran to her mother with her prize. It immediately became a subject of sage speculation, and was eyed by some with superstitious distrust. "Throw it away," said one; "it's Moorish—depend upon it, there's mischief and witchcraft in it." "By no means," said another; "you may sell it for something to the jewellers of the Zacatin." In the midst of this discussion an old tawny soldier drew near, who had served in Africa, and was as swarthy as a Moor. He examined the hand with a knowing look. "I have seen things of this kind," said he, "among the Moors of Barbary. It is a great virtue to guard against the evil eye, and all kinds of spells and enchantments. I give you joy, friend Lope, this bodes good luck to your child."

Upon hearing this, the wife of Lope Sanchez tied the little hand of jet to a ribbon, and hung it round the neck of her daughter.

The sight of this talisman called up all the favorite superstitions about the Moors. The dance was neglected, and they sat in groups on the ground, telling old legendary tales handed down from their ancestors. Some of their stories turned upon the wonders of the very mountain upon which they were seated, which is a famous hobgoblin region. One ancient

crone gave a long account of the subterranean palace in the bowels of that mountain where Boabdil and all his Moslem court are said to remain enchanted. "Among yonder ruins," said she, pointing to some crumbling walls and mounds of earth on a distant part of the mountain, "there is a deep black pit that goes down, down into the very heart of the mountain. For all the money in Granada I would not look down into it. Once upon a time a poor man of the Alhambra, who tended goats upon this mountain, scrambled down into that pit after a kid that had fallen in. He came out again all wild and staring, and told such things of what he had seen that every one thought his brain was turned. He raved for a day or two about the hobgoblin Moors that had pursued him in the cavern, and could hardly be persuaded to drive his goats up again to the mountain. He did so at last, but, poor man, he never came down again. The neighbors found his goats browsing about the Moorish ruins, and his hat and mantle lying near the mouth of the pit, but he was never more heard of."

The little Sanchica listened with breathless attention to this story. She was of a curious nature, and felt immediately a great hankering to peep into this dangerous pit. Stealing away from her companions, she sought the distant ruins, and, after groping for some time among them, came to a small hollow, or basin, near the brow of the mountain, where it swept steeply down into the valley of the Darro. In the centre of this basin yawned the mouth of the pit. Sanchica ventured to the verge, and peeped in. All was as black as pitch, and gave an idea of immeasurable depth. Her blood ran cold; she drew back, then peeped in again, then would have run away, then took another peep—the very horror of the thing was delightful to her. At length she rolled a large stone, and pushed it over the brink. For some time it fell in silence; then struck some rocky projection with a violent crash; then rebounded from side to side, rumbling and tumbling, with a noise like thunder; then made a final splash into water, far below—and all was again silent.

The silence, however, did not long continue. It seemed as if something had been awakened within this dreary abyss. A murmuring sound gradually rose out of the pit like the hum and buzz of a beehive. It grew louder and louder, there was the confusion of voices as of a distant multitude, together with the faint din of arms, clash of cymbals and clangor of trumpets, as if some army were marshalling for battle in the very bowels of the mountain.

The child drew off with silent awe, and hastened back to the place where she had left her parents and their companions. All were gone. The bonfire was expiring, and its last wreath of smoke curling up in the moonshine. The distant fires that had blazed along the mountains and in the Vega were all extinguished, and everything seemed to have sunk to repose. Sanchica called her parents and some of her companions by name, but received no reply. She ran down the side of the mountain, and by the gardens of the Generalife, until she arrived in the alley of trees leading to the Alhambra, when she seated herself on a bench of a woody recess, to recover breath. The bell from the watch-tower of the Alhambra tolled midnight. There was a deep tranquillity as if all nature slept; excepting the low tinkling sound of an unseen stream that ran under the covert of the bushes. The breathing sweetness of the atmosphere was lulling her to sleep, when her eye was caught by something glittering at a distance, and to her surprise she beheld a long cavalcade of Moorish warriors pouring down the mountain side and along the leafy avenues. Some were armed with lances and shields; others, with cimeters and battle-axes, and with polished cuirasses that flashed in the moonbeams. Their horses pranced proudly and champed upon their bits, but their tramp caused no more sound than if they had been shod with felt, and the riders were all as pale as death. Among them rode a beautiful lady, with a crowned head and long golden locks entwined with pearls. The housings of her palfrey were of crimson velvet embroidered with gold, and swept the earth; but she rode all disconsolate, with eyes ever fixed upon the ground.

Then succeeded a train of courtiers magnificently arrayed in robes and turbans of divers colors, and amidst them, on a cream-colored charger, rode King Boabdil el Chico, in a royal mantle covered with jewels, and a crown sparkling with diamonds. The little Sanchica knew him by his yellow beard, and his resemblance to this portrait, which she had often seen in the picture-gallery of the Generalife. She gazed in wonder and admiration at this royal pageant, as it passed glistening among the trees; but though she knew these monarchs and courtiers and warriors, so pale and silent, were out of the common course of nature, and things of magic and enchantment, yet she looked on with a bold heart, such courage did she derive from the mystic talisman of the hand, which was suspended about her neck.

The cavalcade having passed by, she rose and followed. It continued on to the great Gate of Justice, which stood wide open; the old invalid sentinels on duty lay on the stone benches of the barbican, buried in profound and apparently charmed sleep, and the phantom pageant swept noiselessly by them with flaunting banner and triumphant state. Sanchica would have followed; but to her surprise she beheld an opening in the earth, within the barbican, leading down beneath the foundations of the tower. She entered for a little distance, and was encouraged to proceed by finding steps rudely hewn in the rock, and a vaulted passage here and there lit up by a silver lamp, which, while it gave light, diffused likewise a grateful fragrance. Venturing on, she came at last to a great hall, wrought out of the heart of the mountain, magnificently furnished in the Moorish style, and lighted up by silver and crystal lamps. Here, on an ottoman, sat an old man in Moorish dress, with a long white beard, nodding and dozing, with a staff in his hand, which seemed ever to be slipping from his grasp; while at a little distance sat a beautiful lady, in ancient Spanish dress, with a coronet all sparkling with diamonds, and her hair entwined with pearls, who was softly playing on a silver lyre. The little Sanchica now recollected a story she had heard among the old people of the Alhambra, concerning a Gothic princess confined in the centre of the mountain by an old Arabian magician, whom she kept bound up in magic sleep by the power of music.

The lady paused with surprise at seeing a mortal in that enchanted hall. "Is it the eve of the blessed St. John?" said she.

"It is," replied Sanchica.

"Then for one night the magic charm is suspended. Come hither, child, and fear not. I am a Christian like thyself, though bound here by enchantment. Touch my fetters with the talisman that hangs about thy neck, and for this night I shall be free."

So saying, she opened her robes and displayed a broad golden band round her waist, and a golden chain that fastened her to the ground. The child hesitated not to apply the little hand of jet to the golden band, and immediately the chain fell to the earth. At the sound the old man woke and began to rub his eyes; but the lady ran her fingers over the chords of the lyre, and again he fell into a slumber and began to nod, and his staff to falter in his hand. "Now," said the lady, "touch his staff with the talismanic hand of jet." The child did so, and it fell from his grasp, and he sank in a deep sleep on the ottoman. The lady gently laid the silver lyre on the ottoman, leaning it against the head of the sleeping magician; then touching the chords until they vibrated in his ear,—"O potent spirit of harmony," said she, "continue thus to hold his senses in thraldom till the return of day. Now follow me, my child," continued she, "and thou shalt behold the Alhambra as it was in the days of its glory, for thou hast a magic talisman that reveals all enchantments." Sanchica followed the lady in silence. They passed up through the entrance of the cavern into the barbican of the Gate of Justice, and thence to the Plaza de los Algibes, or esplanade within the fortress.

This was all filled with Moorish soldiery, horse and foot, marshalled in squadrons, with banners displayed. There were royal guards also at the portal, and rows of African blacks, with drawn cimeters. No one spoke a word, and Sanchica passed on fearlessly after her conductor. Her astonishment increased on entering the royal palace, in which she had been reared. The broad moonshine lit up all the halls and courts and gardens almost as brightly as if it were day, but revealed a far different scene from that to which she was accustomed. The walls of the apartments were no longer stained and rent by time. Instead of cobwebs, they were now hung with rich silks of Damascus, and the gildings and arabesque paintings were restored to their original brilliancy and freshness. The halls, no longer naked and unfurnished, were set out with divans and ottomans of the rarest stuffs, embroidered with pearls and studded with precious gems, and all the fountains in the courts and gardens were playing.

The kitchens were again in full operation. Cooks were busy preparing shadowy dishes, and roasting and boiling the phantoms of pullets and partridges; servants were hurrying to and fro with silver dishes heaped up with dainties, and arranging a delicious banquet. The Court of Lions was thronged with guards, and courtiers, and *alfaquis,* as in the old times of the Moors; and at the upper end, in the saloon of judgment, sat Boabdil on his throne, surrounded by his court, and swaying a shadowy sceptre for the night. Notwithstanding all this throng and seeming bustle, not a voice nor a footstep was to be heard; nothing interrupted the midnight silence but the splashing of the fountains. The little Sanchica followed her conductress in mute amazement about the palace, until they came to a portal opening to the vaulted passages beneath the great tower of Comares. On each side of the portal sat the figure of a nymph, wrought out of alabaster. Their heads were turned aside, and their regards fixed upon the same spot within the vault. The enchanted lady paused, and beckoned the child to her. "Here," said she, "is a great secret, which I will reveal to thee in reward for thy faith and courage. These discreet statues watch over a treasure, hidden in old times by a Moorish king. Tell thy father to search the spot on which their eyes are fixed, and he will find what will make him richer than any man in Granada. Thy innocent hands alone, however, gifted as thou art also with the talisman, can remove the treasure. Bid thy father use it discreetly, and devote a part of it to the performance of daily masses for my deliverance from this unholy enchantment."

When the lady had spoken these words, she led the child onward to the little garden of Lindaraxa, which is hard by the vault of the statues. The moon trembled upon the waters of the solitary fountain in the centre of the garden, and shed a tender light upon the orange and citron trees. The beautiful lady plucked a branch of myrtle and wreathed it round the head of the child. "Let this be a memento," said she, "of what I have revealed to thee, and a testimonial of its truth. My hour is come; I must return to the enchanted hall. Follow me not, lest evil befall thee. Farewell. Remember what I have said, and have masses performed for my deliverance." So saying, the lady entered a dark passage leading beneath the Tower of Comares, and was no longer seen.

The faint crowing of a cock was now heard from the cottages below the Alhambra, in the valley of the Darro, and a pale streak of light began to appear above the eastern mountains. A slight wind arose, there was a sound like the rustling of dry leaves through the courts and corridors, and door after door shut to with a jarring sound.

Sanchica returned to the scenes she had so lately beheld thronged with the shadowy multitude, but Boabdil and his phantom court were gone. The moon shone into empty halls and galleries stripped of their transient splendor, stained and dilapidated by time, and hung with cobwebs. The bat flitted about in the uncertain light, and the frog croaked from the fish-pond.

Sanchica now made the best of her way to a remote staircase that led up to the humble apartment occupied by her family. The door, as usual, was open, for Lope Sanchez was too poor to need bolt or bar. She crept quietly to her pallet, and, putting the myrtle wreath beneath her pillow, soon fell asleep.

In the morning she related all that had befallen her to her father. Lope Sanchez, however, treated the whole as a mere dream, and laughed at the child for her credulity. He went forth to his customary labors in the garden, but had not been there long when his little daughter came running to him, almost breathless. "Father! father!" cried she, "behold the myrtle wreath which the Moorish lady bound round my head!"

Lope Sanchez gazed with astonishment, for the stalk of the myrtle was of pure gold, and every leaf was a sparkling emerald! Being not much accustomed to precious stones; he was ignorant of the real value of the wreath, but he saw enough to convince him that it was something more substantial than the stuff of which dreams are generally made, and that at any rate the child had dreamt to some purpose. His first care was to enjoin the most absolute secrecy upon his daughter. In this respect, however, he was secure, for she had discretion far beyond her years or sex. He then repaired to the vault, where stood the statues of the two alabaster nymphs. He remarked that their heads were turned from the portal, and that the regards of each were fixed upon the same point in the interior of the building. Lope Sanchez could not but admire this most discreet contrivance for guarding a secret.

He drew a line from the eyes of the statues to the point of regard, made a private mark on the wall, and then retired.

All day, however, the mind of Lope Sanchez was distracted with a thousand cares. He could not help hovering within distant view of the two statues, and became nervous from the dread that the golden secret might be discovered. Every footstep that approached the place made him tremble. He would have given anything could he but have turned the heads of the statues, forgetting that they had looked precisely in the same direction for some hundreds of years, without any person being the wiser.

"A plague upon them," he would say to himself, "they'll betray all; did ever mortal hear of such a mode of guarding a secret?" Then on hearing any one advance, he would steal off, as though his very lurking near the place would awaken suspicion. Then he would return cautiously, and peep from a distance to see if everything was secure, but the sight of the statues would again call forth his indignation. "Ay, there they stand," would he say, "always looking, and looking, and looking, just where they should not. Confound them! they are just like all their sex; if they have not tongues to tattle with, they'll be sure to do it with their eyes."

At length, to his relief, the long anxious day drew to a close. The sound of footsteps was no longer heard in the echoing halls of the Alhambra; the last stranger passed the threshold, the great portal was barred and bolted, and the bat and the frog and the hooting owl gradually resumed their nightly vocations in the deserted palace.

Lope Sanchez waited, however, until the night was far advanced before he ventured with his little daughter to the hall of the two nymphs. He found them looking as knowingly and mysteriously as ever at the secret place of deposit. "By your leaves, gentle ladies," thought Lope Sanchez, as he passed between them, "I will relieve you from this charge that must have set so heavy in your minds for the last two or three centuries." He accordingly went to work at the part of the wall which he had marked, and in a little while laid open a concealed recess, in which stood two great jars of porcelain. He attempted to draw them forth, but they were immovable, until touched by the innocent hand of his little daughter. With her aid he dislodged them from their niche, and found, to his great joy, that they were filled with pieces of Moorish gold, mingled with jewels and precious stones. Before daylight he managed to convey them to his chamber, and left the two guardian statues with their eyes still fixed on the vacant wall.

Lope Sanchez had thus on a sudden become a rich man; but riches, as usual, brought a world of cares to which he had hitherto been a stranger. How was he to convey away his wealth with safety? How was he even to enter upon the enjoyment of it without awakening suspicion? Now, too, for the first time in his life the dread of robbers entered into his mind. He looked with terror at the insecurity of his habitation, and went to work to barricade the doors and windows; yet after all his precautions he could not sleep soundly. His usual gayety was at an end, he had no longer a joke or a song for his neighbors, and, in short, became the most miserable animal in the Alhambra. His old comrades remarked this alteration, pitied him heartily, and began to desert him; thinking he must be falling into want, and in danger of looking to them for assistance. Little did they suspect that his only calamity was riches.

The wife of Lope Sanchez shared his anxiety, but then she had ghostly comfort. We ought before this to have mentioned that Lope, being rather a light inconsiderate little man, his wife was accustomed, in all grave matters, to seek the counsel and ministry of her confessor Fray Simon, a sturdy, broad-shouldered, blue-bearded, bullet-headed friar of the neighboring convent of San Francisco, who was in fact the spiritual comforter of half the good wives of the neighborhood. He was, moreover, in great esteem among divers sisterhoods of nuns; who requited him for his ghostly services by frequent presents of those little dainties and knick-knacks manufactured in convents, such as delicate confections, sweet biscuits, and bottles of spiced cordials, found to be marvellous restoratives after fasts and vigils.

Fray Simon thrived in the exercise of his functions. His oily skin glistened in the sunshine as he toiled up the hill of the Alhambra on a sultry day. Yet notwithstanding his sleek condition, the knotted rope round his waist showed the austerity of his self-discipline; the multitude doffed their caps to him as a mirror of piety, and even the dogs scented the odor of sanctity that exhaled from his garments, and howled from their kennels as he passed.

Such was Fray Simon, the spiritual counsellor of the comely wife of Lope Sanchez; and as the father confessor is the domestic confidant of women in humble life in Spain, he was soon acquainted, in great secrecy, with the story of the hidden treasure.

The friar opened his eyes and mouth, and crossed himself a dozen times at the news. After a moment's pause, "Daughter of my soul!" said he, "know that thy husband has committed a double sin—a sin against both state and church! The treasure he hath thus seized upon for himself, being found in the royal domains, belongs of course to the crown; but being infidel wealth, rescued as it were from the very fangs of Satan, should be devoted to the church. Still, however, the matter may be accommodated. Bring hither thy myrtle wreath."

When the good father beheld it, his eyes twinkled more than ever with admiration of the size and beauty of the emeralds. "This," said he, "being the first-fruits of this discovery, should be dedicated to pious purposes. I will hang it up as a votive offering before the image of San Francisco in our chapel, and will earnestly pray to him, this very night, that your husband be permitted to remain in quiet possession of your wealth."

The good dame was delighted to make her peace with heaven at so cheap a rate, and the friar, putting the wreath under his mantle, departed with saintly steps toward his convent.

When Lope Sanchez came home, his wife told him what had passed. He was excessively provoked, for he lacked his wife's devotion, and had for some time groaned in secret at the domestic visitations of the friar. "Woman," said he, "what hast thou done? thou hast put everything at hazard by thy tattling."

"What!" cried the good woman, "would you forbid my disburdening my conscience to my confessor?"

"No, wife! confess as many of your own sins as you please; but as to this money-digging, it is a sin of my own, and my conscience is very easy under the weight of it."

There was no use, however, in complaining; the secret was told, and, like water spilled on the sand, was not again to be gathered. Their only chance was that the friar would be discreet.

The next day, while Lope Sanchez was abroad, there was an humble knocking at the door, and Fray Simon entered with meek and demure countenance.

"Daughter," said he, "I have earnestly prayed to San Francisco, and he has heard my prayer. In the dead of the night the saint appeared to me in a dream, but with a frowning aspect. 'Why,' said he, 'dost thou pray to me to dispense with this treasure of the Gentiles, when thou seest the poverty of my chapel? Go to the house of Lope Sanchez, crave in my name a portion of the Moorish gold, to furnish two candlesticks for the main altar, and let him possess the residue in peace.'"

When the good woman heard of this vision, she crossed herself with awe, and going to the secret place where Lope had hid the treasure, she filled the great leathern purse with pieces of Moorish gold, and gave it to the friar. The pious monk bestowed upon her, in return, benedictions enough, if paid by heaven, to enrich her race to the latest posterity; then slipping the purse in the sleeve of his habit, he folded his hands upon his breast, and departed with an air of humble thankfulness.

When Lope Sanchez heard of this second donation to the church, he had wellnigh lost his senses. "Unfortunate man," cried he, "what will become of me? I shall be robbed by piecemeal; I shall be ruined and brought to beggary!"

It was with the utmost difficulty that his wife could pacify him, by reminding him of the countless wealth that yet remained, and how considerate it was for San Francisco to rest contented with so small a portion.

Unluckily Fray Simon had a number of poor relations to be provided for, not to mention some half-dozen sturdy bullet-headed orphan children and destitute foundlings that he had taken under his care. He repeated his visits, therefore, from day to day, with solicitations on behalf of Saint Dominick, Saint Andrew, Saint James, until poor Lopez was driven to despair, and found that unless he got out of the reach of this holy friar he should have to make peace-offerings to every saint in the calendar. He determined, therefore, to pack up his remaining wealth, beat a secret retreat in the night, and make off to another part of the kingdom.

Full of his project he bought a stout mule for the purpose, and tethered it in a gloomy vault underneath the tower of the seven floors; the very place whence the Belludo, or goblin horse, is said to issue forth at midnight, and scour the streets of Granada, pursued by a pack of hell-hounds. Lope Sanchez had little faith in the story, but availed himself of the dread occasioned by it, knowing that no one would be likely to pry into the subterranean stable of the phantom steed. He sent off his family in the course of the day, with orders to wait for him at a distant village of the Vega. As the night advanced he conveyed his treasure to the vault under the tower, and having loaded his mule, he led it forth and cautiously descended the dusky avenue.

Honest Lope had taken his measures with the utmost secrecy, imparting them to no one but the faithful wife of his bosom. By some miraculous revelation, however, they became known to Fray Simon. The zealous friar beheld these infidel treasures on the point of slipping forever out of his grasp, and determined to have one more dash at them for the benefit of the church and San Francisco. Accordingly, when the bells had rung for animas and all the Alhambra was quiet, he stole out of his convent, and descending through the Gate of Justice, concealed himself among the thickets of roses and laurels that border the great avenue. Here he remained, counting the quarters of hours as they were sounded on the bell of the watch-tower, and listening to the dreary hooting of owls, and the distant barking of dogs from the gypsy caverns.

At length he heard the tramp of hoofs, and, through the gloom of the overshading trees, imperfectly beheld a steed descending the avenue. The sturdy friar chuckled at the idea of the knowing turn he was about to serve honest Lope.

Tucking up the skirts of his habit, and wriggling like a cat watching a mouse, he waited until his prey was directly before him, when darting forth from his leafy covert, and putting one hand on the shoulder and the other on the crupper, he made a vault that would not have disgraced the most exper-

ienced master of equitation, and alighted well-forked astride
the steed. "Ah ha!" said the sturdy friar, "we shall now see
who best understands the game." He had scarce uttered the
words when the mule began to kick, and rear, and plunge,
and then set off full speed down the hill. The friar attempted
to check him, but in vain. He bounded from rock to rock,
and bush to bush; the friar's habit was torn to ribbons and
fluttered in the wind, his shaven poll received many a hard
knock from the branches of the trees, and many a scratch
from the brambles. To add to his terror and distress, he found
a pack of seven hounds in full cry at his heels, and perceived,
too late, that he was actually mounted upon the terrible Belludo!

Away then they went, according to the ancient phrase,
"pull devil, pull friar," down the great avenue, across the

Plaza Nueva, along the Zacatin, around the Vivarrambla—never did huntsman and hound make a more furious run, or more infernal uproar. In vain did the friar invoke every saint in the calendar, and the holy Virgin into the bargain; every time he mentioned a name of the kind it was like a fresh application of the spur, and made the Belludo bound as high as a house. Through the remainder of the night was the unlucky Fray Simon carried hither and thither, and whither he would not, until every bone in his body ached, and he suffered a loss of leather too grievous to be mentioned. At length the crowing of a cock gave the signal of returning day. At the sound the goblin steed wheeled about, and galloped back for his tower. Again he scoured the Vivarrambla, the Zacatin, the Plaza Nueva, and the Avenue of Fountains, the seven dogs yelling and barking and leaping up, and snapping at the heels of the terrified friar. The first streak of day had just appeared as they reached the tower; here the goblin steed kicked up his heels, sent the friar a summerset through the air, plunged into the dark vault followed by the infernal pack, and a profound silence succeeded to the late deafening clamor.

Was ever so diabolical a trick played off upon a holy friar? A peasant going to his labors at early dawn found the unfortunate Fray Simon lying under a fig-tree at the foot of the tower, but so bruised and bedeviled that he could neither speak nor move. He was conveyed with all care and tenderness to his cell, and the story went that he had been waylaid and maltreated by robbers. A day or two elapsed before he recovered the use of his limbs; he consoled himself, in the meantime, with the thoughts that though the mule with the treasure had escaped him, he had previously had some rare pickings at the infidel spoils. His first care on being able to use his limbs was to search beneath his pallet, where he had secreted the myrtle wreath and the leathern pouches of gold extracted from the piety of Dame Sanchez. What was his dismay at finding the wreath, in effect, but a withered branch of myrtle, and the leathern pouches filled with sand and gravel!

Fray Simon, with all his chagrin, had the discretion to hold his tongue, for to betray the secret might draw on him the ridicule of the public and the punishment of his superior. It was not until many years afterwards, on his death-bed, that he revealed to his confessor his nocturnal ride on the Belludo.

Nothing was heard of Lope Sanchez for a long time after his disappearance from the Alhambra. His memory was always cherished as that of a merry companion, though it was feared, from the care and melancholy observed in his conduct shortly before his mysterious departure, that poverty and distress had driven him to some extremity. Some years afterwards one of his old companions, an invalid soldier, being at Malaga, was knocked down and nearly run over by a coach and six. The carriage stopped; an old gentleman, magnificently dressed, with a bag-wig and sword, stepped out to assist the poor invalid. What was the astonishment of the latter to behold in this grand cavalier his old friend Lope Sanchez, who was actually celebrating the marriage of his daughter Sanchica with one of the first grandees in the land.

The carriage contained the bridal party. There was Dame Sanchez, now grown as round as a barrel, and dressed out with feathers and jewels, and necklaces of pearls, and necklaces of diamonds, and rings on every finger, altogether a finery of apparel that had not been seen since the days of Queen Sheba. The little Sanchica had now grown to be a woman, and for grace and beauty might have been mistaken for a duchess, if not a princess outright. The bridegroom sat beside her—rather a withered, spindle-shanked little man, but this only proved him to be of the true blue blood; a legitimate Spanish grandee being rarely above three cubits in stature. The match had been of the mother's making.

Riches had not spoiled the heart of honest Lope. He kept his old comrade with him for several days; feasted him like a king, took him to plays and bull-fights, and at length sent him away rejoicing, with a big bag of money for himself, and another to be distributed among his ancient messmates of the Alhambra.

Lope always gave out that a rich brother had died in America and left him heir to a copper mine; but the shrewd gossips of the Alhambra insist that his wealth was all derived from his having discovered the secret guarded by the two marble nymphs of the Alhambra. It is remarked that these very discreet statues continue, even unto the present day, with their eyes fixed most significantly on the same part of the wall; which leads many to suppose there is still some hidden treasure remaining there well worthy the attention of the enterprising traveller. Though others, and particularly all female visitors, regard them with great complacency as lasting monuments of the fact that women can keep a secret.

Guests From Gibbet Island

A Legend of Communipaw

FOUND AMONG THE KNICKERBOCKER PAPERS AT WOLFERT'S ROOST

WHOEVER has visited the ancient and renowned village of Communipaw may have noticed an old stone building, of most ruinous and sinister appearance. The doors and window-shutters are ready to drop from their hinges; old clothes are stuffed in the broken panes of glass, while legions of half-starved dogs prowl about the premises, and rush out and bark at every passer-by, for your beggarly house in a village is most apt to swarm with profligate and ill-conditioned dogs. What adds to the sinister appearance of this mansion is a tall frame in front, not a little resembling a gallows, and which looks as if waiting to accommodate some of the inhabitants with a well-merited airing. It is not a gallows, however, but an ancient sign-post; for this dwelling in the golden days of Communipaw was one of the most orderly and peaceful of village taverns, where public affairs were talked and smoked over. In fact, it was in this very building that Oloffe the Dreamer and his companions concerted that great voyage of discovery and colonization in which they explored Buttermilk Channel, were nearly shipwrecked in the strait of Hell Gate, and finally landed on the island of

Manhattan, and founded the great city of New Amsterdam.

Even after the province had been cruelly wrested from the sway of their High Mightinesses by the combined forces of the British and the Yankees, this tavern continued its ancient loyalty. It is true, the head of the Prince of Orange disappeared from the sign, a strange bird being painted over it, with the explanatory legend of "DIE WILDE GANS," or, The Wild Goose; but this all the world knew to be a sly riddle of the landlord, the worthy Teunis Van Gieson, a knowing man, in a small way, who laid his finger beside his nose and winked, when any one studied the signification of his sign, and observed that his goose was hatching, but would join the flock whenever they flew over the water; an enigma which was the perpetual recreation and delight of the loyal but fatheaded burghers of Communipaw.

Under the sway of this patriotic, though discreet and quiet publican, the tavern continued to flourish in primeval tranquillity, and was the resort of true-hearted Nederlanders, from all parts of Pavonia; who met here quietly and secretly, to smoke and drink the downfall of Briton and Yankee, and success to Admiral Van Tromp.

The only drawback on the comfort of the establishment was a nephew of mine host, a sister's son, Yan Yost Vanderscamp by name, and a real scamp by nature. This unlucky whipster showed an early propensity to mischief, which he gratified in a small way by playing tricks upon the frequenters of the Wild Goose,—putting gunpowder in their pipes, or squibs in their pockets, and astonishing them with an explosion, while they sat nodding around the fireplace in the barroom; and if perchance a worthy burgher from some distant part of Pavonia lingered until dark over his potation, it was odds but young Vanderscamp would slip a brier under his horse's tail, as he mounted, and send him clattering along the road, in neck-or-nothing style, to the infinite astonishment and discomfiture of the rider.

It may be wondered at, that mine host of the Wild Goose did not turn such a graceless varlet out of doors; but Teunis Van Gieson was an easy-tempered man, and, having no child of his own, looked upon his nephew with almost parental indulgence. His patience and good-nature were doomed to be tried by another inmate of his mansion. This was a cross-grained curmudgeon of a negro, named Pluto, who was a kind of enigma in Communipaw. Where he came from, nobody knew. He was found one morning, after a storm, cast like a sea-monster on the strand, in front of the Wild Goose, and lay there, more dead than alive. The neighbors gathered round, and speculated on his production of the deep; whether it were fish or flesh, or a compound of both, commonly yclept a merman. The kind-hearted Teunis Van Gieson, seeing that he wore the human form, took him into his house, and warmed him into life. By degrees, he showed signs of intelligence,and even uttered sounds very much like language, but which no one in Communipaw could understand. Some thought him a negro just from Guinea, who had either fallen overboard, or escaped from a slave-ship. Nothing, however, could ever draw from him any account of his origin. When questioned on the subject, he merely pointed to Gibbet Island, a small rocky islet which lies in the open bay, just opposite Communipaw, as if that were his native place, though everybody knew it had never been inhabited.

In the process of time, he acquired something of the Dutch language; that is to say, he learnt all its vocabulary of oaths and maledictions, with just words sufficient to string them together. *"Donder en blicksem!"* (thunder and lightning) was the gentlest of his ejaculations. For years he kept about the Wild Goose, more like one of those familiar spirits, or household goblins, we read of, than like a human being. He acknowledged allegiance to no one, but performed various domestic offices, when it suited his humor; waiting occasionally on the guests, grooming the horses, cutting wood, drawing water; and all this without being ordered. Lay any command on him, and the stubborn sea-urchin was sure to rebel. He was never so much at home, however, as when on the water, plying about in skiff or canoe, entirely alone, fishing, crabbing, or grabbing for oysters, and would bring home quantities for the larder of the Wild Goose, which he would throw down at the kitchen-door, with a growl. No wind nor weather deterred him from launching forth on his favorite element; indeed, the wilder the weather, the more he seemed to enjoy it. If a storm was brewing, he was sure to put off from shore; and would be seen far out in the bay, his light skiff dancing like a feather on the waves, when sea and sky were in a turmoil, and the stoutest ships were fain to lower their sails. Sometimes on such occasions he would be absent for days together. How he weathered the tempest, and how and where he subsisted, no one could divine, nor did any one venture to ask, for all had an almost superstitious awe of him. Some of the Communipaw oystermen declared they had more than once seen him suddenly disappear, canoe and all, as if plunged beneath the waves, and after a while come up again, in quite a different part of the bay; whence they concluded that he could live under water like that notable species of wild-duck commonly called the hell-diver. All began to consider him in the light of a foul-weather bird, like the Mother Carey's chicken, or stormy petrel; and whenever they saw him putting far out in his skiff, in cloudy weather, made up their minds for a storm.

The only being for whom he seemed to have any liking was Yan Yost Vanderscamp, and him he liked for his very wickedness. He in a manner took the boy under his tutelage, prompted him to all kinds of mischief, aided him in every wild harum-scarum freak, until the lad became the complete scapegrace of the village, a pest to his uncle and to every one else. Nor were his pranks confined to the land; he soon learned to accompany old Pluto on the water. Together these worthies would cruise about the broad bay, and all the neighboring straits and rivers; poking around in skiffs and canoes; robbing the set nets of the fishermen; landing on remote coasts, and laying waste orchards and watermelon patches; in short, carrying on a complete system of piracy, on a small scale. Piloted by Pluto, the youthful Vanderscamp soon became acquainted with all the bays, rivers, creeks, and inlets of the watery world around him; could navigate from the Hook to Spiting Devil on the darkest night, and learned to set even the terrors of Hell Gate at defiance.

At length negro and boy suddenly disappeared, and days and weeks elapsed, but without tidings of them. Some said they must have run away and gone to sea; others jocosely hinted that old Pluto, being no other than his namesake in disguise, had spirited away the boy to the nether regions. All, however, agreed in one thing, that the village was well rid of them.

In the process of time, the good Teunis Van Gieson slept with his fathers, and the tavern remained shut up, waiting for a claimant, for the next heir was Yan Yost Vanderscamp, and he had not been heard of for years. At length, one day, a boat was seen pulling for shore, from a long, black, rakish-looking schooner, that lay at anchor in the bay. The boat's crew seemed worthy of the craft from which they debarked. Never had such a set of noisy, roistering, swaggering varlets landed in peaceful Communipaw. They were outlandish in garb and demeanor, and were headed by a rough, burly, bully ruffian, with fiery whiskers, a copper nose, a scar across his face, and a great Flaunderish beaver slouched on one side of his head, in whom, to their dismay, the quiet inhabitants were made to recognize their early pest, Yan Yost Vanderscamp. The rear of this hopeful gang was brought up by old Pluto, who had lost an eye, grown grizzly-headed, and looked more like a devil than ever. Vanderscamp renewed his acquaintance with the old burghers, much against their will, and in a manner not at all to their taste. He slapped them familiarly on the back, gave them an iron grip of the hand, and was hail-fellow well met. According to his own account, he had been all the world over, had made money by bags full, had ships in every sea, and now meant to turn the Wild Goose into a country-seat, where he and his comrades, all rich merchants from foreign parts, might enjoy themselves in the interval of their voyages.

Sure enough, in a little while there was a complete metamorphose of the Wild Goose. From being a quiet, peaceful

Dutch public-house, it became a most riotous, uproarious private dwelling; a complete rendezvous for boisterous men of the seas, who came here to have what they called a "blow-out" on dry land, and might be seen at all hours, lounging about the door, or lolling out of the windows, swearing among themselves and cracking rough jokes on every passer-by. The house was fitted up, too, in so strange a manner: hammocks slung to the walls, instead of bedsteads; odd kinds of furniture, of foreign fashion; bamboo couches, Spanish chairs; pistols, cutlasses, and blunderbusses, suspended on every peg; silver crucifixes on the mantelpieces, silver candle-sticks and porringers on the tables, contrasting oddly with the pewter and Delf ware of the original establishment. And then the strange amusements of these sea-monsters! Pitching Spanish dollars, instead of quoits; firing blunderbusses out of the window; shooting at a mark, or at any unhappy dog, or cat, or pig, or barn-door fowl, that might happen to come within reach.

The only being who seemed to relish their rough waggery was old Pluto; and yet he led but a dog's life of it, for they practised all kinds of manual jokes upon him, kicked him about like a foot-ball, shook him by his grizzly mop of wool, and never spoke of him without coupling a curse by way of adjective, to his name, and consigning him to the infernal regions. The old fellow, however, seemed to like them the better the more they cursed him, though his utmost expression of pleasure never amounted to more than the growl of a petted bear, when his ears are rubbed.

Old Pluto was the ministering spirit at the orgies of the Wild Goose; and such orgies as took place there! Such drinking, singing, whooping, swearing; with an occasional interlude of quarrelling and fighting. The noisier grew the revel, the more old Pluto plied the potations, until the guests would become frantic in their merriment, smashing everything to pieces, and throwing the house out of the windows. Sometimes, after a drinking bout, they sallied forth and scoured the village, to the dismay of the worthy burghers, who gathered their women within doors, and would have shut up the house. Vanderscamp, however, was not to be rebuffed. He insisted on renewing acquaintance with his old neighbors, and on introducing his friends, the merchants, to their families; swore he was on the lookout for a wife, and meant, before he stopped, to find husbands for all their daughters. So, will-ye, nill-ye, sociable he was; swaggered about their best parlors, with his hat on one side of his head; sat on the good-wife's nicely waxed mahogany table, kicking his heels against the carved and polished leg; kissed and tousled the young *vrows*; and, if they frowned and pouted, gave them a gold rosary, or a sparkling cross, to put them in good-humor again.

Sometimes nothing would satisfy him, but he must have some of his old neighbors to dinner at the Wild Goose. There was no refusing him, for he had the complete upper hand of the community, and the peaceful burghers all stood in awe of him. But what a time would the quiet, worthy men have, among these rake-hells, who would delight to astound them with the most extravagant gunpowder tales, embroidered with all kinds of foreign oaths, clink the can with them, pledge them in deep potations, bawl drinking-songs in their ears, and occasionally fire pistols over their heads, or under the table, and then laugh in their faces, and ask them how they liked the smell of gunpowder.

Thus was the little village of Communipaw for a time like the unfortunate wight possessed with devils; until Vanderscamp and his brother merchants would sail on another voyage, when the Wild Goose would be shut up and everything relapse into quiet, only to be disturbed by his next visitation.

The mystery of all these proceedings gradually dawned upon the tardy intellects of Communipaw. These were the times of the notorious Captain Kidd, when the American harbors were the resorts of piratical adventurers of all kinds, who, under pretext of mercantile voyages, scoured the West Indies, made plundering descents upon the Spanish Main, visited even the remote Indian Seas, and then came to dispose of their booty, have their revels, and fit out new expeditions in the English colonies.

Vanderscamp had served in this hopeful school, and, having risen to importance among the buccaneers, had pitched upon his native village and early home, as a quiet, out-of-the-way, unsuspected place, where he and his comrades, while anchored at New York, might have their feasts, and concert their plans, without molestation.

At length the attention of the British government was called to these piratical enterprises, that were becoming so frequent and outrageous. Vigorous measures were taken to check and punish them. Several of the most noted free-booters were caught and executed, and three of Vanger-scamp's chosen comrades, the most riotous swash-bucklers of the Wild Goose, were hanged in chains on Gibbet Island, in full sight of their favorite resort. As to Vanderscamp himself, he and his man Pluto again disappeared, and it was hoped by the people of Communipaw that he had fallen in some foreign brawl, or been swung on some foreign gallows.

For a time, therefore, the tranquillity of the village was restored; the worthy Dutchmen once more smoked their pipes in peace, eying with peculiar complacency their old pests and terrors, the pirates, dangling and drying in the sun, on Gibbet Island.

This perfect calm was doomed at length to be ruffled. The fiery persecution of the pirates gradually subsided. Justice was satisfied with the examples that had been made, and there was no more talk of Kidd, and the other heroes of like kidney. On a calm summer evening, a boat, somewhat heavily laden, was seen pulling into Communipaw. What was the surprise and disquiet of the inhabitants to see Yan Yost Vanderscamp seated at the helm, and his man Pluto tugging at the oar! Vanderscamp, however, was apparently an altered man. He brought home with him a wife, who seemed to be a shrew, and to have the upper hand of him. He no longer was the swaggering, bully ruffian, but affected the regular merchant, and talked of retiring from business, and settling down quietly, to pass the rest of his days in his native place.

The Wild Goose mansion was again opened, but with di-minished splendor, and no riot. It is true, Vanderscamp had frequent nautical visitors, and the sound of revelry was oc-casionally overheard in his house; but everything seemed to be done under the rose, and old Pluto was the only servant that officiated at these orgies. The visitors, indeed, were by no means of the turbulent stamp of their predecessors; but quiet mysterious traders; full of nods, and winks, and hieroglyphic signs, with whom, to use their cant phrase, "everything was smug." Their ships came to anchor at night, in the lower bay; and, on a private signal, Vanderscamp would launch his boat, and, accompanied solely by his man Pluto, would make them mysterious visits. Sometimes boats pulled in at night, in front of the Wild Goose, and various articles of merchandise were landed in the dark, and spirited away, nobody knew whither. One of the more curious of the inhabitants kept watch, and caught a glimpse of the features of some of these night visitors, by the casual glance of a lantern, and declared that he recognized more than one of the freebooting frequenters of the Wild Goose, in former times; whence he concluded that Vanderscamp was at his old game, and that this mysterious merchandise was nothing more nor less than piratical plunder. The more charitable opinion, however, was, that Vanderscamp and his comrades, having been driven from their old line of business by the "oppressions of government," had resorted to smuggling to make both ends meet.

Be that as it may, I come now to the extraordinary fact which is the butt-end of this story. It happened, late one night, that Yan Yost Vanderscamp was returning across the broad bay, in his light skiff, rowed by his man Pluto. He had been carousing on board of a vessel, newly arrived, and was somewhat obfuscated in intellect, by the liquor he had imbibed. It was a still, sultry night; a heavy mass of lurid clouds was rising in the west, with the low muttering of distant thunder. Vanderscamp called on Pluto to pull lustily, that they might get home before the gathering storm. The old negro made no reply, but shaped his course so as to skirt the rocky shores of Gibbet Island. A faint creaking overhead caused Vanderscamp to cast up his eyes, when, to his horror, he beheld the bodies of his three pot companions and brothers in iniquity dangling in the moonlight, their rags fluttering, and their chains creaking, as they were slowly swung backward and forward by the rising breeze.

"What do you mean, you blockhead!" cried Vanderscamp, "by pulling so close to the island?"

"I thought you'd be glad to see your old friends once more," growled the negro; "you were never afraid of a living man, what do you fear from the dead?"

"Who's afraid?" hiccoughed Vanderscamp, partly heated by liquor, partly nettled by the jeer of the negro; "who's afraid? Hang me, but I would be glad to see them once more, alive or dead, at the Wild Goose. Come, my lads in the wind!" continued he, taking a draught and flourishing the bottle above his head, "here's fair weather to you in the other world; and if you should be walking the rounds to-night, odds fish! but I'll be happy if you will drop in to supper."

A dismal creaking was the only reply. The wind blew loud and shrill, and as it whistled round the gallows, and among the bones, sounded as if they were laughing and gibbering in the air. Old Pluto chuckled to himself, and now pulled for home. The storm burst over the voyagers, while they were yet far from shore. The rain fell in torrents, the thunder crashed and pealed, and the lightning kept up an incessant blaze. It was stark midnight before they landed at Communipaw.

Dripping and shivering, Vanderscamp crawled homeward. He was completely sobered by the storm, the water soaked from without having diluted and cooled the liquor within. Arrived at the Wild Goose, he knocked timidly and dubiously at the door; for he dreaded the reception he was to experience from his wife. He had reason to do so. She met him at the threshold, in a precious ill-humor.

"Is this a time," said she, "to keep people out of their beds, and to bring home company, to turn the house upside down?"

"Company?" said Vanderscamp, meekly; "I have brought no company with me, wife?"

"No, indeed! they have got here before you, but by your invitation; and blessed-looking company they are, truly!"

Vanderscamp's knees smote together. "For the love of heaven, where are they, wife?"

"Where?—why in the blue room, up-stairs, making themselves as much at home as if the house were their own."

Vanderscamp made a desperate effort, scrambled up to the room, and threw open the door. Sure enough, there at a table, on which burned a light as blue as brimstone, sat the three guests from Gibbet Island, with halters round their necks, and bobbing their cups together, as if they were hob-or-nobbing, and trolling the old Dutch freebooter's glee, since translated into English:

"For three merry lads be we,
   And three merry lads be we;
   I on the land, and thou on the sand,
   And Jack on the gallows-tree."

Vanderscamp saw and heard no more. Starting back with horror, he missed his footing on the landing-place, and fell from the top of the stairs to the bottom. He was taken up speechless, either from the fall or the fright, and was buried in the yard of the little Dutch church at Bergen, on the following Sunday.

From that day forward the fate of the Wild Goose was sealed. It was pronounced a *haunted house,* and avoided accordingly. No one inhabited it but Vanderscamp's shrew of a widow and old Pluto, and they were considered but little better than its hobgoblin visitors. Pluto grew more and more haggard and morose, and looked more like an imp of darkness than a human being. He spoke to no one, but went about muttering to himself, or, as some hinted, talking with the devil, who, though unseen, was ever at his elbow. Now and then he was seen pulling about the bay alone in his skiff, in dark weather, or at the approach of nightfall; nobody could tell why, unless, on an errand to invite more guests from the gallows. Indeed, it was affirmed that the Wild Goose still continued to be a house of entertainment for such guests, and that on stormy nights the blue chamber was occasionally illuminated, and sounds of diabolical merriment were overheard, mingling with the howling of the tempest. Some treated these as idle stories, until on one such night, it was about the time of the equinox, there was a horrible uproar in the Wild Goose, that could not be mistaken. It was not so much the sound of revelry, however, as strife, with two or three piercing shrieks, that pervaded every part of the village. Nevertheless, no one thought of hastening to the spot. On the contrary, the honest burghers of Communipaw drew their nightcaps over their ears, and buried their heads under the bedclothes, at the thoughts of Vanderscamp and his gallows companions.

The next morning some of the bolder and more curious undertook to reconnoitre. All was quiet and lifeless at the

Wild Goose. The door yawned wide open, and had evidently been open all night, for the storm had beaten into the house. Gathering more courage from the silence and apparent desertion, they gradually ventured over the threshold. The house had indeed the air of having been possessed by devils. Everything was topsy-turvy; trunks had been broken open, and chests of drawers and corner cupboards turned inside out, as in a time of general sack and pillage; but the most woeful sight was the widow of Yan Yost Vanderscamp, extended a corpse on the floor of the blue chamber, with the marks of a deadly gripe on the windpipe.

All now was conjecture and dismay at Communipaw; and the disappearance of old Pluto, who was nowhere to be found, gave rise to all kinds of wild surmises. Some suggested that the negro had betrayed the house to some of Vanderscamp's buccaneering associates, and that they had decamped together with the booty; others surmised that the negro was nothing more nor less than a devil incarnate, who had now accomplished his ends, and made off with his dues.

Events, however, vindicated the negro from this last implication. His skiff was picked up, drifting about the bay, bottom upward, as if wrecked in a tempest; and his body was found, shortly afterward, by some Communipaw fishermen, stranded among the rocks of Gibbet Island, near the foot of the pirates' gallows. The fishermen shook their heads and observed that old Pluto had ventured once too often to invite guests from Gibbet Island.

Designed by Barbara Holdridge

Composed in Tiffany Medium display and Garamond text by Foto-Typesetters, Inc., Baltimore, Maryland

Text printed by Haddon Craftsmen, Bloomsburg, Pennsylvania on 60 lb. Old Forge Opaque, Regular Finish

Full-color illustrations color separated and printed by Longacre Press, Inc., New Rochelle, New York, on 80 lb. coated paper

Jackets and covers color-separated and printed by Rugby, Inc., Knoxville, Tennessee

Bound in paper by Bindagraphics, Inc., Baltimore, Maryland

Bound in Kivar Victoria Charcoal and Kivar Corinthian Red by Haddon Craftsmen, Scranton, Pennsylvania